The SECOND Vendetta

The Maxwell Family Saga (2)

A Novel by
CARL R. BRUSH

BOOKSIDE Press

Copyright © 2023 by Carl R. Brush

ISBN: 978-1-77883-005-1 (Paperback)

All rights reserved. No part of this publication may be reproduced, distributed, or transmitted in any form or by any means, including photocopying, recording, or other electronic or mechanical methods, without the prior written permission of the publisher, except in the case brief quotations embodied in critical reviews and other noncommercial uses permitted by copyright law.

The views expressed in this book are solely those of the author and do not necessarily reflect the views of the publisher, and the publisher hereby disclaims any responsibility for them.

BookSide Press
877-741-8091
www.booksidepress.com
orders@booksidepress.com

Table of Contents

Acknowledgments vi
1 A Feast Of Farewell 1
2 A Letter Of Congratulations 4
3 Back To School 8
4 Reunion With Virginia 11
5 Carolyn And Many Clouds 17
6 Andy At The Dean's Office 22
7 Drinks At The Key Route Hotel 24
8 Many Clouds Starts Home 29
9 Andy Tracks Down Ambrose 35
10 Hellfire 43
11 Andy Meets The President 48
12 Many Clouds Meets Maggie And Willy 51
13 Alliance 54
14 Helpless 57
15 Andy Among The Bohemians 60
16 A Day At The Circus 70
17 Bad Medicine 72
18 Ambrose Again 75
19 Many Clouds Arrives At The Circle M 79
20 The Hearing 83
21 Hale Gentry Drops By The Circle M 89
22 The Decision 93
23 Many Clouds Sheds Her Quills 96
24 The Thinker 99
25 Just Like The Big Top 104
26 Rising Waters 105
27 Getting The Word Out 107
28 Cooper In Action 110
29 In The Sheriff's Office 115
30 Carolyn And Nonny 119
31 Lockup 121
32 Disappointment 125
33 Andy Underground 127
34 An Uncle And Niece Reunion 131
35 Andy Back At The Ranch 136
36 Carolyn In Camp 140

37 Homecoming 142
38 Secrets. 145
39 Politics 148
40 Breakdown 156
41 Hiram Johnson Comes To Breakfast 158
42 Missives. 162
43 Many Clouds Returns 164
44 Frustration 169
45 Carolyn And The Washoes 170
46 Andy And Macintosh At The Railroad Café . . . 173
47 Candidate Coaching 176
48 Camping Out In Green Canyon 180
49 The Candidate's Maiden Voyage 182
50 The Press 189
51 A Crowded Household 192
52 Hiram's Son Returns 194
53 War Council 197
54 Midnight Reunion 199
55 Hope Valley Hoedown 202
56 Doctoring. 210
57 The Press 212
58 Last Marmot 214
59 Changing Of The Guard 216
60 Rooftop Rendezvous 218
61 Markleeville 221
62 The Press 226
64 Roundup 233
65 Fair Warning 235
66 Firing Range 237
67 Ling Chu's Kitchen 239
68 Flouting The Doctors. 241
69 Another Burn 243
70 Riding Into Trouble. 246
71 Hunting Willy 249
72 Hay 252
73 Vigil. 254
74 Over? 256
75 Looking Forward, Looking Back 258
77 The Great Debate. 264
78 The Press 270

79 Surgery	272
80 Beneath The Ground Beneath The Tree	274
81 Soliciting Votes	276
82 Awaiting The Tally	277
83 Cabin Fever	280
84 Tote Board	283
85 Legal Tender	287
86 Injunction (1)	290
87 Injunction (2)	294
88 What Bierce Is Up To	297
89 A Giant Favor	300
90 Where's Virginia?	302

Acknowledgments

These are like Oscar speeches—You're always liable to leave someone out. Not that I've ever given an Oscar speech (maybe some day?) but I want to be sure to honor these folks:

Star billing to my wife, Susanne, for her help and support in this and in all other things.

Les Edgerton, Noir master, mentor and friend. His staunch backing and nourishment of this project and of my writing in general gives him a major share in the creation of *The Second Vendetta*.

Nik Morton, Solstice publishing editor-in-Chief. He was willing to take a second look, and is always there with a prompt and patient reply.

Luis Urrea. Super novelist whose writing and workshop tutelage taught me loads about how to make what went on then seem like its going on right now.

Dan Barth for general inspiration for his *Fast Women, Beautiful Horses...*

Finally, my parents, who made sure I had plenty of exposure to outdoor life in Northern California and taught me how to make the most of it.

ONE

A FEAST OF FAREWELL

"I'm telling you son," his Uncle Cooper was saying, "you better off here on the Circle M. It's going to be different out there now that you a black man."

"Coop," Andy Maxwell replied, "You're talking like you never heard about emancipation. It's 1910, and the University of California isn't a plantation. It's ideas that count there, not race."

"Uh, huh," Aunt Amelia said, "and how many of them professors is colored, Andy?"

Amelia's question stopped him for a moment. Crystal and china gleamed in the twilight. Aromas of roasted meat and baked sweets still hung in the air. It looked as if his farewell banquet was in danger of degenerating into serious discussion now that the town guests had left and only his mother, his aunt, and his uncle remained at the table.

He'd known Cooper and Amelia as his relatives for only two years, the same amount of time he'd known he was half-Negro. For twenty years his mother had attributed his fathering to her darkish, but distinctly caucasian, absentee husband. But in the summer of 1908, the vendetta that had nearly destroyed every last Maxwell had opened the curtain on some family secrets. He smiled across the remains of the feast at his unique family. His mother smiled back, but Amelia and Cooper looked almost grim as they awaited his answer.

"You know, Amelia," he said, "You've got me. I can't think of a single Negro professor." Cooper and Amelia shared a look and a nod. "So why don't

I…" He executed a mock drum roll on the table top, raised his arms, grinned "… become the first one?"

Cooper threw up his hands. Amelia said, "Boy, you're more hard-headed than your daddy, Lord rest his soul."

"That's the truth," Cooper said.

"Uncle, join the celebration. Yellow Squirrel's rampage is over. Mother's healed and back to her old *caballera* self. Thanks to the great job you've done of taking over for Shelby—for father—as foreman, the Circle M is in tip-top shape. You don't need me here."

His mother reached across the table and clasped Amelia's hand. "You know Shelby would have given an arm for the chance at a university education, Amelia. Your brother would have been proud to see Andy standing up for himself."

Cooper said, "That don't change nothing. This boy is so ignorant he's worse off than David going up against Goliath."

"Things worked out all right for David, Coop," Carolyn Maxwell said.

"There was only one Goliath," Cooper said. He folded his arms across his chest.

Why was Mom was sticking up for him now? She didn't want him to go any more than Cooper or Amelia did. He leaned back in his chair. "Hey, Mom, you're finally on my side?"

"Always," she said. "Which is why I agree with Coop."

"But you just said—"

"I've decided to stopped wasting my breath is all."

"People," he said, "I'm just going down the mountain and across the river. Not to the moon. Never more than a telegram and a day's travel away."

"I ain't saying…" Cooper's voice was tight with frustration. "Ah, to hell with it. This conversation always turns out the same." He waved a dismissive hand and rose, digging into his shirt pocket for tobacco and papers.

"No call to be cursing, now," Amelia said.

A chorus of dogs sounded from the ranch yard. All heads turned toward the front door. "Hello the house," called a rumbling bass voice.

"Who the hell?" Cooper said.

Amelia spoke sharply again. "Cooper—"

"I know, woman. But it's Saturday night and all the hands is in town and they's no call to bother a man at suppertime."

Andy rose. "I'll get it, Uncle."

"I'm most there already," Cooper said as he opened the front door. "Probably drifters looking for work." He closed the door behind him.

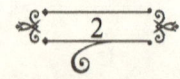

Through the lace curtains Andy glimpsed two horsemen slouched in their saddles near the porch rail. He saw a match flare as Cooper lit his cigarette, heard low murmurs. He sipped his cognac, apprehensive, hoping the strangers would cause no trouble, spoil the evening. He was so eager to catch his train back to school in the morning he could hardly keep his feet in one place. The front porch murmurs turned to shouts.

"Now see here, boy, if you don't bring out the boss man, we'll have your hide on a fencepost right here and now."

"Oh, Mercy," Amelia said, rising to her feet.

His mother started toward the front door, but he got there first, threw it open and stepped onto the porch.

"About time we got a white man out here," the rider snarled. "This fool—"

"Whoa." Andy pointed a finger. "You don't—" Cooper blocked his path.

"Ain't none of your concern, professor. You only a dinner guest, after all."

He turned back to the rider. "You want the boss man," he said, "you looking at him." The cowboys twisted in their saddles. Their horses scuffed nervously, raised some dust. Cooper drew on his cigarette, exhaled. "You gents want to work roundup, come back next month. I got nothing right now."

Finally, the deep-voiced man spoke, his voice low. "Ain't no nigger—"

"Let's go, Slade," the other rider said. "I hear a bottle of whisky calling my name all the way from town." He reined his horse and trotted toward the archway that graced the entrance to the Circle M yard.

The man called Slade said, "My rebel daddy would rise up out of his grave to see me taking orders from your kind." He spat at the ground, then followed his partner into the night.

He watched the spitter cross the bridge out of the yard, listened to his mother comforting Amelia, heard the front door close. "That was scary for a minute," he said.

Cooper smiled. "You ignorant, boy. Like I said." He pinched out the coal of his cigarette, began humming "The Battle Hymn of the Republic," the tune he carried everywhere. He dropped the butt into his tobacco pouch. "Got to see to that new colt now." He trotted down the steps and across the yard, humming as he went.

TWO

A LETTER OF CONGRATULATIONS

Monday morning, angry and grimy, he heaved his foot locker up the stairs to his old room in the same boarding house where he'd spent his undergraduate days. A delay of the train—unexplained mechanical problems—in Sacramento had brought him to Berkeley a full twelve hours later than scheduled. Twelve hours stuck in his railcar—no whisky available—to smart over Cooper's reprimand. Was his leaving the Circle M hurting them all so badly they needed to hurt him back? Then his grandmother had showed up, and he'd been stewing all night over that conversation, too.

While he stood on the porch, irked at Cooper's scolding, she'd sent a melodic greeting floating out of the shadows. "Nonny, hey nonny, my dear Andy."

His grandmother had been Julia Maxwell once, wife of Carter Maxwell, founder of the Circle M. But when the ranch's success pressured her to change from a pioneer woman into a society matron, she balked like a mule at a snake. Not that life, not for her. She "went native." Left ranch, husband, and daughter and took to wandering the forest around Sawtooth Valley in the guise of an itinerant squaw.

To the locals, the appearance of another bizarre-looking Indian in the area caused some curiosity, but no alarm. She became widely known, if seldom seen, and no one ever recognized Julia Maxwell in her deerskins and braids. They dubbed her Nonny, after the melody she chanted as she meandered. Her husband first declared her lost, then dead. Even erected a gravestone. But the vendetta of 1908 had unmasked that pretense along with the secret of Andy's fathering.

"Walk with me, Andy," she said. He strolled at her side as she headed past the blackberry patch toward the pasture.

"You're leaving again," she said. Her tone was conversational. He replied in kind.

"Yes. Back to school."

Silence.

"Aren't you happy for me?"

"You know what happened the last time."

His temper flashed. "Doesn't anyone want me to see any more of the world than this ranch?" He spread his arms.

"Those desires of yours, Andy. "Expectation is the root of all heartache.""

"Ah ha." He grasped her shoulders and spun her around in a little dance. "All I need to do is snuff my desires and everyone's problems will be solved. Thanks, Grandma."

She laughed. "Aren't you the giddy one?" she said. "Well, fine. I suppose we could do with more dancing."

"Remember when Julian and I used to do this one?" He executed a few steps of a clogging routine his father had taught him and Julian to the tune of "The Irish Washerwoman." They'd performed it on demand at family functions, a demand they received so often they'd begun to wish they'd never learned it. It was a dance he'd never before danced alone, hadn't danced at all, since Julian's murder. "Aren't I soooo cyooote?"

His grandmother began clapping, la-dee-dah'ing, and tapping her foot. He finished up on one knee, arms spread while his grandmother applauded and laughed.

"Thank you, Andy. I needed a smile." As they hugged, she whispered, "And I came to tell you she's on her way."

He pulled back. "Who is?" She was silent, watching him. She had a maddening custom of refusing to reply when she thought you should know the answer.

"From Wind River," she said finally. So. Many Clouds was coming from Wyoming. He shifted, folded his hands, watched the hills darken. He felt a shiver, ignored it. "Many Clouds. Why?"

"She gives one reason, but holds the other in silence."

He didn't know Many Clouds' first reason, but he feared the second.
"Is this another one of your riddles?"

"Your heart knows."

He knew he'd lost her now that she'd drifted from her conversational mode to this oracle-like state. Whenever she did it, he suffered a strange sense of abandonment, a shadow of the emotion he'd felt kneeling beside the dying Julian, and beside his dead father. He tried to drag her back to earth, took her arm and resumed walking.

"I know you had fantasies about Many Clouds and me, Grandmother. The vendetta threw us together for a while. A short while. But that storm's over, the sun's out. I've felt like a plow horse in the traces for two years trying to help put things back together around here. It's time for me to frisk a little. I wish everyone else would join the dance instead of frowning on the sidelines."

But did Grandma agree or argue or even stay around to talk about it? She did not. She disappeared into the dark, dissolved like a cryptic puff of smoke.

He dragged his trunk to the foot of the bed. Objections, obligations, distractions. He couldn't afford them. After two years away from the books, he felt like a man who'd been lost at sea and washed up on his home shore at last. He needed to get back in the academic swing. And he needed some fun. Did he even remember how to play?

A letter from the university sat on his study table. At last. He'd been expecting something like it at the ranch for a week, directions regarding his first week orientation into the PhD program. No postmark. Hand delivered, then. Thrifty of them.

He ripped open the envelope. Department of History, University of California. Dated August 15, 1910. He read the letter. Read it again. Sat on his bed. A third time. He was beginning to understand what Coop had meant. "It's going to be different out there now that you a black man."

> *We herein offer our best wishes and inform you that you have been granted an indefinite extension of your leave of absence from our doctoral studies program.*
>
> *Considering the burdens your family circumstances would put on your academic pursuits, we feel sure that this decision is in the best interests both of yourself and of the University.*
>
> *Yours Truly,*
> *John McNulty, Chairman*

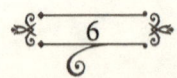

Hypocrites. Spit on them. McNulty and every last one of them. He'd never asked for an extension of his leave, and all their concern they felt for "the burdens of his family circumstances" wouldn't fill a shot glass. The Maxwell family was high-profile, so the assault against the Circle M had been a press sensation. But this letter had nothing to do with the vendetta itself. The intimate details of his parentage and his grandmother's resurrection hadn't found their way into print. Still, rumors were bound to circulate. Apparently they'd circulated their way right into the ivory tower.

Why didn't these charlatans say it straight out? "Now that we know your mother's Negro foreman, not her fugitive Caucasian husband, is your natural father, we've determined that your miscegenated self is no longer eligible for our esteemed program." No matter that the Caucasian lawyer abandoned his family while the black foreman died defending them.

He crushed the letter in his fist until his knuckles ached, imagined he was squeezing Chairman John McNulty's neck. He threw the wad across the room, watched it bounce off the wall and back onto the threadbare rug beside his bed. He pulled a hefty silver watch, memento of his grandfather, from his pocket. Nine A.M. His clothes were rumpled, his face soot-streaked. He splashed some water from the bedside pitcher into its basin, gave his face and hair a once-over, and headed out the door. He didn't look great and probably smelled bad. But not as bad as that letter, and certainly, he vowed, not as bad as McNulty's office would stink by the time he finished with him.

THREE

BACK TO SCHOOL

As he approached the history department office, he saw the globelike figure of Chairman McNulty approaching from the opposite end of California Hall's long tiled corridor. Plummy lips protruded from the professor's hedgehog beard as he studied a sheaf of papers.

Andy stood at the door expecting to be recognized, acknowledged. But McNulty's concentration brooked no distraction.

"Good morning, sir," he said.

McNulty appeared startled twice. Once at the sound of the greeting, at which he stiffened and stopped. Again, when he saw who had spoken.

"Mr. Maxwell. I daresay. I was so… I hardly noticed… terribly busy." His deep voice was staccato and agitated. He sidled into his outer office as he spoke. "Perhaps you can come back later. Talk to my secretary about an appointment, why don't you?" He gestured toward a wizened little blonde fellow who was struggling with the stuck keys of a typewriter. "Sorry not to be more sociable. Mr. Grimes, here, will take care of you. Be a good fellow. Thank you." McNulty turned and walked directly through a large walnut and brass door into his office.

He paused no longer than McNulty, and when the beefy scholar turned to close his office door, Andy stood face-to-face with him. The man smelled strongly of pipe tobacco, faintly of mothballs.

"I won't be long, sir. I have a couple of questions regarding this letter."

McNulty fled as though for protection behind a massive oak desk. "It seems self-explanatory, don't you think? Not much on which to elaborate.

Not much at all." He sat, slid aside a dead briar pipe, reached for a pen, stared at the papers he'd been studying in the hallway.

"Begging your pardon, though. I wonder why I'm being suspended from the department."

"No suspension there. Only a leave. Just as it says."

"A leave I never requested. And I wonder as well what you meant by "family circumstances."

McNulty finally looked up. "My God, son. Your brother murdered. Your mother shot to within an inch of death. Not to mention your father…" McNulty shifted his weight. "Everything your proud family fought for, stood for, disrupted. Nearly destroyed—"

"It's been two years, sir. My mother has recovered. Our affairs are quite in order."

"For a boy to pursue his studies, to concentrate on academic matters so soon after such an upheaval." McNulty shook his head and smiled. "It would verge on the heartless to expect that."

"And what about the letter I received in July accepting my request to return?"

"Oh, well, that must have gotten through a lower level committee before we officially—"

"You signed them both."

McNulty stood. "I sign many things, Mr. Maxwell. I'm a busy man. If I made an inadvertent error and caused you some inconvenience, I apologize. Now I insist that you leave."

He sat down. "I'm looking to pursue my doctorate here, professor. Beginning this year."

"Impossible. Your place has been filled."

"And when do you think I might be permitted to return?"

"As the letter said. Indefinite. You may apply next year."

"Sir, are there any family circumstances aside from the 'upheaval' that influenced your decision?"

McNulty sat back down. Leaned back in his highbacked chair. "Aren't those circumstances enough?"

"Professor McNulty, one the most important ideas I carried away from your lectures is the idea that the heart of what the world calls history is the word "story."

"Yes, yes?"

"You challenged us to write the history of the Napoleonic wars as if we were Napoleon."

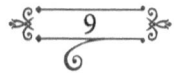

"You did quite well as I recall, Mr. Maxwell. You made his imperialism seem reasonable and justified. I almost felt sorry for him."

"I loved that assignment. Creating a new narrative with old facts. I wonder if you and your colleagues aren't doing the same thing with my application."

"Mmmm. I'm afraid I don't catch your drift, Mr. Maxwell."

"I mean you're telling the story of my so-called leave in a way that makes you look and feel good, but you're ignoring the main issue." Andy waited, hoping to get McNulty to name the issue. If he himself brought up race, he knew McNulty would throw up an impenetrable wall of denial. McNulty proved either too smart or too dense to fall into the trap.

"We consider this a humane decision, of benefit to you and to the department. It is irreversible, and I invite you to go now, Mr. Maxwell. I was not joking about how busy I am."

"I hardly expected you to rescind this decision, McNulty." He tapped the paper, which he had laid on the desk. "I doubt you have the authority. But I did hope you'd at least have the courage—the guts—to tell me the truth."

McNulty didn't change his expression, merely nodded his head in the direction of the doorway. Andy leveled his gaze and held his place in a duel of looks. McNulty returned fire a long while, then eventually lowered his eyes.

"I want my degree, McNulty, and I deserve it. I am going from here to Dean Perkins, and if I don't get satisfaction from him, I'll go to the president. Maybe I should carry a lantern like Diogenes. I might stand a better chance of finding myself an honest man."

McNulty rose, a resigned slump about him as he spoke. "I'm sorry, Andrew," he said softly. "You were a good student. I was looking forward to working with you."

"I can tell you already regret this, McNulty, but I guarantee you'll regret it even more before long. Good day."

FOUR

REUNION WITH VIRGINIA

He left McNulty's office on a tide of rage, and the surge carried him to Dean Perkins office, where he was granted an audience, but not till the next day. He suppressed an impulse to barge past Perkins' secretary, but caught himself. That move would hardly have strengthened his case.

Walking down the hall outside the dean's office, he passed classrooms filled with students, each headed by a professor chalking facts and concepts on a blackboard or declaiming passionate views on a point of history or philosophy. He deserved a place in front of one of those classes, and the denial ached like a boil in his mind. He stood outside for a moment, below the ersatz ramparts of South Hall, suddenly drained, disheartened, at loose ends. For years he'd organized every minute of his life around goals and lists. Suddenly nothing was due, no one required his presence for a full twenty-four hours.

He remembered his resolution to have some fun. How? That he should have to think about that… Berkeley had lately become a dry city, and the nearest bar was now over a mile away. He set off from campus at a pace that in short order, brought him to a ramshackle enterprise called The Merry Widow. The place was filled with a lunchtime mob of hungry men shouldering and elbowing their way to the free sandwiches that fell to anyone willing to fork over a nickel for a pint of beer. The smells of hops and sweat and pickles and salami were nectar to Andy, though he had no interest in a meal. He was however, interested in the other commodity on sale. He squeezed his way to the bar and soon had two boilermakers sitting in front of him.

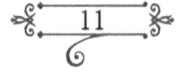

He'd started on his second when a voice called, "Maxwell. Hey, Andy, over here." A dough-faced man about his own age, his cheek bulging with food, waved across the room. He waved back. He was not particularly happy to see a former classmate, but it seemed less awkward to accept the reunion than to avoid it, so he turned sideways to make room for Nathan Cohen to elbow himself an opening at the brass rail. They lifted glasses and traded toasts.

"Great to see you back, Andy. Sorry as hell about all your trouble."

In no mood to revisit the events of the last two years, he changed the subject. "You know, Nathan, I believe I owe you an apology for not responding to your wedding invitation. My life was a scrambled mess when I got it."

"You have been out of touch, haven't you, Andy? There never was a wedding. Vowing till death do us part to Livvy was one thing, but to her father and his law practice? Couldn't. Just plain couldn't. So I'm back in harness at the history department."

"Congratulations, then." They clinked mugs. Drank. "You know, this is a first for me, Nathan."

"What's that, Andy?"

"I don't think I've ever congratulated anyone on canceling a wedding."

"Believe me, the congratulations are entirely in order." They drank a second toast. "What's cash and servitude, I say, compared to poverty and happiness? Say, speaking of love and romance, whatever happened to you and that Virginia girl you were always panting after?"

"How dare you accuse me of panting after Virginia Leavitt?"

"Maybe that is laying it on a bit thick," Nathan said.

"And then again, maybe it isn't." He smiled, nodded.

He'd pursued the blonde daughter of a prominent, corrupt state senator, with a knight-like fervor so excessive in its ersatz chivalry that she'd taken to mockingly calling him "Sir Andrew." Their frustrating relationship had ended shortly after she'd surprised him by accompanying her father on a business trip to the Circle M. He thought her visit meant she was ready to take the next romantic step, had trekked fervently across the steep ranch house roof to her room one midnight. She'd seemed to welcome him, then sent him away. An old pattern. Soon after, she'd cut him off entirely.

Then, not a month later, she'd written to say that she'd broken her father's grip on her life and intended to make her own way in the world as an artist. Angry, hurt, he'd resolved to forget her, but from time to time the last paragraph of the letter he somehow couldn't leave off reading and re-reading, floated unbidden through his mind like a persistent and unwelcome melody.

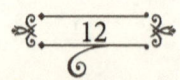

I know it is forward of me. However, if you should choose to contact me at the address below, I assure you that you will find yourself in the company of a very different girl than the one who treated you so rudely in the past.

"I have to admit to some Werther-like behavior in regard to her, but she's just part of my dusty past now." Time to change subjects again. "Hey, you should be close to your degree by now."

"Should be, but they're stalling on approving my thesis topic. Let me warn you. McNulty's turned into a damned Napoleon since they made him department chairman."

"Do tell."

"Yeah. The little emperor all over again. He's going to start going around with one hand stuffed in his vest any day now. They were even saying he was going to boot you out of the university because of some rumor about your parentage. Glad to see you're back after all."

"What rumor?"

"This one is rich, Andy. They were saying you're a nigger."

Andy smiled, lifted his mug, and looked at the mirror glistening behind the bar.

"Goddamn, Andy. It's true?"

"I'm just another lump of coal now," he said as he poured the remainder of his drink into Cohen's lap. He shoved away from the bar.

He heard Cohen's voice pursuing him out of the doorway and down the sidewalk. "Don't go. Wait a minute. Let's talk about…"

As he turned the corner, he caught a satisfying glimpse of Cohen, legs and arms spread wide, gazing at the wet patch between his legs.

* * *

He knew he'd used Cohen as a stand-in for venting his anger on McNulty and Perkins, but he still took guilty pleasure from dumping the beer on him. He nursed his enjoyment and a bourbon-filled flask as he wandered afoot through the warm September afternoon along familiar avenues that exuded a cacophony of sounds and smells—sputtering engines, clattering iron wheels, gasoline exhaust, fresh manure.

Manure. Napoleon. Ghengis Kahn. KKK. Niggers. Jews. Cohen. Why wasn't Cohen getting ostracized? Or maybe he was. Maybe the delay in his thesis approval was just a more subtle method than they'd used on him. They had all kinds of ways, these guys. He'd have to be more careful with Perkins than he'd been with McNulty. Humble himself a bit. Yassuh. Nossuh. But, no, his father had never groveled like that. Yet, he'd never offended either.

How had he done that? Maybe you had to grow up black to understand. Get what you need, but certain things you don't sacrifice.

He drifted into visions of himself as a character in an H.G. Wells fantasy, existing simultaneously on the western frontier and in some imminent future when the Maxwells and the Circle M would be nothing more than a collection of myths and artifacts. Artifacts. Like Virginia Leavitt, the blonde socialite relic of his adolescent passion. Or Many Clouds, the Indian maiden, model of devotion and courage, who had carried a part of his heart with her when she returned to her Wyoming reservation. And now she was coming back?

Talk about opposites, these women. Both lost to him now. Many Clouds at her grandfather's side. No room for him in her world. Nor, truth be told, for her in his, no matter if she returned, no matter what Grandma thought. As for Virginia… Virginia… He dropped back into reality when he discovered that his feet, independent of his conscious will, had carried him to the address he'd memorized from rereading her note for the past two years.

* * *

The boarding house was a shabby-looking place. The tipsy columns, flaking paint, and unkempt yard must be difficult to face for the moneyed girl who'd been his true love once upon a time.

True love. Silly phrase. Would Virginia now think so, too? During the months of their romance, her pink cheeks, blonde curls, and lilting soprano had seemed the fulfillment of his ethereal feminine ideal, an icon of Western civilization. But she was a spicy number, for all of that, loved to make a game of flouting convention, of espousing agnosticism and other radical ideas, even though he sensed she wasn't quite sincere about it all. Her attitude had been too flippant and merry to take her rebellion seriously.

Since their breakup, he'd been treated to the uncomfortable realization that he'd been duped—by his own romanticism. His mother had last summer unearthed a book of nursery rhymes from his childhood, and in it was a picture of Little Bo Peep. Virginia. My God in heaven, he thought, my Platonic archetype was an illustration from a book of toddlers' verses.

Now at her door, he wondered whether he should knock. Maybe Virginia didn't want him to see her in this dilapidated place. Or, he had to admit, maybe he was the one who didn't want to see her this way. He turned to go, stopped, turned back, knocked anyway. The thirtyish woman who whipped open the door was tall, slim, and clad in a blue calico dress covered by a yellow apron. Her dark hair was netted, her voice impatient. She rubbed chapped hands on a towel, and he caught an astringent whiff of lye soap.

"Yes?"

"Virginia Leavitt, please."

"You'll have to wait out here. I'm cleaning, and I prefer not to have men inside anyway." She turned and yelled back into the house, "Miss Leavitt, there's a gentleman here for you." She closed—not quite slammed—the door.

It was from behind him, however, that he heard Virginia's voice.

"Andy? After all this time?" That voice, recognizable, but in a lower, throatier key.

She stood with one hand on the half-opened, waist-high gate in the picket fence. No one would take Virginia for Little-Bo-Peep now. Her face still had the delicate heart-shape, but it was no longer framed with blonde ringlets. In fact, virtually all her hair was tucked inside an orange turban, matched by an orange sash around the waist of a plain muslin, ankle-length dress. The chilly breeze rippled the fur of the fox stole draped across her shoulders, an incongruous holdover he recognized from the wardrobe of her privileged past.

The boarding house door opened again, and he turned to face the woman in calico. She began to explain in her irritated tone that Miss Leavitt was not at home, then stopped in mid-sentence when she spotted Virginia on the front walk.

"You're supposed to sign in *and* sign *out*, missy. I've got enough to do without playing receptionist for you Bohemian ar*teests* who don't care nothing for working folks."

"Oh, Mrs. Cheever, I'm so very sorry. Please forgive—" The slamming door cut Virginia off mid-sentence. Virginia shrugged, squared her shoulders.

"Well, it looks like I've offended the warden again."

"Is it bread and water, now?" he said.

"Maybe once I get out of solitary," she said.

They laughed. Looked at one another. There was an awkward silence.

"This isn't exactly how I'd pictured our reunion, Andy," she said. "In fact, I stopped picturing our reunion some time ago."

"You gave up on me already?" he said. Trying to keep the tone light.

"After two years, and the way I treated you when you came to my window that night, I certainly wasn't holding my breath."

Almost an apology. Surprise.

"If you'd done that, you'd be a pretty blue Virginia by now, wouldn't you?" he said.

A shared giggle.

She hesitated, as if expecting him to say something, then spoke herself instead. "I wonder, did you get my note?"

"I wouldn't be here otherwise," he said.

"I wasn't sure what to think, you see, since you never answered."

A veiled accusation. Something familiar. Part of their old pattern of tease and chase. He'd offer either an objection or an apology. *I'm sorry I didn't write*, he might say. And she'd control the situation from then on, answering with something like, *I suppose you expected me to just pine away.* He'd say, *Of course not, but...* or some other placating idiocy. And away they'd go.

But he surprised and pleased himself now by avoiding the trap. Half drunk, floating between his present and former self, the present and former Virginia, what he said was, "Well, I'm here now." He stepped back, spread his arms.

"I just wasn't sure." She smiled. Slightly. Paused. Maybe she'd walk away now. Maybe he would. The scent of jasmine breezed past from the vine on the fence.

You're different, somehow, aren't you, Sir Andrew?" she said finally.

"Maybe," he said. "I haven't had time to keep track."

"I suppose not. That crazy Indian stabbing, shooting, killing all over the place. She lowered her eyes. "Your... father." She paused. Raised her eyes. "That's caused more talk than anything else, you know." There was an inquiring tone in her voice. An almost flirtatious tilt of her head. His father. The race business. So that intrigued her, like it did everyone else.

"It seems you've been keeping track even if I haven't."

"It would be difficult to avoid hearing talk of the Maxwells."

"So the gossip mill has been grinding away."

"Ah, but talking *of* a Maxwell is not quite the same as talking *with* a Maxwell." That flirtatious look again. "Especially a changeling Maxwell."

He tired of the game. "What would you say to talking about it over a drink?"

"The time has come, the walrus said... Judging by your fragrance, you've been talking of many things already."

"Yes or no?"

She burst into a deep laugh he'd never heard from her before. "Oooh, so forceful. Yes, Andy, absolutely. But I'm due over in the city before long. So let's make it tomorrow. I suggest my favorite establishment de jour, the Key Route Hotel. Only a streetcar ride away, yet miles from the Berkeley temperance fiends."

"So you've become one of us scurrilous wets."

"Let's just say you're more likely to find me holding a tankard than a teacup these days. Tomorrow then? Four o'clock?"

She extended her hand, palm down. He lifted it, pressed his lips to her fingers. Her skin. He'd forgotten how soft it was.

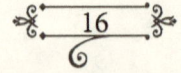

FIVE

CAROLYN AND MANY CLOUDS

Carolyn Maxwell emerged from the Circle M ranch house after several wearying hours over the ledgers. She looked out over the trim green and white outbuildings and corrals, inhaled the aromas of the ranch yard—dust, hay, manure. She needed these smells and sights, the flesh and blood realities the account figures represented, to stay in touch with her land and her heart. She lifted her eyes to the three peaks that gave Sawtooth Valley its name. Numanistic guardians of her Circle M. *Glad you're here, gentlemen. It's a tough job, guarding this place.*

All morning she'd been missing Andy, her prodigal son, constantly at her side these last two years, helping to fill the empty spaces the vendetta killings had left in her life. Now he'd become an empty space as well.

She'd heard nothing from him since the dinner. A merry occasion up to the point when those drifters had ridden up. It had started a bit awkwardly, with only half the invited guests showing up to share a table with such as Amelia and Cooper. Sheriff Halstad. Feifer Gilligan, who owned Sawtooth Wells' livery stable, his wife Sarah and their daughter, Bridget. A wastrel son named Jesse had disappeared and was never mentioned. Only a few left, it seemed, of the legions who had claimed to be Maxwell loyalists before the scandal. Oh, they'd pitched in and helped clean things up after the mess the marauding Indian Yellow Squirrel had left behind. And they'd still do business with the Circle M, something they couldn't help since the ranch was such a presence in Sawtooth Valley. But they didn't have to socialize. And they didn't.

But you couldn't stop a Maxwell party that easily. Everyone had helped Ling Chu clear the empty plates, consolidate tables and chairs, and they'd made an intimate and pleasant occasion of it. But face it. She was lonesome. Without Andy's father, Shelby—her lover, her love—she had no one to share her feelings and fears. Perhaps Amelia, but she'd been unable to crack though her sister-in-law's standoffishness. It seemed they were always smiling at each other, but politely, at arm's length even when they embraced. She didn't understand, hadn't been able to draw it her out of her, her de facto, not de jure, sister-in-law. A problem with class? Race? Something else? Add it to the list of incomprehensibles. Like her mother.

She'd already tried twice to contact her mother since Andy's exit. Perhaps a third attempt would do the trick. It was irritatingly unfair that her mother would not approach the house, that if Carrie—thinking of her mother always seemed to make her think of herself in the diminutive—wanted to see her, she had do what she did at that moment—saddle the old stallion, Sailor, and let him pick his way the two miles up the rocky slope to Granite Spring, and wait. Often, the trip was fruitless because Nonny was always on the move, alone or with the bands of the decimated Washoe tribe who lived hand-to-mouth between the Eastern Sierra and the Nevada desert.

Carrie dismounted and sat in a hollowed spot in a boulder by the clear, granite lined pool. It had been decades since Carrie's father had attempted to hide the secret of his wife's desertion under a gravestone, preferring that everyone, even his daughter—especially his daughter—believe his wife dead become the shamed man whose spouse had gone native. Fear. Shame. Fear of shame. Particularly for the children. The same choice she and Shelby had made. But, inevitably, the secrets came out, and it turned out the harm wasn't in the shame, but in the concealment.

Carrie grew stiff with sitting, knelt to drink, the fresh smell and cool taste of spring water cleared her mind. Sailor chuffed and jangled his bridle. She heard her mother's hey, nonny, nonny melody, scrambled to the top of the boulder and peered upslope into the forest. "Mother," she called. "Mother."

The singing stopped. A figure took shape in the tree shadows, but instead of Carrie's mother, a younger Indian woman walked out of the trees. Her skin recalled the soft brown of Ponderosa Pine, and the buckskin skirt of her dress swayed gracefully with each step. She was not Washoe. Her cheekbones were higher, wider, more those of a plains tribe. Carrie guessed immediately who she was. And knew why her mother hadn't appeared earlier, knew that she'd been arranging this meeting.

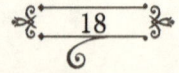

"Where's Mother, Many Clouds?" she said.

The woman stopped, smiled. "She wanted me to come ahead. Alone."

"You're even more beautiful than Andy described you. And well-spoken." Andy had, it seemed to Carrie, devoted an inordinate amount of time to describing Many Clouds when he told the story of his journey to the Wind River reservation in his quest to find the roots of the vendetta. Much as she wished Andy had not chosen to return to his academics, she had no desire for him to ruin his career by relighting the torch he carried for this red girl.

"The missionary teachers were strict with us."

"And apparently you were a ready pupil. Come closer."

But Many Clouds didn't move. Was she shy or defiant? Carrie couldn't tell. "I understood you were in Wyoming with your grandfather."

"Grandfather died. I came to tell Nonny."

"I'm sorry to hear that. Owl Feather was quite a man, for an abductor of women and children."

The light went out of Many Clouds' smile, and Carrie regretted her sarcasm. This young lady had no responsibility for the ten days that she, as a three-year-old, and her mother had spent as captives of Owl Feather's Arapaho band more than forty-five years earlier. She smiled and softened her voice.

"Look, I know it wasn't Owl Feather who did all the murdering—my father, Julian, Shelby. But Yellow Squirrel *was* his son, after all. And if Owl Feather hadn't raided our wagon train and dragged us off in the first place, Father wouldn't have had to rescue us, and none of your people would have been killed, and that criminal uncle of yours wouldn't have… done what he did. Surely you can't blame me for harboring some resentment."

"Nonny doesn't feel—"

"'Nonny,' as you call her, has a real name. Julia Maxwell. In those days she was a young woman with all her wits about her."

"Your mother brought much joy to my grandfather during his last time. He often said he was sorry he never saw you grown up. He admired your spirit as a child." Many Clouds walked toward Carrie, smiling again. "They shared many stories of your adventures among our people."

"You make it sound like a holiday instead of a kidnapping."

Many Clouds stopped, turned away. Carolyn once again regretted her sharpness. She rose and took a step toward the young woman, nearly placed a hand on her shoulder, but the gesture felt too intimate.

"But that's far in the past, isn't it?" She said. "And perhaps Mother, despite her new-found pagan ways, is a better Christian than her daughter." Many Clouds said nothing. Didn't move. "Did she explain why she wanted us to meet alone?"

Still facing away, Many Clouds said, "Nonny said only that you would understand."

"I think I do." Many Clouds turned. Carrie gestured toward a rock shelf above the pool, inviting Many Clouds to sit, but the younger woman stayed put. "I do wish Mother hadn't done this, Many Clouds. You must have an idea what she was about." A shake of the head. "You couldn't be that naïve. She believes you and Andy should be… beaux, doesn't she?"

"Beaux?" Many Clouds said.

"Sweethearts. Perhaps even man and wife."

Many Clouds turned and began walking swiftly back toward the trees. Nonny appeared, her hands extended, smiling, the red and yellow ribbons plaited into her twin braids fluttered as she fairly danced into the scene. Many Clouds tried to avoid her, escape into the forest, but Nonny took her hand, skipped across the space separating them and joined the three of them above the crystal pool.

"My daughter," she said. "You must embrace the one who is to become your daughter."

This is bizarre, Carrie thought. But most things with Mother seem to lead to the bizarre. How much Many Clouds had to do with this matchmaking notion, she couldn't tell, but it must go no farther. She took a cue from her mother's girlishness and led the group to a bed of soft pine needles, where they sat cross-legged. Her mother was singing her nonny nonny song, and Carrie joined in, swaying and bobbing her head with her mother's rhythm. Many Clouds cast her eyes toward the ground.

"Mother," she said finally. "We can't pursue this business of Andy and Many Clouds. Not now."

"Ah, but they love each other, so there is nothing else to do." Her mother's face was soft, serene, smiling.

"It's exactly what we must not do, Mother." She turned toward Many Clouds, who had slid away from the two other women, still gazed earthward. "Many Clouds, I must explain—please look at me. It's disconcerting to talk to the top of your head. It must seem hypocritical of me, when Andy's father… but he's trying to build his career, and a liaison with you—with anyone of another race—given the business with his father…"

"I have no wish to harm Andy, Mrs. Maxwell." She came to her feet. "Good-bye."

"I simply wanted you to understand…"

Carrie watched Many Clouds become a shadow in the trees, then disappear altogether. She turned to her mother, who was no longer smiling, but sat on the ground in small space she had cleared, stacking cedar cones in a circle.

"Nonny, hey nonny no," she sang.

"Mother, why are you trying to force this thing you know can't possibly work?"

The powder-blue eyes of Nonny—Julia Maxwell, Carolyn had to remind herself—looked out from under her dark brows, past Carolyn, to the drifting pool of water.

"Power, illusion, power," she chanted, "dangerous, dangerous." Then she looked directly at her daughter. "I thought you'd have learned that by now."

SIX

ANDY AT THE DEAN'S OFFICE

Dean Perkins of the College of Letters and Science kept him waiting for an hour past his appointed time. Then, once the conference began, Andy's view of Perkins nearly blocked by a pile of disordered paperwork, the squint-eyed, horse-toothed, tousle-haired official stared out the window while Andy detailed his case. The man was interested, apparently, in other matters.

"Is it true, Mr. Maxwell, that you engaged in direct combat, as it were, with Indians?"

"One Indian."

"Extraordinary. Mmm. Guns and knives, I understand?" He smiled, incisors protruding.

"It's a simple doctorate I'm after now, sir."

"You see, we get only rumors, as it were, yellow press accounts of these things. Mmm." He leaned back in his high-backed leather chair and steepled his nicotined fingers. "And you nearly beat to death, as it were, with your bare hands, a man who attempted to prevent your taking command of the family ranch?"

"A fist fight is all it was, one I was lucky enough to win. But, Dean Perkins, how does—"

"And during all this you somehow became involved with, of all things, a Chinese gangster?"

"I arranged to pay some gambling debts my younger brother had incurred before his murder, but—"

"Ah, yes. The murdered brother. Quite a litany of violent proceedings, as it were, Mr. Maxwell, if I may say so. My sympathies." Perkins pulled himself close to the desk, shoved some of the papers aside to gain a clearer look at Andy, began to sense that there was more than race involved in the resistance to his readmission, at least for Dean Perkins. He had become dangerous, somehow, threatening to this world which made a great show of studying wars, but which turned squeamish at the suggestion of actual bloodletting. He moved closer to the desk himself, tried to smile, but felt that he probably managed only a grimace of some sort.

"And about my request, sir?"

"Certainly understandable. But the department's decision—a reasonable and compassionate one in my judgment—was made, and the timing now is certainly, as it were, awkward, so probably a request from you next year is the most appropriate measure. Mmm-hmm." Perkins looked at him a little sideways, as if afraid of being jumped. These people with their indirection, smiles, mouthings of policies and procedures—he had an impulse to shoot them all, firebomb their offices, but it would be useless. Like the ground squirrels on the knoll behind the Circle M ranch house. You could fire every bullet in creation and never get them all. Perkins' next remark set him back on his heels.

"Now, Mr. Maxwell. It's common knowledge that the Maxwells make substantial annual contributions to this institution, and I daresay you might expect some special consideration in that regard. Mmm-hmm."

"Sir. If you please." He felt both his gorge and his voice rising. Struggled to hold both in check. "I expected—expect—to be admitted on my merits." It was as if he had said nothing. Perkins was not about to interrupt his speech.

"You must understand that we cannot allow financial matters to influence academic decisions."

Andy stood, leaned across the desk. Perkins drew back. "What about racial matters influencing academic decisions?" There was a moment of silence. Perkins reassembled the pile of papers as if to reconstruct the barrier between them.

"Perhaps you'd like to discuss this with President Wheeler," he said.

SEVEN

DRINKS AT THE KEY ROUTE HOTEL

The delay in his session with Dean Perkins made him a good half-hour late to his appointment with Virginia. His fury had subsided, but not disappeared, and it was mixed with anxiety about his tardiness and anticipation over renewing his moribund romance.

He took a breath as he entered the hotel. He scanned the lobby, paneled in redwood, painted and carpeted with geometric Indian designs, then caught sight of her in the lounge beyond the lobby, a blonde curl trickling artfully from under her turban. All the emotional turmoil he'd carried through the door dissipated, dissolved by the old infatuation, newly fueled by the hope of quashing their old pattern of approach and repulse. He hurried toward her, vaguely aware of a calming décor of dark walnut, brocade upholstery and drapery, glad she was still here, hoping she wouldn't be upset at the long wait.

In fact, she didn't seem upset at all. And she had someone to keep her company. The two women were perched on a small settee. Two sherry glasses of a Venetian design in green laced with gold graced the small table in front of them.

"Meet my mentor, Andy. Evelyn Withrow. You've heard of her."

"No, I'm sorry," he said.

"Well you will. She's the most marvelous painter. On a par with Mary Cassat and Berthe Morisot." Evelyn saved him from further stammering.

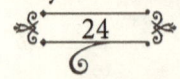

"Whom you've obviously not heard of either." She rose to her feet, gripping a beaded reticule. She was older, but by only a few years, than Virginia and he. She wore a turban like Virginia's, lavender instead of orange, topped by an ostrich feather. "I have, however, heard a great deal about you, Mr. Maxwell."

"Andy, Miss Withrow."

"Evelyn, then. Pleased to meet you." She extended her hand, which he grasped briefly, then sat. "Virginia assumes our artistic proclivities are shared by the world at large. Would it were so. But to balance her excess enthusiasm, she has abundant talent, and," She turned to Virginia, "excellent taste in men." Turning back to him, she said, "You've lived up to your billing. I'm very pleased to meet you." She leaned toward Virginia, pecked her cheek, stroked it lightly. They locked eyes, "Thanks for the peek," in a whisper loud enough that he couldn't have missed it. "Later?" she said out loud. Virginia waggled her fingers. Together they watched Evelyn Withrow steer a mincing way through the mostly unoccupied tables and disappeared into the lobby.

Virginia patted the cushion her friend had just vacated. "This seat's still warm, Andy. Come on over." He did as he was bidden, bussed Virginia's proffered cheek. She signaled a waiter. "What's your choice of libation? Whatever you want, I'm buying. Well, the first round, at least. Starving artist, you know."

She smiled, glowing with excitement, a familiar glow in which Andy basked as he had during former times. He did note with a shadow of discomfort that she'd taken charge of the situation.

"What was that all about?" he said, gesturing toward the door where Withrow had just exited.

"You are something of a celebrity, you know. Scholar, rancher, Indian fighter."

"Negro."

"Oh, Lord, Andy, don't mope so. Accept your place in the sun. You could have fun with it if you tried."

"Maybe I should have done a minstrel routine for her," he said.

"That would have been terrific," she said.

"It's not too late." He stood and danced a short circle, providing his own "Irish Washerwoman" music, sat. She laughed, clapped. Two women from a nearby table joined in the applause. He tipped an imaginary hat to them, sat down.

"Very nice, Andy. The only thing missing was the blackface."

He turned serious. "Oh, we've always got our blackface on, don't you know?"

She recoiled, turned to the waiter, recently arrived. "A pint of your Anchor Steam, please." He ordered the same, bourbon back. The waiter grunted and left.

"Evelyn has a wide following, you know. She could help you."

"In what conceivable way?"

"I couldn't say right now. It's good to know people."

"Ah. The politician's instinct. Like your father, the senator." The waiter made a show of laying drinks and peanuts before them. "Keep the tab open," he said. He raised his glass. "A toast." Virginia raised hers as well. They clinked. "To fathers," he said. She hesitated, looking at him over the rim of her glass, then sipped.

"You're really angry about my inviting Evelyn, aren't you Andy? I'm so sorry if I offended you. I just thought sharing a little of my new life might help bridge… well, just please believe I didn't mean to upset you."

"I'm sure you didn't. I'm probably a bit thin-skinned after my meeting with the estimable dean Perkins. It went much the same way, thank you very much, as this encounter with your Evelyn. He, too, took an almost prurient interest in my exploits—"

"Prurient? That sounds exciting." She leaned forward. He warmed to his story. "It was as if the slimy little rat-faced horse—" He stopped, glanced at Virginia, said, "dropping— "she laughed the deep laugh he was beginning to enjoy, to expect.

"Why, Sir Andrew, thank you for so gallantly protecting my tender ears."

"You know I'd never utter a crudity like "turd" in your presence." The laugh again. "Anyway, you'd have thought he was drooling over a stack of French postcards." He assumed a lascivious sneer and a French accent and laid the imaginary cards one by one on the table. "Ze Indian fighting. Ze Chinese gangsters. Ze combat *main á main*. And on and on, and all the while I'm trying to turn the conversation to the PhD. Then, when he finally starts talking about that, he twists my words—not even my words, come to think of it. He created the whole story out of nothing—accused me of blackmail."

He threw down the shot of bourbon and signaled the waiter for more. Virginia drank some more herself, then settled back in her chair, glass cradled in her lap.

"Don't stop now, Andy."

"He brought up how much money our family contributes to the university and implied I might turn off the faucet."

"Now there's an idea worth considering," she said.

"I admit it seemed like a great notion, once he raised it, but I played the noble Good-Knight Andrew, insisted I wanted to be judged only on my merits. And I kept my temper on a short leash right up until he said he couldn't allow financial matters to influence academic decisions."

The waiter arrived, did his job, left.

"And then what happened with your temper, Sir Andrew?" Virginia was leaning forward, a light of anticipation in her eyes.

"Slipped the leash entirely. I looked into his beady, rodent eyes and said, 'What about *racial* matters influencing academic decisions?' It was rather comical, the way he wheeled back in his big chair and squeaked at me like he had a noose tightening around his neck." He mimed the noose. "'Perhaps you'd like to discuss this with President Wheeler.'"

"So you're going to see the renowned Benjamin Wheeler?" Virginia clapped. "Surely that's good news."

He shrugged, drank beer, then bourbon, then more beer. "I'm sure the donkey at the grist mill thinks he's going somewhere besides around in a circle, too. At any rate, the next person who treats me like a sideshow freak is liable to get a taste of my notorious pugilistic tendencies."

"Meaning you'd prefer not to be introduced to any more of my friends?"

"Not as a carnival attraction, no."

"I certainly didn't intend to put Evelyn at risk of a punch in the nose."

She drained her beer, signaled the waiter for another. He raised his hand as well. The tables were beginning to fill with late-afternoon customers.

Virginia's soft and merry features had turned stiff with anger. Even so, watching those limpid blue eyes and blonde curls, remembering how long and at what cost he'd pursued them, he wasn't ready to give her up. But he wasn't going to give up his pride either. He'd never intended to threaten Evelyn, hadn't threatened her, in fact. This was another of her tactics to put him off balance.

"'Teach not thy lips such scorn, for they were made for kissing, lady.'"

Virginia turned back toward him. Her features softened, eyes sparked. "Going to use Shakespeare on me, are you? Let me see. How about, 'Where did you study all this goodly speech?'"

"'It is extempore, from my mother wit.'"

"So what comes after that? 'Best beware my sting?'"

"'Then my remedy is to pluck it out.'"

"All right," she laughed. "I give up. Your shrew is tamed."

"Already? It took Petruchio three more acts to seduce Katharine." He moved closer, arm around her shoulders, smelled a hint of violets. She didn't turn away from the kiss he placed on her lips."

"Well," he said. "It seems we've reestablished contact."

The waiter placed a new round of drinks discreetly on the table, disappeared. Virginia slid away, turned somber. She sipped at her beer, eyes down. He couldn't recall seeing her in this contemplative posture before, and there was something disturbing about it. She suddenly lifted her eyes to his and smiled softly.

"Well, Andy Maxwell," she said.

He smiled back. "Where are we, then?"

"That remains to be seen, I suppose. It's a warm place." She patted his arm. "But a little unnerving, too." She stood. Put a hand on the arm of the settee. "Dear me. Even in my new debauched life, that's more beer than I'm used to."

"I'll see you home."

"No. No, thank you, Andy. I'm not so far gone that I can't ride a streetcar a few blocks."

"It's more than a few blocks, and it's not—"

"Please, Andy. I have to say no thank you, and I don't want you to be angry with me." She kissed her fingertips, caressed his cheek with them, put up her palm when he moved toward her. He grasped her hand, put it behind him, and kissed her lips again. This time she pulled away and slapped him smartly. Heads turned at the other tables. Virginia smiled at her audience, tugged her skirt into order and walked through lounge, lobby, and out the front doors, back straight, steady and sober.

He remained standing, sensed the other patrons' eyes upon him. Was it too much to ask that life move in straight lines once in a while? He wasn't too many drinks down to know the answer to that one.

EIGHT

MANY CLOUDS STARTS HOME

The deerhide tumpline tugged gently on Many Clouds' forehead, and the weight of her basket rested comfortably on her back as she trudged northward. The air was warm, the forest trail smooth. She chanted a childhood song about coyote and the moon and worked on keeping foremost in her mind thoughts of her return home to the Wind River reservation. Without that effort, her thoughts spun toward the failures of this journey west.

At the pace she was moving now, she stood an excellent chance of making it over the mountains before the snow. She would have to be lucky, but a month should suffice if she met enough freight wagons with Indians at the reins who would allow her to ride. If she could find enough saloon-keepers or boarding house owners who would pay her for scrubbing floors, clothes, dishes so she could buy a train ticket. If the weather held.

When the chanting didn't keep her mind off the Circle M and everything and everyone associated with it, she found herself mired in pain over the ugly events of the last few days—the grudging hospitality of the Washoes and the surrender of the burro she'd brought to help her get to Wyoming—their clandestine price, she was sure, for the few days they'd fed and sheltered her. She should have expected it. She was Indian, but she was a stranger, and they had little enough for themselves. Then came the terrible confrontation with Andrew's mother. And, finally, the realization of her own self-deception.

When her grandfather died she had genuinely wanted to bring Nonny the news of his death. But, she admitted now, it was really Andy—no, better to think of him as Andrew—she'd come to see. All the while she'd known the futility of it, which is why she'd hidden the idea even from herself. She would return to Wind River and hide it again. For good.

The trail roughened, filled with rocks and roots. The day was warmer now. Not even noon, and would soon become hot. The trees thinned, replaced by rocks and shrubs. She climbed to an intersection with a wagon road, which skirted the hillside as it inclined to a ridgetop. Her singing faded. She would be forced to follow the road to the top or scale an impossibly steep hillside. With sheer hills rising on one side of the road and sheer cliffs dropping off on the other, she was vulnerable to any man who wanted to take out today's bad mood on a squaw. But there was no help for it now, and there would be many such stretches before she got home, so she drank from her water skin, began her song again and stepped into the public way.

The walking was easier in this deep dust along the graded road than on the last stretch of trail. After what she judged to be an hour or so, she had nearly reached the ridgetop, where she hoped to find a foot trail down the other side, a way to get off the road. Eager to be back in the cover of the trees, she quickened her pace.

A rider appeared on the crest. Big bay horse, frock coat, flat-crowned hat. Then, just behind him, another. Sorrel horse. Same outfit, but no cravat. She hadn't noticed the cravat until she saw the one without it. She scampered to the edge of the road and stepped off. She half-ran, half-skidded to the scant shelter of a bitterbrush clump, held her breath, waiting for the riders to pass. They stopped instead. Through a scrim of twigs, it appeared they were looking directly at her. She stilled herself.

"What do you think, Deacon?" The man on the bay horse spoke in a deep, cultured voice. "She worth the trouble?"

"Looked comely to me, Mr. Caller." The accent of the sorrel's rider stabbed her with fear. The sharp, thin twang of the soldiers who had killed her father, of the men who had burned her family out of their villages or beat them for walking through town instead of around it.

"Might be some amusement would pep us up for your preaching tonight."

"You echo my own thinking, Deacon, as usual. Perhaps the Indian maid would like to join us for lunch."

The other man raised his voice, said, "We know you're down there, squaw girl."

She didn't answer, frozen like a frightened rabbit. She imagined her grandfather's voice from girlhood lessons in stalking. It applied equally whether you were prey or hunter. Not a twitch, not a breath.

Both men dismounted, let their horses' reins dangle in the dust. The horses didn't move. Trained to ground hitch. These men were accustomed to being obeyed. "Maybe she doesn't understand our language, Deacon."

"She's sure to understand this." Deacon leaped off the roadbank feet first and skidded down the hillside at a breakneck rate, like a boulder landsliding right past her. Still she didn't break cover, hoping, hoping he would somehow miss her. But when he finally braked himself against a boulder and looked back uphill, she had no cover.

"Right there she is," he said, pointing.

She couldn't move uphill without running directly into Caller. Her only chance was to outdistance Deacon in a downhill race. She tossed the basket aside and dived. He cut her off before she got ten yards, slugged her in the belly, then managed to get his belt around her ankle and dragged her, breathless, uphill until loose gravel robbed him of footing.

"Toss me a rope, would you there, Mr. Caller." In short order, she was lying face down in the roadway with the two men standing over her. Deacon withdrew a huge knife with a curved blade from a scabbard at his belt. He held it to her throat while Caller turned her over and tied her hands in front of her. He jerked her to her feet and tied the other end of the rope to his saddle horn.

"The cool shade of that grove we just passed near the spring at the ridgetop should do nicely, Deacon."

Both men led their horses up the slope, Many Clouds stumbled along beside Caller's horse. The animal was so tall she was nearly on tiptoes. As they neared the top, a wagon, heavy with sacks and barrels appeared. The driver was occupied with trying to control four mules as his rig headed downslope. Nevertheless, he reined in as the odd procession approached. Deacon and Caller seemed unperturbed. Caller tipped his hat. "Howdy. Hot day for a journey, isn't it?" The driver simply nodded, his eyes on Many Clouds. Caller thumbed over his shoulder in her direction. "Sheep killer," he said.

"No call for treating someone that brutal," driver answered. "Especially not a woman." He was young, wispy mustache, same accent as Deacon, but apparently of a different temper.

"They're lying," she said. She heard the panic in her voice, hated it.

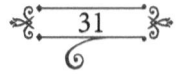

"And a minute ago she didn't understand the language," Deacon said. He had circled to the other side of the wagon, and the driver's attention was now split between him and Caller.

"They're devious by nature," Caller said. "We would have given her and her man a meal if they'd asked. But they'd rather steal it. We can't allow them to slaughter our stock."

"Not true. Not true," Many Clouds cried.

"Been tracking her all night," Deacon said. "Her man got away, but we'll deliver this one to the first law we see."

The driver reached toward the wagon boot below his feet, but froze when he saw Deacon's pistol leveled at him. "Hope that ain't a firearm you got down there. Man's got to protect his property."

The driver sat up slowly. "Wouldn't hurt you to put the girl on a horse."

"You know, Deacon, the man has a point. We perhaps got a bit carried away in our anger and all the trouble she put us to." He lifted Many Clouds by the waist into the saddle quickly, in a single movement, as if she were light as a toddler. He climbed up behind her. "Indeed, sir, our Lord himself tells the Pharisees in Matthew twenty-three 'whosoever shall exalt himself shall be abased; and he that shall humble himself shall be exalted.' Praise be."

Deacon waved his gun barrel, the driver's cue to continue down the hill. Caller and Deacon watched him around the bend.

"And for that little indiscretion, my dear. You will pay," Caller whispered.

The grove was secluded. Travelers passing by on the road would see nothing. Caller tossed Many Clouds off the horse, still tied to the saddle horn, wrenching her arms and shoulders painfully. Her face jammed against the horse's flank. Deacon trotted up behind her with his knife. Panting, he slit her dress from neck to hem. Many Clouds screamed. Deacon silenced her with a fist to the side of her head.

Groggy, she heard as from a distance, "Turn her around, Deacon. Use that bowie on the rear. I'd like another view." She was sagging from Deacon's blow. She feigned unconsciousness, thinking to keep him occupied holding her up or perhaps laying her down. Either way, she might spot an opening. In the moment, he chose to prop her up. The pain from the bindings and the yanking on her joints flamed through her. They twisted her around. The knifepoint nicked her chest as Deacon went to work. She felt blood dribble between her breasts.

"Oh, gave you a little scratch there," Deacon said. "Let me fix that." He dipped the finger into the blood and wiped it across her forehead. Then he took the knife to the dress. She felt it drop in two halves.

"There you go, boss. Complete with the sign of the cross on her forehead."

"She's damned near unconscious you fool. I'm no necrophiliac."

"You ain't what?"

"Never mind. Give me that canteen." He sprinkled water over her. Many Clouds' head cleared a little, but she remained limp, eyes closed. She felt the remnants of her dress hanging from her shoulders, the chill mountain air washing across her bare skin, they eyes of Caller and Deacon crawling up and down her body. Like worms. She thought she could give herself over to unconsciousness, but that would mean giving up the idea of escape. Not yet.

Caller's arms wrapped around her and pulled her to him. "Wake up, damn you," he said. "Fight like the heathen beast you are." Her instincts told Many Clouds to struggle, but she refused give her attacker what he wanted, so she continued to pretend she was barely conscious. "Drop her," he ordered Deacon. "Maybe if she gets some blood in her brain."

On the ground, her hands and arms began to prickle as circulation returned. She lay on her side, unbound, neither man touching her, though she felt their boots at her back. She opened her eyes a crack, saw horse hooves. An Arapaho war cry exploded from her as she rolled under the horses. The animals jumped and kicked, and a hoof clipped her backside. It would hurt later, but for now, it propelled her out from under and sent her spilling down the hillside. The horses broke their ground-reining, pitched and whirled and whinnied. She could hear Deacon and Caller yelling as they tried to control them. She gathered the rags of her clothing to her in a bundle as she ran, not out of modesty so much as to avoid tangling them in her feet. She couldn't pause to shed them.

The seeping spring water had created something of a swamp downhill, engendered a thicket of willows and bear grass. She plunged in, tried to ignore the twigs and roots that scraped her on all sides. She was out of sight for the moment, but there was no use trying to lie low. The area was too small. The spring water opened a narrow channel through the vegetation, and she followed that till it slowed to a trickle and the greenery closed in again.

Behind her, she heard Caller yelling with rage. She heard "Squaw bitch." And she heard, "Humiliate." And she heard, "Blaspheming filth." She burst from the thicket and fled downhill, hoping the willows still screened her. She followed an old trail across the slope for a few yards, doubtless created by Indians collecting water at the spring. She was running north now, paralleling the road above. Below, the trees broke into a mixture of conifers and oaks and shrubbery. Not much cover. She slipped the halves of her dress off each arm as she ran, then threw one as far down the trail as she could. Tossed another on to a branch of a rabbit bush, hoping it would appear it had snagged there as she fled in that direction.

She dropped off the trail, leaping as far as she could downhill so that her turn from the beaten track wouldn't be too obvious to someone in a hurry. Her goal was a live oak tree a hundred yards or so away. The lowest branches appeared low enough to allow her to climb quickly into the cover of the greenery. People looked for their prey in circles, but seldom looked up. Maybe Caller and Deacon wouldn't either.

By the time she reached the tree, she could no longer hear her pursuers. However, the branches were too high to catch by jumping as she had planned. She wrapped herself around the trunk and gripped tightly with arms, knees and ankles trying to shinny up. This was a big, old tree, though. Too large to get the grip she needed. Behind her was a thin jack pine, its trunk maybe a foot thick. She sprang for it and clambered up. The cover was thin, and the branches barely strong enough to give her a foothold. She hugged the trunk, tried to keep still. The tree swayed whenever she shifted her weight. Uphill, the voices returned. Maybe they had found where she left the trail. Downhill, she peered into the branches of the tree she'd tried to climb. Green eyes stared back. Cougar.

NINE

ANDY TRACKS DOWN AMBROSE

The lunch crowd had gone, and he'd managed to secure a table to himself. It had been three days since his session with Dean Perkins and his altercation with Virginia. She hadn't responded to the note of apology he left at her boarding house. Maybe her truculent landlady had failed to deliver his regrets, but maybe she was still in a huff. Either way, he didn't want to go back so soon and appear to be begging.

He sipped at his boilermaker, penned a quick note to his mother, mentioning nothing of his dilemma. He didn't like withholding information from her, but she could do nothing to solve this and would not only worry but would likely renew her campaign to bring him back to the ranch. Time enough to tell her the story when it was all over. The note written, his day was suddenly empty as a desert landscape. His meeting with President Wheeler was still two days off. Once again, he was in an infuriating limbo.

In an attempt to fill an hour with something at least minimally productive, he'd picked up copies of both the big San Francisco papers—the *Chronicle* and the *Examiner*— intending to catch up with current events. Actually, it was the *Chronicle* he wanted for news. The *Examiner* he bought for Ambrose Bierce's column, "The Tattler." If not for Bierce's wit and intellect, he would have boycotted the paper. He himself held the unpopular opinion that the Spanish-American war was a colonial venture unworthy of the U.S.

and that *The Examiner's* publisher, Yellow-Journalism Hearst, had played a key role in promoting the conflict with his sensationalist coverage of the explosion aboard the battleship Maine in Havana harbor.

He'd just folded the paper to the Bierce column when a chair scraped, the table shuddered, and he looked up to find himself staring into the round, pudgy face of Nathan Cohen, the erstwhile recipient of a lapful of his beer. He slapped down his paper and stood. Cohen clasped his hands as if in prayer.

"Andy, Andy, I'm here to apologize. If you'll let me."

"Sure. My table is open to any two-bit kike who walks through the door."

Cohen started to rise at the insult, then sat back down. "All right, I deserved that. I'll leave if you want, but I need to tell you how bad I feel about what I said. You can imagine I've endured my share of that kind of talk, and why I would get into it myself I can't imagine."

The two stared at each other for a moment. "Can you at least accept that I didn't call you that myself? That I was repeating other peoples' words?"

"You're not serious."

Cohen's eyes went to the ceiling. "God this is hard."

"I'm bleeding for you."

Cohen took a huge breath. "So, anyhow, I've said it." He turned and walked away. Andy refolded the paper, sat back down and resumed his reading. A few moments later Cohen's voice intruded once more.

"Least I can do is buy you a drink." He shoved another boilermaker across the table, sat down again and lifted his own beer. "Cheers?"

Andy left his own drink untouched and held up the newspaper as a barrier between himself and his tormentor. But he couldn't concentrate. He had to admit what had happened with Cohen didn't belong in the same category as the letter from McNulty and all the rest of the aspersions he'd endured lately. He himself had just returned Cohen's insult with one of his own, so maybe they were even. But he still wanted to be left alone.

"I see you're in the middle of Bierce's column," Cohen said.

He kept the paper in front of his face. Didn't answer.

"I haven't been looking over your shoulder. I can tell by what's on the fold I can see from over here. I never miss that guy."

He remained silent.

"Today's item about the mayor is especially sharp." Cohen kept talking as if Andy was engaging with him. Despite himself, he scanned the page till he came to the passage Cohen had mentioned.

We herein note the recent proposal of Mayor P.H. McCarthy to raise the wages of city workers by some 50 per cent from two dollars to three dollars per day. In view of his close alliance with labor terrorist Kearny, who purports to lay all on the line for the good of the working man, we may be forgiven if we wonder at the audacity of offering those sheltered in the confines of taxpayer-funded corruption a salary three times more than those on the outside can expect. That wage is, of course, a hundred per cent more than any Oriental person can expect in this state for any work whatsoever thanks to the exclusion laws championed by Messrs. Kearny, McCarthy, et al. Mr. McCarthy seems bent on living up to his jocular nickname, "Pinhead."

Appropriate to the above, we believe, are these excerpts from a soon-to-be-published volume authored by Yours Truly entitled The Devil's Dictionary.

PREJUDICE, n. A vagrant opinion without visible means of support.
WHITE, adj. and n. Black

"What's this dictionary he's talking about?" he said.

"You must not have read the column for some time."

"Nearly a year, I guess. Papers were days late getting to the ranch, and I got out of the habit."

"He's been leaking little excerpts from this book he's writing. Coming out in a couple of months, I guess. I can't wait. Do you know what he said about the university? No, of course you don't. 'Academe: In ancient times a school where morality and philosophy were taught. In modern times, a school where football is taught.'" They laughed.

He realized that he'd been lonesome to talk to someone about all this, someone besides Virginia, who could never really appreciate the situation and apparently wasn't talking to him anyway. Cohen wasn't exactly a friend, but he wasn't exactly an enemy any more either, and he was available.

"You know what, Cohen? This part about the mayor. Bierce isn't just describing Mayor Pinhead. He's talking about McNulty and Perkins and the whole crowd of mountebanks. And this… he… I believe Ambrose Bierce is the man I've been looking for."

"For what?"

"And I didn't even know I was looking for him till just now. Thanks, Nathan," he clapped Cohen on the shoulder and headed toward the door of the saloon.

"Thanks for what?" Andy heard him repeat as he passed through the doorway.

* * *

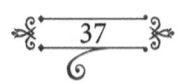

Andy, Virginia on his arm, entered the Palace Hotel's Garden Court, where Bierce was known to hold forth at all hours. Virginia's answer to his note had been awaiting him in his room. He thought it might be awkward to bring her to his *tête-a-tête* with Bierce, but he was loath to pass up a chance to reconcile with her.

Bierce didn't make appointments, but the word was that he made himself eminently accessible. The court seemed as big as a railway station, covered by the same kind of expansive skylight. Greenery abounded, and the place had the ambience of a tropical courtyard, liberally adorned with marble, silver, crystal, and white linen.

Instantly recognizable from his photographs, curly dark hair, the eminent journalist stood near a table laden with oysters, champagne, Peking duck, potatoes au gratin, a healthy serving of beefsteak tartar topped with a raw egg and a carafe of cognac. He was flourishing a cigar and pontificating to a slim, nattily attired Negro man who stood stiffly and without expression in response to the writer's expostulations.

"You know I admire your work, sir, and would never—" Bierce was saying. He interrupted himself when he noticed Andy. "Ah, Mr. Maxwell, isn't it?" Andy was mildly surprised that Bierce knew who he was right away. He recalled Virginia's remarks about how to handle his new-found fame, tried to act as if such public recognition was his as a matter of course.

"Yes, sir. And this is my friend, Miss Virginia Leavitt."

"Excellent. Let me introduce you two. He laid one hand on the man's shoulder and extended the other, still holding the cigar, toward him. "Andrew Maxwell, this is Joseph Francis, one of our state's most distinguished journalists, editor and publisher of the esteemed newspaper *The Elevator*."

Distinguished journalist. Yet he'd never heard of him or of his newspaper. He shook hands with Francis. "A pleasure," he said.

"Likewise," Francis answered. And their eyes locked for a moment. No doubt the man recognized his name, knew his situation. Was he sympathetic, amused, scornful? Francis' face betrayed nothing. He wished his Aunt Amelia and Uncle Cooper were there to consult. Francis turned back to Bierce.

"Thank you for your time, sir. We'll talk again soon, then?"

"Yes, yes. Joseph. Certainly. The matter is by no means closed." Francis walked with small quick steps as he wove his way through the tables toward the exits. "One would like to help, of course. But there's only so much… But, now to you, Mr. Maxwell, our frontier Galahad."

Andy decided to step right into the momentary gap in the conversation as the man named Francis left.

"Good afternoon, Mr. Bierce. Forgive me for interrupting, but I have some urgent business. And may I present, Miss Virginia Leavitt."

"Pleased to meet you both," Bierce said. "Please sit down and help me consume this extraordinary feast while we discuss your urgent business."

He signaled to the waiter, who immediately set champagne flutes before Virginia and Andy and poured them full.

"Thank you for your hospitality," Andy said. He had decided to get straight to the point out of respect for the man's time. "As I said, I have important business and was hoping to enlist your help."

"Ah, I'm disappointed already."

"Sir?"

He lowered his voice and leaned forward. "I was hoping you'd come to offer me an exclusive on your next deed of derring-do."

Bierce stared intently, but Andy thought he discerned a twinkle in his eye. Then he winked. "I hope there'll be no need for any of those in the near future," he said with a smile and a chuckle.

"Ah, well. Hopes dashed, day spoiled, but one goes on. What help are you enlisting?"

"Something you said in a recent column," Mr. Bierce." Bierce settled back, clamped his dwindling cigar in his teeth, and waited.

"The item about Mayor McCarthy. Particularly the reference to Chinese laborers and the definition of prejudice. I felt they applied to a fix I'm in at the moment." He waited. Bierce jammed his cigar butt into a bucket of sand already bristling with a small forest of other stubs.

So he did go on. While the waiter poured the champagne, he explained the situation as succinctly as he could, struggling to suppress the anger that boiled harder the more he talked.

Bierce sipped his champagne, lowered his glass and smiled. "Mr. Maxwell, why do you care?" His tone was sympathetic.

"I don't understand."

"It's an obvious question, isn't it? And a sincere one. You have land and fortune aplenty, many ways to make a mark in the world. What do you care about these terriers yapping at your heels?"

A fashionable couple stopped to greet Bierce, obviously basking in his glow, giving Andy a chance to sip and contemplate. They cast sidelong glances at him, but Bierce didn't introduce him, and he was glad to remain anonymous. The champagne tasted thin compared to the diet of boilermakers he'd been consuming lately. He cautioned himself against misjudging the potency. Seems he'd cautioned himself a great deal lately without any discernable effect.

"Apologies for the interruption, my boy. Go on."

"It's human, isn't it, sir? We're always reaching, aren't we? Beyond ourselves? In different directions?"

"Well a bit of a philosopher as well as a warrior. Am I right, Miss Leavitt?"

"I wouldn't argue with that," Virginia said.

"Always check with the woman, Andy, especially if she's pretty. Keeps a man from going astray. As for your philosophical observations, The Buddhists tell us that such desires are the source of all pain. The object of existence is to transcend those yearnings so that we will no longer crave, say, Peking Duck. Or wine. I'm afraid I'm a few incarnations short of that state."

"As am I, young man." Bierce lifted his glass. "Now, reaching beyond philosophy and theology, tell me your errand."

"To be frank, Mr. Bierce, I'm not completely sure what I'm asking of you. My thoughts ran all the way from requesting an item in the column to a letter of support."

"And what influence do you imagine I might have with these learned canines?"

"I'm not sure, it's just—"

"You realize I'm not a great admirer of the academicians, nor they of me." He waved his glass to the waiter, who refilled his empty glass. Andy was amazed to discover that his glass was also empty, considered refusing the offer, but allowed the pour.

"You've made that amusingly clear. But you have a forum, and, as you know, people read you and listen to you. These men might not care much about what you write for its own sake, but I believe they're very sensitive to public criticism."

"Censorship in the very temple of intellectual inquiry and open discussion?" He drank. "Shocking."

"Shocking, oh, yes, indeed. Shocking." He laughed. He was starting to relax in the presence of this famous man.

"Mr. Bierce, Mr. Bierce," piped a thin voice. A young boy in a flat leather cap and lederhosen rushed to the table with an envelope for Bierce. He tore it open, scribbled something on it with a pencil, then sent the messenger on his way. Two dozen oysters arrived, arranged on a crescent-shaped bed of shaved ice. Bierce dipped one in horseradish, popped it in his mouth, gestured to Andy to follow suit.

"Young man." He swallowed. "No, let me address this to the young lady. Miss Leavitt, do you know why people read my column?"

"You write with great style and wit, Mr. Bierce."

"You are too gracious, young lady. Although what you say is certainly true, there is something even more essential." He turned to Andy. "Do *you* know what a journalist does, Mr. Maxwell?"

"He reports the news."

"And what constitutes *news*?"

"Facts. Events." He felt as if he were in a classroom. Except he'd never attended class while he was tipsy. This ought to be interesting.

"So the public believes." Another oyster. Two. More champagne, the bottle empty now, another on the way. There was no hope of keeping up with Bierce or of keeping sober. Another silk-hatted denizen stopped by the table just to say hello and shake the journalist's hand. He went on as if they hadn't been interrupted at all. "Not just facts, but important facts. And what are facts? And which of them is important, which not? A journalist faces these questions every day. Every minute.

"Ah, the duck at last. We're lucky to be living in California in a paradise of Chinese cuisine, Mr. Maxwell. To the uninitiated, Chinese food means the likes of chow mein, which was only some terrified chef's scraping together of leftovers to please a drunken miner. But to those in the know, Mandarin cooking rivals the French." To the waiter, who was lifting a slice from the breast of the plump bird, "Serve the young man first. He looks quite starved."

And the more food that came, the hungrier he got. The serving done, the chewing and drinking began again, along with Bierce's discourse. "Take your story, Andrew. I can call you Andrew?"

"Andy would be better," he said.

"Andy, then. And you, of course, must call me Ambrose. As pretentious a Christian name as there is, so I don't lower myself at all by offering it. It means 'immortal,' you know. A vain hope."

"Perhaps you'll achieve immortality through your writing, though," Virginia offered.

"Much as I appreciate the sentiments, young lady. I'm afraid it's a most vain hope, though devoutly to be wished. But..." He leaned over the table and whispered, "I am, indeed, a vain man, so I continue to hope in the heart for what the mind knows is futile. *In vino veritas,* In wine, there is truth, Andy, my boy, but those words must never stray beyond this table."

"Safe with me," he said.

Bierce leaned back. "But as to your story, Andy. At this moment, it is not, to me, a fact. It is fictional as a dime novel. It won't become fact until I interview the principals you name, then the ones that they name. And do you believe your story from their lips will match your version? Of course not, and then I will have to compare and confirm. And then, should I undertake all that, I'll have facts. And what comes next, do you suppose?"

What came next was the potatoes, followed by the tartare. The waiter carried the oyster platter away. How had they all disappeared? And the duck as well. More champagne. Was this the second or third bottle? He reached for his glass, misjudged, toppled the crystal stemware to the tiled floor where it smashed. A waiter was there in a trice to clean the mess, replace, repour.

"Sorry," he said. Bierce was concentrating on his plate, dismissed the apology with a wave of a fork.

"Perhaps Miss Leavitt can help us. What do you think comes next, my dear?"

Andy noted that Virginia stiffened slightly at Bierce's "My dear," but forged on as if the sobriquet was a natural part of the conversation.

"I would suppose you must decide whether the story belongs in your column or not," she said.

"Ah, we might have a natural journalist on our hands, Andy. Well put, young lady." Bierce went on. "Eight hundred words I'm allotted each day. I could write triple that, but I must choose." He took a mouthful of tartare, closed his eyes and smiled in appreciation. Washed it down. "You say you have a meeting with President Wheeler."

"The day after tomorrow," he said.

"Come see me afterwards. Let me know how the meeting goes."

He was confused. "Are you going to help or not, Ambrose?" He sounded more combative than he intended.

"An impertinent question, wouldn't you say, from one with his legs under another man's table?"

He held his breath, tried to clear his head. Was he going to spoil this somehow?

"I'm interested in your *tête-a-tête* with Wheeler."

"Thank you, Ambrose."

"Nothing to thank me for yet. In the end, we might be thanking each other. Or quite the opposite. Suspense, boy. The bread of life and literature ever since Eve wondered what in the world was inside that juicy apple.

"Now. You haven't done justice to your beef, my boy. You'll need some blood in your veins to confront the eminent"—he affected a British accent—"president of the Athens of the west."

"My compliments to you both." He shook Andy's hand, kissed Virginia's, and bade them both farewell.

TEN

HELLFIRE

Many Clouds barely moved for what seemed like hours. Except for an occasional brandishing of its considerable tail, neither did the lion. A glance at the sun told her not much time had passed at all, but her wounds and cramped muscles wrapped her in pain, turned minutes into seeming hours.

Was the lion not hungry or waiting her out, knowing she'd have to come down eventually? Cougars love a chase, would rather attack a fleeing victim than a recumbent one any day. Caught between the beast and her human pursuers, she didn't dare leave her perch. Yet she wondered how much longer her failing strength would allow her to stay in the tree. Voices from uphill.

It had taken them a while, but they'd tracked her, all right. Deacon was good. He kept his eyes to the ground like a bloodhound, occasionally stooping to examine a broken twig or a puddle of leaves. Caller followed him, surveying the ground ahead. They followed her trail right down to the base of the live oak tree, and they looked up into the branches, just as she'd counted on them not to do. If she'd made it up that tree, she'd have been trapped. Any minute, she feared, they might turn uphill and spot her among the scant fringe of pine needles. They didn't turn uphill, though, because what they saw in the big oak was that same pair of green eyes she'd been staring into for so very long. And the cat was no longer still or quiet. It was snarling, poised to strike.

"Stand your ground," Deacon cautioned Caller.

But the sound of the cat's roar and the sight of its fangs were too much for Caller, who declared himself anxious to retrieve his rifle and scrambled up the hill. The lion bunched at the shoulders and hips, prepared to leap. Perhaps Deacon and Caller would be chewed to pieces. She'd have been happy to watch. However, Deacon was more savvy than his boss. He yelled, fired his pistol twice, and the beast retreated behind the trunk. Deacon backed slowly uphill toward the trail, yelling continuously, firing occasionally, finally disappearing into the uphill trees. The cat waited a while, then sailed to the ground, slinking along Deacon's trail, leaving the way clear for Many Clouds.

* * *

As sunset haloed the treetops, Many Clouds crouched naked behind a redbud bush near a shacklike farmhouse—clapboard, unpainted, maybe two rooms. Tired and frightened from scuttling bareskinned over a circuitous route on faint trails through the countryside all afternoon, she thought to find refuge with the small Indian band encamped outside Auburn, where she had stayed overnight on her way from Wyoming. If they were still there, that is. And if she'd judged her direction correctly. But she couldn't continue without clothing. Dwellings became more frequent as she neared town, and her nudity was both a danger and an embarrassment. Women in her village at home often left breasts uncovered, but always wore at least a skirt. And her years at the mission school had imbued her with more inhibitions than most of her peers.

She'd never imagined wearing a pair of men's B.V.D.'s. But that was all that hung on the twine clothesline outside the farmhouse. Right now, they seemed more than inviting. They wouldn't be dry, of course. The grizzled and skinny farmer had rinsed them at the pump and draped them over the line barely a half-hour earlier, stripped himself in the early evening's heat to do it. The sight of his unclothed body might have uneased her another time, but in the current situation she was not moved even to look away.

He entered his cabin, his border collie following, and left the B.V.D.'s untended. She felt lucky. Stupid thought. Lucky to be stripped and pursued by the worst kind of men? Yes, lucky to be at least free and alive.

She wrapped her arms around her knees. Her body was sticky with blood from seeping lacerations and abrasions. She wanted to wait until the kerosene lamp went out inside the cabin, but there was that dog. The farmer was likely to let it out for protection when he retired, so she'd have to act now. Crawling on all fours, she circled the clearing and approached from the rear

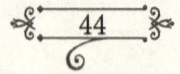

of the building. Hens clucked inside a small coop, but raised no alarm. She reached the clothesline, grabbed a leg of the garment and pulled. Too wet to slide down easily. She stood slowly and reached, then barking started and the cabin door opened and in a moment she was standing frozen in lantern light with the black and white collie swirling around her feet and the bearded farmer, still as unclothed as she was, and staring.

"Good Lord," he said. "A naked woman."

She snatched the garment from the line and ran, the dog on her heels. Then he was in front of her, yapping, snarling, trying to herd her like an errant sheep. She dodged left, right. The dog not only stayed with her but seemed to anticipate her moves.

"Jasper, come," the farmer called. "Back here, now." Then, "Thanks to you, girlie. You can keep them long johns. They was worth the look."

And she was alone with her damp treasure.

* * *

She stumbled exhausted and hurting through the stand of manzanita and scrub oak where the few Indian families, thank God, still huddled. She'd gathered some firewood on her way through the chaparral, knowing that if she came bearing something useful they'd be more willing to accept her, especially given her odd apparel. But she had no food to offer. All her supplies had rolled downhill during the struggle with Deacon and Caller.

Taking her at first for a white man, they scurried into the brush at her approach, but a few words of the Washoe language she'd picked up served her well, though she couldn't move her mouth well with both jaw and lips swollen where Deacon had slugged her. Before long, though, they recognized and remembered her. Fingers traced the wounds on her face, and the gooey bloodiness of the rest of her. They quickly provided sympathy and sponged her wounds. As they ministered to her, they chattered in a mixture of stumbling English, Washoe, and sign language, heating water for a deliciously bitter tea from the manzanita leaves.

The men were off hunting. The only shelter in camp was a crude brush ramada, for this was a temporary refuge until the salmon began running in the fall, when they would provision themselves for the winter and join other families at a more permanent village. Two of the younger women had found work in town and would probably return later unless something kept them. Once again, Many Clouds appreciated the relative safety and certainty of her Wind River home.

Eventually, the women from town arrived, and they brought a prize—a couple of pounds of bacon, their wages for a day of helping a butcher slaughter a pair of hogs and flush the offal from the guts, from which he'd make sausage casings and filler for his "pure" ground beef. Soon a sparse meal became a jolly feast, replete with songs and jokes and rollicking children. One of the town women suckled an infant. Many Clouds wondered if she would ever do that. If so, who the father would be. Which thoughts brought back images of Caller and Deacon. But she tried to remain cheerful, and the little clearing was full of warmth and friendship.

When it came time to retire, not wishing to intrude on the families' privacy, she found a niche somewhat removed from the others. She gathered a few pine boughs for bedding and, despite the chill, dropped into an exhausted sleep. She dreamed, as she did often, of her father being dragged by a rope behind the trooper's horse while she watched helplessly. In her dream, the soldier's horse left the ground and pulled her father into the sky, blood pouring from his body, till horse, and rider vanished like smoke. In reality, her father had ended up bloody and broken on the ground in front of their teepee while the soldier and his companions laughed over the corpse. In her dream now, she fought to close her ears to the familiar voice, which she began to realize was not the voice of the imagined murdering trooper, but that of the man from the mule-drawn wagon. And he was rushing through the bushes, calling in a loud whisper.

"Get out, you all. That preacher's got them likkered up and ready to kill. Everyone. Get out. Scatter. Move. Now."

Many Clouds scuttled downhill toward the bottom of the canyon. There was no moon, so she couldn't see her way, just slid downwards feet first. She skidded over sharp rocks and vicious snags. Something raked her calf. Something else stabbed, ripped the small of her back. Deep and hard. Above, she heard exultant hoots and hoofbeats. A woman screamed, stopped suddenly. Shouts of glee. More screams. Torchlight bounced off the chaparral leaves.

"Vengeance upon the heathen." Caller's voice. "We shall wash our feet in the blood of the wicked."

"I saw one runnin' down here." The voice was close. Deacon's. A collision with a tree slammed the breath out of her. Torchlight came closer, and she hugged the tree, fighting for air. The light of the flame burst full, and a shadow loomed. "Got you, redskin." Then the shadow twisted. She heard a panicked "Whoa. God*damn* it," and the man's silhouette dropped downhill past her tree. He lost hold of his torch, which shot ahead of him into the bushes, and almost instantly the bushes themselves became torches.

The falling man screamed as sheets of flame and smoke rolled up the hillside toward him from where his torch had ignited the brush.

She had barely caught her breath, and suddenly there was no air to breathe, and a searing heat enveloped her, calling to mind the word-pictures of hell drawn by Wind River's Christian missionaries. Was this to be her life through eternity? She pushed off from her tree and scrambled along the canyon wall, away from the flames, away from the yells, the screams, and the thundering roar that had become louder than all of them together.

* * *

The dawn air, heavy with ash, choked her. Black smoke rolled uphill and south, in the opposite direction of the dry creek bed where she lay exhausted and scorched. Among the thousand burning smells round her, she recognized that of her own singed hair. She raked her fingers through the tangles, found it half gone on the left side. The pain of blisters on her legs and arms, added to the cuts and scrapes of the day before, overshadowed even that of the gash in her back. She couldn't see how deep that cut was, but probing it with her fingers was like touching raw meat, and the red tinge on her fingertips told her she was still seeping blood. She stumbled to her feet and headed north and east. She was no longer thinking of Wind River. She was thinking only of her pain and her thirst. She didn't feel lucky.

ELEVEN

ANDY MEETS THE PRESIDENT

The pale-eyed, mustachioed, and bespectacled scholar-commander of the university didn't hide behind his desk as Perkins had. Nor was his desk messy as Perkins' was. All was ordered as neat and tidy as a hospital operating room. His voice thin and his manner diffident, Benjamin Wheeler pulled their chairs close and poured drinks as if the conversation were to be purely social. He asked him to reiterate his request. That done, he placed his hands atop his thighs and studied the carpet for a moment. Then snapped him a look so intense that his eyes seemed to deepen their color behind his glasses.

"And if you are denied, you're threatening to withhold your family's money?"

He was taken aback, but delighted that at last someone was speaking directly. "Absolutely not, sir."

"That was Dean Perkins' impression, Mr. Maxwell."

"A misunderstanding, President Wheeler. My application stands on its own." Andy refused to drop his eyes before the man's piercing gaze.

"And you conducted yourself in a threatening manner?"

"I intended nothing of the kind. I want only a fair hearing on my petition."

"You don't believe you've had a hearing? After all, both the History Department Chair and the Dean of Letters and Science have opened their busy schedules for you."

"Mr. McNulty's letter granted me a leave I never requested. If I was qualified for the program a year ago, I'm qualified now. Doesn't it seem self-evident that that a fair hearing would result in a favorable ruling?" That gaze again. He met it once more.

"You must realize, Mr. Maxwell, that your case has implications far beyond your individual circumstances."

"And what implications might those be?" he asked.

"In my position, I must anticipate the ramifications of my decisions, ramifications which you may be unequipped to comprehend."

"Ramifications?"

Here's what I'm prepared to do, sir," Wheeler said. "Not in response to your attempts at intimidation. A university needs money to run, but it can't let itself be run by money." He nodded, appeared pleased by his aphorism. "No, I'm taking this measure purely in the interest of *fairness*. A three-man committee of the academic senate will hear your case. A decision—a final decision—will be forthcoming soon after. I trust that is a satisfactory arrangement?"

"I believe I am entitled to reinstatement without—"

"I am not in the habit of second-guessing my subordinates, Mr. Maxwell. I hire good men and leave them to do their jobs. This hearing is an extraordinary measure."

So. A *pro forma* tribunal. A setup. The decision preordained. But why this extra step when Wheeler could have denied him on the spot? Perhaps they were a little afraid of him. Or, more likely, of losing the Maxwell money, else why all the conversation about a subject he'd never broached? He could imagine their discussions now—the pros and cons of academic miscegenation versus the loss of income. Both consequences unacceptable. But, someone would have said, there was no need to choose. Not if they made sure he couldn't run loose, claiming he hadn't had due process. A special committee was the perfect window dressing.

All right. He'd appear in the little star chamber. But he would do his best to see that it wouldn't be the tidy proceeding they were planning.

"Then I suppose I must be satisfied, sir."

"Details from my secretary, and good day to you."

* * *

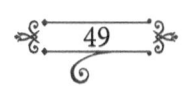

It was late in the afternoon when he emerged from the president's office. Across a tranquil bay, the sun glowed a rainbow behind the San Francisco hills. A pretty sight, but he was in no mood to commune with nature. This struggle to get back into school was more like combat than like the reasoned argument he'd imagined.

He burned to discuss the Wheeler meeting with someone, to share the plan that was brewing in his mind. Nathan Cohen. He might find him at the Merry Widow. If not, at least he could have a drink or two, a little merriment even with strangers would release some of the anxiety building inside him like a head of steam. And Virginia's boarding house was on the way. Or could be. Cohen or Virginia? Maybe both, maybe neither. Suspense. Delicious.

At Virginia's boarding house, a third option presented itself. Virginia herself was, once again, not there, and the careworn Mrs. Cheever was as hostile as ever. However, just before she slammed the door in his face, she stopped herself. "Oh," she said. "Your girly left an envelope for you. Said to give this to you if you ever showed up. As if I was her servant or something. If I didn't need her rent…." She shoved the envelope at him and this time she did slam the door.

Elegant typeface on embossed card stock invited him to "Share in the revels of the Women's Sketch Club's annual bacchanal. Costumes and masques encouraged, but not obligatory. Festivities begin one hour after sundown and continue until the revelers tire." There was a San Francisco address and a date. Two nights hence. "I hope you can drop by, Andy," she had added in her own hand. As if nothing at all had happened. "I left an invitation at your boarding house, but got no answer." Perhaps he had some communication problems with his own landlady. At any rate, the suspense had just intensified. A bacchanal. He'd never been to one of those. Costumes. Carousing. Time for his first.

TWELVE

MANY CLOUDS MEETS MAGGIE AND WILLY

She tried every trick she knew for staving off thirst. She ran her tongue around her teeth to stimulate wetness, bit down on the inside of her lips and cheeks. Carried small pebbles under her tongue. She managed to find some moisture under a seemingly dry patch of sand. None of it was enough to keep her lips from cracking, her tongue from swelling.

She recalled the last time she'd been in a fix like this, when it was her mother who'd been the sick and wounded one. It had been Andy—Andrew—who'd helped them then. No chance of him appearing now. He wouldn't even know if she died here amid the scrub oaks and dry grass of the Sierra foothills.

She was resting again. A hundred steps. Then sit down for a count of two hundred. Judging by the sun, she'd been doing that for at least two hours this morning. She'd spent most of the day before the same way, but her efforts hadn't brought her far. By the time darkness settled, she could still see smoke from the fire. Or maybe she'd come farther than she thought, and the fire had grown.

She'd spent a restive, painful night amid a scatter of boulders on top of a low hill, then resumed her halting journey at dawn. She'd skittered down into a ravine, was now climbing out the other side. She had no clear goal, knew only that she couldn't stay put. Most roads ran east and west between the mountains and the Sacramento Valley. She'd keep heading north, hoping to encounter someone who was helpful instead of dangerous. She pushed herself up and began once again to make her skidding, gravelly way uphill. On the fifty-fifth step, she tripped over a rock and fell flat. Her nose in the dirt, awash with pain, she allowed herself a twenty count then lifted her head. A road. She was on a road. It was a narrow and infrequently traveled judging by the faintness of the wagon tracks, but perhaps someone… She scooted back downhill, behind the thin cover of a few strands of poison oak. She was the color of dust now, a natural camouflage if she remained still. Still as a rabbit hiding. And listened for who or what might appear on this seldom-used thoroughfare.

* * *

"Do you suppose she's dead, Willy?"

It was a child's voice that woke her. How could she be so careless as to fall asleep? But she was still alert enough not to move. She heard no answer to the question. She did hear scuffling, the dribble of gravel down the embankment.

"Don't go touching her, Maggie. Don't. Don't."

"I ain't. But we can't just leave her here."

"But don't touch."

Many Clouds felt a prod in her ribs. Didn't move. These children wouldn't be alone, and until she knew more—"No," she yelled. The child had managed to poke the open wound in her back. She dragged herself back up to the road. The children had disappeared. Now she felt in danger not just of falling asleep, but of fainting.

"Kids," she called. How weak her voice sounded. She took a big breath and tried to shout. "Maggie. Willy. I won't hurt you." It was louder, but still weak. Silence. "If I could just have some water." Silence still. "You don't have to come close. I'll turn my back. Just leave it where I can get it."

She buried her face in her hands and started to count to a hundred, but lost count somewhere in the middle. When she reopened her eyes, there was a tin cup sitting in the middle of the road. She tried to stand and walk toward it, but dizziness forced her to crawl. The water was sweet. Very. But there wasn't much. She held the cup high.

This time, a scrawny, brown-skinned, girl of maybe six or eight appeared from behind a boulder, a dripping canteen in her hand.

"Maggie?" Many Clouds said.

"How do you know our names?"

"I heard you talking. Could you refill my cup, please?" She set the cup out at arm's length and pulled back to give the girl plenty of clearance,

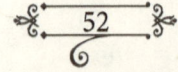

but Maggie bypassed the cup and held the canteen close enough for Many Clouds to take. Many Clouds glimpsed a younger child inching from behind the same boulder. "Thank you," she said.

"You're welcome. Are you hurt?"

"Yes."

"You should go to the doctor."

Many Clouds laughed at the idea of finding a doctor willing to treat a squaw. Still, both these kids with their dark hair and flat noses looked to be at least part Indian. Maybe they knew someone. "I think so, too," she said. "Do you know where I can find one?"

"Ma didn't go to the doctor, and she died." The little boy had stepped up behind his older sister.

"Don't be stupid, Willy," Maggie said. "You make it sound like she didn't want to. It's just cause Pa couldn't find one, so I guess I can't find one neither. Sorry."

"That's all right. Thank you for the water. I'll just rest here a little while then be on my way."

"Why are you wearing them long johns?" Maggie said.

Many Clouds didn't want to answer that question.

"Where you going?" the boy said.

"A long ways. But I need to rest first." Many Clouds nestled into a crevice in the shade behind the rocks. The water had calmed her thirst, but she was still desperate for sleep. If her pain would allow it.

"That ain't no bed," the boy said.

"You could come to the cabin," Maggie said.

"Is your pa there?"

"Pa gone off on a job," Maggie said. "He won't be back for a spell longer."

Many Clouds hadn't seen a cabin, but it had to be near. What kind of a man was this father, a father who would leave children untended in this place? She didn't intend to wait around long enough to find out. But the offer of a real place to rest was too tempting to pass up. There might even be a little food.

"Can you show me where the cabin is?" she asked.

Each of the children took one of her hands and led her uphill toward a small stand of pines a quarter mile away. Many Clouds hoped she could make it that far without collapsing.

THIRTEEN

ALLIANCE

Nathan Cohen was indeed at the Merry Widow, and this time it was Andy who hailed him down rather than the other way around. There were no tables available, so the two elbowed their way into a corner where, though barely able to hear one another, they managed a degree of privacy.

"Does this mean you've forgiven me, Andy?"

"Forgiveness, Cohen? A complicated subject and not what I had in mind."

"That pretty much fits the script of my life these days. Sorry I asked." He took a gulp that nearly drained his beer mug. Andy marveled at Cohen's ability to turn every conversation to himself. He knew he would never get a proper hearing unless he listened to Cohen's troubles first.

"What's happened?"

"McNulty denied my thesis topic. He wants me to come up with something more original and scholarly than Talleyrand's role in the American Revolution."

"Did Talleyrand have a role in the American Revolution?"

"See?" Cohen said. "Even you don't know about the friendship between him and Alexander Hamilton and how that—but never mind. The point is, it's a valid topic, and I can't understand why he won't accept it."

"What did he tell you, exactly?"

"That the connection was weak and not worthy of scholarly exploration."

"That's perfect," he said. Cohen stiffened. "No I didn't mean what you think. I mean what McNulty did to you fits exactly into why I came to see you. I believe, my friend, that you and I may be in somewhat the same boat."

"How's that?"

"Ever been to a bacchanal?"

"A what?"

"Bottoms up," he said. "Let's get out of here. If this crowd will let us through."

* * *

It was a balmy early fall evening on the bay, and quite pleasant on the deck of the ferry. Discussing his quandary with an understanding soul was like lancing a boil. He found himself repeating every word, every nuance of his conversation with Wheeler. Cohen, despite limited experience in academic politics, understood instantly what the special committee meant.

"That hearing is a fraud, Andy, a smoke screen. The bastards are never going to let you in."

"Not if they can help it, just as McNulty will never approve your thesis."

"What do you mean?"

"They'll stall until you quit, Nathan. Neither the tribe of Ham nor the tribe of Israel is welcome in this university."

"Of course. Damnation. Why didn't it ever occur to me? Didn't want to believe scholars would care about anything but scholarship, I guess." He stood and paced the deck. Andy drew a flask from his coat and offered it to him. He took a generous swallow, breathed, took another. "Damnation."

"Well, they may not welcome us, but they may not have a choice. You wondered where I went after you showed me Bierce's column?" Cohen nodded. "I went straight to Ambrose himself."

"He agreed to see you?"

"There are some advantages to being infamous." He took a drink for himself, waggled the flask. "We're going to have to get this thing refilled before we go to the party." He handed it toward Cohen, who waved it off.

"For Christ's sake, Andy, quit changing the subject. What did he say?"

"After I explained everything, he said for me to come back after the meeting with Wheeler."

"So you think Bierce might be willing and able to convince him it's immoral, what he's doing to us?"

"Not just us, Nathan. Let me ask you something my Aunt Amelia asked me a few days ago. How many colored professors can you think of?" Cohen considered for a moment, then shook his head. "Jewish?"

"Not that I know of."

"Of course not. When I went into that meeting with Wheeler, I was thinking about my own degree and nothing else. Now, I'm thinking this has much more to do with power than morality, and I seriously think they're afraid of us, Nathan."

"Be serious, Andy. We're annoying, maybe, like gnats. But that's about it."

"By ourselves, maybe. But why fight us even this hard if we don't represent a threat beyond just us? I mean imagine the time and trouble they've gone to planning each encounter with me. The alternatives they combed through before they set up this silly committee. From their perspective, we're a serious problem."

"And what would that be, Sir Andrew?"

"I'm not sure, but it must have to do with power and money, and we've got to fight it."

"All right, general. Call forth your troops and charge."

"I'm not playing, Nathan. There's no army yet, but I think we can make some trouble. And speaking from experience, when there's trouble, secrets pop right out of the woodwork. Are you with me?"

"Trouble for McNulty? Do you even have to ask?"

"Good, because between you, me, and Bierce I think we can create a hell of a mess. And if there's anything those so-called gentlemen hate worse than niggers and Jews, it's mess."

The ferry landed. Passengers headed toward the exit, waiting for the gangplank to be lowered. Andy and Cohen remained on the fantail a few moments passing the flask back and forth until it was empty. Andy leaned toward his new confederate.

"It's party time, Nathan."

FOURTEEN

HELPLESS

Many Clouds had intended to be gone from the cabin by sundown. The children's finding her had been a stroke of luck. She figured she had one coming. In their innocence and despite their poverty, they had offered her a little cheese and water without the reluctance or suspicion a white adult might have had. A small spring and a couple of goats seemed to be all the resources the little homestead possessed. A short rest was all she needed to give her the strength to carry her to where she might find more help. Another Indian rancheria, or even a town with a doctor willing to treat her. Apparently, though, her normal ability to sleep and wake almost at will had deserted her. The sound of Willy and Maggie yelling, "Papa, papa" from outside broke her slumber. The sun had long since disappeared. The children's father would surely be angry to find his children harboring a squaw who was consuming their scarce food. There was only one door to the cabin, and the sounds were so close she knew she would never escape that way. A small window in the rear might be just large enough. It was her only chance. She felt dizzy as she scrambled toward it, but managed to resist succumbing long enough to force her head and one shoulder and arm into the opening. Then time ran out.

"That's her," she heard Maggie say from the doorway. And she knew it was no use. The window was too small, and the effort had drained her in any case. She pulled herself back inside and turned around to face a man with a lantern followed by the children.

"No need for that," the man said. "Ain't nobody here going to hurt you." Noting the kindness of his eyes and voice, Many Clouds recognized the very man who had made the futile attempt to rescue her from Caller and Deacon.

"Kids tell me your name's Many Clouds," he said. "That right?"

She nodded.

"Mine's Miller," he said. "Miller Fitzpatrick. I recognize you now. You're the girl them two phony preachers had tied up, ain't you?"

She nodded again.

"And I guess you been hurt some?"

She nodded yet again.

"Well, let's see what we can do for you." He held out his hand, which she took reluctantly, and he led her back to the floor palette on which she had been sleeping. "Where's it at?" he said.

"A cut on my back," she said. "Lots of burns."

"Oh, lordy, you was in that fire, wasn't you? You had a rough couple of days. Maggie, would you get that stove going and put on some water? That's a good girl. Now, Many Clouds, if you want, maybe you can tell us later how you come to be wearing these B.V.D.'s, but right now I'm going to have to cut away a little piece from the back to get a good look at that wound, okay?"

She nodded and gripped the mattress in anticipation of the pain, grieving over her helplessness. He pulled a hunting knife from a sheath at his belt. She flinched.

"Ah, don't worry none. Said I ain't going to hurt you, and I ain't." She felt a tug and twist, heard the fabric tearing as he opened the area around the cut. "Ugly business, what them fellers did. But you was lucky in a way. They was a woman and a baby burned alive."

Many Clouds jammed her face into the mattress. Although they'd only spent a couple of evenings together, she suddenly felt that the mother and child had been part of her family.

"Dear, oh, dear. I may have to break my word about hurting you. Hang on," Fitzpatrick said.

Then she arched her back and screamed, for Miller Fitzpatrick's probing of her wound had sent a tornado of pain twisting through her body.

Willy started crying. Maggie said, "What are you doing, Pa?"

Fitzpatrick stood and gathered his children around him. "Many Clouds has an infection and it hurts, is all. We're going to fix it up."

"Is she going to die, Pa, like Mama did?" This was from Willy.

"No, boy. Now you go on over and make sure that fire stays hot. Maggie, girl, how's that water doing?"

"It's boiling, Pa," she said.

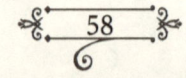

"All right then. I'll just rip the arms off this here old shirt. Ain't nothing much but rags anyhow. And you boil it up while I stick my knife in the coals. Sorry, Many Clouds, I ain't got nothing to give you to ease things."

He trussed Many Clouds' hands and feet together and inserted a gag between her teeth, explaining that it would keep her from flailing around and hurting herself or interfering with the operation, "For I guarantee you're going to want to kill me before this is over," he said. Once everything was prepared, Fitzpatrick retrieved his knife from the stove and knelt beside his bound and gagged patient.

She could smell the seared metal as Fitzpatrick lifted his sterilized knife over the infection on her back, recalled the hot desert afternoon two years earlier when Andrew had heated a knife to slice open the fester on her mother's leg. It seemed as if her own screams, her own pain, now merged with her mother's in a horrible unity that would last for eternity. Then oblivion swallowed her.

FIFTEEN

ANDY AMONG THE BOHEMIANS

Virginia and Andy were walking along the embarcadero, arm-in-arm, headed toward Telegraph hill and the headquarters of the Sketch Club, a group of women artists who were nurturing Virginia's career as a painter, also the organization that had organized the bacchanal for that evening. They hadn't seen one another for two days since their meeting with Bierce, which now seemed an age ago.

"Well, that meal with Ambrose was up near the top of the scale for exciting lunches," Virginia said.

"So it's 'Ambrose' now, is it?" Andy said

"Why not?" Virginia said. "It was his idea."

"All right. Granted. Yes, the meal the talk were exciting, sure," Andy said. "But I could do with less of his precious suspense. Do you think Bierce is going to help out or not?"

"Why do you doubt it, Andy? All that blather about facts and so on was just a cover. He's a man of instincts, and you impressed him. "

"You can read him that well?"

"I'm not a politician's daughter for nothing."

"If anyone impressed him, though, it was you."

"We could make quite a team, don't you think?" They shared a look of intimacy that frightened him and excited him at the same time. He slid his hand down to grasp hers, squeezed slightly. She answered the pressure.

At the base of the hill sprawled the Barnum and Bailey Circus layout of tents and flags and rail cars. Part way up the slope, they took a moment to gaze on the spectacle. They heard a band. A show was in progress inside the big tent.

"Care for a day at the circus?" she said. "I've never been."

"Another time," he said. "My life is enough of a circus at the moment."

"This is quite a sight, you must admit," she said.

"It smells a bit like the Circle M barnyard."

"You're no fun, Andy. You know that?"

They arrived at the bottom of the steps that led to the Sketch Club's house. It was a converted house—mansion, really—perched halfway up the hill and served as both workshop and, at various times, residence for the bevy of artists—all female—who used the space.

"We could put that theory about my fun-loving nature to the test." He raised her hand to his lips, kissed it. She giggled, slapped his shoulder lightly, but she didn't pull her hand away. Then Nathan Cohen appeared at his elbow. He'd wanted Virginia to himself, but had invited Nathan to meet them at the party. He figured it was an opportunity to cement their friendship as an assurance that he wouldn't pull out of the fateful proceedings with the faculty committee.

"Hello, Nathan," Virginia said. It seemed to Andy that she didn't fully approve of Cohen's presence, but decided not to object. Come in, you two," she said, "and see what we're all about."

They climbed the steps, and entered a foyer. Virginia told them to wait, promising to return quickly. She disappeared up a stairway.

Bacchus, he thought, would have enjoyed this party. Virginia's sketch club advertised itself with a picture of a group of three women standing before easels, paintbrushes poised, on a bluff overlooking the ocean. Breezes ruffled their skirts as they transferred the *pleine aire* scene to canvas. The scene in this dim basement, however, looked more like something out of Hieronymus Bosch or the kind of Barbary Coast den he'd frequented with Julian.

"Andy, Andy," Cohen whispered loudly, elbowed Andy's ribs and wagged his head in the direction of a corner couch. He meant the gesture to be surreptitious, but he was obvious as if he'd aimed his nose like a pointer at an amorous couple on a corner couch, a couple that did not include a man. Andy wondered whether bringing Cohen had been a good idea. He himself was a step or two short of sober, but Cohen was on the verge of slurring and stumbling. On second thought, what was he worried about? Getting thrown out of an orgy?

"That would make quite a sketch for all these artists, wouldn't it?" he said. "Why don't you do some exploring, Nathan? I want to see where Virginia's got to."

"Exploring. Ah, yes. Dr. Livingston ventures into the great unknown. See you later, Andy." Cohen made as much of a beeline as he could manage in his inebriated state toward a tall woman in a black dress and sequined mask who leaned against a pillar smoking a cheroot. Cohen approached her, pointed at her mask, perhaps asking for a peek. Good luck, Nathan, he thought. He scanned the foyer to make sure wasn't there, then climbed the stairway where she had disappeared.

At the top of the stairs, he found himself at a hallway that led in two different directions. For no particular reason, he turned left. He could see that a number of the rooms, once parlors, now classrooms, afforded bay vistas, which were rendered with varying degrees of skill on canvases set on easels or hanging on walls. Sketch pads, paint tubes, charcoal pencils, and the like lay boxed and stacked, ready for the next session. But art was on no one's mind this night. Nearly every room and alcove housed goings on that would have shocked and enraged the right and proper.

His sexual experiences had been limited to a few exciting and entertaining commercial excursions, usually guided by Julian, and two romantic experiments with otherwise proper girls during his freshman year in college. His frustrated pursuit of Virginia had often reminded him of one of those silly medieval courtly love tales like Troilus and Cressida where it takes the knight years to earn his virgin's favor. Now he was pursuing her through this brothel-like place? Nothing added up.

He wandered the mazey hallways, loins stirring, heart racing at the tableaus of bare breasts and intimate writhings he glimpsed through open doorways. The air was thick with the sweet, intoxicating fumes he recognized from walking through Charley Hung's opium den on his quest for Julian's killer. A pale-skinned woman with honey blonde hair and a massive chin ran toward him. She was not quite naked, but not quite clothed, either, clutching her teddy top to her chest and shrieking in delight. A man and another woman pursued her. "Oh, no you don't," the man called. He was shirtless, as was the woman. They all shouldered past him, the teddy-clad partner of the *ménage-a-trois* allowed herself to be cornered at a turn in the corridor, and the shrieks and giggles became grunts and moans.

He could have joined in any number of such liaisons, even turned down two direct invitations. Is this why Virginia had invited him here? He had mixed feelings about that idea. Isn't that what he'd been after all this time? He'd certainly fantasized her trim body without clothes often enough. But, he realized, this promiscuity wasn't exactly what he'd been seeking. Then what? His body had become a throbbing pulse. He couldn't think.

Finally, he climbed a short stair to a space whose ceiling-to-floor shelves of books proclaimed it a library. He saw Virginia reclining at the feet of an older woman wearing a dress with a lacy collar, curls piled high. She sat on a maroon leather couch, reading aloud from a leather notebook. The audience was all female, and all the ladies were fully clothed and reverential. It was like coming on a church service in the middle of a whorehouse.

Virginia herself wore a plain white blouse buttoned to the neck. Her turban was a color he thought they called mauve. No feathers. No fox fur. At a party where everyone else was extravagantly costumed or undressed, she chose puritan simplicity. Ever the non-conformist.

Even though he hadn't read Ina Coolbrith's poems, he recognized her from her press photos. Virginia didn't see him enter the room, lean against the ebony wainscoting, and take a pull from his flask as he listened to the final lines of the poet reading from a paean to the rise of San Francisco out of the ruins of the 1906 quake.

> *But I will see thee ever as of old!*
> *Thy wraith of pearl, wall, minaret and spire,*
> *Framed in the mists that veil thy Gate of Gold—*
> *Lost City of my love and my desire.*

He smiled, nearly laughed aloud, at the stilted, quaint verse, at Coolbrith's melodramatic reading. He had to admit, you couldn't beat a bacchanal for entertainment. The group applauded and Virginia asked for another, but the poet demurred, pleading fatigue, thanked her audience, and walked toward the stair, three or four devotees trailing. Others, Virginia among them, drifted toward the back of the room where a heavy walnut table bore a cut glass bowl of punch. He joined them.

"Why, Andy, I'd lost hope."

"Not again," he said. "I thought you'd learned never to do that. Thanks for the invitation. This is some organization, this Sketch Club." He ladled Virginia a cup of punch. "What would your father say?"

"Or your mother?" she said.

"*Touché.*" He augmented his punch with a dollop from the flask he and Nathan had had refilled at a bar on their way to the party. He offered a share to Virginia. She accepted.

"What did you think of Ina?" she said. Before he could answer, Evelyn Withrow's voice trilled through the room.

"Ah, my bonny lass and laddie." She floated toward them, costumed, he supposed, as Marie Antoinette, panniers wide enough to yoke a team of oxen. She leaned over to Virginia and hid both their faces both behind her fan. But she spoke plenty loud enough for anyone in the vicinity to hear. "A reservation has been canceled. Therefore, my dear, the room with the blue door is yours. I know you'll make good use of it." It was clear from their profiles and the sound that she and Virginia took a moment to share a lip-to-lip kiss. Odd, but everything seemed odd in this house on this night.

Withrow snapped her fan shut, gave him a wink, and turned her back. She reached into her décolletage and withdrew an ornate gold key on a blue ribbon, handed it over her shoulder to Virginia. Another wink. "Ta-ta." She sidled out, turning what might have been an ungainly exit into a little dance, and disappeared merrily down the stairs.

"The blue door?" he asked.

Virginia remained silent and still for a time, regarding the key, then turned. "When I invited you to the party, Andy, I was very enthusiastic for the blue door. Now with this key in my hand, I wonder are we—am I—ready after all?"

"You could at least let me know what you're talking about," he said.

She looked back and forth between him and the key. "I don't suppose a little peek would do any harm," she said finally.

He followed her down the hall and up a flight of stairs to the third floor, where, on a landing at the end of a short hallway, he saw a dark blue door embellished with gold stars and a leering, winking moon. Winking seemed to be the primary gesture of naughtiness around here. Whatever lay behind the door was full of lascivious promise, and his body throbbed with yearning. Virginia looked at him with a slight smile, started to insert the key in the lock, stopped. She handed it to him. "You should do the honors." He took the key, hesitated. For some reason his ardor began to dissipate.

Giggling and shouts exploded from the hallway. "Laura, come back here," a man yelled. Into the hall burst a pretty blonde in a red Arthurian costume carrying a belled and beribboned jester's scepter. Giggling, she ran to a corner on the landing, ignoring Andy and Virginia, concealed the scepter behind her back. The jester followed. Virginia's face pinched, her body became taut. The jester all at once forgot his Guinevere and his scepter and said, "Oh, Virginia."

The whole atmosphere tensed. He felt as if someone had asked a question in a language everyone understood but him.

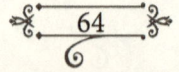

"Aren't you going to introduce me?" the jester said.

"I don't think so, no," Virginia said.

"Then I'll have to do it myself." He thrust a hand forward. "Tom Redmond," he said.

Andy took a cue from Virginia's hostility, and rather than extend and shake, held the key with both hands. But he did tip his head and say, "Andy."

Redmond covered Andy's refusal of his open hand by sweeping toward the woman in the corner, who had stepped forward, scepter now wielded like a weapon, eyes and lips tightened in anger as she glanced back and forth between Virginia and Redmond. "And this is Laura Adams," Redmond said. Laura nodded.

"We're acquainted," Virginia said. "I understand congratulations are in order."

The remark appeared to startle Redmond. "Why?" he said.

"Oh, hasn't Miss Adams told you about the upcoming exhibition of her photographs?"

"Oh, that," Redmond said. "Of course."

"Oh, that?" Laura was yelling. Her cheeks inflamed. "Oh, that? Dismiss my life's work as 'oh, that?'" She swung Redmond's scepter, bells jangling, delivered a blow to his face, then dropped the scepter and fled the room. Blood dribbled from Redmond's nose. He wiped with his wrist.

"Oh, dear me," Virginia said, smiling, mischief in her eyes. She opened her reticule and held out a hanky. "Would the wounded warrior like something to staunch the flow?"

"To hell with you, Virginia," he said. He made no move to accept the hanky, stomped on the scepter and ground his foot as if he wished it were Virginia herself under his heel. "I wish you luck, Andy. You'll need it." Redmond stormed off.

"What was that about?" he said.

"In the past. And none of your business." She stuffed the hanky back in her purse.

He tried to stuff his irritation as well. "All right. If you say so." He pointed to the door. "Let's see what's on the other side of this absurd moon."

"I've never been inside," she said.

"But you know." She nodded, lowered her eyes. "And you're embarrassed."

"No," she said. She lifted her chin and looked him in the eyes. "No. What embarrasses me is the whole idea of embarrassment. What's natural and human should never be embarrassing." She delivered the speech like a recitation, more from memory than conviction.

"Natural and human," he said. He inserted Withrow's gilded key in the lock and bent it back and forth till it snapped. He flung the remains to the floor beside the mutilated scepter and gestured down the hallway. This is an astounding place," he said."

"A lot of wonderful work gets done here."

"Speaking of which, may I see some of yours?"

She looked surprised.

"Well, it's hardly… But if you're really interested,"

"Of course I'm interested," he said. "I'm interested in everything about you."

"Well, come on, then." She took his hand and led down the corridor.

Virginia ushered him into a small studio. The setting sun was a red disk parked on the horizon. Easels circled a platform in the center of the room on which stood a small chaise lounge.

"We're doing life drawing at the moment. My sketches are over here." She pointed to a wall near the doorway. "The upper section there." Andy followed her gesture. "It's not my strong suit, so please don't judge me too harshly."

All the sketches were in charcoal. His eye fell first on an unfinished rendering of a nude woman, a Rubenesque beauty reclining on the very chaise that stood in the center of the room.

"I've had such trouble with the angle of her hands and arms," Virginia said. "She's only coming for two more sessions, and I'm afraid I'll never finish."

"You've done quite well with *him*, however." Andy pointed to a drawing of a man sitting, elbow on thigh, chin on fist. Rodin's "The Thinker."

The model was endowed with the prodigious muscles of the original statue, and Virginia had done an admirable job of reproducing every detail of the whole nude body.

It struck him that if this was what all her art classes were like, she'd have gazed on quite a number of bare cocks. Cocks. A little embarrassing to even think a word like that around Virginia. Suddenly, the idea of her looking at all those men angered him. Why should it? They were only models. What's more, despite their promising reunion, he and Virginia had made no commitments to one another. Beware Othello's green-eyed monster, the predator "jealousy."

"That fellow has quite a physique," he said. He tried to sound casual.

"I knew it," she said.

"Knew what?"

"Male students drawing female nudes is fine, but doing things the other way around puts everyone in an uproar." She put her hands on her hips.

"Was I in an uproar?"

"I thought better of you, Andy. I'm disappointed." She turned her back, stepped to the window. The sun was below the horizon now.

He had an impulse to apologize, but that was the road to their old relationship. If ever there was the time to move past that, it was now.

"How about drawing me?" he said. He closed the door, slid the hasp to, then leaped to the platform and began unbuttoning his shirt.

She turned from the window. "What are you doing?"

"You said you needed more practice." He tossed his shirt to the floor, sat on the lounge and began tugging at his boots.

She held up her hands and turned her back. "Oh, no, Andy. This is entirely too fast."

"What do you mean? If you think about it, we've been an item for three years. Besides, it's just art, isn't it? *Voilà*. He stretched out on the lounge, trying for a rough imitation from the Sistine Chapel. He fought mentally against the erection that would have made the effect rather comical. He didn't succeed entirely, but enough to avoid humiliation.

"Well, aren't you even going to look?"

She did turn then, reddened, started giggling.

"What's the matter?"

"It's just… why Andrew Maxwell you're bald."

He sat up, looked himself up and down, rubbed the top of his head. What was she talking about?

"Are you Jewish and Negro both?" she said.

"Oh, He grinned, looked at his crotch. His tumescence deflated. "You're talking about my circumcision. I had no say in the matter. My mother says she was following some modern medical advice of the time. Maybe if I did another statue." He imitated The Thinker. She laughed. "Well, aren't you going to draw?"

"I'm laughing too hard." He jumped down. Cradled her face in his hands and kissed her soundly on the cupid bow lips he had sought for so long. She at first merely accepted the kiss, then pressed her lips to his.

"Your turn," he whispered.

She shook her head. "I'm the artist, Andy, not the model."

He kissed her again. This time, she tentatively placed her hands on his bare hips.

"What if Mona Lisa had refused Leonardo?"

"You're not Leonardo, and Mona kept her clothes on," she said. She was laughing again.

"Irrelevant and immaterial," he whispered. Another kiss. She pushed away.

Andy, I'm not just some Roberta Roundheels who's going to flop over backwards just because you're worked up."

"After all this time, why would I think that about you?"

"Anyway, I can't here."

Andy was starting to smolder with aggravation and disappointment. "As if the Thinker were watching?"

"Maybe."

"I can take care of that problem." He reached up and tore the sketch from the wall, dropped it fluttering to the floor.

She squealed, jumped, flailed, managed to catch the paper before it landed. "Andy that was juvenile," she said. She smoothed the sketch against her dress, turned her back again. "Now get dressed, please."

"All right," he said. She turned, tipped her head in that flirtatious way she had.

"We're going for a walk, he said."

"A walk?" she said.

"Follow me," he said.

* * *

Soon, they stood in the pale glare of a gas streetlight a few blocks away from the Sketch Club house.

"What do you see, Virginia?"

"What's this all about, Andy?"

He pulled her to him and stroked her cheek. "Please humor me," he said. "It's important."

She smiled. "All right." They stepped apart. "I see a boarded up window. A Padlocked door. A steet light. A concrete sidewalk."

"Through my eyes, Virginia, that padlocked door and boarded window will always open into a crowded bar called the Fandango. The sidewalk is not concrete, it's a boardwalk. And lying right there under the gas light is my brother, Julian. My half-brother, actually, but I didn't know that then. One minute he stumbles, happy and drunk as a lord out of that bar. The next he's lying in his own blood, his belly sliced open from his belt to his breastbone, and a huge Indian is standing over him with a knife that looks as long as my arm. I'm looking at it all from about here, a few steps away, nearly as drunk as Julian. I'm paralyzed."

"My goodness, Andy, you certainly know how to set a romantic mood for a girl."

Oh, I realize this isn't exactly moonlight and roses and chocolates, but you said yourself that I've changed, and you were right." He took her hands in his. "I want you to understand how and why, and it all goes back to that night."

"I discovered two things: First, I thought I was tame and civilized, but if I could have moved, I'd have gladly carved up Yellow Squirrel like a prime rib roast." She dropped her eyes, his hands.

"And the second thing?"

"Before Julian's murder, everything in my world was known and permanent. After, nothing was. So I no longer sit and wait. And now I'm wondering about that Redmond. Is there a future for us, Virginia, or not?"

She stepped back, turned away. "Blunt, aren't you?"

"Life is blunt."

"Andy, I don't have a crystal ball."

"It's a decision for your heart, not a fortune teller."

"I wish..." she whispered.

"Is it Redmond.?"

She smiled, shook her head. "No. No. It's... more complicated than that."

"I won't wait," he said. "Can't."

She turned and walked back up the hill toward the club house. He watched a moment longer, was about to turn away when she reappeared. Some distance away. She stopped.

"Andy?" she said.

He said nothing, stood wondering and hoping. She opened her arms. He came forward. They embraced and kissed. The kiss finished, she snuggled up to his shoulder.

"I was thinking," she said.

"Yes?"

"My first pose could be 'The Naked Maja," she said. "If that's all right with you.

SIXTEEN

A DAY AT THE CIRCUS

Michael Yellow Squirrel shouldered his way into the Barnum and Bailey tent that had been raised near the San Francisco waterfront. He enjoyed the resentment he stirred among those he bumped and shoved. No one was going to seriously oppose the progress of a six-foot-two, angry-looking, two-hundred-and-fifty pound man as he worked his way through the crowd to the front row of the bleachers. If anyone tried, well, he always welcomed a good fight. A box seat is what he wanted, but an Indian couldn't buy one of those even if he had the money. Add that to the list of reasons he'd dedicated himself to a life of revenge against the white men who had stolen his peoples' land, defiled their women, destroyed their way of life.

The band played a fanfare, and the ringmaster in top hat and red tailcoat announced the parade. The marching music started, and the clowns came tumbling in, followed by the high-wire troupe. The women wore those sparkly little costumes that revealed more flesh than many of the strippers dancing in the Barbary Coast bars. Yet the same people who wanted laws passed against the one brought their kids to this. Typical white hypocrisy.

He enjoyed the circus. All of it. But what fascinated him most was the big cats. They prowled. They roared. They clawed the air. Most of all, though, they waited. They waited for an opening, a moment, a chance to grab and destroy the man with the whip who ruled their lives.

It happened every once in a while, and he'd even seen it once himself. In Manila. It had almost been worth the trip—the involuntary "cruise" from San Francisco arranged by Andrew Maxwell and Charley Hung, who'd bought and sold him like a sack of grain. Maxwell had turned him over to Hung to pay off his brother Julian's gambling debt. Hung had sold him for cash to the captain of the *Heavenly Happiness,* bound for Shanghai via Manila and Bangkok. Both had undoubtedly expected never to see him again, certainly not so soon. But he was like those cats, sharing their secret of how at one and the same time hate waiting, but savor the anticipation.

He shifted in his seat for a better look at the lady climbing the ladder to the trapeze, the change in angle provided a view of the plump rear cheeks peeking out from under her brief skirt, but the movement caused a sharp pain to knife through his hand and arm. He rubbed the scar where Maxwell had stabbed him, pinning the arm to the ground. Something inside it had never healed, and his left hand was weak, painful. He was glad for the pain. It kept his revenge hungry, urgent, even through the waiting. He had waited for his chance to jump off the *Heavenly Happiness* in the Thailand and hire on to a freighter back to San Francisco. Not neglecting to slip a blade between the ribs of the first mate before he dropped overboard.

They'd shot that lion in Manila, naturally. He'd clawed and chewed the trainer, smashed him against the bars of his own cage, then they'd blown the poor animal's brains out. But the cat had had his revenge. Had tasted the blood of his enemy. Yellow Squirrel wondered how that blood had tasted to the lion. Maybe one of the beasts would get loose today. He hoped so, the same hope he brought to every circus performance he attended. In the meantime, he, like they, could wait. Had been waiting. And the waiting was almost done.

SEVENTEEN

BAD MEDICINE

"You done almost slept the clock around," Miller Fitzpatrick told Many Clouds when she awoke. She felt weak and sore, but she was clean and salved and bandaged. Her hands and legs were wrapped in clean cloths as if she were a swaddled papoose. She wore a simple buckskin dress she had never seen before.

"It was Swallow's, my wife's" Miller Fitzpatrick said. "Don't worry none. We managed to get it on you without no embarrassing moments."

"It warn't easy, neither," Maggie said.

Many Clouds tried to picture the process. Smiled to herself. "Thank you," she said. With his hat off Fitzpatrick looked thin and vulnerable. His hair was the color of pine cones, and he wore a scant moustache. He smelled of warm summer earth.

"And we washed up your B.V.D's. They need some mending, though, 'cause they was burned here and there. Thought you might like to do the repair work yourself."

She wanted nothing more to do with the longjohns, but didn't want to reject the kindness. "Thank you for that also," she said. "I can be on my way soon."

Two days passed, and she gained strength. The pain receded, and she was able to take short walks. She watched Fitzpatrick at his chores—cutting wood, planting winter vegetables. She patched the B.V.D.'s, using tools and fabric scraps left behind by Fitzpatrick's wife. Miller seemed to appreciate the refurbished underwear.

"You're mighty handy with a needle," he went on. "Maggie could use a lesson or two."

"It's the least I can do to repay your kindness." She was suspicious—no, certain—that Fitzpatrick was suggesting more than a couple of sewing lessons, and she certainly owed the family a great deal. But entanglements with white people, even well-meaning ones, even if they were part Indian, always seemed to end in trouble. She had set in her mind a departure date of a week, thinking that with luck she would still be able to spend winter at home. "I'm sorry to cause so much trouble."

"Ain't your fault," he said. "Any more than it was Swallow's fault she caught the pneumony. And wasn't her fault no white doc would touch a redskin woman calico or no calico. And it ain't our kids' fault they daddy has to leave 'em alone for days at a time to go off and earn a living. So I got a seven-year-old girl's looking after the five-year-old boy. Ain't that a crime? And who's fault is it I can't get help from nobody red or white to help with a half-breed kid?"

In a way, Many Clouds felt that she and the Fitzpatricks were alike, both separate from their people, like moons floating above and outside the world. But she kept her feelings to herself. "Maggie and I trapped a squirrel this morning," Many Clouds said. "I'll help her fix it for supper."

On the morning of the third day, Fitzpatrick readied his wagon and scrawny horse for a hauling job, promised to be back in a couple of days.

"It's an enormous comfort," he said, "having you to look after the young 'uns."

"They are the ones looking after me, I'm afraid."

"Look, Many Clouds. I come to know something about different Indian tribes, and you sure ain't local, so I'm thinking you're on your way to your folks somewhere a ways off, and I ain't got any right to ask nothing of you. But Maggie and Willy, they could use some caring for, and if you'd be willing to stop over a spell..."

She would never get used to the way white people just spoke their minds in such direct ways. It was rude to force people to declare themselves, leaving no way to save face. The best thing to do was ignore Fitzpatrick's request and hope he would catch the hint.

"You don't need to say nothing now," he went on. "Soon's I get those logs over the hill, I'll be back and you can decide then. I'm sure you got your own people are needing you, but the way things are with us, you'd be welcome as the first rain after a drought."

Many Clouds smiled, lowered her eyes.

"In the meantime, we'd be grateful if you accepted something from us." From under the bed he pulled a small trunk—a wooden ammunition box, actually, spruced up with varnish and nickel-plated hardware for hinges and a handle. Inside on top were several objects he removed and laid out on the bed. A tintype of an older Indian man (Swallow's father?), a small buckskin bag, a necklace and bracelet of amber-colored beads.

"These is all we got left of Swallow," he said. "But this is what I was talking about." He lifted out a Calico dress, lavender and white, with puffed sleeves and a lace ruffle on the skirt. "She used to wear this to town. It seemed she was treated a mite better by the storekeepers and such than if she wore her Indian getup. I'm sure she'd want you to have it after what you done for the children."

A lump rose in her throat. A bribe? Ugly thought. "Thank you," she said softly.

She said nothing more to Miller Fitzpatrick about his request to stay the winter. She helped him complete preparations for his journey, then wished him well as he guided his wagon down the hill and on to the road.

The next morning, the wound on her back began throbbing, the pounding spreading in every direction. She remembered Andy's words as they knelt together in the desert over her suffering mother. The wound isn't nearly as dangerous as the infection. She picked up an empty pail and started for the water pump. Her vision blurred, legs weakened and she collapsed at the cabin door.

Maggie yelled, "No."

"She's gonna die," Willy said.

Willy's words were the last she heard before she sank into dark fatigue.

EIGHTEEN

AMBROSE AGAIN

"Andy Maxwell, you already know Mr. Joseph Francis, I believe." When Andy entered Ambrose Bierce's office on Tuesday morning, Nathan Cohen in tow, he found the columnist once again meeting with the publisher of *The Elevator*. And Francis was not alone.

"Very nice to see you again, Mr. Maxwell," Francis said as he shook hands. "Please allow me to present my associate, Miss Deborah Beasley." A demure Negro woman in her late twenties or early thirties extended her hand without rising from the wingback chair.

"Your reputation precedes you, sir," she said. "I'm honored."

He introduced Cohen, then said, "We didn't mean to interrupt. Should we wait outside?"

"Not on our account," Francis said. "We have a newspaper to publish." He helped Beasley rise from her seat.

"We'd be honored to have you call on us at *The Elevator*," Beasley said. "A visit might be advantageous for you as well, considering everything."

Advantageous? Considering everything? There was something mysterious in the way Beasley looked at him. Cooper, Cooper, he thought, you were more right than I knew. "Thank you kindly for the invitation, miss. Perhaps I shall," he said.

The second the two journalists were out the door, Cohen started gushing. "I'm a great admirer of your work," Mr. Bierce. And I can't wait for *The Devil's Dictionary*."

"Well, my young admirer, you won't have to. He reached into a box in the corner of the office and slapped two books on the desktop. "Advance copies. Autographed."

"You don't mean it," Cohen said.

"How much do we owe you?" Andy said.

"Your price, gentlemen is to become my clarions, singing the praises of this slight volume to all and sundry at every opportunity."

"That is not a price," Cohen said. "It's a privilege."

A knock on the door. "Enter," Bierce said.

"Mr. Bierce, I... oh, excuse me." Tom Redmond faltered when he saw Andy and Nathan, but he recovered quickly.

"Well, this is a surprise, Mr... "

"Maxwell," he said. "And my friend, Nathan Cohen."

"Maxwell? Andy? Andrew Maxwell. Of course. The hero of the Circle M. What kind of a reporter am I not to have recognized that straightaway?"

"You were rather distracted as I recall."

"True enough, and don't remind me. But I'm honored to meet you."

Honored. For the second time in ten minutes. He wished the folks on campus felt that way.

Cohen seemed ready to burst. "I recall seeing your name, Mr. Redmond. In 'The Tattler' if I'm not mistaken."

"Mr. Bierce sometimes mentions me when we work together on some matter or another."

"*E Clampus Vitus* was the last subject as I recall," Cohen said. "You stopped some hooligans from breaking up a parade."

"A trifle, Mr. Cohen, but I'm flattered you recognized me." He turned to Bierce and handed him an envelope. Here is the information you requested, sir." He turned. "I believe it will interest you as well, Andy."

"Thank you, Tom," Bierce said. "And I have here a request from Mr. Hearst." He handed Redmond a slip of paper. "Some activity at the Hall of Justice, I believe."

"As always. Good morning, sir. Gentlemen." And he was gone.

Bierce opened the envelope, glanced over its contents, and slid the paper across the desk. "These are the names of your special committee."

Bierce had been unavailable the previous day when he and Nathan had first tried to see him, and they had spent the entire day scouring every source on campus they could imagine to track down the information he had just handed them.

"Already? I haven't even had a chance to tell you about my meeting with Wheeler."

"I'll be delighted to hear your impressions, but Mr. Redmond, notwithstanding his romantic peccadilloes, is a most effective investigator. I trust you'll recognize these names?"

McNulty, the history dept chair. Of course. He'd detected a softness in the chairman, but it had been fleeting, and he doubted the man would have the fortitude to buck what was obviously an institutional decision. Dean Perkins. Two votes against him right there, no matter how strong his arguments. The third member was an unknown. George MacIntosh, Chair of the English Department.

"It's stacked, of course," he told Bierce. "You know I've already talked to McNulty and Perkins. I don't know about MacIntosh, but why would he be different?"

"I'd say your assessment is on target, Andy. MacIntosh is new both to the position and the university. They hired him during the summer of '08, while you were journeying into the wilderness to track down the source of that vendetta. He's a Harvard import, brought in to add a patina of Eastern prestige to Wheeler's western Athens. The word is that there was some resentment because he was placed above several other local candidates, but no one could argue his credentials, so the resentment simmers. He holds his position at the pleasure of the administration, rather than that of his colleagues."

"And did Redmond's inquiries confirm my version of the encounters, sir?"

"Surprisingly, yes."

"Surprisingly?"

"The usual tendency is to demonize one's adversaries, distort their ideas and their remarks. Not you. You'd make an excellent reporter, Andy."

"Then you're willing to write me a letter of support, Ambrose?"

"Here." He handed over a stack of envelopes. "A copy for yourself and one for each committee member. I suggest you introduce them only after the hearing has progressed a while. It will give the gentlemen less time to cook up a unified response."

"Thank you, sir, thank you."

"The gist is this. I ask the committee to remember that people should be judged on their merits rather than extraneous criteria."

"This should help immensely."

"No it won't. It might fluster them a bit, but won't change the vote."

"Then why—"

"Because you interest me, Andy. You're a unique animal. A child of privilege, yet the offspring of the despised. It's entertaining to help you stir the tranquility of the pompous and pretentious."

"Sometimes a few questions from someone like Redmond can evoke enormous activity, like stirring an anthill with a stick, but in this case the disturbance was minor. You observed that these gentlemen do not like 'mess.' However, they don't yet believe that you—we—can create one. Perhaps after the decision is final I can do more. Right now, they can hide behind the shield of 'case pending.'"

Andy stared at the letters. Interesting, Bierce had said. Entertaining. But ineffective? By themselves, maybe.

"Ambrose, perhaps you're wondering why Mr. Cohen is here."

"I assumed you'd get to that when you were ready."

"Mr. Cohen has his own troubles with the university administration."

"They don't like Jews either, I presume," Bierce said.

He nodded. "So we would like to take some liberties with this hearing. We'd like to widen its scope, raise the stakes, so to speak."

"Stakes? Poker now, is it?" Bierce said. "I never play if I can't win."

"Then let me show you the deal," he said.

The conversation went on for another hour. When he and Cohen left Bierce's office with a new, revised, set of letters, he was excited, and he was frightened. He was about to shove all his chips to the center of the table, and he was not at all sure of his hand.

NINETEEN

MANY CLOUDS ARRIVES AT THE CIRCLE M

Carrie had just finished lunch. She had timber on her mind, specifically the forest along the slopes of the Circle M's western boundary. The Maxwells had drawn on the firs, pines, and hemlocks there to construct every building, corral, and fencepost on the ranch. But they'd never sold a tree. Her father had even built his own mill, powered by a Pelton water wheel, a miracle piece of machinery in its time. *Preserve the forest, you'll always have lumber,* he'd said. *Depend on no man if you can help it.*

Carrie, however, was considering a break with Carter Maxwell's motto. The thought made her uncomfortable, but foreign competition had driven down beef prices while California's growing population had driven timber prices sky high. It took cash to run a ranch these days. The railroads weren't as open to a handshake and promise of future payment as they used to be. Neither was anyone else.

She was preparing to mount Sailor and ride to the trees to see if she could stomach the thought of steam shovels and trucks moving into the relatively pristine hills. Her thoughts were interrupted by the chorus of barking and yelping dogs that always greeted new arrivals. Perhaps one of the timber brokers she had been putting off had decided to try again. Irritated, she stepped on to the veranda and observed a buckboard bearing a man and two youngsters pass under the archway and across the bridge that led into the ranch yard. Not what she'd expected, and not one of the local families. A ranch hand vaulted over the rail of a corral from which he'd been shoveling manure, jumped into the dusty moil of animals and quieted them with a few well-paced kicks and shouted commands. The driver jumped down from the seat.

"Thanks, pardner. We got trouble here. Need help." He was breathless.

"What kind of trouble?" Carrie hurried down the steps.

"Hello, ma'am." The man touched his broad hat brim. "Badly injured lady in the wagon. She keeps asking for the Circle M."

When she peered over the sideboard, she was astonished to see Many Clouds lying in the wagon bed on an improvised mattress composed of a couple of quilts. Her arms and legs were wrapped in dirty rags. The children had been bathing her face with cloths dipped in a bucket of water. Her lips were so cracked, her cheeks so flushed, there was no need to check her fever by touch. Annoyed as she'd been with her mother for bringing the young Indian girl to her, anxious as she had been to be rid of her, the sight of her in such misery filled her with compassion.

"Many Clouds, what in the world?" she said.

"You know her name?" Maggie said.

Carolyn didn't respond to Maggie's question. Instead, she turned to the girl's father.

"Who are you?"

"Miller Fitzpatrick, ma'am. And this here's Willy and Maggie."

"Enoch," she called to the ranch hand who had shooed off the dogs.

"Ma'am?"

"Help Mr. Fitzpatrick carry this young woman into the house. Andy's bedroom. Then ride into Sawtooth Wells and bring back Doc Robinson. On second thought, let's leave Doc Robinson out of this. I don't trust him in this situation."

"Thank you, ma'am," Fitzpatrick said.

"I'm sure there's a story to be told here, Mr. Fitzpatrick, and I'll be anxious to hear it, but Many Clouds needs immediate help."

While the two men approached the wagon, she flew into the house. "Ling Chu," she called as she flung open the door. "Bring your medical equipment to Andy's immediately."

The Maxwell ranch house was constructed of full round logs, and everything was on a scale which reflected the grand design and mentality of her father. The supporting columns were bark-stripped fir logs three feet in diameter. The fireplace was large enough to accommodate a tall man wearing a large hat. A stuffed mountain lion strode its mantel. Heads of elk, deer, and bear adorned the walls.

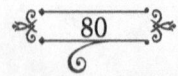

Parallel stairways led from the main floor to opposite ends of a balcony off which opened the doors to four bedrooms. A third stairway led from the balcony's center to more bedrooms on the upper floor. Fitzpatrick and Enoch, doing their best to be gentle, carried a weakly-whimpering, half-conscious, Many Clouds in a blanket sling up the stairs where Carolyn ushered them into the first door on the left. Ling Chu, the Maxwell's cook and factotum, nearly stumbled over Maggie and Willy when he ran into the room awkwardly carrying a small, but obviously heavy chest.

"Who you?" he yelled. "Out of way."

Maggie and Willy darted behind the oversized couch.

"It's okay, Ling, just hurry up here. You youngsters, I'll be down in a minute to fix you some lemonade or something."

Ling Chu, objected. "No, Miss Carrie—"

"I can make lemonade without destroying your precious kitchen, Ling, now get in here."

When she followed Ling Chu into the room, she found Fitzpatrick and Enoch standing helplessly over a silent Many Clouds. Ling Chu knelt beside the bed, touched, poked, prodded.

"Ice," he said. "Need ice."

"There's still a few blocks left in the pumphouse," Enoch said. "I'm on my way." It was a treacherous ten mile sleigh trip from Shingle Lake where Carter Maxwell had begun cutting, transporting, and storing a supply of ice the same year he'd built the Circle M's little sawmill. Packed in sawdust, the hoard usually lasted only until August, but this had been a cool summer.

"What happen?" Ling Chu said.

Miller said, "She was trying to get away from a wildfire. A sharp rock or limb or something stabbed into her back, left a hole the size of a railroad spike. I doctored her up, but then infection got in anyhow and what to do then was beyond me."

"You might have tried a doctor," Carrie said.

"Ain't no doctor in my neck of the woods going to treat a red woman. I'm short one wife on account of that."

"I... of course," she said. She should have known. Exactly the reason she'd decided not to call Doc Robinson.

"She commenced to talking real wild, and the only thing she said that made sense to me was 'Circle M. Circle M.' So I brung her along. My horse has seen better days, and it took us a while. She's been more or less passed out pretty near two days."

Ling Chu had been unwrapping the bandages Fitzpatrick had fashioned for Many Clouds' legs and arms. There was also a patch behind her left ear where the hair had burned away and blistered the scalp.

"Dirt. Need soap," Ling Chu said.

"Raised lots of dust in that buckboard," Fitzpatrick said, "but I figured I couldn't afford to stop."

Carrie hurried out the door and down the stairs. She saw that Maggie and Willy were still cowering behind the couch. "Follow me, children. Your lemonade will have to wait, but you can help me heat water and gather cloths. What are you gawking at? We have a life to save."

TWENTY

THE HEARING

"I can't do it, Andy," Cohen said. The two huddled outside California Hall where the hearing was to take place.

"Now? After you've come this far?"

"They'll blackball me, Andy. It's fine for you to take the risk with all your family money and connections. But if this doesn't work for me, I'm back behind the counter in my father's grocery store."

"They won't let you in anyway, Nathan. Don't you understand that yet?"

"We don't know that for sure, Andy. But I do know if things go against us here, I'm finished."

"And we don't know *for sure* the sun will set tonight."

"I'm sorry."

"You certainly are." He checked his watch. Fifteen minutes until the starting gun. He tripped up the steps, more determined and—he was surprised—more invigorated than ever.

Two hours later, he was still waiting. The committee had come up one member short owing to Professor McNulty's sudden attack of influenza. Suspicious to say the least. How many other delays would they concoct? It was four o'clock by the time the two remaining hearing officers—Dean Perkins and Chairman MacIntosh—had contacted the absent chairman, tried to persuade Andy to postpone the hearing, then agreed at his insistence to hold it anyway.

Perkins and MacIntosh seated themselves behind a table on a raised platform at the front of a lecture room rearranged into a faux courtroom.

He was accorded a straight back chair on the floor below the improvised dais. Perkins squinted even more at this greater distance from Andy than he had from across his desk in his office. Probably needed spectacles but was too vain or parsimonious to wear them. MacIntosh, on the other hand, was clear-eyed and composed. His neatly plastered hair, fashionably grey at the temples, contrasted markedly with Perkins' disarrayed tonsure. His voice was deep and sonorous enough for the stage, and it was he, prompted by Perkins' nod, who opened the hearing.

"Mr. Maxwell, let me begin by saying that since professor McNulty is the faculty member most familiar with your work, we feel it would be to your advantage to wait until he is available. However, let the record show that we are, at your request, proceeding without him. Would you, also for the record, so that there can be no possibility of future misinterpretation, like to explain why you want to go ahead at this point?"

He wondered what "record" MacIntosh was talking about since no stenographer or secretary was present. The high collar and silk cravat he had donned for the occasion strangled him. Despite his discomfort, however, he was amused. He hoped he wasn't smirking. It would become clear soon enough why he didn't want to wait. He tried to put himself in the mind of a revolutionary war militiaman, a sharpshooter in the forest, waiting to pick off the neatly-aligned redcoats.

"My case is strong, and I'm anxious to get to work on my degree," he said, "so let's get on with it."

"Very well," MacIntosh said. "According to these documents, it appears you wish to rescind your leave and gain admission to the history doctorate program even though it is beyond the application period. Is that correct?"

"Not precisely, sir. I want to claim the place in the program that was already mine, per the letter from the department committee, well before the application period closed."

"But," said MacIntosh, "Were you not granted a mercy leave owing to your—"

"Owing to my 'family circumstances,' circumstances which applied when I requested a leave two years ago but which are no longer relevant. Last year, I requested reinstatement as of this term. My request was granted in writing. Then came the expulsion letter."

"Expulsion letter?" Perkins said. "There was no expulsion letter."

"What else would you call a leave forced upon me without my request, pushing me out on the street along with a phony invitation to apply next year on the same basis as every other random undergraduate in the country?"

Perkins smiled at MacIntosh. "You see the problem, this attitude."

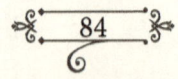

"Uh, yes, I'm beginning to understand," MacIntosh said.

Perkins went on. "Do you know how many applications for leaves like this we reject each year, Mr. Maxwell, and how extremely fortunate you are to be granted one?"

"I only know that mine was imposed, not granted, and for reasons that have nothing to do with the statements in this letter."

"And why, Mr. Maxwell," MacIntosh said, would you think a group of men such as Dr. McNulty, Dean Perkins, President Wheeler, what conceivable reason might they have to take actions which threaten your academic career?"

"I'll answer that question with another. A simple one. What changed between the time I received this letter of acceptance…" he brandished that letter in his right hand "and this one?" He brandished his "leave" letter in his left.

Perkins answered, a mock weariness in his voice, "As we've stated, Mr. Maxwell, your mother's health, the responsibility of running a large ranch—"

"All in the past, sir, as well you know. My academic qualifications are exactly the same as they were when I applied, and if those were acceptable then, they should be acceptable now. What changed is that you discovered, or someone of influence raised an objection to the fact, that my father is a Negro and that I was born of an illicit love match." He leaned back in his chair. Perkins was angry, MacIntosh puzzled, squinting. Hadn't they told him the whole story?

"No such thing—" Perkins was on his feet again. He himself remained seated, continued as if the dean had never spoken.

"And that, Professor MacIntosh, is the answer to your question about why these gentlemen are interested in destroying my career."

MacIntosh turned to his colleague. "This matter of Mr. Maxwell's parentage, did you know of this when the original acceptance was issued?"

So MacIntosh didn't know. McNulty's illness. The hearing was never to have happened, so they hadn't bothered to tell him. An opening. How to take advantage?

Perkins was speaking. "Well, I'm not sure when that came to light. It's more or less common knowledge now, but we wouldn't—"

"Yes, indeed, you would. And did." Andy said. "Let me introduce you to someone." He walked toward the back door of the classroom. He hoped Cohen had changed his mind, or this part of the planned theatrics would fall very flat.

"Mr. Maxwell, there is no provision for outside parties to participate in this deliberation," Perkins said.

His hand on the doorknob, he asked, "Is there any provision against it?"

"It is understood, sir."

He opened the door. The hallway was empty. So Cohen really had deserted. That weakened his assault, but he was still a minuteman. Keep dodging through the trees. Keep shooting. He walked back toward his seat.

"Apparently, you have your way, Dean Perkins. There is no outside party." He stood behind his chair. "And I've outlined the substance of my appeal."

"Very well, then," Perkins said. "We will adjourn and take the matter under advisement. A decision will be forthcoming."

Once again, he ignored Perkins' remarks. "However, in case my own self-interested views are insufficient to sway you, perhaps you'd be willing to consider an appeal from a neutral and interested citizen of some standing in the community." He approached his inquisitors and placed one envelope before each of them. He laid a third between them. "And perhaps you'd be kind enough to deliver Chairman McNulty's copy to him."

"Your tactics grow more outrageous by the second, Maxwell." Perkins wrapped his fist around the envelope and slammed it on the table top. "I've already called adjournment."

MacIntosh, however, was opening his envelope. "You know, Dean Perkins, I'm curious. Let's take a look, shall we?" An open breach in the enemy lines.

Perkins started to object, but stopped. Glaring at Andy, he ripped open his own envelope.

"It seems you've secured the backing of a celebrity, here, Mr. Maxwell," MacIntosh said. "However, Mr. Bierce's letter puzzles me. He first asks for a fair and balanced decision, which it goes without saying we're here to deliver, are we not, Dean Perkins?"

"Of course," Perkins said. "Outrageous to suggest that we wouldn't And look at this. The next paragraph makes demands that seem to reach beyond the purview of this committee. "Not only that, it implies a degree of extortion. 'I look forward to your positive decision regarding the admission of all qualified applicants regardless of race or religion so that I can applaud you in print.' Suggesting obviously that a negative decision will bring adverse publicity."

"Mr. Bierce put it to me this way, Dean Perkins," he said. "He acknowledged that a considerable portion of his audience would be happy with a decision that would keep the university free of pollution by coloreds and Hebrews. However, many others would be offended at their exclusion. Thus, controversy. And controversy sells more newspapers than truth ever did."

"Mr. Maxwell," there was a deadly calm in Perkins' voice. "You had no right to take your petty argument to the press. To the streets. As if this were some kind of seamy commercial transaction."

"I am only asking for an even-handed decision based on evidence, not prejudice."

"This has become a travesty," Perkins said. "We are adjourned." He stood and turned toward the room's other exit. A door closed in the back of the room. Andy turned. Nathan Cohen advanced to the front of the room. Andy mentally cheered, but tried to proceed as if this as all part of the plan.

"Chairman MacIntosh, dean Perkins, this is Nathan Cohen. He has important information to add."

"These proceedings are null and void."

MacIntosh had stood, but now sat back down. "I agree, Dean Perkins, that matters have turned too chaotic to continue in any official way. However, I'm still curious. If you don't mind, I'd like to stick around and hear, unofficially of course, what Cohen here has to say."

"You're free to do as you like, sir." Perkins said. He stormed toward the door, but stopped with his hand on the knob.

Andy jumped into the opening MacIntosh had provided. "I'm sorry Chairman McNulty isn't here. However, you can check the veracity of Mr. Cohen's story with him later. Go ahead, Nathan."

Now Perkins was caught. He didn't sit, appeared poised to flee the room. But to leave MacIntosh here alone would create an even greater fissure in the wall of authority. Andy enjoyed his adversary's obvious pain. More fun than a bacchanal.

Perkins stood at the door while Cohen described the multiple delays in his thesis approval, explained that he'd begun to suspect that, like Andy, he was being delayed until he became frustrated enough to quit the program. Not until the last rejection had he combed the records and noticed that there were no other Jewish students in the program. Had apparently never been any.

"That's hardly evidence of anything," MacIntosh said. "None may have applied, or those that did apply might not have been qualified."

"Perhaps not," Andy said, "but I believe it falls into the category described by Mr. Thoreau when he commented that some circumstantial evidence is very strong, as when you find a trout in the milk. He drew another envelope and held it high in the air before MacIntosh. Mr. Chairman, I would like to include this petition for redress in the packet of materials I've already filed. It demands, in conjunction with the remarks by Mr. Bierce, not only my own reinstatement and equitable treatment for Mr. Cohen, but that equal consideration for the applications of all Negroes and Jews become university policy and practice." He dropped the envelope. "I have sent copies to the Board of Regents."

Perkins was nearly screeching. "Regents? What possible interest would the regents have—"

"Thank you for the opportunity to present my side of things, dean Perkins, Chairman Macintosh." He dipped his head in a slight bow.

"And my thanks as well," Cohen said.

Perkins continued. "Let me warn you, Maxwell. If you and that despicable muckraker, Bierce, think you can get away with desecrating the name of this university, you are sadly mistaken."

"If such a desecration occurs, it will be neither our responsibility nor Mr. Bierce's. Good day." They trooped out of the room. Andy closed the door and pressed his ear to the frosted glass. He heard raised voices, and, though he could understand no words, he threw up his arms like a victorious prize fighter and danced in a circle.

"What's going on with you, Andy?" Cohen said.

"I'm not sure," he said. "But somehow this seems like a victory."

"Seems to me all we did was make them mad," Cohen said.

"Which means they're paying attention," he said. "It's hard to beat an enemy who doesn't know you exist. And we have them in a crossfire. If they accept us, we've won. If they deny us, we can make a stink with the regents."

"Maybe."

"Thanks for coming back, Nathan. I know it took guts."

"The more I thought about it, the more it seemed that life among the vegetables wouldn't necessarily be the end of the world," Cohen answered.

"Yea or nay, I somehow don't see that as your destiny."

"Well, the only destiny I'm interested in right now is the Merry Widow." Cohen started to toward the exit.

"None of that, my friend. We're going to the Key Route Hotel. Dinner and drinks on the Maxwells."

"First you ruin me. Then you feed me."

"Cohen, must you suffer so?"

"Of course. Or I wouldn't be Jewish."

They laughed, embraced. They exited the building. The muffled yelling continued in the room behind them. As they emerged, he saw Virginia standing the bottom of the steps. How had she known where to find him? He shot a questioning look at Cohen, who stared at the heavens in mock innocence.

Virginia waved tentatively. Smiled. She wore an ostrich plume in a turban of violent purple. He waved back. Virginia and Andy at the Key Route. This was shaping up to be a merry little party.

TWENTY-ONE

HALE GENTRY DROPS BY THE CIRCLE M

Carrie and Ling Chu stood at Many Clouds' bedside on the second morning after her arrival. Her fever had abated significantly, but had not disappeared. She was still unconscious. Mumbling, dreaming, incoherent. Ling Chu leaned down and began to rearrange his acupuncture tools. A glass of some vile smelling herb concoction stood on a bedside table.

"What do you think?" she said.

"I think she be okay."

"I mean when," she said.

"Walking around one week. Almost normal one month."

Then what? She thought. Logically, Many Clouds would return with the Fitzpatrick's to their homestead. She wondered if it would be that simple. They'd erected a tent to house Miller Fitzpatrick and his children for the time being. It had been a long time since the Circle M had seen a tent, not since the winter of 1864-65 when Carter Maxwell, his wife, and the Carrie Maxwell of three years old had lived in one until they moved into ranch's first structure—the barn—the following winter.

There was no snow on this bright September morning when Carrie left Ling Chu with Many Clouds and sat on the porch to read Andy's letter, his first since returning to Berkeley. Miller Fitzpatrick, Maggie, and Willy, each with a bucket in hand, walked toward the barn.

"Mr. Fitzpatrick, we appreciate your work, we do. But those poor children," she spoke with a smile.

"They'll get some play time after the chores," he said.

"Of course. And maybe a cookie or two as well if they happen by the kitchen."

Willy dropped his bucket and started running toward the house.

"Ah-ah-ah." Carrie said. "Only when your father gives the word."

"Back here, Willy," Miller said. "Thank you, ma'am, kindly."

She waved and watched the little procession disappear into the barn.

She tore open the envelope, able to afford only a few minutes of relaxation. She'd soon have to saddle up for an afternoon of checking the cattle roundup in some of the high pastures.

"Lemonade, Miss Carrie." Ling Chu extended a tray bearing a ceramic mug and a plate with two ginger cookies.

"Before I even knew I wanted it, Ling Chu. You're a marvel. Please set it on the table. Sit down. Tell me about the state of the kitchen." Ling Chu remained standing. She knew he would. But even after twenty-five years on the Circle M, she hadn't given up trying to get him to relax his formality a bit.

"I have list. I'll take the Model-T to town tomorrow."

"Why not the wagon? You can carry so much more. Make fewer trips."

"Car faster. Don't have to wait so long for getting things. Don't wear out the animals."

"Well, it wears them out to bring in the fuel drums we need to run that automobile."

"Only five miles to Sawtooth Wells. Not so much gas." Ling Chu started to launch into his usual objections that she was exaggerating the matter of the fuel, but she held up her hand. She'd never argue him out of his devotion to his new mechanical beast, and she actually enjoyed seeing some naked enthusiasm break through his iron restraint.

"I give up, Ling Chu. Do as you think best."

"Yes, Miss Carrie. I understand." Ling Chu made a quick bow and stepped back toward the house, but stopped when a cry of "Hello the house," came from the direction of the arched entrance to the ranch. Carrie heard a small gasp escape Ling Chu and wondered if one had escaped her as well. The man who had called was waving his hat, and his blond hair glowed in the sun. He wore black leather studded with silver conches, rode a white stallion, and smiled with teeth white as his horse.

All flash, Carrie thought. Like a certain fallen angel. "I suppose there's no lemonade for Mr. Gentry, Ling Chu?"

"Oh, all gone," Ling Chu said. He smiled.

"As I thought." Ling Chu disappeared. Gentry started to dismount. "Whoa, there, Mr. Gentry," she said. "I don't recall inviting you to light and set."

Hale Gentry hadn't set foot on the ranch since his public humiliation two summers previous when he'd declared that he loved Carrie and tried to use their acquaintance to force Andy aside and assert mastery over the Circle M. Carrie had been unconscious, near death from her Yellow-Squirrel-inflicted bullet wound at the time, but her son hadn't needed her intervention. He'd surprised everyone—even himself, she thought—by pounding Gentry into submission, then outsmarting him when he'd tried to organize a lynching of Yellow Squirrel. Since then, Gentry had stuck close to his Sawtooth Wells Saloon.

"As you wish, Carrie," he said. He swung back onto the saddle with a performer's grace.

"Mrs. Maxwell."

"I'm on official business," he said, "so I won't be long."

"Official business."

"I'm running for the state assembly."

"You mean Southern Pacific is so desperate for legislative votes they're putting the likes of you up against Harvey Cox? Why, you haven't a prayer."

Since Andy had bested him, Gentry had begun using his ownership of Sawtooth Wells' only saloon as a front for a dozen clandestine operations all across the region, operations ranging from brothels to cattle rustling. The enterprises were too large and distant for the local sheriff to control, yet too small, his part too cleverly disguised, to pique the attention of California's Attorney General. Gentry had sworn revenge on the Maxwells, but had so far confined his retribution to spreading tasteless rumors. Given a legislative platform, though… but it was impossible.

"It's just we Democrats feel like the Republicans have had their way with this district too long. We're going to put up a fight this year."

"And when Hiram Johnson becomes governor they figure they need every vote they can buy to keep him from squashing their monopoly. Well, if you're looking for votes out here, you're plowing the wrong field."

"Your personal feelings are your business, *Mrs. Maxwell*. But are you going to deny your hands the right to the information they need to be good voters? As Thomas Jefferson said, 'a democracy depends on an informed and educated citizenry.'"

"You can talk to my workers—or try—on their time off. But they all know that every arbitrary shipping rate hike the railroad barons impose cuts into their wages."

"Surely, as an astute businesswoman, you understand the necessity for businesses to adjust to market forces."

"And as an astute businesswoman, I can spot a greedy monopoly when I see it. So around here, it's Harvey Cox for assembly and Hiram Johnson for governor and Hale Gentry off my property. You're trespassing."

"As you wish, *Mrs. Maxwell.*" He doffed his hat, and cantered away, still smiling. Carrie had almost forgotten how invulnerable the man was to criticism. When he rode out the gate, it was almost as if a huge crowd had left the premises. She exhaled and sat, gazed up at the Sawtooth Peaks in their indifferent solidity until her calm returned. She sipped the lemonade, put an entire cookie in her mouth, and opened Andy's letter.

Dear Mom,

Just a quick note. It's exciting getting back into the academic swing. A doctoral candidate has mountainous obligations, and things are very busy here, what with meetings with the chairman, the dean, and the president. Yes, the president. I'm scheduled to sit with a faculty committee next week. Quite an honor for a neophyte like me.

I miss you and the Circle M. Take care of the place, now, and I'll see you around the holidays.

Your loving son,
Andy

A shadow of the old fear passed over her like a cloud over the sun. The fear that he would dive into his books and never come up. Never come back to her. But this letter. It was wrong. Andy liked to put the best face on everything. Nothing new there. But he was not a boaster. Why this braggadocio? This was not a matter of "best face." He was covering something. It wasn't hard to guess. Whatever was really happening down there had to do with exactly the kind of trouble her brother-in-law had warned against. She rose to her feet and hurried across the yard.

"Coop," she called as she headed toward her brother- and sister-in-law's cabin. "Amelia. We need to talk."

TWENTY-TWO

THE DECISION

"Curse me for an errant knave, Andy. I should have foreseen this." Bierce passed President Wheeler's letter back to him. "We've been outflanked. Outflanked and outfoxed."

"But they've outfoxed themselves, haven't they? If the Board rules in our favor, it doesn't matter what Wheeler or any of them think."

"We geared ourselves for a decisive fight on a defined battleground, Andy. Or to invoke our other analogy, a final show of the cards. What we have instead is the enemy melting into the shadows or the dealer transferring the game to another location and daring us to track him down."

"Ambrose, Ambrose. You, of all people, giving up? The letter says their next meeting is in November, right after Thanksgiving. We can appear then, get a decision, and I'll be back in class by spring semester."

"It also says that Wheeler will present the case at the next available space in the agenda of that august body. I'd wager every penny of my nonexistent fortune you'll find the November agenda is full and with the next available space at the meeting in June. You'll also note that the letter speaks only of Wheeler's presentation to the board. There is no mention of your appearance."

"Surely they can't deny me that."

"Let's hope they do. There might be a story in it."

He started to protest. Bierce held up his hand. "Look, Andy. Like you, I pictured us embarrassing a bunch of self-righteous stuffed shirts into reversing an unjust decision. Pounding some clay feet into dust. People love that. Now…" He lifted the letter and dropped it back on the desk top. "We've got closed door meetings and non-decisions that will drag on for months. Ho-hum. We need trouble, a *cause célèbre*, a riot."

"Maybe I should get myself thrown in jail."

"Over this? They wouldn't bother. I'm sorry, my boy. I hold myself responsible for this delay, but it's only a delay. These pedants are so smug, they're bound to slip up soon, and when they do—"

The door to Bierce's office flew open, and Tom Redmond rushed in.

"Maxwell. Great coincidence to find you here. You'll love this. Ambrose, Charley Hung is dead."

"Our Tong leader? How?"

"They found him hanging from a light post at California and Grant with two of his underlings."

"Right in front of the cathedral?" Bierce said.

"Kitty-corner from St. Mary's, yes. They don't know who or why, but the police suspect a new tong war is breaking out."

"Get on it, Thomas," Bierce said. "See if you can find out anything about internecine disputes with other gangs. Odds are there's some official corruption involved, too. Go. Mr. Hearst will want something for the afternoon edition."

"He's got it. And a picture, too."

"Are you saying I'm the last to know, Thomas? Are you forgetting who butters your bread around here?"

"Not my fault. I was the first reporter on the scene because it's only a couple of blocks from my apartment. Mr. Hearst jumped me on my way through the copy room."

"All right, all right. We'll go after all the stories behind the story. You to the police precincts, I to Chinatown and City Hall. Meet me at Jack's for dinner to compare notes."

"Jack's is it? Oh, you can bet on me for that." And Redmond vanished as quickly as he'd appeared.

"See that, Andy? What's the pale knavery of Benjamin Wheeler compared to this? A capital crime. A mystery. A victim who's also a villain." He sprang from his chair, pulled coat, hat and cane from a rack in the back corner of the office and dashed out the door.

Andy sat stunned, staring at the letter in his lap. He'd come to Bierce to launch a new campaign, but his general had abandoned him. Still, why wasn't he rejoicing at Redmond's news? With Charley Hung dead and Yellow Squirrel gone, every scoundrel in the vendetta was defunct. He should be celebrating.

Celebration. Virginia. Their night at the Key Route had been sensational. Between couplings, under shadowy gaslight, amid sweet, musky aromas, laughter, and relentless tumescence they'd posed one another as famous paintings, statues—she, the Naked Maja, he, David, she Botticelli's Venus, he the Discus Thrower. The breasts he'd fantasized about for so long had turned out to be small, ripe, perfect. Her passion was genuine, not feigned like his parlor house whores. Even the Chilean twins, who'd been so good at it. But now he knew the difference.

That had been a week ago, and they'd not seen one another since, though they had exchanged notes. He caressed his inside pocket where lay the filigreed, artfully calligraphed message of thanks "for a memorable experience." It was time for their relationship to enter a new phase where they could share goals and dreams instead of superficial repartee and insults. He'd find her at the Sketch Club, take her to lunch, share his new dilemma, trade insights and ideas. They'd become confidents as well as lovers.

He headed up Market Street, down the Embarcadero toward Telegraph Hill. The day was brilliant, the salty breeze cool as a mountain valley evening. Past the colorful flags of the Barnum and Bailey tents. The animal smells evoked the Circle M. Country and city merged. Just like him. His life was a circus. A sense of imminent danger crept through his gut. Was he afraid of Virginia? No. Then what? He shook the feeling and headed up Telegraph Hill.

TWENTY-THREE

MANY CLOUDS SHEDS HER QUILLS

Many Clouds couldn't imagine where she was. Feather quilt, feather mattress, window glass streaming with rainwater. Thunder cracked, shook the building. She raised up, propped herself on her elbows.

"No, no, missy. Stay, stay."

A Chinese man padded to her bedside, placed a hand on her shoulder. She pulled back, raised her own hand to ward him off. A bone twig was sticking out from the back of her hand, like a porcupine quill. She reached to pull it out. Saw a quill poking from the other hand as well.

"Aiyee. Father," she cried in Arapaho. Confusion and fear washed through her.

"All right, Missy, all right, make you well," the Chinese man said, trying to push her back down.

Many Clouds barely heard, let alone understood him. She clawed out all the twigs she could find, threw the covers aside, and jumped out of bed. There were still a number of quills all over her, like tiny arrows. She yanked them out as she ran to the door. The Chinese man blocked it, his back to her.

"Miss Carrie," he yelled. "Miss Carrie, come quick."

She pushed and pulled at the man. She screamed and sobbed in a mixture of English and Arapaho. "Let me go. I need to go home. Let me go." More thunder.

She finally managed to pull him aside and launched herself out of the room. She was on a walkway, a balcony, looking down into a huge room. A lodge, she thought, or a giant house made of trees, and coming up the stairs toward her, running, was Carolyn Maxwell, and she knew if she didn't get out she was doomed. She saw another stairway at the other end of the balcony and ran toward that.

"Many Clouds, please. You'll hurt yourself, please," Carolyn called.

She could hear the pad-scuff-pad slippers of the Chinese man right behind her. But she was fast. The fastest girl in her village, faster than some of the boys. She knew she could get out. She used the banister to vault past several stairs and on to the main floor. Carolyn Maxwell blocked her way to the front door, but there had to be a back way. Through the living room, where stuffed heads of sacred animals menaced her from the wall. Another room, huge furniture, a kitchen, a door to the outside. She flung it open and jumped over the few steps into the downpour. She was barefoot and dressed only in a flannel gown, but if she could reach cover, she'd find a way to build a fire, survive. The pine grove just past those corrals.

"Stop her, Enoch," Carolyn yelled.

A stout man emerged from a building that stood between her and the trees. He took a moment to figure out the situation, then lumbered to intercept her. Lightning flashed above. She and Enoch were on a collision path. He reached out, but Many Clouds jumped sideways, and Enoch grabbed only air and rainwater, threw himself off balance, and sprawled in the mud. Thunder crashed.

"Aiyee," she exclaimed again, a mixture of victory and fear, as she fled past the cursing ranch hand and continued her dash toward the grove.

Centuries earlier, a huge ponderosa pine had been felled and burned by lightning, its stump hollowed out by flame, sunk deep below the level of the surrounding earth. Into that stump, pulling in branches behind her to cover her refuge, Many Clouds dived and stilled herself. She heard boots. Voices. Near, then far, then near again.

"Poor girl." It was Carolyn speaking. "Like a frightened animal. She'll freeze to death out here."

"She can't be too far, ma'am. Not with bare feet and sick as she is. Besides, the storm's almost passed. See the blue yonder?"

They talked of a search, of bringing other men. Maybe dogs. She knew she was at the Circle M now. How she came here, she didn't know, just knew she didn't belong. Too often, white people, even with the best intentions, it always ended badly. Even with Andy. Especially with him. Clouds covered the sun, so she hadn't been able to tell anything about the time in her flight across the ranch yard. If she could hold out till dark, she could somehow make her way to the Washoes. Water pooled around her at the bottom of the hole, fed by a rivulet. She began trembling. Cold. Pain in her back. Tired. Very tired.

TWENTY-FOUR

THE THINKER

His knock at the Sketch Club door produced a matronly woman of middle age dressed in a red muumuu. Virginia? In life drawing class. Ten more minutes, if he'd care to wait here in the parlor. The parlor was the size of a large closet, a couple of paces square, furnished with two chairs of faded, worn red velvet, a coat rack. Things had certainly looked more sumptuous around here in the bacchic candlelight. He felt restless and curious how the rest of the place stood up to the light of day. He decided he didn't care to wait as the muumuu lady had suggested and wandered off down a hallway. Students in one room were painting the bay view. In another, a still life of fruit and flowers. And then he came to the life drawing class. On a pedestal at the center of the room, a man sat, elbow on thigh, chin on fist. Rodin's The Thinker. A half dozen women were arranged in a circle around him, each drawing from her own perspective. A short, elderly instructor strolled the room, peering at the canvases, kibitzing, demonstrating. The model had the prodigious muscles of the original statue, and Andy could see every knob and slab of them because the guy was stark naked.

Virginia had her back to the door where he stood. The model faced them both. Virginia was putting the finishing touches on her version of The Thinker's foreskin. His cock. He would have hesitated to use that word thinking about her before, but they'd both used it and others like it liberally during their soirée. She'd spoken it first, regarding his circumcision. Surely she was telling the truth. Wasn't she? A question not to be asked or answered, silly bareheaded boy.

If this was what all her art classes were like, the number of bare cocks she'd gazed on would be a big one. The idea angered him. Why should it? Over a model? He tried to step into neutral emotional territory, but it was a tough road. He was acting, or at least feeling, as if Virginia had betrayed him. But not only was this a completely unromantic situation, they'd made no promises to each other anyway. Nevertheless, it seemed that Othello's green-eyed monster had seized him.

He told himself to turn away, go back to the parlor and wait. But he didn't. And when the instructor called an end to the session, when the students boxed their pencils, when the model began donning his trousers, when Virginia removed her canvas from the easel and turned, she fairly yelped at the sight of him. The sound pierced his mood, and he mustered up a smile.

"Feel like a drink?" he said.

She hesitated a moment. Then, "I'll meet you in the parlor."

"Excuse me." The Thinker wanted to exit, and he was blocking the doorway. He stepped aside, trying not to let his eyes linger. The model looked ordinary in his clothes. A couple of inches shorter than Andy. Mousey. You'd never guess about those muscles.

"Good bye, Matthew," Virginia called after him. "Well, go on, now, Andy." She blew him a kiss. "I won't be long."

And she wasn't. Presently, they were arm-in-arm, a happy young couple in the sunshine.

"You know, my dear, you do take some getting used to. You're so full of surprises."

"Is that so?" she said.

"But you're worth the trouble," he said.

She stopped. "Trouble now, am I?"

He tried to recover. "Effort, I should have said."

"Trouble, effort. Is this a romance or a job of work?" She resumed walking. Slower now.

He felt that they were back in their old pattern, he at the bottom of a hole he hadn't even known he was digging.

"You know that's not what I meant," he said.

She stopped. "There was a time," she said, "When that wouldn't have mattered to me at all, but now for some reason I feel as if I owe you an apology. Can you explain that?"

"No, but I think I owe you one as well."

"Well, then, can we consider the apologies offered and accepted and just go on?"

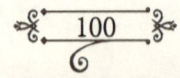

"Okay by me," he said. Cradled her head in his hand and kissed her. She opened her eyes and smiled.

"Now, where are we going?" she said.

"An old favorite of mine. The Brass Monkey." He didn't mention that the bar had been a favorite of his and Julian's. She might accuse him again of living in the past.

"Oh, I love that place, Andy. And you know what I like most about it?"

"I think I can guess. The Cathedral?"

"You, too? To be drinking and sinning practically right under the clock and that silly motto."

He held up his arm and proclaimed, "'Son, observe the time and fly from evil.' Julian and I used to laugh over that one." Now he'd mentioned Julian and ruined the new mood. But no.

"I'll bet you did, with all those brothels in the neighborhood."

So she knew about those, too? Well, why wouldn't she? Everyone did. He was still treating her in his mind like the image of Little Bo Peep. "Those priests wanted prayer, they got laughs. It's not easy getting people to do what you want."

"People should be left to do what *they* want," she said.

They were at the bar now. He gripped the handle, sculpted to match the establishment's name, and pulled open the door. He lifted his eyes, caught sight of the lamppost across the street, the iron tree from which three bodies had swung earlier in the day. It looked ordinary as a fencepost now.

The Brass Monkey was a rowdy place after the sun went down, when a little oompah band struck up "Ta-Ra-Ra Boom-De-ay," and the like, inviting a boisterous crowd, which largely ignored them, to sing along. But in mid-afternoon it was an ideal place for serious conversation. In a booth, across tankards of Anchor Steam, Virginia spoke first.

"I'm glad you came by, Andy. I have something to talk to you about."

"I have news, too," he said. "Rather big news, actually." The voice of a newsboy hawking the afternoon *Examiner* penetrated the quiet. "And this is part of it. Your Mr. Redmond got himself quite a scoop today."

"He's not my Mr. Redmond, Andy. And I hope you don't think one night in the hay, no matter how much fun it was, gives you any rights over me."

"Or vice-versa," he said. He held up the front page for her to see. Just above the centerfold was a shadowy photograph of a silk-robed body suspended under a dim gaslight. Redmond, with his incorrigible jocularity, had entitled the story "The Hanging of Hung."

"Oh, my," Virginia said.

The image also showed two other bodies, one on each side of Charley Hung. He flipped the paper and started reading Redmond's article. The young reporter described the other figures only as Oriental males, said one of them had only one ear and that the other wore a red skull cap. Charley Hung's bodyguards. He had become well-acquainted with that pair, had even come to admire them somewhat during the vendetta struggles. It would have taken more than one man to best those two, and skilled fighters at that. He was surprised to feel sorry about their demise.

"That picture was taken right outside here," he said. "And since it's such an old story to you, I'm sure you know all these guys were part of that vendetta I keep reliving." He regretted his sarcasm, but only for a second.

"If you're going to hog the paper, Andy, the least you can do is read it to me."

He tried for a melodramatic reading appropriate to Redmond's purple-prose catalogues of the tong boss's underground exploits. Virginia sat transfixed. He was glad to see no mention of himself or of the Maxwells, but the penultimate paragraph silenced him. He read it again, silently. Then again.

"Well?" Virginia said. "What?"

"Our Oriental crime boss," Redmond had written, *"was discovered in a most unusual posture, an attitude one can only assume derives from some ancient and mysterious ritual of the yellow race. With apologies to the sensitivities of our more squeamish readers, this reporter must use the image of a gutted trout to describe the manner of his stabbing. After eviscerating their victim, the malefactors suspended him by a silk cord tied to the ends of an ivory handled sword driven through the pectoral muscles.*

He knew little or nothing about Asian torture and execution rituals, but he knew the method of Julian's knifing exactly matched Hung's. And he knew that the Indian ritual of the Sun Dance which Yellow Squirrel's father, Owl Feather, had been performing when Andy discovered their Wyoming camp two summers ago, closely approximated the way Hung had been suspended.

"Virginia, this has nothing to do with a Chinatown gang war. Yellow Squirrel is back."

"That Indian you sent to Shanghai? Are you sure?" She sat back, looking skeptical, took a sip of her beer.

"He hates all things white, especially the Mission school. He thought they force-fed him Christianity to destroy his spirit. Here, look at the photograph again. Remind you of anything?"

Virginia leaned forward to examine the picture. After a brief moment, she said, "Calvary?"

"Our friend, Tom, missed that, didn't he?" He shoved his beer aside and stood. "I have to get back to the Circle M immediately."

"Don't you want my news?" she asked.

"Sure, sure."

"Sit down. I know you're in a hurry, but this will take barely a minute." He did so, reluctantly. "I'm leaving town. Oh, don't look so shocked. Not permanently. Evelyn has organized a group to take a train down to Monterey and Carmel for a *pleine aire* expedition. I wrote you a note, but I hadn't mailed it yet. Now you've saved me the trouble." She handed him an envelope. "Or should I say saved me the *effort?*" She smiled, reached for his hand. "Good luck with all this, Andy. For god's sake be careful. Don't try to do it all alone. If I can help… I mean I don't see how I could, but keep me posted anyway."

He clasped her hand in his and kissed it. They shared a look that recalled, if not recaptured, the warmth of their recent tryst. "I promise," he said. Then he hurried out the door and downhill toward the Ferry Building.

TWENTY-FIVE

JUST LIKE THE BIG TOP

An Indian had a hard time finding a hotel. A closet-like room in Chinatown was the best Yellow Squirrel could do, but he didn't mind. In fact, it was perfect. A corner lookout, across from St. Mary's, down the block from Hung's headquarters. Ideal for scouting the movements of Charley Hung and his bodyguards as well as for clocking the rounds of the beat cop. He was proud of the care he'd taken. Patience went against his nature. He liked to settle his scores as quickly and dramatically as possible. But he was also the son of Owl Feather, legendary for his planning and persistence, and he had years of his father's instruction under his belt.

He had acted only after he'd determined the perfect moment. It had taken a mere couple of minutes to slit the throats of Hung's bodyguards and gut the Tong leader himself. Then came another fifteen or twenty minutes of crouching in the alley with the corpses until the policeman turned a corner. Then the hanging.

He didn't sleep, watching and waiting in his room for someone to discover the bodies. Finally, an hour before sunrise, a priest. The man crossed himself a dozen times and went knocking on doors. Then came the crowd. Cameras. Reporters. Police. It was like watching his own circus. It must be something like this for P.T. Barnum. When enough people had gathered for him to pass unnoticed, he joined the throng. He heard words like "Savage." "Brave." "Horrible." And he savored them all. The only thing missing was him at the center of the spectacle. But that time would come. He had just started.

TWENTY-SIX

RISING WATERS

How long Many Clouds had been asleep, she didn't know, but it was nearly dark. The water was up to her waist as she crouched in the hollow. She tried to rise, but her legs and feet were numb, and the weak effort only rolled her on her side. She tried to push against the stump, but couldn't lift her body out of the water. She clawed at some branches, pulled weakly. No. The hole was filling up. She could drown here. Or freeze. Thoughts of escape began to fade into despair.

"Aiyee." She tried to call, but couldn't hear even herself. She took a deep breath. "Help," was what she tried to say, but barely a whine emerged. She listened. Only the wash of wind through the trees and the liquid splatter of rain. She shoved, pulled. She had some feeling in her feet now, but they only pushed deeper into mud, not out of the hole.

"Aiyee. Help." Oblivion again.

When she awoke the next time, she found she'd slid deeper into the mud. Water had climbed nearly to her chin. More clawing and kicking. The shade outside the pit was deeper still.

"Help."

"We can't give up." It was Maggie's voice. A friend.

"Told you she was gonna die." Willy was whining. He sounded as frightened as Many Clouds herself.

"Ain't either."

"Pa told us not to come out here, Maggie."

Maggie called again. "Many Clouds."

"I'm cold. Let's go back," Willy said.

"Maybe you should, but I have to keep going," Maggie said.

"I'll get lost." He was whining now, frightened.

"Then stay with me. Many Clouds, where are you?"

"Help," Many Clouds thought she was speaking loudly but the children seemed not to hear. Then came another voice.

"Shhh," Maggie said.

"I didn't hear nothing."

"I said shhh." Then came another voice. Nonny's,

"This way, children. Yes, nonny, hey nonny."

"Help," Many Clouds said again.

"Who are you?" Willy said.

"No matter. I am a friend. Now come."

Willy said, "I'm scared."

"Where is she?" Maggie said.

"Follow me," Nonny said.

Many Clouds summoned all her strength. "Maggie."

Willy said. "I heard it that time."

Many Clouds heard rustling. Branches moving. More light, then Maggie's face appeared through the branches.

"Howdy, Many Clouds," she said. "I knew we'd find you." Nonny's humming faded into the distance.

TWENTY-SEVEN

GETTING THE WORD OUT

On his way to the ferry, Andy ducked into a Western Union office and loosed a flurry of telegrams.

* * *

MRS. CAROLYN MAXWELL
    YELLOW SQUIRREL BACK ALERT SHERIFF HALSTAD STOP ON MY WAY STOP

* * *

AMBROSE BIERCE, EXAMINER
    HUNG'S KILLING NOT TONG WAR MORE SOON STOP

* * *

NATHAN COHEN
    CALLED AWAY STOP URGENT YOU FIND OUT HOW CONTACT REGENTS SECRETARY STOP IN TOUCH SOON STOP

* * *

He fairly sprinted to the ferry, thinking as he ran. The wind was cooling, picking up speed. A few whitecaps sprinkled the greenish bay waters. After all the battles of words he'd fought in the last weeks, physical action felt good. Maybe he belonged to the ranch life after all.

It bothered him to leave so many issues floating unresolved, but it was funny how something like this Yellow Squirrel business reduced matters to their essence. He'd considered running to Bierce for a sit down, or dropping a note at the *Examiner* office, or even telephoning, but all that took too much time. Besides, it occurred to him that the teasing message in the telegram might make the great man stew a bit. Andy would have some leverage. First time for that.

The telegram he had the least faith in was the one about the regents' secretary. He had to force his way on to the regents' November agenda, and he had to start with the secretary, and although he knew nothing about the protocol, it was surely well past any deadline. Cohen was not a rock of dependability, but who else did he have? Maybe dean Perkins would help out? Sure. He smiled to himself. An idea like that. Did it mean he was hanging on to his sense of humor or maybe going a little crazy?

What about the San Francisco police? The idea flew through his mind like a dark cloud chased by a gale wind. He would never forget the San Francisco sheriff's refusal two years earlier to deal with Julian's murder as anything but a bar fight between a couple of drunks. Too, Sheriff O'Neil had broadcast far and wide his displeasure that Andy had bypassed his office so that Charley Hung could ship the big Indian to Shanghai. Another lecture from the martinet O'Neil? Why? There was small chance Yellow Squirrel was still in San Francisco anyhow. Much more likely he was on his way to the Circle M. Perhaps following him there right now. He looked over his shoulder as he shuffled to the top of the gangplank. Yellow Squirrel was tall enough to spot in most any crowd. He didn't see him. Maybe he'd gotten on the ferry first. He thought he'd put the life of the hunter/hunted behind him. Seemingly not.

* * *

He stopped at the boarding house, threw together a few necessaries, and headed for the train station. He nearly ran over the postman at the front door. A letter from the English Department, with the name "MacIntosh" handwritten under the printed return address. Now there was a surprise. He wanted to tear the envelope open right there, but day was dimming, and he couldn't afford the time.

From the trolley going down University Avenue, he could see the steam plume from the train's smokestack swirling along the bay's edge approaching Berkeley from Oakland. He would make it just in time. Suitcase in hand, he sprinted across the platform toward an open car. A hand clamped his shoulder. He dropped his suitcase, turned, prepared for combat. He found himself facing a large man with a huge mustache topped by a natty bowler, which was about half-size too small. The effect was rather comical, but there was nothing comic about the man's attitude, or about the badge he held at eye level.

"Mr. Maxwell," he said, "Sheriff O'Neil would like a word, if you please."

TWENTY-EIGHT

COOPER IN ACTION

Everyone was gathered around the Fitzpatrick buckboard when the telegram came. Even Carolyn's mother knelt in plain sight on the hill above the yard, though she wouldn't come any closer to such a crowd. Early morning cast its brightness over Ling Chu, Cooper, Amelia, Miller Fitzpatrick and the children. Even Enoch. In the short time they'd stayed, the little family had almost become a fixture on the ranch.

There were hugs and good wishes aplenty. The buckboard was piled high with supplies and gifts. Maggie and Willy perched atop the load of new riches. A younger, healthier horse stood in the traces in place of the one that had struggled to pull a much lighter buckboard through the archway when they arrived. Miller Fitzpatrick had let himself be talked into trading away his older animal, which Carrie insisted would be useful to help train younger horses for wagon work. But he refused further help.

"One last time, Miller," Carrie said after he had shared handshakes and embraces with everyone else, "I'd be honored to buy out your homestead and give you and Maggie and Willy a permanent place here."

"And one last time," Miller said, "your offer is most kindly and generous, but it's just a tad too much like charity, and we've had more of that from you than all the thanks in God's world could express."

"Hmpff. Pride. But remember. We refuse to be strangers. You're the next thing to family now. You should expect a visit soon, and plan to return on a regular basis."

"That, ma'am, I am most proud to accept." He shook her hand as and put a boot on the wheel hub. Then stopped. "Where's Many Clouds?"

As if she'd heard her cue, Many Clouds emerged from the house into the sunlight.

"I'm coming," she said. She wore a simple calico dress, moccasins, and her hair was braided into a single plait down her back. As frightened as she had been, as much as she had alarmed everyone else, her excursion into the rain had not only caused no significant setback in her recovery, but the sympathy and nurturing she received afterwards began to dissolve her fear of Carolyn Maxwell and the Circle M and to replace it with a glimmer of trust.

Her step was firm, though she occasionally sought the precautionary support of a post or railing. Carrie hurried to meet her as she reached the bottom of the steps, and there the two women did something neither of them thought they ever would. They shared a long embrace.

"Thank you, ma'am," Many Clouds said.

"Now, I've told you to please call me Carrie," she said. "My very best wishes. I hope we'll see you soon."

"Yes, ma'am. Carrie." And they crossed to the buckboard arm in arm. Miller boosted her into the buckboard, then swung up himself.

Carrie, standing beside Amelia, said almost under her breath, "Who would have guessed I'd be welcoming that girl into my home?"

"Maybe," said Amelia, "but unless I miss my own guess, part of you ain't too sorry to see her go."

Carolyn had no chance to reply because a rider appeared on the hilltop at a gallop.

"That there's Billy Mays," Cooper said. "And them telegrams of his ain't never good news."

The rider pulled up outside the ranch yard, his horse dancing in a circle while he waited to let the buckboard clear the little bridge under the archway. The second he had space, he spurred the horse toward the porch, reined in, leapt to the ground as if he were in a rodeo or a circus.

"Telegram for Mrs. Maxwell," he bellowed, his mouth opening like a megaphone through his thick black beard. He waved a yellow envelope in his upraised hand.

"Right here, Billy," Carrie said. She held out her hand. "As you can plainly see."

"Yes, ma'am. Sign here if you please." Signature gathered, he leapt on his horse and sped away.

"Someone should tell that boy the Pony Express is out of business," Cooper said.

"Good God in heaven," Carrie said.

"What?" Amelia said.

"It's from Andy. Yellow Squirrel is on the loose again."

"I knew he wouldn't stay in no Shanghai," Cooper said. "What else it say?"

"Andy's coming home."

"At least that part's good."

"You should have let me go get him, Cooper." Carrie knew her remark was a *non sequitur*, that her going to Berkeley to rescue her son from whatever difficulty she inferred from his letter would have had no influence on the Yellow Squirrel situation. But she was still angry with Cooper for stopping her, or with herself for allowing him to do so, or both.

"Like I said, Miss Carrie, some things a boy got to learn on his own. Didn't I tell you once he learned them things, he'd be back? And here he sure enough comes."

"Whether he learned those things or not has nothing to do with Yellow Squirrel and therefore nothing to do with Andy's coming home."

"And not with whether you was there or not, either, do you think?"

This was not something Carrie was going to acknowledge aloud. "Well, he won't be here for a day or so, but Yellow Squirrel might, so we have to get ourselves ready."

"Yes, ma'am." He stared at the heavens for a few moments, humming the Battle Hymn a like a little prayer. When he spoke it was with the assurance of a general. "First thing, no one goes out alone. Amelia, you and Ling Chu ride into town. Squirrel man won't shoot at you cause he don't know you's family."

"You are off your head Cooper Duprée," Amelia said. The thought of getting shot don't bother me nearly so much as that noisy, smelly machine."

"No help for it. You all got to talk to Sheriff Halstad. Tell him to order up some of them guards from Folsom prison for us."

Amelia started to object again, but Ling Chu said, "Don't worry, Miss Amelia. Very safe with me." Ling Chu was smiling, as he always did when he talked of driving the Model-T.

Cooper kept talking. "Enoch, you and Jordan get out to the roundup camp and warn everyone. Don't stop the work, just do everything in pairs or better. He might try to take a hostage even if it ain't family or he might try something else ain't none of us thought of. Then come back here pronto. We're going to set up sentries round the clock. Well, go on, now."

The crowd dispersed. Ling Chu, trotting and jabbering beside Amelia, who kept waving him away as she stomped toward the shed which housed the automobile.

Carolyn felt disturbed for a moment at how forcefully Cooper had taken charge. She was used to running the ranch, and she didn't like losing control.

"We had sentries everywhere last time, too, and he still—"

"You didn't have me, Miss Carrie. You didn't have a sniper's viewpoint."

"Please, Cooper, you aren't about to tell me again how your were the best sniper in your division and how General Kettleman himself sought you out after Little Big Horn and how—"

"No ma'am I ain't gonna tell you none of that. What I am gonna tell you is a sniper learns certain things about where to be, how to see what's the best field of fire. I been scouting around in case anything like this ever come up again. Now what I understand, you had a man up in the barn before."

"That's right."

"And two on the housetop."

"Yes. That gave a good view of the ranch yard and the road coming in."

"Now, that's what I'm saying. Even with all that, he put you near to shaking hands with your maker." Cooper started walking, pointed toward the shade of the porch, continued talking. "You could see everything, but so could he and he figured a way around it. There's more to sniping than sharpshooting." They were at the porch rail now, and he pointed past the barn up the hill toward the slope at the bottom of Sawtooth Peaks. "You see that there fir tree a bit up the trail that runs behind the barn?"

"Which one, Cooper? There must be a couple of dozen."

"See, now, that's what I'm saying. There's one in particular gives the best view of the yard, but it don't stick out. So you don't take notice."

"Hide yourself in plain sight, in other words?" She was irritated at the way Cooper was leading her by baby steps, but he spoke with the pride of a skilled craftsman, and she appreciated that.

"Now was I to take up in that tree, and Enoch in one of them cedars up yonder, ain't nothing could get past us."

"You can't be up there twenty four hours a day."

"That's where Zeke and Michael come in. See that's what I'm saying. You done mighty smart to put me in charge of hiring because I made sure everyone not only was cow savvy but that some of them was gun savvy also. Enoch took some training, but Zeke and Michael, they put in cavalry time like me."

"You, know, Cooper, military thinking is kind of fun once you get started. What do you say to this? The men we borrow from Folsom, we station in the yard, just like before. That way, it'll look easy to him. You and Enoch and the others are our secret weapon."

"You know, Miss Carrie, I do believe you hit on a great idea. I like it just fine."

From the smugness of his smile, the humming of "Mine eyes have seen the glory," she discerned that this had been his plan all along. He was letting her take credit. Well, that was all right. She had thought of it herself, even if he had thought of it first.

"There's only one piece not taken care of."

"That be you, Miss Carrie?"

She nodded.

"You ain't gonna like it."

"I'm not going to sit in this house all day."

"No, you going to hide out with your mama."

"That's ridiculous. I can't live like she does."

"She just, poof, vanish all the time. Let her teach you."

"But half the time I don't even know where she is."

"She always know where you is, Miss Carrie. Now I know you know I'm telling the truth."

And she did. Damn Cooper. Damn him to hell. It was perfect.

"No time to waste, then," she said. "You get on with your part of things. It looks like I have to get in costume."

TWENTY-NINE

IN THE SHERIFF'S OFFICE

The clock in Sheriff O'Neil's anteroom had just struck eight P.M. The anteroom was long and narrow, resembling a hallway more than a proper room. Pew-like benches lined unplastered brick walls. The bricks seemed dry to the touch, but the place smelled dank, musty. A clerk's desk sat at one end, unoccupied, typewriter silent. At the other end, the big detective, undersized bowler still perched on his dark mane, stood near the exit door. Not blocking it, exactly, but a step away and scowling. He clearly meant his position and manner to discourage egress.

"You said he'd be here an hour ago," Andy said. "If I'm not under arrest, I'm leaving."

"You ain't under arrest," said the detective, who'd identified himself as Lieutenant Brogan.

"Then tell O'Neil we can talk another time." He moved toward the door.

"Not advisable." Brogan blocked the doorway now.

"And why is that?" He hoped at least to learn what O'Neil wanted with him, something Brogan either did not know or refused to divulge.

"Because I'd be obliged to place you under arrest," he said.

"You said I wasn't under arrest." He raised his voice in frustration. Brogan didn't raise his voice. If anything, he lowered it.

"You ain't. Yet."

"And what would the charge be?"

The big man shrugged. "My orders don't go that far," he said.

"All right, have it your way." He threw his hands in the air, turned his back, and made to sit down on one of the benches. Halfway there, he turned and feinted to the left. Brogan went for the feint, stepped over to block his way to the door, but Andy jumped to the right instead, and managed to squeeze through the door and sprint toward the stairway.

"Hey, guard, stop him," Brogan's voice roared and echoed through the brick caverns of halls and stairwells. From previous encounters with O'Neil and his minions, he remembered that there was a back stairway that mirrored the public one, used for transporting prisoners. The door between the two wells were supposed to be locked, but if someone had gotten careless, he could get out the back way. O'Neil's office was on the third floor. The doors on the first two landings were locked. However, with the sound of a hubbub in the lobby rising, just as he reached to grab the handle of the doorway he sought, the door started to open. He yanked hard, threw the man who had been pushing from the other side off balance, and dived through. He was in the stairwell he'd wanted to find, but he collided immediately with a man in uniform, tried to disentangle himself and roll toward the stairs. He rose to his feet and gathered himself to leap downward, but something hammered at his ankle, and he plummeted down the steps, landing in a pile on an intermediary landing. Two men in blue pinned him, and he heard the ratchet as metal handcuffs bit into his wrists. From above, came a voice he recognized well, no doubt the voice of the man he'd run into at the top of the stairs.

"Good work, boys," he said. "Now please help mister Maxwell up to my office."

* * *

He knew the bruises and contusions would hurt for a while, and he was chagrined that he couldn't keep from limping as he crossed to the chair in O'Neil's office. Two officers flanked his chair.

O'Neil still didn't come in right away, but kept him waiting for another half hour. Andy could hear snatches of conversation as he discussed matters with Brogan and other assorted officers in the anteroom. Finally, he sat at his own desk and waved the two guards away. He was not an imposing fellow, with his long, sallow face and narrow shoulders.

"We can do without the handcuffs, don't you think?" Andy said.

"Nothing personal, Mr. Maxwell. Protocol with a prisoner who attempts to escape."

"I wasn't a prisoner. I wasn't even under arrest, as I'm sure detective Brogan told you."

"We'll leave the handcuffs on for the time being." His voice was low and cold. "At least until you tell me what you know about Charley Hung's murder."

"What makes you think I know anything about it?"

O'Neil said nothing. Watched. Andy watched back. The whole thing went on for what seemed like five minutes, was probably less than two. Finally, O'Neil turned to the desk. Andy congratulated himself that the sheriff had broken first. The satisfaction did not last long.

"Hung's killing not tong war," he said. "Stop." He put the telegram back down. Looked at Andy again.

"That wasn't addressed to you," he said. Rage welled up in his gut.

"It didn't have to be. A crime has taken place in San Francisco, Mr. Maxwell, and I'm entitled to all evidence. You've been rather casual about observing that principle in the past, but I'm about to cure you of your neglectful ways. Now. What do you know?"

"The telegram says it all," he said. "Almost all anyway. Uncuff me, and I'll tell you the rest." He was determined not to blink. It wasn't hard. Through his eyes, he fired bullet after mental bullet. O'Neil had been complicit in the vendetta. By refusing to take Julian's murder seriously, by refusing to treat Yellow Squirrel as a severe threat to the Maxwells, he'd cost trouble, money, lives. And had he acknowledged his errors in the end? No. He'd accused Andy of obstructing justice for arranging Yellow Squirrel's Shanghai voyage. With Yellow Squirrel gone, O'Neil could only make noise and raise dust about the matter, which impotence seemed to make him all the more malevolent. For all these reasons and on the principle that he was in his entirety a nasty piece of work, Andy despised him.

"It's late, Mr. Maxwell." O'Neil's eyes didn't waver, but he had spoken first. There was some satisfaction in that. "Let me explain what you're looking at when you look across this desk. You're looking at obstruction of justice, assaulting a police officer—four counts—and resisting arrest."

"Is that all?" He felt none of the bravado he tried to display.

"No, but it's all I need to lock you up until your arraignment."

"Arraignment?" The consequences of O'Neil's threat were just beginning to sink in. He wondered about the wisdom of holding out like this. He didn't really have much to tell. It would cost him little to give up the information, and it would help O'Neil little to know it. But that wasn't the point. He tightened his lips.

"Did you think we'd write you a citation and let you go? Arraignment is the automatic next step for felony arrests. Yours will be in the morning, or perhaps the next morning depending on how full the judge's calendar is." O'Neil's eyes hadn't wavered. "Care to change your mind?"

His look remained steady as O'Neil's. "Care to change yours? Those charges will fall to pieces faster than a five dollar suit."

"It's not up to me, Maxwell. And it sure as hell isn't up to you." He rose and opened the door for the officers waiting in the ante room. It wasn't long before he found himself back in the stairwell he'd so frantically sought an hour before. This time, however, he had company. One man on each arm, and his manacle chains jingled happily, incongruously, against the concrete as he descended toward the cell blocks. Well, he'd promised Bierce to get himself thrown jail hadn't he? Maybe this was the trouble they needed.

THIRTY

CAROLYN AND NONNY

Carolyn left home afoot at sundown, and she knew she was overloaded. She didn't plan to carry all of it very far, though, would arrange a cache or camp for some of it soon. She carried a blanket rolled inside a slicker across her shoulders and two canvas bags of necessaries tied to her waist. Inside the bags were matches, a small slab of bacon, a small loaf of bread, and a couple of handfuls of dried apples. By a strap over one shoulder, she slung an empty canteen under one arm. Water was close by. She'd fill the canteen later and save the weight for now.

For weapons, she carried a bone-handled knife, one of her father's favorites, in a scabbard on one hip. She carried a Colt .45, a peacemaker, in a holster on the other. She figured it best to carry only one weapon and had considered lighter firearms—the Sharps .22 four-barreled derringer she liked for close-range encounters such as city crowds. Or the short-barreled .25 revolver, unerringly accurate, a gift to her father from a Belgian nobleman. However, nothing packed the wallop or had the range of the Colt. With its nearly six-pound weight and terrific recoil, it was a hard pistol for most people to handle, but it was the weapon Carter had taught her to shoot with. *If you learn to control this, you can take care of anyone.* The dreadful noise, the mule-like kick, the leaden heaviness had brought her to tears many times. Even as an adult, she found it cumbersome. She wasn't quick on the draw. In fact, she used both hands in most situations. But she never missed. Yellow Squirrel was a hard man to stop. She'd need all the firepower she could muster and she'd just have to hope she'd have the time to use it.

It was only a couple of miles to Granite Spring, where she'd met Many Clouds and her mother, and she'd traveled it hundreds of times. Today, though, it was no easy jaunt. Heeding Cooper's advice, she kept off the trail wherever it lacked cover, which made for longer distances over more difficult terrain. Thanks to both the weight and awkwardness of her load, she stopped often. Rested, readjusted everything.

She wore leather trousers and blouse, an outfit she often used for working roundup and fence lines. The most difficult decision about her preparations had been her hair, her long ebony hair—the gray streaks that had appeared lately, she contended, merely highlighted its crow's-wing blackness—had become one of her vanities.

It would have been rational to cut it, keep it out of the way and save the time it took to care for it. Sure, she rode and roped and wrangled like a man many a day, but most nights found her indoors, robed and civilized as any Nob Hill matron, and she hadn't spent any length of time in the wilderness since her teen years, when she'd defy her parents and disappear into the Circle M's vast acreage for a week at a stretch.

So the hair had become an emblem of her vitality, as if she were some female Sampson. She hadn't realized all this till she picked up a pair of shears. Then put them down. She took a cue from her mother and plaited it into two braids that hung nearly to the middle of her back. That ought to keep it out of the way long enough to survive even another Yellow Squirrel assault.

By the time she arrived at the spring, twilight had dwindled to darkness. No moon. She sat at the waterside, munched on a few slices of dried apples. Not far below the spring, stood a cedar grove, and that's where she planned to spend the night. She thought if she remained secluded in this area, her mother would eventually appear. And it was a place Yellow Squirrel would be unlikely to look, even if he knew she was gone from the ranch. Which would likely not be for some time.

From dust we come and to dust shall we return. From out of the forest primeval, her family had built this small empire. And here she was returning to the forest. All day, she'd been thinking of this excursion as a temporary exile, a romantic interlude like Rosalind's in the forest of Arden. As she gathered boughs to lay her blanket on, she began to feel strangely at home here, began to wonder if her journey might turn out to be something more meaningful than a brief Rousseau-like interlude with nature. She lay down and counted stars through the tree branches till she drifted into sleep. And into a dream in which her mother stroked her hair and sang a soft melody at her bedside. She felt another body snuggle up beside her, still singing, and she knew it wasn't a dream at all.

THIRTY-ONE

LOCKUP

The morning came and went. No arraignment. They'd put him in a cell with four other inmates who had, apparently, participated in some melée, were bruised, cut, and surly. Snarling at each other. Two of them—a sharp-nosed man with stringy hair nicknamed Rat and a bulky no-necked fellow called Bull—fought over whose turn it was to use the honey bucket and strewed waste over the floor. The other two, a nondescript pair named Adam and Billy chose sides and started shoving each other, but their hearts weren't in it. They soon retired to a scrap of unbesmeared floor and sat in sullen gloom. Bull and Rat gave up their fight presently as well, and a silent, odoriferous pall settled over the room. Until the guard's nightstick clanged its way across the bars.

"Stand back, gentlemen. Door's opening. Time for court." The freckle-faced, boyish-looking officer flourished a large key, made a production of turning it in the lock and swinging the door back, pointing his stick. "You. You, You, You. *Not* you." He directed the last words to Andy, followed them up with a poke in the chest.

"But I'm—" He raised his hand to brush push away the stick.

"Uh-uh," the guard said. He dropped his hand. "Back." Another poke. The door swung shut, and the procession disappeared down the hallway.

O'Neil couldn't keep this up for long. There were laws. *Habeus corpus*. Plus, he had resources. Less than a mile from this cell sat Harry Barker behind a massive walnut desk, for decades on a Maxwell family retainer to take care of their legal business. Seldom had that business been in a criminal court, but soon, despite O'Neil's shenanigans, Andy would get Barker a message. Wheels would turn, and he would be free. He wondered what might happen if he had no standing. If he were just a black man off the street instead of a Maxwell black man.

He paced through he stink, thought of famous dungeon tales—Byron at Chillon "consigned to fetters and the damp vault's dayless gloom," was how that went. *The Pit and the Pendulum*. Napoleon marooned on St. Helena. Men driven mad or to heroic deeds. Romantic foolishness. He wasn't in such a dire situation, but it probably wouldn't take long to change even a strong man in a spot like this.

His cell mates were gone for over an hour, and they returned even angrier than they left. *Five hundred dollars bail. Might as well be five million. Turd. If it hadn't been for you. Shut up, stupid bastard.* Bull and Rat were about to square off again. The guard swung his nightstick against Bull's kidneys, kicked the feet out from under Rat. They both sprawled on the floor, slid through the filth. The door slammed shut. The guard hadn't said a word. Bull and Rat, still cursing, tried to wipe themselves clean. Adam and Billy had retreated to their corner.

Since his previous accusations and threats hadn't worked with the guard, Andy decided to try politeness. "Sir, if you please, would you mind bringing me a pen and paper? I'd like to send a message."

"A message is it?"

"I have the right, I believe."

"Oh, you believe so, do you?" The babyfaced grin revealed blackened teeth. "Well, I believe it is my right to tell you to shut that pie hole of yours."

A short staredown. So he'd have to push harder. He retreated, mumbling.

"They could at least get someone to clean the floor."

"Do you have something else to say?"

"Maybe if you gave us a mop, we could—"

"Maybe If I gave your head a shove into that bucket."

"And maybe you'd like walking a night beat on the waterfront. I could arrange that, you know. Do you know how cold it gets on the waterfront?"

In answer, the guard smiled, pulled out his big key, and made for the cell door. Andy braced himself. The other prisoners drew back against the cell walls.

It was what he'd been aiming for, but now he was not so sure how good an idea it had been. The guard was no taller than he, but outweighed him by a good twenty pounds. And he had that night stick.

He flung the door wide, closed and locked it behind him. He put the key ring on his belt, gripped his handcuffs like brass knuckles, and strode toward into the cell, grinning his rotten-toothed grin. He lifted his stick high and brought it down toward Andy's head. Andy blocked the man's forearm with his own, managing to avoid the nightstick. But he didn't avoid the uppercut to his gut, enhanced by the handcuffs.

Pain radiated from his solar plexus, and he couldn't pull in a nickel's worth of air. He collapsed into the slime. His face was inches from the guard's polished black boots. He watched one of them draw back, knew it was about to fly into his face. His hands gripped his stomach. The other prisoners were yelling now. He couldn't tell who they were rooting for. He rolled away from the kick. The guard missed, and the miss threw him off balance. Andy grabbed the other ankle and yanked. Now they were both on the floor.

He had dodged the kick, but he couldn't see that he was any better off. The guard was on his hands and knees now, his uniform dripping with muck. And he was no longer smiling. Savage was the word for the look on his face. He made to push himself to his feet, but a pair of hands pushed him back down.

Suddenly, the guard had new problems. The other prisoners were closing in, circling, Rat and Bull in the lead.

"Hold it. Hold it," Andy gained his feet gasping, fighting for breath. He held his arms wide, palms down.

"You kidding?" Rat giggled. "He started it. We're all witnesses. This guy had no reason—"

"You can't win this," he said hoarsely. "You know that." He leaned down next to the guard's ear, whispered loudly. "You have one chance to keep us quiet about this. I want to be on a telephone to my lawyer within ten minutes. When he arrives, we'll be arranging bail for these gentlemen."

"I don't have the authority."

"Someone does. Find him. Persuade him."

He motioned the other men back. They looked at each other, murmuring, smiling. He offered a hand to help the guard to his feet, but he spurned it, crawled to the door and used the bars to pull himself to his feet. Careful not to turn his back on the prisoners, he pulled out the key and let himself out of the cell.

A merry whistling echoed through the cellblock, and another guard entered hallway.

"Sorry I'm a little late, Michael," he called. "That old woman of mine—Hey, what in the world happened to you?"

Guard Michael glowered. Andy spoke. "We were complaining about the mess in our cell," he said. "Officer Michael here came in to make an inspection. He slipped."

"Get somebody down here with a mop," Michael said. "My shift is over." He strode off down the hall trying to find a clean place on his uniform to wipe his hands. He gave up and just waved them around.

"Thank you, officer," Andy called, his own body soaked with excrement, "We won't forget you."

THIRTY-TWO

DISAPPOINTMENT

VENDETTA CELEBRITY ARRAIGNED

by Thomas Redmond

    Mr. Andrew Maxwell, charged with obstruction of justice, resisting arrest, and four counts of assault on a police officer stemming from an incident in the Hall of Justice two evenings previous, was arraigned today in an extraordinary afternoon session of the district court of Judge Hugh Bailey. Mr. Maxwell's counsel, Harry Barker, a respected barrister of this city, entered pleas of not guilty to the charges on behalf of his client. Bail in the amount of $5,000 was arranged, and Mr. Maxwell was released.

    However, the drama did not end there. Assistant district attorney Elihu Harris called for Mr. Maxwell's re-arrest as a material witness in a murder investigation, claiming the defendant held important information anent the killing of tong boss Charley Hung, information he had unlawfully refused to divulge. As evidence, Mr. Harris asserted that Sheriff O'Neil's office had intercepted a telegram from Maxwell implying deep knowledge of the crime. Asked to produce the telegram, the prosecutor declined, asserting that making it public at this time would jeopardize the investigation. Judge Bailey determined that absent the telegram or other evidence, there was no lawful cause to detain Mr. Maxwell, which decision brought Sheriff O'Neil to his feet, but Bailey gaveled him down and dismissed the proceedings.

That gavel, however, did not end things after all. Mr. Barker begged successfully to extend the session to arrange bail for four clients, cellmates of Mr. Maxwell, who had been arraigned at an earlier session, charged with public drunkenness, disturbing the peace, and brawling, but who had remained incarcerated until trial due to their inability to post bail. Prosecutor Harris objected that the four men, Sylvester MacEnroe, Harold Billings, William Givens, and Adam Gordon were flight risks and dangerous to the public safety. Judge Bailey, however, answered that bail had been set and met and that he had no recourse but to release them.

Finally, Mr. Maxwell requested and was granted permission to address the court. He used his allotted time to commend one of the jail guards, Officer Michael Pendergast, for his professional and sympathetic conduct toward him and his cellmates during his time behind bars. Judge Bailey's gavel this time did succeed in concluding the session, and the parties went their separate ways.

* * *

Michael Yellow Squirrel was relieved to read of Andrew's release. Ordinarily, any Maxwell trouble was cause for cheer, and he would have rejoiced to see his adversary in jail. Now, though, the incident interfered with his plan, a plan which required that all the Maxwells and their minions gather at the ranch. He knew his quarry would understand the message he'd left via Charley Hung, would head for the ranch immediately. He'd concentrate all the forces he could at the focal point of Maxwell power. Circling the wagons, so to speak, to make their strongest possible stand against him.

The arrest had meant a delay. He hated delays, and his tolerance for it was thinning. Luckily, though, it had not turned out be a long one, thanks to the Maxwell money he was sure. He'd bought his way out. Well, that was fine this time. The better for Yellow Squirrel. *I'll meet you in the mountains, Mr. Maxwell.*

THIRTY-THREE

ANDY UNDERGROUND

Redmond accosted him on the way out of the courtroom. He refused to talk.

"No questions now. Let's go to Bierce's office."

"You won't find him there," Redmond said.

"Where, then?"

He'd anticipated one of Bierce's sumptuous venues like the Tadich Grill, where his retinue could gather and fawn over him. Now, though, Redmond led him to a subterranean dive on North Beach lacking any sign to announce its name. The light was dim, the ambience and the clientele odoriferous. The bar was a booth in one corner. A glassy-eyed prostitute gave them a grin and a lookover as they walked through the room. Redmond walked straight toward what, in the darkness, appeared to be a solid wall, reached out and slid aside a black curtain.

Bierce sat in a small booth before a bank of candles. He was writing in a journal. He looked up when the curtain opened. Dismay crossed his features. "Can I find solitude nowhere? Nowhere at all? If my dictionary is never completed, Redmond, it will be on your head, and my ghost will haunt you like a Mexican muerto."

"I know, I know, and you scare me to death. You do. However, Mr. Maxwell here claims to have the story you asked for."

"Oh, does he now? Well, sit down. Let's have it." He slammed the journal shut.

He asked, "Did you get a telegram from me day before yesterday?"

"I haven't received a telegram from anyone for days," he said.

"Then I think I have two stories," he said. He told them first about O'Neil's interception of the telegram. "Until this moment, I didn't know whether O'Neil was showing me a copy or an original in his office. Obviously, he not only wanted information from me, he wanted to keep it from you."

"For a man like me who makes his living off information, that is a serious offense, and we can arrange to make the officious fool pay for his misdeed. A good story, indeed, Andy. You say you have another."

He nodded, smiled. Now to the main subject. What he was about to say carried the sweet taste of revenge. Maybe this is what Yellow Squirrel felt like when he strung up Charley Hung. He didn't like admitting to an impulse like that, but a man couldn't help what he felt. Besides, he wasn't planning to kill anyone. Not planning to, anyway.

"Here's what the telegram said: *Hung's death not Tong war*." He watched Redmond and Bierce, waited for the obvious question. He realized he was using O'Neil's interrogation techniques and, abashed, prepared to continue. But Redmond broke the silence first.

"If it wasn't a tong war, what was it?"

"I'll need a favor," he said.

"Andy, Andy," Bierce said.

"All right, Ambrose. I didn't mean to make it sound like blackmail. But I guess it did. It's just that—never mind. I'll give you the scoop and trust you'll do the right thing." He told them what he suspected. Knew. About Charley Hung's execution. They were suitably impressed. Enthralled, actually. Redmond pounded the table.

"How in God's heaven did I miss the savior-and-two-thieves pattern?"

"Context, my boy, context. We rarely see what we don't expect, no matter how obvious," Bierce said. He drummed his fingers and stared into space. "A juicy story," he said. "But I hesitate…"

"Why, for God's sake?" Redmond said.

"Because of Andy, here." Bierce answered. "If we print the story, it will be obvious where we got the information, which will in turn constitute strong evidence to support O'Neil's charge of obstruction."

"I thought of that," Andy said. "I was not a witness. I have no hard evidence, no direct knowledge of anything. What I deduced—the Calvary configuration, the sun dance, Yellow Squirrel's hatred for the white man—it's all public knowledge. Good researchers, journalist and scholars like you and Redmond could put it all together yourselves. A trip to the library and to your own archives and you would have all the quotes and background you need. Strictly speaking, it's more speculation than evidence anyway."

"Mr. Maxwell, you amaze me," Bierce said. "We'll certainly consider it."

It was not the enthusiastic commitment he had hoped for, but he felt he'd won, even if Bierce didn't say so directly, so he decided to leave the subject. "Now, can I make my request?" he said.

"Well, we've got the quid, so what's the pro quo?" Redmond laughed. Bierce frowned.

"Another Latin massacre by the Redmond regiment. Well?" Bierce said.

"Help Nathan with our appeal to the regents. I'm going to be busy, and he's kind of at sea by himself. I'm not asking you to publish anything. Just help him with contacts, protocol, wording of letters. That sort of thing?"

"A pleasure," Bierce said immediately.

"Thanks. Thanks. Now, I've got to catch the last ferry or I'll miss my morning train." He rose, but Redmond put a hand on his arm.

"Hey, I have an idea. How about I go with you?" he said. Andy felt as puzzled as Bierce looked. Redmond turned to his boss. "Sure, I could follow him around while he combats this Indian. I'll file reports. It'll be like a dime novel serial. Sell papers like Tadich sells oysters."

"A novel idea," Bierce said. "And if I could spare you, you'd have my blessing."

"But—" Redmond's objection got no farther. Bierce raised his hand.

"Out of the question, Tom. You've got to storm Mayor McCarthy's barricades and get the goods on the grafters and grabbers we've been pursuing. You're getting close, and it's no time to quit."

What about me?" Andy said. They both looked at him blankly.

"I'll file reports. I can't promise how regular they'll be, and some things I'll have to keep secret for obvious reasons, but I'll give it a try." The more he could do for Bierce, he was thinking, the more he'd be able to capitalize on his good will as he battled with the regents. And then he was suddenly thinking this would be fun. Fun? Odd notion, but there it was.

"Send in the reports, then," Bierce said. "No more than eight-hundred words. I've seen no samples of your writing, so I warn you we'll likely edit them heavily. If we publish them at all."

Redmond pounded the table. "This is quite unfair, Ambrose. It was my idea."

"And a fine idea it was, Tom. And you'll probably get to put your own signature verbiage into the editing."

"But not the byline."

"Look, I don't want to make trouble," Andy said.

"No trouble," Bierce said. "These details can be worked out. Now, don't you have a ferry to catch?"

"Indeed I do," he said. "Gentlemen." He drew back the curtain, and fairly jogged out of the bar.

THIRTY-FOUR

AN UNCLE AND NIECE REUNION

Many Clouds still hadn't regained her full energy, but it was returning. She wrote to her father, Standing Oak, explaining that she needed a little time to heal from an injury before she could return to Wind River. She assured him she was safe, but mentioned nothing of how she was hurt or of her present circumstances. If he knew everything, he'd turn angry, might even come find her. Ever since her mother's death two summers ago, Standing Oak had been protective, possessive. This situation with Fitzpatrick, Maggie, and Willy—he would say she was a servant to a white man, would suspect she had become Fitzpatrick's concubine.

The missionaries would have said God sent Miller Fitzpatrick her way, and she would have made no effort to refute them. He provided a home, shelter, and asked in return only that she care for Maggie and Willy. Sleeping under the same roof with him in the one-room cabin—temporary, he said, till he could build her a space of her own—that did make her nervous. But he had yet to make a romantic overture. She wasn't sure how she would react if he did. It was hard to imagine a better man for her, or for any woman.

Standing Oak would be even more distressed to know the real reason for her reluctance to think of Fitzpatrick as a mate. Avoiding a relationship with a white man was the right thing to do, of course, but to know that it was another white man who stood between her and this family? She wouldn't let herself imagine his reaction.

She understood her feelings for Andy were futile. Her indirect inquiries at the Circle M revealed only that he was away at school, and she sensed she shouldn't ask more. She supposed she would have to decide about Miller at some point. But for the moment, it was enough to enjoy the satisfaction of her time with this little family.

Miller had planted a small garden on the south side of the cabin, which got plenty of sun, but his days-long hauling trips left him scant time to tend it. Many Clouds worked with the children to enlarge and enrich the plot, adding winter vegetables to help feed them during the long rainy season. They seemed happy to take direction from her, though Willy sometimes tearfully compared her ways to his mother's. Maggie always soothed him and helped prod him to accept the new circumstances of their lives. Quite a girl, Maggie. Many Clouds felt privileged that the children allowed her to help tend their mother's grave, beside an apple tree Swallow herself had planted.

Miller's extended absences had also left scant time for Maggie's and Willy's schooling, so Many Clouds began setting aside an hour or so each day to work with them on their letters and numbers, helping them scratch out lessons with chalk on improvised shale slates.

During one of these lessons on a sunlit hillside behind the cabin, on an afternoon when broken clouds drifted through a brilliant sky, a shadow fell across the little group in as they worked on subtraction of two-digit numbers. Many Clouds thought another cloud had slid between them and the sun, but Maggie and Willy clutched their slates close and stared upward. Something was behind her. Someone. She leapt to her feet and turned. Yellow Squirrel.

"Look where I find you, Many Clouds. A schoolteacher for white children. Your grandfather would be disappointed."

"Not all white," she said.

A cowardly answer, she thought. Yellow Squirrel had always frightened her, ever since she was a girl. He'd enjoyed great esteem in the tribe. A handsome man, a superior hunter, dancer, athlete. But for her, there'd been a menace about him that made her uneasy when he approached, relieved when he left. During all the trouble with Andy, he'd proved himself willing not only to ignore the direct commands of his father, Owl Feather, but to put him and the rest of the family in danger to chase his dream of destroying the Maxwells. She'd come to think of him as a sort of Lucifer, heaven's brightest angel fallen, a traitor to those who gave him life. She'd been grateful to Andy for erasing him from her life. Now he was back, and her throat tightened with the old girlhood fear.

"I'm surprised to see you," she said.

He displayed that familiar smirk of his, delight at her discomfort.

"I'm full of surprises," he said. "And so are you. For example, I'm surprised you would call such mongrel children anything but white." She'd last seen him in the garb of an old-time Arapaho warrior—war paint, breechclout, eagle feather—racing away on horseback in pursuit of Andrew. Now he could pass for a ranch hand with his broadbrimmed straw hat, pointed boots, denim pants and shirt. He couldn't have come far on foot in those boots, but she saw no horse or wagon nearby. "You have fallen far from our people."

"What do you want?" she said.

"You see what I mean? None of the traditional hospitality we are obligated to offer even to a stranger, let alone a beloved uncle." He had begun wandering as he spoke, peeking through the cabin window. Casting glances at Maggie and Willy, who cowered behind her now.

"We have very little to spare," she said. "Of course, if there is something in particular you'd like, I'll do my best." She followed him at a distance as he circled the cabin, moved toward the garden. He stepped quite deliberately in the freshly turned earth, where stakes indicated fresh planting.

"Oh," he said. "Careless of me. I hope I haven't ruined anything." Many Clouds edged toward a shovel leaning against the cabin wall. "You won't need that," he said. "Not that it would do you any good." She tried to push the children toward the cabin, but they wouldn't move. "And they can stay here," he said. "I just came for information."

"Oh?" She was beginning to glimpse his purpose.

"You just returned from the Circle M."

"Yes." So he had returned to complete the job he'd failed at two years earlier. "I was sick."

"They were there, too?" he said, indicating the children.

Now what was he getting at? She remained silent.

"And your white man. All of you were there long enough to learn a great deal about how the place operates."

"I was in bed, sick, most of the time. As soon as I could travel, we left." She met his eyes. Difficult.

"But these ones and their white daddy. They weren't sick. They were all over the place, helping with the chores? Playing? Isn't that right?" This last, he directed straight to Willy and Maggie. They'd been peeking from behind Many Clouds but dodged behind her when he addressed them. Now he took a step forward, Many Clouds spread her arms protectively.

The smirk reappeared.

"Now, here's what I need to know. How many in the house? How many in the bunkhouse? The schedule. I could get all this by watching, but it's nice when a man has family around to help."

The questions went on for another fifteen or twenty minutes, Many Clouds and the children squeezed back against the cabin wall, Yellow Squirrel pacing through the garden as he spoke, trampling stands of lettuce, spinach, squash.

"When you left, did they know I'd come back?" he said finally.

Many Clouds shook her head, remembered the rider who had galloped in as they'd crossed under the archway, but she'd attached no significance to him at the time.

"What's that?" he said sharply. "You're hiding something."

She shook her head. "You know all we know."

He paused, eyes boring into her. "Come here, Willy," he said.

Willy had been peeking out at Yellow Squirrel. Now he ducked behind Many Clouds again.

"You see, I've been learning things from listening to your lessons. Like your names. Your daddy's name. Come, on, don't be shy." He darted forward quick as a snake and snatched Willy up into his arms. Willy struggled, but Yellow Squirrel held him too tight to move much, stroked his head.

"Uncle—" Many Clouds said.

"Oh, Willy's fine, aren't you, boy?" Willy said nothing. "Aren't you?" Yellow Squirrel squeezed harder. Willy nodded.

"It was nothing," Many Clouds said. "A man riding fast to the ranch as we were leaving. I don't know what he wanted." The eyes again. The smirk again.

"All right," he said, finally. He dropped Willy to within a few inches of the around, held him with one hand, dangling by the wrist. "You know, Willy, if you truly are an Indian, you should come with me. You won't learn warrior ways staying here." Willy yelled. He flopped and wriggled.

"Stay still, Willy. You'll hurt yourself, now." Yellow Squirrel lifted the boy higher.

"Oww. Let me go."

"Any pain you feel, boy, comes from your own doing."

"Please, Uncle," Many Clouds said.

Yellow Squirrel tossed the boy to the ground with a quick twist of his wrist. Many Clouds knelt and opened her arms. The boy buried his face in her bosom.

"This seems like a fortunate little situation for you, Many Clouds. I'm glad to see you doing well. You shouldn't do anything to spoil it. Like telling anyone. Anyone at all. That I was here." He touched his hat brim and headed uphill into the pines and brush behind the cabin. She listened for a horse, but heard none.

"Is he really your uncle?" Maggie asked after a long while.

"Yes," said Many Clouds.

"He's a bad man," she said.

"Come here." Many Clouds knelt, brought Maggie into the same protective circle that cradled Willy. "He won't hurt you," she said. "I promise." She had never made a promise she felt less capable of keeping.

THIRTY-FIVE

ANDY BACK AT THE RANCH

Two envelopes awaited him at his boarding house after his rendezvous with Bierce and Redmond. One was no surprise, though the closing sentences were intriguing:

> *I know your feelings about waiting and hope I am not trying them too horribly. I look forward to seeing you. We have much to discuss, do we not?*
>
> *Affectionately,*
> *Virginia*

Yes we do, my blonde bohemian. We most certainly do. In the normal course of things, he could have been righteously angry about her sudden departure, but not when he had made such a sudden departure of his own. Not that hers was as justified as his. Or so he might have contended.

During his sophomore year, he'd studied the Greek tragedies and become a believer in fate. Oedipus, Orestes, and all the rest drawn ironically toward their disastrous ends despite their best efforts to redirect the universal will. He'd later decided the whole philosophy was superstition or artistic manipulation. Now, with Virginia, he began to wonder if it didn't apply after all. Useless speculation. He turned to the other envelope, which was a complete surprise.

"MacIntosh" was hand lettered under the embossed return address of the university's English department. The note inside was short and mysterious.

> Mr. Maxwell,
>
> I believe it would be in our mutual interest to meet at your earliest convenience. Please contact me at the Shattuck Hotel rather than at my university office.
>
> Sincerely,
> George MacIntosh

Why the subterfuge? It was almost enough to make him take delay his return to the ranch still farther. Almost, but not quite. MacIntosh could prove crucial to his doctorate, but Yellow Squirrel was life and death. He hoped a telegram would suffice to keep the chairman waiting. If O'Neil didn't intercept it. He felt like a general forced to split his armies, unable to properly supply either one. Well, it had worked out for Lee at Chancellorsville, maybe he could make it work for him as well. Not that he had a Stonewall Jackson to help out.

He got the MacIntosh telegram off barely in time to catch first morning train:

* * *

ANXIOUS TO MEET STOP EXTREMELY URGENT BUSINESS AT HOME STOP PLEASE TELEGRAM OR WRITE IMMEDIATELY STOP

* * *

He arrived in Placerville around noon and hurried to Feifer Gilligan's new livery stable, where the Maxwells boarded several horses. Gilligan had owned the only such stable in Sawtooth Wells for years, and Carolyn had lent him the money to open another in Placerville after the vendetta.

Gilligan wasn't there when Andy requisitioned the hardy Appaloosa he saddled up for his ride to the ranch. He drew on the emergency trunk of necessaries the Circle M kept in the loft. After shipping out Yellow Squirrel two years earlier, he had felt safe again in his home territory. However, after all that had happened, he and his mother had determined to be always prepared.

He took a canteen, some pemmican, a slicker, a .30-.06 Remington, and a brand-new .45 caliber double action Colt revolver. The pistol was a model the U.S. Cavalry had adopted after previous sidearms had proved ineffective against the Moro insurgents in the Philippines.

He decided not to take the main road, but to travel trails and back roads in case his nemesis awaited. It more than thirty miles and a climb of about two thousand feet from town to the ranch. The slower and steeper route would delay his arrival until well after dark. But that might be an advantage as well, to approach at night and observe the defenses Cooper and his mother had devised.

He noticed thunderheads as he topped the ridge surrounding Shingle Lake. He sipped from the canteen, tore off a chunk of pemmican. The sun was descending at his back, pinking the tops of the dark-bottomed towers which been gathering in the eastern sky while he'd been ascending the western wall of the canyon he'd just put behind him. The thunderheads were moving his way. The lightning started a couple of miles past the lake, near the entrance to Green Canyon with its massive cinnabar deposits, ore his mother had once considered mining. Might have to consider it again if the financial situation didn't improve. The clouds began to empty fifteen minutes after he donned his slicker. In another fifteen minutes, the sun disappeared, and he was riding through liquid blackness.

After it passed Green Canyon, the trail wound for ten or twelve miles around the slopes of the ridges that marked the western boundary of the Circle M before it passed behind the barn and dropped into the ranch yard itself. It was well-marked and stable in ordinary times, but could become treacherous in a downpour. He began to wonder if he'd make it home before midnight, make it home at all tonight. He got his answer shortly.

The horse stopped and shied. Andy couldn't tell why, but knew better than to ignore the animal's nervousness without checking the source. He dismounted and walked along the trail for a few yards, then nearly stepped into space. A virtual river poured down the hillside, washing out the trail for, as far as he could see in the darkness, at least ten yards. Probably more. This was the softest stretch of the route. He pictured the detour that would be required to get past it. Downhill, across some pastureland, through a half mile of gravel-and-boulder screeland, and a steep climb up a root-tangled hillside before regaining the trail. A good five miles. At least two hours. Dark as it was? Be realistic. He'd be out here somewhere when the sun rose. Nothing for it, though, but to get started.

The way was too steep for riding, so he led his mount carefully down the hillside through brush and trees, slipping and cursing. The horse tossed and snorted. Andy didn't blame him. Finally they gained a sloping but navigable pasture, a favorite summer grazing area for Circle M cattle. It would be one of the last to be cleared of animals during roundup. He wasn't sure whether the hands had gotten this far or not yet. There were no cattle to be seen now. Not surprising. He couldn't see his own hand at the end of his arm except when the lightning flashed, and if there were any animals around, they'd all be sheltered in the brush. Then one flash showed him cattle after all. In the middle of the pasture. Lying down. No.

Two yearlings. A heifer and a bull. Butchered. The Washoes? Although his grandfather never countenanced it, punished any Indian he caught, Carolyn Maxwell turned a blind eye if the starving Washoes slaughtered Circle M beeves once in a while. As long as it was not a regular occurrence, as long as they were eating, not selling, the meat. But these animals had not been killed for food. They were slit up the belly, their innards spilling out on to the ground. In the precise manner of Charley Hung. And Julian. He saw all this in fragments, like a series of photographs tossed before him by the lightning.

The rain had rinsed the blood into the mud, so that the guts were a grey slime now. Yellow Squirrel had begun his assault. He wondered if he'd been meant to find these carcasses, if the Indian was watching him right now, though he couldn't be. He wondered these things and more, but most of all he wondered what he'd find when he reached the house.

THIRTY-SIX

CAROLYN IN CAMP

Nonny tore a strip from the squirrel's tenderloin and handed it to her daughter. Carolyn took the offering and stared for a moment at the stringy, greasy fragment between her fingers. An odd breakfast to say the least. But they'd been lucky to snare the animal. Last night's fierce storm had probably dulled its instincts, prompting it to take corn that had lain untouched for several days previous under the figure-four trap.

"Eat, Carrie," her mother said. And she did. Chewing gratefully, thankful for a variation from pine nuts and juniper berries. "We'll go see our Washoe friends today."

"No, Mother," she said. "No one must know I'm here but you."

"Yes, yes. You won't come into their camp, just wait outside. They might know something of Yellow Squirrel."

Suddenly, Carolyn found herself anxious to leave. If the Washoes did know something, the sooner she and her mother found out the better.

They consumed the rest of the meat and buried the skeleton. A large rock's natural bowl still held rainwater in which they rinsed their hands. Even afterwards, though, she felt dirty, her fingernails crammed black with soil. She needed a bath, a change of clothes. She needed. She needed. Yet her mother seemingly needed nothing beyond the light meals that left her hungry every time. As she shook her hands dry, she glanced over to find her mother gazing at her. It was a loving look, a tilt-headed smile. She smiled back and reached out. They grasped one another's hands for a moment, then started out.

As they passed Granite Spring, she paused to look down on the Circle M ranch yard. Home. A miniature from here. Sunlight glinted off puddles the rain had left behind in the yard. The buildings looked washed and fresh. More washed and fresh than she felt. Much as she felt warmed and nourished by her mother's company, she wished she were down there. Maybe soon. Something told her that this visit to the washoes would be fruitful, perhaps decisive.

If it hadn't been for the wet earth, she would have seen dust long before she heard the noise. As it was, her first hint of something unusual approaching were the sounds mysterious clicks and splutters, somewhat like Ling Chu's Model T, but with a different tone. Then at the top of the rise, appeared a long, steel-gray convertible touring car with three banks of high-backed seats carrying three men. She could discern almost nothing about the occupants, only that the passenger in the front seemed older and heftier than the driver. The man in the second seat was scooted so low she could tell nothing at all about him.

Right behind the car rode Billy Mays, unable to pass because the driver kept swerving to avoid ruts. Unable to leave the road because the sides were fenced. The poor man was probably apoplectic.

"Mother, you go ahead, please. I'll meet you here in the morning. You can tell me what you found out."

"My girl, you mustn't. You said yourself how dangerous it is." Nonny clutched her arm.

"It is, yes. But there's somebody important in that car, and it's not Yellow Squirrel. I don't know if Andy's returned yet, but whether he has or not, I'm needed down there. I know it." She removed herself from her mother's grip, kissed her hand and began working her way down the hill.

"I'll be here if I can," her mother called.

Carolyn turned. "Please don't play hide and seek, Mother. Not now."

"If I can," her mother waved. Then disappeared.

Down below, Enoch had emerged from the bunkhouse and was walking toward the car, kicking at the dogs and chickens that swarmed around it. A man on the porch, one of the prison guards they'd borrowed from Folsom, held his rifle butt at his shoulder, barrel pointed at the sky, but ready to level at a moment's notice.

A movement on the trail above the barn. Someone on horseback. Yellow Squirrel. No. She couldn't tell much through the trees, but whoever it was wasn't trying to hide. He stopped, lifted his hands. Another man stepped out of the trees, rifle trained on the rider. The car, Billy Mays, the strange rider, the confusion. All of it needed her attention, and, safe or not, she hurried down the trail.

THIRTY-SEVEN

HOMECOMING

Of all the fearful things he'd imagined when his all-night ride finally ended at the ranch house, a Locomobile touring car carrying three official-looking occupants had never occurred to him. He hadn't planned on Billy Mays, either, but he was much more in the realm of possibilities than the other. It was unnerving to have been forced to dismount and walk into his home yard with a rifle pointed at his back, but he felt reassured that security had been taken care of.

As he and his challenger rounded the barn, he saw Enoch talking to the three men, or rather to the oldest of the three who had disembarked from the automobile. The two younger men stood behind him. Billy Mays was standing behind all three, waving a yellow envelope. Ling Chu stood on the porch, along with Amelia. Where was Cooper? Ling Chu spotted him before he had a chance to hail the house.

"Mr. Andrew," he called. He hurried down the steps. "Come quick, Mr. Andrew."

Billy Mays jogged toward him as well. "Telegrams, Mr. Maxwell. Had a devil of a time getting here between the storm and this infernal contraption, but you know me. Never miss a delivery. Sign right here."

"Stand back, y'all," said the man whose rifle was trained on Andy.

Enoch said, "Never mind, Fetters. Andy here owns the ranch. You can go back to your post."

Fetters lowered his rifle reluctantly. "And good job, Mr. Fetters," Andy said. "Stay alert." He clapped the man on the shoulder. Fetters smiled and turned, began trudging back up the hill. "But, oh," Andy said. "I would like my pistol back." He held out his hand.

Fetters pulled the gun from his belt and handed it over. "Sorry, plumb forgot I had it," he said.

Andy had barely holstered his weapon before Mays shoved the telegrams and the receipt book, pencil dangling from a string, in his face.

"Hang on, Billy," he said. "Let me catch my breath."

"Oh, yessir. It's just I'm so behind schedule now, I'm fair beside myself."

"Enoch," he called, "would you mind finding someone to take care of my horse? He's had a rough night."

"You bet, Mr. Maxwell," Enoch said. "So long, gents." He tipped his hat at the three men. As he took the appaloosa's reins, he said under his breath, "Rather deal with a horse than those stuffed shirts any day."

"Who are they?"

"Someone named Johnson's all I got," Enoch said. "But, listen, get rid of them quick. I got a lot to tell you."

"Where's Mom? And what about Cooper?"

"Not with them around," Enoch whispered.

"Mr. Maxwell." Billy Mays again, thrusting paperwork toward him. "I need to be on my way."

He signed the book and grabbed the telegrams. "So begone with you, Billy," he said. Mays sprinted back to his horse, vaulted into the saddle, and lifted a hand high in a showy farewell as he cantered out of the archway.

Tearing open the telegrams as he walked slowly toward the automobile, he noticed the leader of the three motorists walking toward him, hand extended.

"If I'm not mistaken, sir, you are Mr. Andrew Maxwell." The man's voice was tenor, pitched higher than one might expect from a man of his heft and girth, but it was the voice of an orator even in a conversational situation like this one.

"And if I'm not mistaken," Andy said, perusing the telegram, "you are Hiram Johnson. Apparently you travel faster than Western Union. Forgive me for not recognizing our Republican candidate for governor. I've seen your picture in the paper, sir, but not wearing a hat."

They shook hands, and Johnson doffed his grey fedora. Andy had never seen a man who impressed more at first glance. Johnson's icy blue eyes demanded attention, even obedience. His smile, on the other hand, invited friendship and trust. Here was a man with tremendous force of personality. Even his wire-rimmed spectacles, which would have weakened the initial impact of most men, rendered him more forceful.

"And here," Johnson waved the hat to summon his two companions, "let me introduce my son Jack, also my campaign manager, and this is my aide, Jeremiah Peabody." There were handshakes all around. "So my arrival preceded the telegram announcing that I was on my way. Beastly storm. I do apologize, but I assure you my business is urgent. I must speak to you and your mother immediately." A shout from Enoch behind the barn interrupted them.

"You. Squaw. What are you doing skulking around here? Away, now."

An Indian woman with long black braids, shuffled from the barn, across the yard, and out under the arch. Her head was down, in obvious fear and humiliation. Enoch followed her, making shooing motions with his hands and stood watching till he was sure she was headed down the road.

"No need to be so severe, Enoch, is there?"

"They've been getting awful bold lately, Andy, and what with all the rest that's going on, we'd rather be safe than sorry, wouldn't we?"

"Of course, Enoch. Excuse me, gentlemen." He turned toward the house. Aunt Amelia, Ling Chu, this is Mr. Hiram Johnson and his son, Jack, and Mr. Peabody. Ling Chu will you please make our guests comfortable while I bathe and change? We'll meet out here in an hour or so. I'm quite anxious to find out why you're here."

Everyone trooped up the steps. He read the second telegram.

* * *

MUST MEET EARLIEST POSSBLE PLS ADVISE STOP MACINTOSH

* * *

Another urgency. How many did that make? No use counting.

He muttered as he passed Amelia, "Let's go to the office, Amelia. I'd love to find out what's going on around here."

"Andy, honey, I'll tell you everything, but you're still not going to believe it."

THIRTY-EIGHT

SECRETS

It was late in the morning, two days after Yellow Squirrel's visit, that Miller Fitzpatrick approached the cabin in the buckboard. Many Clouds yearned to keep Yellow Squirrel's visit a secret, but she knew that for Maggie and Willy to bottle up something so horrendous would be impossible, even in the face of the savage warning.

Once he found out, Miller would want to take some action, and whatever he did would endanger himself and his children. He wouldn't understand how devious, ruthless, dangerous her uncle was. Nobody could who hadn't met with him, lived with him, fought him. She would flee if she thought that would divert Yellow Squirrel's attention from the little family, but he wouldn't forget about them. If she ran, he'd more likely double whatever cruelty he'd planned for them. She was reminded again of the cost of taking up with white folks.

Amid the greeting hugs and smiles, Many Clouds fought the impulse to pull Miller aside right away, but she couldn't until the preliminaries were over. She'd just have to hope the children wouldn't break the news immediately.

"Maggie and Willy, would you please go play for a few minutes? I have to talk to your father. Then we'll have a nice lunch."

"It's about your uncle, isn't it?" Maggie said.

"Yes," Many Clouds said. "Yes, it is." Miller looked puzzled. "But we still have to have a grown-ups talk."

"Just like mama," Willy said. "Grown-ups talk. No fair."

"Go on, now," Miller said. "Kids is kids and grown-ups is grown-ups, and that's all there is to say. Go on, now, I tell you."

Many Clouds stood with Miller and watched as the children sulked their way to a swing Miller had rigged from a live oak tree up the slope. Then Miller turned to her, a question on his face.

"While you were gone," she said, "My uncle came here."

"Your uncle?"

"Yellow Squirrel. The one who tried to destroy the Maxwells."

"That man was your uncle? Why didn't you tell me?"

"Please don't be angry. I thought he was gone. There was no reason to mention it." She had never seen Miller's features so rigid and dark.

"What did he want?" Miller said.

"He wanted to know everything about the Circle M. I'm sure he has another plan to kill them. He warned us to keep quiet that he was here," she said.

"Well, we ain't about to keep quiet. First thing, we're going to warn Mrs. Maxwell."

"I'm sure she already knows. Miller—Mr. Fitzpatrick—we must keep away from the Circle M. If he thinks… Yellow Squirrel won't stop with the Maxwells, and because of me, you, and Maggie and Willy…" She was crying now.

"Because of you, Maggie and Willy have someone to love and care for them for the first time since their mother died, so don't give me that line of baloney. But we got to think about this. All right. The sheriff—"

"He can't protect us."

"Guess not. Actually, better question is, would he? He might be interested in helping the Maxwells out, but we don't count for nothing. Still and all, we can't go on like normal. I can't leave you alone, and we can't all just hang around here waiting to be attacked."

"I will leave," Many Clouds said. "Go home. I'll find a way to get across the mountains."

"Don't be silly. He ain't going to leave us alone just because you ain't here. Near as I can tell, only one thing to do." He paced his way back and forth for a few moments, hands on his head. Then he stopped and turned. "Yessir, only one thing for it."

"Mr. Fitzpatrick?"

"We're going back to the Circle M. Let's pack up the buckboard." He headed for the cabin. "Come on, kids, roll up your beds, we're hitting the road again."

Many Clouds hurried after him, yanked on his sleeve. They stopped and faced each other at the cabin door. "That's where Yellow Squirrel will be."

"Exactly so. But if I know them folks, they'll have an army of protection around them, and we ain't got none."

"He'll be watching the roads."

"But once we're there, your uncle's gonna have to go through all of them to get to us, so where's our chances gonna be better? Here or there?"

And Many Clouds had no answer. So, it was back to Carolyn Maxwell's house. And this time Andy was sure to be there. She and Carolyn had grown fairly close during her illness, but that was during his absence. The memory of her first conversation with Carolyn at Granite Spring still burned. How could she step into that situation? How could she not? Once again, she had no answer. But she had no time to contemplate the matter, for here came Willy came struggling toward the door, trying to manage a quilt several times his size and half his weight.

"Many Clouds, will you help me?" he said.

"Of course I will," she said. "Of course."

THIRTY-NINE

POLITICS

Andy ushered Amelia into the office, closed the door, then invited her to sit in the big oak wheeled chair.

"You forgetting something," she said, holding out her arms for an embrace.

"Grimy as I am?"

"It's just dirt, and I do want to hear how you came by it." He had to lean over to hug her, and her arms encircled him about waist high.

"I've missed you," he said.

"Boy, don't tell me." She waved her hand and sat. "You sure took your sweet time getting here."

He pulled up a bent wood chair. "I'll tell you that story later," he said. "Right now, I want to start with Mother and Cooper."

"Cooper's in his tree," she said.

"Tree?"

"Yes, his tree. He's got him that whatever rifle his daddy took off a Confederate sniper in the war."

"The Whitworth? That obsolete muzzle loader?"

"That's the one. Has to make his own bullets, but 'If I can see it, I can kill it,' is what he says. And him and Enoch taking turns sitting up in a tree behind the barn waiting to shoot up that Yellow Squirrel. Perched on a limb at his age, even in all that wet and cold. Catch his death. How they going to see anything in the dark? 'In the lightning,' the fool says. Mmm. Mmm." She shook her head.

"Enoch done took his shift, too, after midnight. 'Cooper can do it, so can I,' is what he said. 'Course them two others Cooper had trained to shoot had the sense to take off for parts unknown the minute they heard about Yellow Squirrel, so it's just my lame-brained husband and Enoch to cover the whole clock. Cooper climbed back up there at dawn."

"I thought Enoch looked a bit peaked," he said. "I have to admit it's a line of defense we didn't have the first time around with Yellow Squirrel. But a shooter in that position dare not miss." Cooper's Whitworth was rumored to have a killing range and accuracy of eight hundred yards. "I suppose all these extra men are from Folsom?"

"Yep, twice as many as what was here in '08 is what Cooper says," Amelia said.

"What about Mother?"

"And this is the thing you really going to find hard to believe," she said, shaking her head again, smiling.

The office door swung open. Both he and Amelia jumped to their feet, backed away. The door slammed, and there stood Andy's mother. Except not really his mother. Her long hair was braided, a style she never wore, and it was tangled, as it never was even after her hardest day on the range. Her outfit he now recognized as one she often wore for riding, but grimy as it was, he had not recognized either the clothes or the Indian woman who had scuttled across the yard a few minutes earlier.

"Mom?"

"Miss Carrie," Amelia said. A hand flew to her mouth.

He reached out a hand. Took a step in her direction. Stopped.

"Yes, for Pete's sake, of course it's me. No, no closer, Andy. Much as I'm glad to see you. I'm not fit to touch anyone who's had a bath in the last six months."

"Amelia and I just discussed all that, and we're not accepting that excuse."

"Blame Cooper," she said as they completed their embraces. "Hiding out with Mother isn't good hygiene, even if it is a good idea."

"I didn't know your husband was so full of bizarre notions," Andy said to Amelia.

"He ain't even got started yet," Amelia said.

"Never mind," Carolyn said. "What's Hiram Johnson doing here? Why was that man pointing a gun at you?"

"Second question first. The sentinel system seems to be working. No one rides down that trail without a confrontation, including me. First question? Johnson's a mystery to me as well. I had Ling Chu offer him some hospitality to buy time till I could get up to date. Frankly, I'm glad to find the place still standing." He told them about the slaughtered cattle in the high pasture. "And that, Amelia, is where I came by all this mud."

"So, he's truly returned," Carrie said. "Mother may find out something more from the Washoe today, but I think we've put ourselves in a ridiculous position. Yellow Squirrel is just one man."

"Yet we're hiding out like he's an army," Andy said. "I think you and I are in tune with our thinking, Mom. What say we get rid of Mr. Johnson then convene a strategy session?"

"Whatever you decide," Amelia said, "I pray it don't include sitting up in no trees."

* * *

"It's an amazing vehicle, that Locomobile," Jack Johnson was saying. He took a sip of lemonade. "Marvelous lunch, by the way, Mrs. Maxwell. Never had a better stroganoff even at The Pushkin out on Lombard, and your man a Chinaman at that. Such a treasure. Marvelous. Yessir, that automobile has carried us up and down this state without a problem, places where no train could have gone."

Jeremiah Peabody, the young man Johnson had introduced as a campaign aide, said, "Southern Pacific gives free rail passes to politicians, but Hiram doesn't want to be beholden to any of the railroad interests, you see, so he refuses to accept them."

"You know I am in full support of your candidacy, Mr. Johnson," Carrie said. Her hair was clean, gathered from her face with a lavender ribbon and spilling down the back of a ruffled white cotton dress with a lilac print. "I must say, however, that it puzzles me with the election barely a month away why you're hunting votes in these hills. Why we have more cows than people in this district."

"I'm here because if I'm to fulfill my campaign pledges, I'll need every legislative vote I can muster," Johnson said. Andy noted that he had stood to speak, as if he were addressing a crowd instead of a few people on the steps of the ranch house.

"And our Harvey Cox will stand with you in the assembly," she said.

"Oh, Lord, You haven't heard? They haven't heard, Dad," Jack Johnson said. He leaned forward in his chair.

"We've been… preoccupied," Andy said.

"Harvey Cox is dead," Peabody leaned forward as well. "His heart gave out, right there on the Capitol steps, three days ago."

"My goodness. That means Hale Gentry is unopposed?" Carrie said. She balled her fist and pounded the table. The lemonade pitcher jumped, sloshed. It was Andy's turn to stand.

"Hale Gentry? That incompetent peacock is on the ballot?" Andy was standing himself now.

"Oh, yes. He dropped by a short while ago to inform me personally," Carrie said. "As if I would be interested."

Andy sat back down, stared up at the peaks.

"Yes, yes," Johnson said. "Poor Cox was a stout ally and he gave us Republicans one of our few secure districts. The Democrats put Gentry on the ballot as a throwaway opponent, doubtless by some corrupt arrangement having to do with his liquor interests. But now, the way is clear for him unless we can field a viable opponent immediately, Mrs. Maxwell."

"Disturbing. Very disturbing. But how does that involve the Maxwells?" she said.

Johnson remained silent, watching. He made eye contact first with Carolyn, then with Andy. And in that glance, Andy limned the man's purpose.

"May I be frank?" Johnson continued.

"If it gets us to the point, please do." She said. So she hadn't guessed yet.

Johnson returned to his seat now, elbows on his knees. Intimate. "My first choice would be you, Mrs. Maxwell."

"First choice for what?" she said.

"You and your politics are well-known and respected in this area."

"Respected? Leaving aside my escapades as a miscegenating adulteress, of course."

"Very old news. Of little political consequence, locally, I'm told." He cast a questioning glance at Peabody, who nodded. "Of no consequence at all compared to the antipathy for Southern Pacific in these parts. You'd be a natural, were it not for your sex."

Carolyn laughed. "And what, pray, is the matter with my sex?" she said.

"Women's suffrage is just around the corner. I'm sure you know it's part of the Republican platform, but it's not here yet, even in this finest state in the union. Women candidates are, I fear, even farther down the road."

"Well, that's a relief," she said.

Everyone except Andy joined in the ensuing laughter. Once the amusement had died, Johnson continued. "And that leaves you, Andy, as the man of the hour."

Startled, Carolyn stood and crossed to here son. "Absolutely not," she said, wrapping his arm in hers. "I won't risk him. Not him, too." She turned to him. "You won't, will you?"

"Mr. Johnson," he said, "when was the last time a colored man was elected to the California legislature?"

"But you're not entirely—"

"Oh, not entirely. I suppose from what my father told me I'm no more than about one-fourth, perhaps one-eighth, black. But that's more than enough to get a man lynched in certain parts of the country, and more than enough to incite putrid language even here in what you call the finest state in the union. Hell, I can't even get into a university now that everyone knows my background. And, oh, you can add to my debits my recent encounters with the legal authorities in San Francisco."

"What encounters?" she said.

"Later, Mom." He said. "My candidacy, Mr. Johnson, seems like a stroll across hot coals to no purpose."

Johnson rose and paced the gallery, his back to them now, seemingly addressing the heavens. "I myself am a political neophyte, but I have had some success in the courtroom, and that has taught me the value of boldness and timing. My instincts tell me you are the person we need in this place, at this hour."

The man's theatrics, his grand gestures and rolling consonants, seemed almost ridiculous here in the peaceful afternoon. Andy supposed climbing on the stump at any moment was an occupational hazard for a politician, but that didn't make it any more appealing to be treated like a crowd instead of an individual. And the idea that he might become such a person himself struck him as comical.

"You smile, sir," Johnson went on. "Your skepticism is noted. Let me continue to be frank." He turned and looked directly at him.

"In person, you're not the imposing fellow I imagined from all the tales of derring-do that appeared in the papers."

"There, you see?" he said.

"No, no. It means your actions are bigger than life. In the public arena, how you project yourself is at least as important as who you are. And what's more, you appear no more Negroid than your garden variety Italian or Greek, am I not correct?"

"I have been told so."

And you are an honest man, are you not?"

"Well—"

"Of course you are. We'll need an army of such men as you, brave and staunch, to dethrone the robber barons. And an Indian fighter. Almost a legend in your own modest way. And you would love to de-tentacle this octopus railroad that's been squeezing us dry for decades, would you not?"

"I can't argue with that, no." He found himself willing to answer in a way that would allow the man to go on with his entertaining rhetoric.

"And. You are a Maxwell. In another district, any of the negatives you've named might disqualify you. But not here, Mr. *Maxwell.* Not in Sawtooth Wells, Mr. *Maxwell.* Not in District four, Mr. *Maxwell.* As for your altercation with Sheriff O'Neil. More in your favor than against. Hometown denizen versus the big-city politician. It's perfect."

Andy tried to imagine himself on the campaign circuit, surrounded with bunting and dignitaries, speechifying to a crowd, a crowd filled with drunks and bullies trying to shout him off the platform. He was deemed a competent classroom lecturer, but those were captive audiences in defined circumstances. The political stump—it would be like going from a refereed boxing match to a freestyle street fight. Absurd. Then he realized he was allowing himself to entertain the idea enough to argue against it. Carrie's voice interrupted his thoughts.

"Since you're so well-informed," Mr. Johnson, "you know we're again under attack from the same man who earned Andy his dubious reputation as a warrior. Putting him on a political platform would make a public target of him. And even if he survived that, win or lose, we'd be subject to utter vilification in the press. They will make considerable hay over not only the matters we've already discussed, but over my mother's decision to run off and live with the Indians. We'll be portrayed as a pack of mongrels devoid of morals and cursed with insanity. And that's only the version we'd see on the printed page. You can imagine the language they'd use in alleys and back rooms. Why would we subject ourselves to all that?"

It was the longest, most passionate speech Andy had ever heard from her. She was used to delivering perfunctory orders and pronouncements. She would, indeed, make a formidable candidate. The Johnsons and Jeremiah traded glances. Jack slouched, seemed ready to leave. But not Hiram. He turned his back for a moment, seated himself, then leaned back in his chair.

"I understand how painful such attacks can be." His jaw tightened. "I will never forget my father's dark fury when I announced I was leaving his law firm, nor his public denunciations of my anti-railroad speeches. I was painted as a traitor to my class, my party, my family. So yes, I understand the ugly humiliation. For myself, it counted for next to nothing. But for my dear Minnie and for Jack here, I will never forgive the suffering those savage pundits caused my nearest and dearest. Yes, I understand that pain."

He rose from his chair, his fists clenched at his sides. All his oratorical pretension was gone now, and Andy thought he was here seeing and hearing the real man. "But I understand as well how important it is to meet them head-on. Why would you subject yourselves to these assaults, you ask? Because to ignore them would be to leave the field to the enemy. And from what Jeremiah and Jack tell me, that is not the Maxwell way, is it?"

He met his mother's gaze.

"How many years have you fought the railroads, Mrs. Maxwell? How much more difficult has their bullying domination made it to build this magnificent establishment?"

Johnson was back in his speechmaking mode now. He swept his arm and eyes across the ranch yard and up the peaks. "What you Maxwells have created here is emblematic of why this Golden State is, yes, Andy, the finest in the union. But the Stanfords and the Huntingtons and the Crockers and the Hopkins—they mean to replace enterprise and ingenuity with monopoly and corruption, and we must join to thwart them."

"An impressive address, Mr. Johnson. And persuasive," he said.

"But things being what they are," Carrie was talking now, "we think not. If a new Republican candidate is so important, you need to climb in that automobile and get rolling. You're wasting your time here."

Johnson smiled, nodded, sighed. "As one who has walked a similar road, I can't blame you. I couldn't swear I would choose it a second time myself." He sighed again. "Well, boys, I guess we'd better get on. I'm sorry to have bothered you, Mrs. Maxwell, Andy." He walked toward the steps, Jack and Jeremiah trailing. He was about to step off the porch when he turned back. "And Hale Gentry?" he said.

"What of him?" she said.

"Are you prepared for a nefarious tool of the Southern Pacific to represent your district—represent you and your son, represent the Circle M—in the legislature?"

A silence hung there, and Johnson let it. Andy looked beyond Johnson to the patch of dusty ranch earth where, two years before, he'd beaten Gentry down. All the man's small time racketeering didn't amount to beans now, but what might he attempt with corporate power to back him up? And beside that threat, he could not deny an eagerness to watch his enemy writhe in the dust again."

"Certainly my son is not the only possible candidate," she said.

Johnson turned to Jack, who shrugged, then said, "If you have another suggestion, we'll happily entertain it. However, as you pointed out, this is a small district with few gentlemen of his stature or intellect, none with his notoriety."

He felt all eyes upon him, waiting for a cue. The descending sun had begun to etch Sawtooth Peaks against the western sky. He found nothing to say. Johnson finally broke the silence.

"Do you have an answer for us, sir?"

"My mother and I need to confer, Mr. Johnson. We can discuss the matter further over breakfast. Make yourselves at home. Ling Chu will attend to your needs."

Johnson beamed. As if he were assuming victory. Presumptuous beyond reason. Maybe that's what it took to succeed in public life. Or anywhere. "We appreciate both the hospitality and the consideration you're giving to our request. Mind, we'll need to be off early in the morning. Time—and voters—wait for no man. Or no woman, either."

FORTY

BREAKDOWN

It had not been a particularly deep rut, just a shallow, dry ditch that spring runoff had scooped out of the roadway months ago. And Miller had been careful to approach it from the safest angle. But the axle snapped just the same.

"Damnation on this creaky old thing," he said. "Didn't expect the iron parts to disintegrate. And nothing I can do. Not right here. We're afoot the rest of the way. Near dark, too."

Maggie and Willy moaned. Many Clouds had mixed feelings. She was not afraid of the walk, was in no hurry to get to the Circle M and the uncomfortable situation she was sure to confront there. On the other hand, she wished even less to confront her uncle when they were so vulnerable. Too much useless pondering. She focused her attention on the problem at hand.

"We can tie most of our load on the horse and carry the rest. But what will we do with the wagon? We can't just leave it," she said.

"That's for sure. Someone's plumb certain to steal the wheels, or haul it off for firewood or some such. Onliest thing to do is shove it downslope and hide it in the brush as best we can until I can get back here with what I need to fix it. Many Clouds? What's the matter?"

Many Clouds had followed Miller to the edge of the road, followed his gesture toward the willows where he proposed to conceal the buckboard, and her breath caught in her throat. A short time ago, she'd fled through those same willows, Caller and Deacon pursuing her.

"I... nothing. We'd better hurry."

"Wait. Wait." Miller lifted his head and looked around. "I'm understanding now. Just over that there hillcrest. Isn't that where I first saw you? Saw you tied to that preacher's horse?"

She ignored his question, steered away from her distress to concentrate on practical obstacles. "Down the hill on the other side, there's a trail," she said. Even as she spoke, she couldn't take her eyes off the spot, couldn't blot out the scene, the fright, the humiliation. "It's a trail that goes almost all the rest of the way to the ranch. We'll probably be safer from Yellow Squirrel there than we would be on the main road anyway."

Miller grasped her shoulders and turned her away from the hillside. "I'm sorry as can be," he said. "Let's get ourselves out of here quick as we can." His arms drew her toward him. There was great comfort there. She answered his embrace with one of her own.

"Daddy," Willy called. "Are we going to eat pretty soon?"

FORTY-ONE

HIRAM JOHNSON COMES TO BREAKFAST

"**B**oy, you even crazier than you were when you left out of here," Cooper was saying. "Leave this whole place open? He'll burn it flat."

They'd gathered in the kitchen, out of earshot of the Johnson company, who were enjoying after-dinner cigars and brandy in the living room. Ling Chu laid a plate of steak and fried potatoes and a bottle of beer in front of Cooper, who had missed the meal, having just come down from his roost.

"Hear him out, now, Cooper," Amelia said. "And eat your supper. You'll fall right out of that tree without your nourishment, which doesn't include no beer."

"And your eyes look as red as if you've been on a three-day binge," Carrie said. "You can't keep up this schedule much longer."

"Like Mom says," Andy said, "Yellow Squirrel's just one man, not the whole cavalry. And we're acting just like we did two years ago when we knew nothing about him. Now we know exactly how he operates, so why not take advantage of it?"

"We know he's sneaky, devious, and loves killing. So what?" Cooper said.

"Don't talk with your mouth full," Amelia said. Cooper shot her a look. She grinned.

"We also know he doesn't really plan. He hangs around, looks for an opening, then charges in."

"So we don't leave him no openings," Cooper said. "Simple." He shoved a bite of steak in his mouth, washed it down with beer, gave Amelia a defiant look.

"But that's not really possible, is it?" Carrie said. "Think of those butchered cattle. We have hundreds more in the lower corrals we'll have to drive to the railroad in Placerville soon, and all those fresh-branded calves?"

"Cows ain't people," Cooper said.

Andy chose to steer around this remark. "I know it sounds contradictory to put up a defense that seems like no defense at all. But the idea is to make it look like there's an open door, then jump him when he comes through it. We move all the guards inside— the house, the barn, the line shacks—so it looks like business as usual."

"In the first place, You can't hide them fellows completely," Cooper said. "Everyone got to use the outhouse." He took his last bite of steak, hummed absently while he chewed.

"You ain't got to talk about all that," Amelia said.

"Chamber pots," Carolyn said.

But Cooper wasn't finished yet. "Second of all, why is he going to believe it? The guards are gone, but then that leaves you two," pointing at Andy and his mother, "wandering around for him to pick you off like a couple of squirrels."

Carrie made a sour face. "I'll be back in the woods with Mother," she said.

"I'll be somewhere else also," Andy said. "We'll know more after we talk to the Johnsons at breakfast tomorrow."

Cooper finished his beer, looked toward Ling Chu, who looked to Amelia, who nodded. Ling Chu retrieved another beer from the pantry. "Thank you, Ling," Cooper said. "Thank you, Wife."

"You was going to drink it anyhow, wasn't you?" she said.

Cooper winked and smiled. "Maybe so, maybe not." He turned back to mother and son. "You ain't answered my question, though. He gonna know something's up. Now, since you know Mr. Squirrel so well, what's gonna bring him through that door you talking about?" He pulled on his beer.

"That's the part that involves Grandmother," Andy said.

"Grandmother?" Cooper stopped the beer bottle halfway to his mouth.

"And you," Carrie said.

Cooper took a gulp of beer, smiled. "You know, I wouldn't be surprised if you thinking of those Washoe folks, are you?"

"Uncle Cooper," Andy said, "you must be a mind reader."

Cooper turned to his wife. "You see?" he said.

"Oh, Lord, Andy," Amelia said. "Do you *have* to go and tell him stuff like that?"

* * *

Ling Chu served breakfast on the gallery, quite cool on fall mornings, a tactic to ensure the party didn't linger. The eastern sun had begun to pink the spires of Sawtooth Peaks, but most of the yard still lay under shadow.

Unlike the day before, Andy felt himself the master of the situation. He waited until the perfunctory greetings were finished and until Johnson had a cup of coffee in front of him and a sausage on his plate before he spoke.

"I'd like to make a request, " he said.

"As you know from our conversation yesterday, my boy, it's a seller's market here. What is it you want?"

"If you win," he said, "I'd like an appointment to the Board of Regents."

The three Johnson crewmen stopped and stared.

"Whether I win or not," he said. "If I survive, of course. Remember I'd be making a target of myself."

"Is your mother going to join us here?" Johnson said.

"She sends her regrets. Other urgent business connected with this threat from Michael Yellow Squirrel."

"I see. I see."

He brought Johnson back to the subject. "The governor does appoint the board, "And there will be vacancies, so I suspect it would be no great problem to seat me."

"You're rather young for—"

"Don't demure, sir. I remind you once again of the great risk to me and my family."

"All right, Andy. Once again, let us be frank," Johnson said. He had shoved his plate aside now and leaned across the table.

"As always."

"Why the regents?" He was prepared to explain himself, but Johnson was ahead of him.

"Your antipathy toward President Wheeler and the others is understandable, and it would be a coup for you to become, as it were, one of their superiors. However, for me to inaugurate my governorship by appointing an opponent of theirs to such a position would be problematic at best."

"It's a question of justice, not personal animosity," Andy countered. A half-truth. Not even an official candidate yet, and he'd entered one of those political grey areas between principle and personal gain. "That alone would make the run worth it for me. Otherwise, we'll just have to suffer whatever slings and arrows Mr. Gentry sends our way. At least he won't be shooting at us the way Yellow Squirrel is."

Johnson tossed down his napkin. "You're quite a negotiator, Mr. Maxwell. Pack your bags. We've no time to waste turning you into a candidate."

"But Pa," Jack said. "I've barely even started—"

"No time," Hiram said. "Wrap something in a napkin if you have to."

It was Andy's turn to stand. "Ling Chu. Amelia." Ling Chu appeared immediately, suitcase in hand, Amelia close behind him. He set the luggage down and performed a perfunctory bow.

"Good luck, Mr. Andrew," he said.

"Take care, Ling." He stepped past him and cupped Amelia's head in both hands. "And you, too. Especially you."

Tears dribbled down her cheeks. "Lord, boy, I hope you know what you doing."

"I'm not sure I do," he said softly. "But everything depends on my acting like I do. Understand?" She nodded, stood on tiptoes and kissed his cheek.

"All right, Mr. Johnson. Show me what that Locomobile can do."

FORTY-TWO

MISSIVES

PROFESSOR MACINTOSH
PLEASE MEET SACRAMENTO RAILROAD CAFE TOMORROW NOON STOP

* * *

Dear Mr. Bierce,

Please find enclosed the first of the articles we discussed. I leave to you, of course, whatever background preface you think necessary.

I have also included a piece which, after gleaning whatever information you find useful, I ask that you pass on to Mr. Francis at the *Elevator*.

* * *

The Second Vendetta—I

by Andrew Maxwell

I write this from the Circle M ranch in the Sierra Nevada. Less than twenty-four hours ago, I hurried home from San Francisco after learning that Michael Yellow Squirrel, perpetrator of a savage vendetta against my family two years ago, has returned from exile to resume his campaign against us. I sit scribbling—in a different room than I would ordinarily use for such work—by the light of a kerosene lamp. I have drawn the drapes, hung a quilt over the window, and tacked the edges to avoid light leaks. Such is our siege mentality.

Is this caution truly necessary? I deduced Michael Yellow Squirrel's return from recent events in San Francisco. But can we be sure that he has already arrived among us at this lofty altitude? We could not be more certain. Last night I discovered two of our herd of cattle slaughtered in a manner unique to this man who fancies the Maxwells the perpetrators of all wrongs against his family, his people, and himself, their self-appointed avenger. Certain marks on the butchered animals, signs I cannot reveal here, assure that one represented my mother, the other myself.

Yellow Squirrel lurks and watches. He murdered my grandfather, my father, my brother, and nearly succeeded in killing my mother and me. He intends not only to complete his work, but to induce every possible anxiety and dread before he commits the final act. At this point we can do little but wait like the Romans for Hannibal's approach and hope our preparations are sufficient to ward off the inevitable attack. I vow to prevent him from adding to his catalogue of horrors, and to tell the world as his doom unfolds.

It is my hope that the resolution will be speedy, but I fear otherwise. Our enemy enjoys the suffering he inflicts as much as a cat enjoys the throes of his captive mouse. But we are not mice. I bid you farewell until my next missive and ask you to keep us in your thoughts and prayers.

* * *

Special to the *Elevator*

COLORED MAN TO STAND FOR ASSEMBLY

Andrew Maxwell of Sawtooth Wells has announced his intention to become a candidate on the Republican ticket for the Fourth District Assembly seat in the upcoming November election. The seat became vacant recently owing to the sudden death of Republican Assemblyman Harvey Cox. Rather than allow the Democratic Candidate, Mr. Hale Gentry, to run unopposed, Mr. Maxwell decided to pick up the banner of the fallen warrior, Mr. Cox, and attempt to preserve the seat for the Republicans. He counts himself a strong supporter of Mr. Hiram Johnson and expects to follow that candidate's philosophy if elected.

The Maxwell family has long been prominent in the district. The fact that Mr. Maxwell's murdered father was of Negro heritage became known to the public as well as to himself only two years ago. He trusts and believes that the constituents of district four will not allow that fact to influence their votes.

FORTY-THREE

MANY CLOUDS RETURNS

They traveled on foot with only starlight and a new moon for guidance, keeping off the roads, planning to skirt even the Washoe camp, to stay away from anywhere Yellow Squirrel might find them. Miller carried a rifle on a strap on one shoulder, a canteen on the other. An old revolver rode on one hip. Many Clouds carried a small basket on a tumpline filled with a bundle of jerky and a few apples plucked from the small tree outside the cabin. Bedding and a few other supplies were strapped to the horse, which Maggie was currently leading, Willy riding. Many Clouds had been over the trail only once each way, in the daylight. She could not claim to know it well, and she did not welcome the responsibility of leading the little family through a barely-familiar countryside. Little as she knew of the geography, however, Miller knew even less, so she became leader by default.

She was terrified of wandering off onto one of the many spurs that deviated from the main route, a route that sometimes dwindled to a scratch in the dirt. A wrong turn might lead them over a precipice or into a secluded camp inhabited by men like Caller and Deacon. It was far more than a scratch in the dirt, but a wide and well-beaten track that veered slightly to the left of the course they'd been following at one point. Not a sharp deviation, well within the range of natural meanderings of a forest trail. After the fork, though, the path continued hooking to the left, but then zigged back to the right, and Many Clouds felt they were still moving in the right direction.

"Let's change places," Maggie said.

"Can't walk no more," Willy said.

"Don't be such a baby," Maggie said.

Miller lifted the boy from the horse to his shoulders, helped Maggie aboard the horse.

"You aren't a horse, Mr. Fitzpatrick," Many Clouds said.

"You comfortable up there, Champ?" Fitzpatrick said to Willy.

"Yes, Pa."

Fitzpatrick grasped the horse's lead. "Okay, then, let's go."

"Pa, it's gone," Maggie said.

Miller spoke without turning around. "What is, Maggie?"

"The quilt. The one Mama's box was wrapped up in."

Fitzpatrick stood without speaking for a long moment, then inspected the load on the horse's back. He held a length of frayed line aloft. "Must have scraped off on a tree or boulder."

"We'll go back," Many Clouds said. "It can't be far."

"No, we'll come back," he said. "Maggie and Willy's our main worry for now."

Many Clouds doubted they'd find their way back here, but she knew there was no arguing with Miller, and she didn't disagree with him. At the same time, she knew how much it must have hurt him to lose the few keepsakes he had of Swallow.

They walked another half hour before they ran into the massive boulder. An often-used fire pit lay at its base, and there seemed to be no way around it, cliffs dropping off on both ends. It was a place easy to defend and shelter, and some one or some group had used it regularly. The trail they'd been following, the one Many clouds had thought was the main path, had led straight to this destination. A dead end. Their only choice was to retrace their steps.

Miller pulled from his pocket a worn gold-plated timepiece, found a sliver of moonlight to illuminate the face.

"Nigh on to midnight. How much farther do you think, Many Clouds?"

She'd been dreading this question. It was one she'd been asking herself and received no answer. "If we make no more mistakes, we may reach the Washoe camp in perhaps two or three hours. The Circle M will take us another hour or more."

Maggie and Willy both slumped against the rock. Maggie was fighting to keep her head up. Willy was actually snoring lightly.

"I'll put both the young 'uns back aboard the horse for a while," Miller said. "Though truth to tell he's near as tuckered as they are."

"If we don't reach the ranch by daylight…" she said.

Miller finished the sentence. "We might as well paint targets on our backs. So, kids, up you go, but you may end up afoot again before long."

So it was back to the main trail, a left turn, and they trudged on. It wasn't long before the horse stumbled, and both Maggie and Willy barely escaped tumbling to the ground. Miller hoisted Maggie, and Many Clouds swung her basket from back to front and carried Willy piggy back. Then came the thicket.

It was a right turn that led them astray this time, and by the time they realized they were off course, they were in the middle of a stand of manzanita so dense there was no telling what was a path and what wasn't. There was barely room for a human to squeeze through, let alone a horse. Only the animal's fatigue could have allowed it to submit to the humiliating pushing, twisting, and pulling it took them to shove and thread their way through the nearly impenetrable brush. When they finally emerged, they were joyful to see that they'd found their way back to the main trail, however accidentally. Their joy turned to discouragement, however, when they realized they were no more than ten yards from where they'd taken the wrong turn. It was back now to Maggie on Fitzpatrick's shoulders and Willy on Many Clouds' back.

The smell of a campfire warned them that the Washoe camp was close. It warned them as well that sunrise was close. Miller shook Willy awake.

"Come on, Champ. We've got to hustle."

"Okay," was all he said.

"Good boy," Maggie said. Her voice sounded vague.

They'd reached familiar territory now, and Many Clouds led them quickly around the outskirts of the camp. Yellow Squirrel could be there. Or the Washoes might be sympathetic to his cause. Or he might have terrorized them into submission.

The eastern sky was beginning to lighten when they reached Granite Spring. As they descended the hill from the spring toward the ranch, a shadowy form rose like a hulk from the forest floor a few yards downhill from them. Yellow Squirrel. Many Clouds turned and motioned everyone to lie down and keep quiet, hoping the horse would blend into the shadows, remain quiet. If they'd come on it in full darkness, as Many Clouds had intended, they might have stumbled right into their enemy.

He stood against a tree to urinate, then turned uphill in their direction, sniffing the air like a bear. Many Clouds nearly cried out in fear, prayed the children would be able to contain themselves. They lay still for a long time. Lay still for even longer after Yellow Squirrel had slung his necessaries across his back and headed away without detecting them.

When they finally began moving, Miller drew his pistol and started after him. Many Clouds stopped him.

"Not now. Not with the children," she whispered.

"He could be waiting for us," Miller said.
"I know a back way," she said. There was a long pause.
"Okay."
"I'll go alone. You wait." Another pause.
"Okay."

* * *

She crept up behind the barn and peered into the yard. She saw no one. There were the usual smells of hay, manure, dust, the dark sweat of horses. It was perhaps a bit early for the morning chores—feeding, watering, gathering eggs—but why were there no guards, men with rifles and lanterns?

Voices sounded from the direction of the bunkhouse, dropping her to the ground and pushing her to the barn wall. More voices. A narrow path led behind the buildings on this side of the yard, and she followed it past the barn, the tack shed, the smokehouse. She could see downslope to the the small clearing that was the Maxwell family burial plot. Sounds of digging. Three men, one holding a shovel, staring at a pile of freshly-dug earth. One was armed, looking uphill. Humming. A tune she knew but could not name. She dodged behind the bunkhouse, strained to hear.

"That'll have to do it for now." Cooper's voice.

"He should have a Christian burial, though." Someone she didn't recognize.

"He will, but later," Cooper said. "Enoch don't care no more. God won't either." A pause. "But we can at least say a word before we leave. Know any?"

"All right, then, yes," Cooper said. "And I know you know it, too. Come on, now."

A discordant, ragged male trio sang "Glory, glory Hallelujah; Glory, glory hallelujah; his truth is marching on." Cooper spoke, concluding the little service.

"Lord is my shepherd that leads me beside still waters in the face of my enemies. And he restores my soul. Please take Enoch's soul to heaven, Lord. Amen."

"Amen."

"Now let's get on," Cooper said.

She stepped around the corner of the smoke house as the men departed the fresh grave. "What happened to Enoch, Mr. Cooper?" Cooper nearly ran into her. The armed man brought the rifle to his shoulder. The third man raised his shovel. Cooper raised his hand to stay them.

"Ain't smart to sneak up on men with hair-trigger nerves, miss," he said. "And I reckon you can guess the answer to your question."

"Yellow Squirrel."

He nodded. "And I got a question for you."

"He threatened us also—Mr. Fitzpatrick and the children. We thought we'd be safer here at the Circle M."

Cooper snorted. "Ask Enoch about that," Cooper swung his chin in the direction of the fresh grave.

Many Clouds squatted on her heels, leaning against the bunkhouse. She was remembering Enoch's kind, round face. The many small ways he'd helped them all during her sickness, how he'd tried to save her from running off into the rainy woods. "He was a kind man," she said.

Cooper nodded. "Where are your folks?" Many Clouds pointed uphill. Cooper nodded again. "Get everyone in the house. Amelia will take care of you. He ain't likely to try anything else so soon after Enoch, but you can't tell. We'll watch till you're across the yard. Ain't a twig or a stone of cover there. Then me and these boys got to get down to the branding pens."

Many Clouds was stilled by fear and shame. Disgraced, menaced by one of her own family. Yellow Squirrel's evil tainted all his relatives. In days past, the family itself would have exacted blood redemption, something she couldn't imagine herself doing. Perhaps her father? But Standing Oak was far away. Did that mean it was up to her after all?

"Move now, girl." Cooper pushed her gently.

So she started walking, propelled by a mixture of affection and duty to protect the charges she had left in the woods. Still mystified by what her duty might be toward her predatory relative.

FORTY-FOUR

FRUSTRATION

From a hillside boulder, Yellow Squirrel watched Many Clouds herd her minions across the yard into the house. He was furious with her, with the situation, and unhappy with himself. He would have liked to take a shot at her, but held back. Enoch's killing served well as another warning to the Maxwells, but it had none of the circus power he craved, and neither would the shooting of Many Clouds. It was all teasing, like parading tigers around the ring in wagon cages. You could only keep that up so long before the crowd lost interest and went home. At some point you had to open the cage doors.

He should have waited until he found out why the guards had suddenly disappeared from the yard and the rooftops. Waited until he found out why he hadn't seen Carolyn Maxwell for three days. Waited until he found out the meaning of the automobile that sped in one day and out the next, carrying Andrew with it. None of this was going as he'd expected, which meant he wasn't in control, which angered and worried him. There was a trap hidden in this new direction of events, and he had to be careful not to step into it before he figured out a way to capitalize on it. Yellow Squirrel didn't like being careful.

FORTY-FIVE

CAROLYN AND THE WASHOES

Carrie and Nonny sat cross-legged on grass mats beside a central campfire in the middle of the Washoe camp. Bark wikkiups surrounded the communal grounds where the stone-ringed fireplace was placed. Carrie had never imagined herself here, sitting on the ground like just another squaw. She wasn't, of course, just another squaw. If she were, the other women—men, too—wouldn't have scattered to the bushes when she entered the village.

"They're afraid of you, Carrie," Nonny said. "It was the same with me when I first came among them. Now I'm just harmless, crazy, Nonny. But earning their trust took quite some time."

"Why afraid?" she said. "I've never done anything to hurt them. I've tried to help when I could, given the men jobs, allowed them to hunt on our land—even to kill cattle during lean times. Ling has never turned anyone away from the kitchen door."

She nodded, smiled, shook her head. "It's not so much you yourself. We all of us depend on the order of things. When something upsets the order, it's frightening. Otherwise you wouldn't be here, would you?"

Upsetting the order of things. She'd done a lot of that over the years. Just ramrodding the Circle M had violated notions of a woman's proper place. And her affair with Shelby had violated not only notions, but taboos. Now,

Yellow Squirrel was doing plenty of upsetting. Was it the same thing? Not at all. Once she thought about it a bit, Yellow Squirrel was very much in the order of things. Evil was always in the order of things, and fighting it—and him—was necessary to stave off the chaos that threatened always to overwhelm.

Her father had talked about that often. In some ways, the Circle M had been like a crusade to him, a crusade to impose boundaries and definitions on a random wilderness. That's why every building, corral, fenceline, stood in a geometrical pattern. Nothing thrown up in the hasty, ill-planned manner of many of the surrounding ranches. That her mother had refused to follow his preconceived pattern for their—her—life, a life of politics, power, prestige, violated his passion for organization and coherence. Not to mention his concurrence with St. Paul's admonition that a wife was properly subject to her husband's will.

She liked to think she'd inherited Carter Maxwell's passion for order, but not for convention. Still, she'd never felt comfortable with her mother's going native. It wasn't the attire or the primitive conditions. It was the confusion of role and—she had to admit it—status that disturbed her. It hadn't been so bad during the couple of days when only she and her mother had shared a campsite, but here in the sight and sound of strangers, even strangers from a primeval society, she felt herself plunked down in the middle of confusion, and she wanted out.

"What do they know about him?" she said.

"He's been here, and he's asked them to spy on the Circle M, just as he did two years ago."

"And?"

"They agreed, but they will do as little as possible."

"Do they know his plans? Where he's camped? Anything to help us track him down?"

Nonny shook her head. "He tells no one anything. He moves constantly. He's threatened them as well."

She thought for a moment. "Suppose one of them overheard a conversation that I've gone to hide in San Francisco," she said.

Nonny shook her head and smiled. "First, no one will believe you would desert the ranch, least of all Yellow Squirrel. Second of all, a direct lie is not their way. They'd rather appear to comply out of politeness and respect, then do the minimum to uphold the promise."

"No wonder no one trusts them," she said.

"Because they won't lie?" Nonny said. "Listen to what you're saying, Carrie."

"What kind of truth is that?" Her mother started to speak, but she waved her away. "Never mind. Mother, you've lived among these folks for over thirty years. What do you think they can do to help?"

"Winter is coming. Perhaps something for the hungry months," Nonny said.

"Mother, I was asking how *they* could help *us*."

Nonny reached out and laid her hand on her daughter's. "If there were a bear attacking your cattle, what would you do?"

"Hunt him down, naturally. Trap him."

"And what would you give to the one who did so?"

"He'd get the meat, the pelt. Probably some cash, too."

"Good," she said. "I'll explain." She stood. Carrie did likewise.

"Explain?" she said. Nonny grasped her cheeks and kissed her forehead. Then she waved and disappeared into the bushes like the rest of the villagers.

She stood alone, turned a full circle trying to spot movement, failed. Something had happened, and she felt it was positive, but she felt confused as ever, though in a different, indefinable way.

FORTY-SIX

ANDY AND MACINTOSH AT THE RAILROAD CAFÉ

"I'm sure I can get you reinstated, you and Cohen both," George MacIntosh said. "Full status, no recriminations." Steam billowed past the windows outside the café as a locomotive heaved to overcome the inertia of a string of freight cars. MacIntosh bit into his roast beef sandwich, tore a bite out of a tough piece of meat, sipped from a mug of black coffee. Andy poked his fork into the hangtown fry on his plate, dragged the food back and forth while he talked.

"Recriminations? For demanding my rights?"

"Ah, what naïve astonishment you affect, Andrew." MacIntosh chewed hard, swallowed. More coffee. "You're a historian. You know there's always a struggle when might meets right."

"So, I'm struggling," he said. Two flatcars loaded with fir logs crawled past the window.

"You angered some fairly powerful people, Embarrassed them. That's not to say your charges aren't justified." He shoved his sandwich away and waved for service. "It's to say that you can't expect proud men to willingly swallow a mouthful of crow. They're more liable to spit it in your face." To the approaching waiter, he said, "I've bitten into rubber more tender than this bull meat. Do you think you can find something edible back there?"

The waiter stiffened. His face puckered as if he'd caught a whiff of something rotten. "Perhaps the ham, sir?"

"Perhaps," MacIntosh said. "Plenty of mustard, if you please."

"Yes sir." He executed an almost military about face and strode toward the kitchen.

"Take that fellow," MacIntosh went on. "He had nothing to do with creating that monstrosity of a sandwich. If he and I were fellow diners, he'd rail against it as energetically as I did. However, he's caught between me and his boss, and he can't express his real feelings to either of us, so he'll be furious with both. He'll build up a head of steam like that locomotive out there, and God help who or whatever's around when he blows. Same with Wheeler and the rest. They'd rather this didn't rise to the level of a discussion among the regents, but they also feel they can't honorably back down when you take such a militant stance. So give them a way out. Withdraw your demand for a regents hearing and you'll be admitted in the spring semester just as I've described."

He was silent. The professor's sandwich analogy was nonsense. McNulty and the rest had plenty of responsibility for the meal they'd put in front of him. You'd think a man who made a living teaching literature could do better. But he couldn't deny the point about the head of steam.

"It's funny, doctor MacIntosh. A month ago I would have jumped at this offer."

"But now?"

The waiter appeared again, slid before MacIntosh a plate bearing a thick ham sandwich, fat whole pickle on the side. MacIntosh said nothing. He handed the waiter his empty coffee mug and pointed. The man did his same military about face, this time more abruptly. The steam was building. The tension between Andy and MacIntosh billowed like a cloud between them now.

"It doesn't seem attractive at all. I'm grateful to you, truly I am. It must have cost you a good deal of time and effort to negotiate this idea and bring it all the way up here."

"Not to mention the influence I've squandered in campus politics." MacIntosh's lips were tight.

"I'll take the deal if it's a policy, not just me."

"It's not in their power."

"Then argue the regents into changing the policy."

"They'll lose the argument, and in the fight, they'll lose momentum on other priorities."

"What other priorities?"

"Well, among others, there is the question of expanding the humanities program. You know a big chunk of the university curriculum has been a tool of the mining and timber concerns, who have little interest in literature and languages, ancient or modern. That would be to your advantage, wouldn't it?"

"And to yours, of course," he said. The waiter returned with a full mug of coffee. MacIntosh didn't give the steaming black liquid a glance, but gazed across the table with eyes hard as porcelain. The ham sandwich lay untouched.

"Sir," Andy said, "you must think I'm a hard-headed, ungrateful son of a bitch," he said.

"You omitted 'arrogant.'"

"I told you I was grateful for what you're attempting to do here, and I am. I won't try to excuse or explain myself. You'll just have to be satisfied with my thanks. Perhaps if I win the election—"

"Election?"

"The announcement should come out today. I'm running for the assembly." This was the first time he'd said that sentence out loud in public. It sounded odd.

"So now you're the academic, Indian fighter, politician. Is there no end to your versatility? Or your audacity?" MacIntosh stood. He did likewise. "I'm sure your *thanks* will provide warm comfort to those of us who expended our energy so fruitlessly on your behalf." The professor's spin-around and exit was every bit as crisp and sudden as that of the angry waiter.

The café door slammed. Heads turned, and the waiter presented him with the check MacIntosh had forgotten to pay. He smiled as he laid bills on the table. On second thought, he doubted the professor had forgotten at all.

FORTY-SEVEN

CANDIDATE COACHING

It was a few minutes before his appointed hour of three o'clock when he appeared in the office of Meyer Lissner, Hiram Johnson's chief aid. Lissner's secretary looked up from his paperwork when Andy gave his name.

"Oh, yes," he said, "Mr. Lissner wanted to see you the moment you arrived. A murmur and creaking of furniture arose in the crowded office, and a nondescript man who appeared to be in his forties jumped to his feet.

"Here I've been waiting for three hours, and this young pup waltzes in without a by-your-leave and steps to the head of the line? It's not right."

The secretary stood, well over six feet in height, rolled his eyes, opened a gate in the counter, and motioned Andy toward the door behind his own desk. "That way," he said.

He felt a little like a fugitive escaping a lynch mob, but he stepped toward the inner office, trying to appear as if such privilege were his expectation and his due. The sort of technique one might use to keep a mountain lion at bay.

Meyer Lissner stood from his seat behind a scarred pine desk and extended his hand when Andy entered. It struck Andy that no one had ever looked more Jewish. It bothered him to notice, but he couldn't help being taken with the prominent nose and large ears on the man and with how the small, round, dark-rimmed spectacles emphasized the outsized features. He was nearly a caricature of himself. Virginia, with her artist's eye would have had a field day with his fashion mistakes. For all the disadvantages of his appearance, though, Lissner had been successful in business and politics, and Hiram Johnson had instructed Andy to listen to him well.

"I see you made it intact past all the spoils beggars, Mr. Maxwell," Lissner said as they shook hands. "That's an accomplishment in itself. Let's escape down the backstairs and head over to the theater."

"Theater?" he said.

"You'll find that politics and show business have more in common than you might think. Some believe I'm an unlikely fellow to be showing anyone the secrets of the stage, but with your first campaign appearance in less than twenty-four hours, I'm all you've got."

"Twenty-four hours? No one told me."

"No one knew until I finished arranging it a couple of hours ago. A crew will start nailing up posters any minute. High noon tomorrow in Sawtooth Wells. No place like home to start out, eh? Are you ready? Of course you're not. Not yet. But you will be."

They were hurrying down K Street, Andy pushing a little to keep up with the rapidly-striding Lissner. "I have about an hour to give you, Mr. Maxwell, then you're on your own. Mr. Johnson said you might need more, but I've got to get back to Los Angeles. We'd have Mr. Bell down there out for the count by now, but for the lies Harrison Otis prints in that damned rag of his. Refuting the *Los Angeles Times* is a full-time job in itself. It seems I have several full-time jobs. Here, to the right. See? Grand Theater. It's early, so it's all ours for a while. Let's make the most of it."

Lissner took them down an alley, knocked on a steel-sheathed door. A janitor opened it presently and escorted them to the stage. A single bulb glowed atop a long pole.

"Ghost light," Lissner explained. Burns all the time so people can find their way to backstage. But it's all we need. Thanks, Fred," he called to the retreating janitor. Lissner hopped off the stage and into a seat. "All right. Walk for me."

"Walk?"

"Yes. One side of the stage to the other. Just walk."

He complied, feeling self-conscious the while. Lissner stopped him before he'd covered half the thirty-foot distance. Suddenly, Lissner was back on stage and beside him.

"That amble will never do. No energy to it. Crowds thrive on energy, starve without it. If you look attractive from the beginning, folks will start voting for you in their minds before you say a word. Here. Watch this."

Lissner took off with a long, quick stride that covered the stage in a few seconds. The unimpressive figure behind the desk transformed into an attractive, compelling man. Lissner then took the same distance at half-speed, in a relaxed manner, which somehow drew attention to his diminutive size and Jewish features. The effect was magical.

"See the difference? Now you. You're about to give a speech. The podium's over there. Go."

He tried to match the stride he'd just seen from Lissner, but felt awkward. This was the kind of thing his murdered brother would have accomplished with ease. Maybe Julian had been destined for the stage.

Lissner interrupted his thoughts. "No, no. Never do. Never do. You look like a fencepost with legs. People won't vote for a fencepost. Try a jog. Imagine you're hurrying to get to your class on time."

Lissner's admonitions were definite and clear, but not offensive or personal. The whole project was alive with the feeling that they were together working out the solution to a problem, not trying to repair faults in him. He did as he was told, found it easy to accept direction from the man.

"Good, good, Maxwell. No hesitation in that. Gets you there fast, and no time to let the stage fright grab you. Now how about your speech?"

"I've only had time to make a few notes." He pulled a sheaf of rubber-banded cards from his inside coat pocket.

Lissner leaped back up on the stage, took the cards and shuffled through them, nodding, shaking his head, scratching and slashing with a fountain pen as he went. When he handed them back, a full half of Andy's notes had disappeared.

"This isn't the university, Maxwell, it's the streets. A least figuratively. You know the area around your ranch. The Circle something?"

"Circle M."

"Yes. How many voters in a given audience you'll address will have made it through high school? See what I mean? Clear and simple. Not a lot of reasoning. Just common sense. Straight-line cause and effect. The railroads have made life hard. Elect me, your life will get easier.

"But there are other issues I think need attention. Don't you believe—"

"Not in this election." He pulled a gleaming gold watch from his waistcoat pocket. "Now I've got to get back to my desk and deal with a few more matters before I catch my train."

They hurried past the janitor, whom Lissner favored with a quick wave, out the stage door and back on to the street. "There's one more essential matter. You're a rancher, so you do wear a ten-gallon hat or something, don't you, out on the range?"

"I do have working clothes at the house, sure, but what I've been wearing lately is more appropriate for the classroom."

"For crying out loud, Maxwell, stay off that university stuff. This guy Gentry you're running against, he's a bit of a dandy, is that right?"

He nodded, the image, the very thought, of Hale Gentry's black leather and silver conches floated through his mind evoking enough anger to tighten his throat.

"They all know you beat the snot out of him a couple years ago, but no one will believe it if you look like a schoolteacher, so you're the working stiff, understand? The guy who can throw a loop or brand a steer or whatever you guys do, with the best of them. This Gentry, he wanders around playing cowboy. He's a dressup pretender who wouldn't know a horse from a goat if it bit him on the nose."

They were in the alley behind Lissner's building now. Lissner shook his hand, said, "A pleasure," and began racing up the back stairs to his office.

"But what do my clothes have to do with my ideas?" he called.

Lissner stopped, looked at the sky, gathering patience. Then he dropped his gaze back to Andy. "Your costume, my boy, has to do with getting elected. The ideas can wait."

He had a sudden thought. "One more thing, Mr. Lissner."

"Yes, yes, yes."

"You're obviously a very intelligent man. Did you ever attend the university?"

"In Berkeley? Hah. They'd never let a Jew like me near the place if they saw me coming. But now I'm going to help appoint the people who pay their salaries. How's them apples, eh, Maxwell?" He hurried up the stairs and disappeared into the doorway.

And I'll be one of those, too, he thought. He pulled out his notecards and shuffled through them as he stepped out of the alley to the busy sidewalk. He wondered if there was still time to call this off, then a newsboy shoved a headline in front of his face.

* * *

MAXWELL HAT IN DISTRICT 4 RING.

* * *

So no, it was much too late to quit.

FORTY-EIGHT
CAMPING OUT IN GREEN CANYON

No one ever came up here—no cattle, no cowboys—so it was a perfect place to keep watch on the Circle M without risking exposure. Evening shadows dropped early over the site where Yellow Squirrel kept his small fire under the cliff's brow, inside one of the exploratory tunnels that had been blasted into the walls of Green Canyon when Carolyn Maxwell had toyed with the idea of allowing miners to exploit the rich cinnabar deposits. Cinnabar yielded mercury, and mercury meant big money in the gold business because it attracted like a magnet the precious yellow metal from the detritus of the diggings. The extra cash would have given the Circle M some leverage over Southern Pacific at a time when transportation was eating into the profits from cattle sales. In the end, Carolyn had decided the spoilage and the turmoil was not worth the extra money and that she would have to find other ways to break the railroads' stranglehold.

Roasting over the fire was a marmot, his third stringy, greasy critter of the week. Another reason to get this over with quickly. He watched Wing-Without-Feathers work his way up the trail toward the camp, hoping the little Washoe brought some information that would unlock the mystery of the apparently-abandoned Circle M. He gestured vigorously, waved the flask of moonshine he used as bait for his diminutive spy. He couldn't see that his urgings had any effect, but maybe they did, for when the man arrived, he was winded to the point where he couldn't speak.

"What do you have, Wing?"

The man shook his head, beckoned toward the flask. Yellow Squirrel handed it over, watched him start drinking, then pulled it away, refused to return it despite the reaching, pleading hands.

"Not until I know something you didn't when you walked in here. Something important," he said.

In answer, Wing-Without-Feathers lifted his felt hat and removed a piece of paper from the inside band. He shook out the folds and held it before Yellow Squirrel, who promptly handed the flask back.

"You've done well, my friend," he said, taking the simple poster advertising Andrew Maxwell's political debut. "You've done very, very well."

FORTY-NINE

THE CANDIDATE'S MAIDEN VOYAGE

There hadn't been time to construct a proper platform, so Andy's first political stage would be the bed of liveryman Feifer Gilligan's most elegant freight wagon. Gilligan had also dug the Fourth of July bunting and flags from out of their trunk in the hayloft. The wagonbed had room for four chairs—one for the candidate, one for Gilligan, who was also Sawtooth Wells's mayor, one for the itinerant Methodist pastor, Reverend Norbert Moreland, and one for Sheriff Michael Halstad. Sheriff Halstad would descend inconspicuously from the platform soon after the speech began to join and supervise the security arrangements.

At eleven A.M. Andy stood just inside the livery stable door, dressed, per Lissner's instructions, as if he were ready for the roundup. The churchbell sounded, and he heard chatter from the glade behind the stable as congregants emerged from the services at Reverend Moreland's church. An hour to go. Everything had been arranged so hastily, he must have forgotten something.

He hadn't had time to visit the ranch, but had been able to get word to Ling Chu, who sped the clothes to town in his beloved Model-T. He'd also brought another outfit, this one improvised by Cooper at the Circle M forge.

"Mr. Cooper say you now Mr. Knight-of-armor," Ling Chu said as he handed him a metal cylinder designed to fit around his body, supported by leather suspenders across his shoulders. There was also a matching cap. "You supposed to wear under shirt and hat, stop bullets."

He laughed. "Cooper. Cooper. Oh, Lord. I might be safe, Ling, but how would I ever get a vote? Look." He fit the armor over his clothes. "I'll look like I'm wearing a steel barrel."

Ling Chu did not share in the laughter. In fact, wore a stern and cloudy look as he took back the clumsy apparatus. "Maybe nobody shoot you during speech, then you wear in car home."

"We'll see. I appreciate the work you all went to." He asked Ling Chu if his mother was still in the hills. A nod. Whether Amelia and Cooper were okay. Another nod. Ling Chu never told you more than he thought was good for you, especially when he was miffed. Usually, that frustrated him, but for once he was grateful. He had more than enough on his mind.

He'd been able to practice his speech only to Gilligan. Sheriff Halstad, always the stickler for procedure, had recused himself as a test audience because he felt it might compromise his impartiality. The other candidate, after all, was also from Sawtooth Wells, and Gentry hadn't asked for the lawman's advance opinion of the speech he'd delivered a couple of weeks earlier.

He gazed around the street, the trees, the roof of the café, the roof of the livery stable above. He imagined Yellow Squirrel sighting down the barrel of a .30-.30 at his heart, or perhaps his head, ready to pull the trigger on his political career—and his life—before it started. Here was one of those doors he'd bragged to Cooper about. Come in, Yellow Squirrel. Come right in. He patted the holstered .44 at his side.

"No sidearms inside the Sawtooth Wells limits, Andy, you know that." The voice was Halstad's.

"It's a prop, Sheriff, for my speech." Halstad held out his hand. Andy handed over the weapon.

"If it's a prop, no need for bullets, then, is there?" He swung the cylinder out and emptied the chambers. "You can pick them up after. Good luck, boy." He headed into the street and worked his way through a gathering that was increasing in size by the moment.

"Pretty good crowd, Andy." Feifer Gilligan walked up from behind and clapped him on the shoulder. "Bet there's nigh on to a hundred afore it's done. You're gonna wow 'em, boy, and make no mistake."

"Keep talking, Feifer," he said. "I might just turn tail out of here."

Gilligan laughed and clapped him on the shoulder again. "Nothin' more important than a sense of humor, son. Lemme see that hogleg for a second." He took the gun, surreptitiously loaded it, handed it back.

"I hate to pull something like this on Sheriff Halstad, Feifer," he said.

Gilligan smiled, winked. "You didn't pull nothing, Andy. Sheriff can't play no favorites, but he no more wants you out there without protection than a preacher would go to church without his Bible."

"Should have known," he said. "And look, Feif, here's something else. I've changed my mind about using that chair you set out for me. A fellow down in Sacramento told me it'll work best for me to run up on stage, so just introduce me, and I'll trot out from here. Is that all right?"

"Sure. I'll go out and take it away right now before we get started."

"Okay. No, wait. Just leave it there empty. It might create some suspense."

"You're the boss, Andy." He checked his watch. "Quarter to. Time to strike up the band."

The band consisted of a bass drum, trumpet, and trombone. All that could be gathered at the last minute. They wore no uniforms, only a motley collection of their personal Sunday best, but their renditions of "The Stars and Stripes Forever" and "The Star Spangled Banner" were at least heartfelt, and the ascension of the pastor, the sheriff, and the mayor to the platform evoked warm applause. Then came Pastor Moreland's benediction. Energy seeped from the audience as the preacher called down blessing after blessing on the assembled and punishment after punishment on those who would do them harm. The collective response that greeted his final words was as sincere an "amen" as ever was uttered.

Gilligan got overly wound up with his address as well, and Andy sensed he'd have a job to boost the enthusiasm of the gathered when he finally heard "our esteemed, our renowned, our own" and jogged out the door toward the platform. He'd grown unaccustomed to the pointed toes on his boots, and he never used them for running anyhow, so he was careful mounting the steps. No tripping. While he was watching out for the toes, though, the high heel betrayed him, caught on the platform edge he thought he'd already cleared. He recovered with a little skip that he hoped looked playful and joyous rather than clumsy. He heard no laughter, so he guessed he hadn't disgraced himself.

He scanned the crowd, making eye contact with at least one person in each area. Create connections, Lissner said. Movement in a far corner. An orange turban. Impossible that Virginia would be here, but there she was. And a dark face on the other side under the shade of a large-brimmed hat. Deborah Beasley of *The Elevator.* Startling to see her here as well. He swallowed, smiled (Did it look like a smile? It felt more like a grimace.)

"It's wonderful to see so many friends as well as so many who will become my friends before this campaign is over. I won't keep you long. I'm just going to tell you little story, a true one, about greed and power destroying innocence and hard work."

"Get out of town, nigger." The shout came from immediately below him. He recognized one of Hale Gentry's crew. From the back, another call.

"Black bastard."

From the corner of his eye, he caught Halstad moving toward the loudmouth who'd made the first catcall. He drew his own weapon, stared down at the man, who hit the dirt at the sight of the pistol. The crowd shifted, some rose from their chairs. He lifted his eyes and resumed speaking.

"Don't worry, folks. I'm not going to shoot anyone." He glanced back down at his heckler, who was getting to his feet, dusting himself off as the sheriff arrived to hustle him away. In the back, deputies did the same with the second troublemaker.

"This," he waved the gun barrel in the air, "is all part of that story I was talking about."

He went on to describe how Southern Pacific had stolen land all over Sawtooth Valley by jacking up transportation prices until farmers couldn't get their goods to market, then buying their acreage for a fraction of its value.

"You remember that two hundred acres that used to be Jackson Powell's farm?" He pointed the pistol at a location over the crowd's head. "Pow. Dead as if someone had put a bullet through its heart, and, in a way, through the heart of Mr. Powell himself. An honest man who poured heart and soul into that farm, and he's now a landless laborer supporting himself by whatever odd jobs he can beg.

"And Harvey Milstead's farm? Pow. Murdered as well. By Southern Pacific in exactly the same manner. Located right next to the Powell place, isn't it? Now what a coincidence that is. And what about Widow Langston's little plot? Her husband dead for our sakes at San Juan Hill? What does she get from Southern Pacific? Pow. There goes her land. And suddenly the railroad owns eight hundred adjoining acres and water rights to boot and the rest of you are paying more for the irrigation that is the lifeblood of your crops. Am I right?"

Cautious applause. The caution was understandable. There was some danger in skylining yourself as an enemy of the railroad, and you could never tell who might be watching.

"Now, who is in jail for these crimes? Why no one, of course. Because the railroad men have arranged it so that these murders are perfectly legal. Legalized murder? In California? In America? I must be joking. Not at all. It's legal because the legislature says so, and the legislature says so because they are in the pay of the murderers themselves. I know you don't want any more names added to this list of victims, especially not your own. It needs to stop now, and that's why Hiram Johnson must become California's governor and why Andrew Maxwell must become the assemblyman from your fourth district."

Most of his attention went to delivering his speech and to assessing its effect on the people before him. He found himself lifted by his own rhetoric. Hell, he was enjoying this. Surprise. The bookish scholar extolling the masses? As unprepared as he'd been for public speaking, he'd been even more unprepared for this exhilaration, this thrill. It didn't make sense, but there it was, undeniable. He had his audience's attention, he was sure of that. Their gazes fixed on him. He thought they believed him, were ready to follow him, though he couldn't have said why he thought so. He reminded himself that he had no practice reading crowds.

A part of his concentration, however, remained alert for signs of Yellow Squirrel, for indications that he might need to use his weapon for protection instead of only for effect. By the time he finished to what seemed like enthusiastic applause and even a couple of cheers, nothing untoward had occurred aside from the disturbance at the beginning. He was almost disappointed.

Amid the post-speech crowd, feeling fairly good about it all, he accepted congratulations, shook hands. He knew many folks, of course, this was his home town. He tried to remember as many names and faces of strangers as possible. He realized he was not yet much of a hand at this aspect of politics. It seemed he forgot one new name almost the minute he turned to receive another.

Both Virginia and Deborah Beasley seemed to have vanished. He did notice a number of folks skulking away. They didn't like him? Didn't like what he had to say? Were put off he by his race? If it was that, why did they come? They surely knew beforehand. And it was in this mood of shaky confidence that he stepped back from a stiff conversation with a wagon driver twice his size and turned to find himself face to face with Virginia.

"Surprise, surprise," she smiled and waved.

"Never a bigger one," he said. "That's certain." He saw Halstad approaching from behind her. "Don't go away."

The sheriff was scanning his surroundings as he walked. He pulled Andy to the base of a large Ponderosa which would protect their backs. He said, "I think we're clear here, Andy." He handed him the six .45 cartridges he'd confiscated earlier. "Remember not to load up till you're out of town." Andy noticed he refrained from casting his eyes down, where he couldn't have failed to see that that the pistol had already been reloaded.

"My everlasting thanks, Sheriff. Particularly for rousting those jokers."

"All in the interest of public order and safety," he said. "You knocked them off balance pulling that gun, but next time it won't be a surprise, so be careful. Hope Valley's over there in Kirkwood County, you know, outside my jurisdiction. I can't follow you around to every town." He strode off toward his office.

He turned back toward Virginia. She was so immediately behind him he almost bumped into her. "Jesus, Virginia."

"Sorry. I just had to listen in. This is all so fascinating."

"Is that what brought you up here? Fascination?"

"That. And a memory or two," she said.

"The memory of when I practically killed myself crawling across the Circle M roof to your room only to have you slam the window in my face?"

"That was before, Andy. Before we came to mean so much to one another. I cared for you then, too, only I didn't know it. I had to get away from Father to realize… a lot of things." A moment of silence. "That was a wonderful speech. I had no idea you were an orator."

"Hardly that," he said. "But you thought it was okay?"

"Better than that. People talk about how big and bad the railroads are in a way that makes them sound like a distant monster. You made it so personal."

"It is personal."

A series of clatters and chugs drew their eyes across the street to where Ling Chu was sprinting from the crank at the Model-T's grill to the driver's seat, having spun the engine into life.

He waved his goggles in their direction and yelled, "We must return, Mr. Andrew." He made a couple of other mysterious adjustments and the vehicle began to amble in their direction. He had considered returning to the ranch via horseback to stay off the main road, but remained convinced that evasion would play into Yellow Squirrel's game, not theirs. They needed to lure him into the open. He'd ride in the open car, even clad in Cooper's metal shirt if Ling Chu insisted.

"I'm being called," he said to Virginia. She smiled and nodded. An awkward silence. He'd assumed Virginia had arrived in one of the many hired and private buggies that had come into town for the event, but they'd all disappeared by now.

"Virginia, I'm pretty sure there's no transportation scheduled out of here this afternoon, is there?" She shrugged. "Are you planning to stay in town here somewhere?"

She reached behind her, retrieved a small carpetbag and her sketch pad, which had sat concealed behind her skirt, held them in front of her with both hands. She shrugged again, held his gaze, smiled. "I wasn't sure," she said.

He shook his head. "Oh, no. Not safe. Not at all. Haven't you heard I'm a hunted man, a walking target? I'll talk to Feifer. He can—"

"No, Andy. I quit playing it safe a couple of years ago, if you'll recall. So if you don't want me, say so. If you do, I'll take my own chances with your vengeful redskin." She made a melodramatic taunt out of "vengeful redskin." Giggled.

"Well then, I guess it's climb aboard," he said. He opened the car door for her. Ling Chu looked from him to Virginia, smiled. Ling Chu never smiled.

"Mr. Andrew?" he said.

"Yes?"

"No matter now, Mr. Andrew. Too late."

Andy held Virginia's hand while she found her way to the back seat. Ling Chu dropped the smile and handed him the armor.

"That stuff is going to be so hot and—"

"Better than bullet in heart," Ling Chu said, shoving it into his chest.

So he relented, sneaking behind a tree to don his unwieldy shield. He hurried back to the car.

"Hurry, Ling Chu, before someone sees me."

Virginia convulsed with laughter in the back seat. "You're a walking tea kettle," she said.

Ling Chu shot her a look which shut her up immediately. Then he started them on their bouncing five-mile drive to the ranch. It wasn't long before the mysterious smile returned to Ling Chu's face.

FIFTY

THE PRESS

The Second Vendetta—II

Special from Mr. Andrew Maxwell

Our stealthy assassin made another appearance. I suppose it would be more correct to call it his usual cowardly lack of appearance. This time, he did not stop with livestock. One of our most dependable ranch hands, Mr. Enoch Randle, was cruelly butchered while performing his duties as a faithful employee of the Circle M. His body was desecrated in the manner that has become so distressingly familiar to readers of this series. It is not necessary to delve into more perturbing detail than to say that beasts in a slaughterhouse are treated with more dignity than Michael Yellow Squirrel showed Mr. Randle.

Ugly as this event is, I can report that our efforts to bring our nemesis to justice show encouraging signs. Discretion forbids outlining particulars, but we expect them to bear fruit in the near future. Rest assured that when the matter is concluded, we will reveal in full how we accomplished our aims.

Some say I could and should have ended this terror two years ago, should have encouraged vigilante justice and allowed a mob to hang Michael Yellow Squirrel. Perhaps. But my father told me a story once of a town full of good people who got caught up in mob hysteria and lynched a man. According to my father, the collective guilt of that awful act destroyed more lives, more souls than the victim's. People could no longer face each other. Half the residents moved elsewhere, A cloud of sullen quiet and shame hung over those who remained. I did not wish that for Sawtooth Wells. Of course, I did not wish for nor anticipate Yellow Squirrel's return, either. But he is back, and there is no profit in regret.

It could be that my campaign will enhance the murderer's chances of success in exterminating the Maxwell family. Let me assure him—and you—that the opposite is true. Our plans are so well-laid that we are confident of thwarting his every scheme. We invite him to lay on his very best. His defeat is certain.

* * *

MAXWELL OPENS CAMPAIGN

Special to The Elevator *by Deborah Beasley*

Taking the stump in his hometown of Sawtooth Wells, Mr. Andrew Maxwell launched his campaign for the fourth district assembly seat vacated by the recent death of Mr. Harvey Cox. Mr. Maxwell concentrated on what he termed the abuses of Southern Pacific in forcing small farmers out of business in his district, asserting that the railroad conspired to buy up land and water rights in order to extort higher prices for transportation and irrigation from ranchers and farmers in the area. The speaker used the startling device of a drawn firearm to illustrate how less-powerful landholders are being deprived of their livelihood.

The speech was interrupted at the outset by racial epithets called from the crowd, references to Mr. Maxwell's Negro heritage, which was revealed two years ago when it was discovered that he is the natural son of a black foreman on the Circle M ranch and the ranch's owner, Mrs. Carolyn Maxwell. Sawtooth Wells Sheriff, Michael Halstad, and his deputies promptly quelled the disturbance, and the speech was not disrupted again.

The Elevator *hopes to include comments from several bystanders and from Mr. Maxwell's Democratic opponent, Mr. Hale Gentry, in future articles.*

* * *

The SECOND *Vendetta*

REPUBLICANS MOUNT 4TH DISTRICT OPPOSITION

Special to The Sacramento Union

by *Harold Finch*

    Stunned by the sudden death of longtime Republican Assemblyman Harvey Cox, Republicans began a desperate attempt Sunday to salvage the Fourth District seat for their party. Mr. Hale Gentry, the Democratic candidate, a prominent Sawtooth Wells businessman, is expected to win the election handily. However, apparently unwilling let the seat go completely uncontested, the Republicans have fielded at the last minute young Mr. Andrew Maxwell, son of well-known ranch owner, Mrs. Carolyn Maxwell.
    On Sunday past, Mr. Maxwell appeared in Sawtooth Wells before a small audience on a rude platform improvised from, of all things, a wagon. Though he gave it a game try, he showed his oratorical and political inexperience by brandishing a firearm as an amateur prop to illustrate his allegations that Southern Pacific is intentionally killing off small farms in the area. Mr. Maxwell issued that and other hackneyed charges against the railroads, but added a new wrinkle, coming dangerously close to slander as he used words like "murder" and "criminal" to describe their imagined offenses.
    It will be recalled that Mr. Maxwell was recently discovered to be a Negro of illegitimate birth. The Union *has also learned that he was recently accused of inappropriate conduct relative to an academic dispute with the University of California, and that he is out on bail from felony charges brought by the San Francisco district attorney. None of his bodes well for his candidacy or for Republican chances of retaining the fourth district seat in next month's election.*

FIFTY-ONE

A CROWDED HOUSEHOLD

"That girl's no more a housekeeper than Cooper is," Amelia was saying to Andy. "All these folks jammed in under one roof, a body's got to keep up her end."

"It was only one plate," he said. "And it was a great breakfast. Thank you."

Amelia nodded at the compliment, but she wouldn't leave the subject. "Plate don't mean nothing. It's attitude."

"She's trying, Amelia. Surely you can see that," he said. "She just, it's that nobody ever taught her. Her mother died having her."

Amelia rolled her eyes to the heavens. "Your will, not mine, Lord."

Many Clouds entered with two fistfuls of clean silverware, headed for the breakfront. She steered a course around the far side of the table, eyes to the floor.

"Got to finish up in the kitchen," Amelia said. She swatted Andy on the shoulder. "Git on, now." And she left. What was that all about?

"Many Clouds." He crossed to her, stood behind her as she slipped the various utensils into their proper cubbyholes. "It was a big surprise to see you here," he said. "A wonderful surprise. How are you?"

"I'm fine, Mr. Maxwell. I'm sorry for all your troubles."

"Surely I'm not Mr. Maxwell to you, am I?"

"Andrew, then." She began shuffling the silverware back and forth aimlessly.

"From what I understand my troubles hardly measure up to yours. It must have been horrible. The burns and all."

"They're healed now." She shifted her attention to the glassware, rubbing imaginary spots off on her skirt.

"We have a lot of catching up to do, you and I. Why don't we go out on the veranda where we can talk?"

"Cooper says it's dangerous outside the house."

"The screening they threw up will keep us safe on the porch."

A voice called from the stairway. "Andy, can we talk, please? Privately?"

He turned to see Virginia, her face in a pout. "Perhaps a bit later?" he said.

"I'm about to burst," she said.

He turned back toward Many Clouds, but she had already sneaked away and was halfway to the kitchen. A trout slipping off the bank, back into the stream.

"On the veranda, then, Virginia," he said. "We should be safe out there."

FIFTY-TWO

HIRAM'S SON RETURNS

"**H**ere comes that politician's boy, Andy," Amelia announced. It was late afternoon, a couple of hours before Carrie was scheduled to sneak in for a reunion and planning meal.

"Jack Johnson?" He put down his notebook, still refining his speech, and joined Amelia at the window. Jack Johnson's touring car jounced across the bridge, under the arch and into the Circle M yard.

"I hope he has enough sense to walk up on the porch on his own," Amelia said, "because you sure as shooting aren't going out there to meet him."

Johnson did, indeed, have that much sense. In fact he was looking over both shoulders and turning in all directions as he leaped out of the car and jogged up to the house. Andy opened the screen door.

"Safe," Johnson ducked inside. "You don't know what it's like out there in the open, never knowing if you're going to get a bullet any minute. On second thought, I guess if anybody knows how it feels, it is you. I read your bit in the paper, Maxwell. Exciting stuff."

"So *The Examiner* published my piece?"

"Well, not exactly," Johnson said.

"What do you mean?"

"They had a little box on the front page with a few words of yours, then telling folks to go buy *The Elevator* if they wanted the whole thing."

Had Bierce judged his writing below standard? Johnson didn't give him time to think about it, but hit him with another piece of news that reminded him how isolated he'd become.

"What was in the *Examiner*, though, was Ambrose Bierce and that reporter Redmond laying the killing of that Charley Hung fellow on Yellow Squirrel. They said O'Neil was way off base talking about a tong war."

"That must have made the sheriff happy."

"Happy enough to threaten arrest them for colluding with you to obstruct justice and several other felonies. They just said any fool could have looked up the information about how Yellow Squirrel made his kills just like they did."

Andy smiled, but again Johnson didn't give him time to think before launching into his next speech."

"Anyhow, that's not the important subject. Pa sent me here with a message, and I've got to deliver it and get back down the mountain."

The whole time Johnson had been rattling on, Amelia had guided him to a seat at the table, then she'd disappeared, undoubtedly to fetch tea or lemonade.

"Slow down," Jack. "You're not making sense."

"You're right. Need to catch my breath. That's what Dad always says. Breath. Oxygen. Can't do anything without it."

"Your dad's right. How about some liquid to go with the air?"

Amelia carried in one of Ling Chu's patented lemonade and cookie trays. She frowned at Johnson. "Andy, don't let this fool get you in no more situations. Things are bad enough." She strode back to the kitchen.

Johnson drank half a glass of lemonade at a gulp, chomped on a cookie, unfazed by Amelia's remark. His mouth full, spewing crumbs, he said, "Got to jump right back in that Locomobile and get down to Placerville so I can drive Dad over to Auburn for a speech tomorrow morning. Lord, what a pace." He swallowed the cookie, washed it down with the rest of the glass of lemonade, took another.

"Here's what I came to say. Good reports on you from yesterday. Keep it up." He swallowed half the second glass of lemonade, which Amelia had, he felt sure, intended for himself. Finished the second cookie. They're expecting you at Hope Valley tomorrow, then Markleeville on Saturday."

Andy nodded. Why was Johnson telling him what he already knew?

"At Markleeville, you challenge Gentry to a debate. Anywhere, anytime. Make like he's a coward if he doesn't come out. Afraid you'll whup him all over again. We'll deliver him an official written version of the challenge. You just have to sign right here."

He pulled out an envelope, pulled out a blank sheet of thick white stationery, Hiram Johnson's letterhead, shoved the paper to him.

"What am I signing?"

"They haven't had time to do the exact wording yet and get it all typed up. It'll lay out all the conditions and rules and whatnot, then Gentry counters and then you negotiate is how it goes."

"I'd rather do it myself, I think," he said.

"Hey, you want to get elected, leave it this stuff to the pros," Jack said.

"I don't know."

"Lissner's not going to be happy," Jack said. "Dad either."

"Tell Mr. Lissner hello and thanks. His advice worked out well. But on this one, it's a personal thing I have to do. I'll send you a copy."

Jack looked at him for several long moments. He gulped the last of the lemonade and rose. "You know what, Maxwell? If it was just about anyone else, I'd try to talk them down about this, but I don't know." He started for the door. "After everything that's happened and reading your piece in the newspaper and all, maybe it is best you do this on your own, and I don't have time to argue anyhow. Got to get back behind the wheel. Duty and Daddy both are calling me." He turned at the screen door, waved, jumped down the steps and fled to the car, glancing and turning around the whole way.

FIFTY-THREE
WAR COUNCIL

Carrie crept into the house after dark. She, Cooper, Amelia, and Andy huddled around the dinner table, away from the windows, lamplight low. Carrie thought her son looked terribly thin. He probably thought the same of her, though. She hadn't felt particularly hungry living off the land, but she couldn't deny that ribs poked out where none had protruded before. Nevertheless, hunger was not a problem. What was a problem was the alien and painful sneaking, the sense of victimhood. So what Andy was saying made perfect sense.

"Mom and I will both appear at every event from now on out."

"That's just what the fool wants," Cooper said.

"He's looking to pick off both of you at once," Amelia said. "And you want to make it easy for him?"

"I want to get him out in the open."

"I don't know why you don't get some dogs and just track him down," Cooper insisted.

"He'll just disappear till they're gone," Carrie said. "He wants us both together and in a time and place that will make a splash. If we do it Andy's way, we'll look as if we're playing into his hand, but he'll really be playing into ours."

Cooper began humming, his hand keeping a martial beat.

Amelia said, "What if you don't have him divined so well as you think?"

"His actions tell the story," Carrie said. "He's teased us with the cattle and with Enoch. Mother's been hiding, but Andy's been out and about quite a lot, and Yellow Squirrel's made no move on him. And he won't as long as we stay separate."

"Then stay separate, I say," Amelia said.

"And live this dodgy, outlaw life?" Carrie said. "No more."

"Better than no life at all," Cooper said. He quit humming and slammed the table.

"Not much," she said. "Look, you two, I know you're only trying to keep us safe. But we're neither safe nor are we getting rid of the threat."

Andy picked up where she left off. "We'll be out in the open, but well-guarded. I use a pistol during my speech, so I'm ready to retaliate immediately."

"Why you think he gonna attack if you so well-guarded?" Cooper said.

"Because we have divined him so well," Carrie said, smiling.

"Well we'll be right there and be part of the well-guarding," Amelia said.

Andy shook his head. "We can't spare you from here. He could still attack the Circle M."

"But you just said—"

"Just in case we don't have him divined so well after all," he said.

A silence. Cooper nodded to Amelia, and they both rose and left the table. Carrie lifted her hand toward them, then dropped it. She was sure she was doing the right thing. But then why did she feel she'd betrayed two of the dearest people in her life?

FIFTY-FOUR
MIDNIGHT REUNION

Andy lay sleepless on top of his covers. He knew he had to go forward as if he had no misgivings, but at the moment misgivings were all he had. The political campaign seemed like a child's fantasy. The scheme to entrap Michael Yellow Squirrel had all the promise of drawing a jack of spades to fill out a royal flush. He slapped the air, trying to brush aside the negative thoughts. The tapping on the window sounded like thunder. He rolled off the bed to the floor, reached up to retrieve his pistol from the nightstand.

The tapping sounded again. Then a voice. "Andy, for God's sake, open up." Virginia. Damn her. He reached up from the bottom of the curtain to turn the window latch, doing his best not to draw any part of the curtain from the window.

"Slip straight down. Be careful you don't expose the inside of the room."

They sat on the floor, their backs to the bed. "What do you think you're doing?"

"I wanted to see what you went through to get to my window two years back. If I'd known, I'd have been much more impressed. A couple of times I was afraid I'd seen my last starry night."

"It's plenty steep and those slates are slippery, all right," he said. "But that's really not the answer to my question."

"I wasn't too happy with our little talk this afternoon." Her tone was businesslike.

"In what respect?" he said.

"In the respect that I poured out my heart and soul and you didn't respond at all," she said.

"I didn't have much to say. Or I guess I was afraid to say much."

"Afraid?"

With all the other issues on his mind, he didn't feel up to an emotional confrontation with Virginia, but she was forcing it. "Afraid of speaking when I'm angry. It usually gets me in trouble."

"What did you have to be angry about? I'm the one who's being shown no respect."

"All right, let's review your grievances. You resent being asked to help clear the table."

"Of course not. I just like to be *asked* instead of having it assumed. I mean that aunt of yours just up and said 'You get that end, Ginny.' I'm not Ginny, and I most decidedly am not the maid."

"Neither is she. Everyone works here, especially now."

"I just don't like to be taken for granted."

"Jump in and help and you won't be."

"I'm not sure this was such a great idea, Andy."

"Ling Chu can take you back into town tomorrow." He was nowhere near as angry as he thought he would be. He actually felt rather detached.

"Are you going?" she said. Her voice sounded hopeful.

"Mother and I are going to Hope Valley on horseback. It's the quickest way."

"What about Pocahontas?"

"Who?" He knew, but he couldn't believe she'd said it.

"The Indian girl. Is she staying here? Going with you?"

"Why in the world are you asking about her?"

"Isn't she Yellow Squirrel's daughter or something?"

"His niece."

"How do you know she isn't a spy?"

Now he was getting angry. "You think we'd let her in here? She's as much his victim as anyone. More so."

"That's what I thought," she said. "Exactly." It sounded like an accusation.

"What's what you thought?" As usual with Virginia, he'd lost the thread of the conversation, and he suspected he was about to be put in the wrong.

"You have feelings for her. Perfectly natural after all you went through together, I suppose, but still…"

"What do you know about what Many Clouds and I went through together?"

"You keep acting like you're not famous, Andy. It's common knowledge, the saga of your trek across the desert, the struggle to save her dying mother, your time together at her grandfather's camp in Wyoming. She's very pretty in an exotic, aboriginal sort of way, so it's no surprise you're drawn to her."

So that's what this conversation had been about. Not that the altercation with Amelia over chores was completely insignificant, but the core upset was over Many Clouds.

"Well, Virginia, I'm very flattered."

"Flattered? I don't understand."

He reached over, found her hand in the dark. She pulled away the hand, then shifted her whole body. He followed with his own.

"I'm flattered that you would be so jealous." She stiffened.

"You deny you have feelings for this Fluffy Clouds?"

"Many Clouds. As you pointed out, all that happened between us happened years ago, and I hadn't seen her again until last night. So what that could have to do with us, I have no idea."

"Sometimes you're so naïve about romantic matters you scare me to death."

"I'm not so naïve about romantic matters between thee and me." He reached out, stroked her cheek. She began to relax.

"So you're not going to send me back across the roof?"

"You could sleep on the floor," he said.

"A gentleman would let me have the bed." She took his hand and pressed it to her lips.

"Hmmm. All right. You can have the bed." He brought her hand to his own lips.

"All to myself?"

"I'm not that much of a gentleman."

"Good." She threw her arms around his neck and snuggled close. The thoughts that had haunted him earlier faded and dissolved in the wet and warmth of Virginia's eager kisses.

FIFTY-FIVE

HOPE VALLEY HOEDOWN

He hadn't been to Hope Valley for years, and it was even less of a town than he remembered it. If you counted buildings, streets, apparent commerce, there was less to it, even, than to Sawtooth Wells. A large general store, but no cafés, no churches, a community corral instead of a livery stable. Yet, it was worth a campaign ride because it was an important hub for the area surrounding Caples Lake, on whose shores it rested at an elevation of 7800 feet. Everyone and everything that headed east climbing toward Carson Pass or west descending from Carson Pass went through Hope Valley. Few ranchers braved the high-altitude winters to live in the valley year-round, but plenty used the valley for summer range. Thus, a goodly number of voters would probably gather to take in his first foray out of his home town. He wouldn't have Halstad's corps of deputies for protection here, but they'd been assured a contingent of Folsom Prison Guards would turn up, so he felt reasonably good about the security.

Virginia had persisted in her request to come along, and he was tempted. He savored the dew-fresh memory of their night together and her narrow escape from his room when they overslept, not awaking till Ling Chu rang the bell to call everyone to breakfast. She'd scampered back to her room undetected and managed to emerge looking respectable without too much delay. And the adventure gave them another secret to bond them. But he argued that he couldn't afford the distraction, and the notion that he would be unable to concentrate around her proved flattering enough to convince her to stay behind. He didn't really think she wanted to ride across the mountain trails anyway. Wasn't sure she could have even if she had wanted to. Many Clouds would have made the journey with no problem. But that was neither here nor there.

"Where are you going to speak from, Andy?" Carrie said. And it was a good question. There was no sign of platform, wagon, flag, or any other convenience or decoration. The speech was set for four p.m. It was shortly after noon, and if anyone had made any preparations, they weren't evident.

They dismounted in front of the store and headed inside. He did see a poster announcing the event on a bulletin board near the entrance. The store appeared empty.

"Hello," he called.

Silence.

"Hello." Louder. Still no answer.

"I think I hear something out back," she said. There did indeed seem to be some bumping and grunting coming from that direction. She walked to the rear of the store and opened a back door. Quickly shut it, and returned. "We'd better wait till they're finished," she said.

"Finished what?" he said.

"Just... finished."

"Oh." Andy said. "Mom, we should go." He grabbed her arm. She pulled away.

"Go where?" she said. "We need information, and there's no one else around to ask."

"But you shouldn't..."

She smiled, laid a hand on his arm. "It's gallant of you to protect me, Andy, but I'm unlikely to be harmed by a little glimpse of... we'll just wait, as I said."

A few minutes later, a tall, obese man with long, dirty blond hair waddled through the door, shouldering one of the straps on his overalls. He registered no surprise or embarrassment, paused not at all, when he saw them.

"Help you folks?" he said.

Andy stepped between the man and his mother. "I'm supposed to be giving a speech here this afternoon. Maybe you could direct us to whoever's in charge of the arrangements," he said.

"Jack Larson never did like me, and now he cost me plenty of business," he said.

Another fat man came in the back door, this one shorter and younger. Also in coveralls. "George, that pump's acting up again," he said.

"Not now, Phil. I got customers." The man called George did not turn in Phil's direction when he spoke.

Phil shrugged. "No never mind to me, if you don't want no water," he said.

"Later," George said. His voice was sharp this time, and he did turn in Phil's direction. Phil shrugged again and exited the same way he'd entered.

George went on. "They was going to hold the speech right outside the store, but Larson decided to move it to his ranch, about five miles east of here." He pointed as he spoke. "And whatever Larson says no one dares say no to."

"Straight down that road?" Carrie nudged Andy aside.

"Big sign out front. Can't miss it. You like some jerky or a soda or something to carry you along? Got Cokey Cola on ice."

Andy started to accept the offer, but Carrie cut him off.

"We're in a great hurry," she said. "No one told us about the location change, and we don't want to be late."

"Thanks for the help, anyhow," Andy said. He started to reach for a handshake, but Carrie wrapped both her arms around one of his and pulled.

"We have to hurry," she said, and fairly propelled him out the door. Outside, she said, "What in the world's gotten into you?"

"What do you mean?" he said.

"Here you were going to be my protector and you were about to accept a drink and shake hands with that man? Someone you don't want to touch or touch anything he's touched? Sometimes you act so naïve you scare me to death." *What? Naïve? Again? No time to think about that now.* She mounted quickly and was trotting down the road before he'd even made it into the saddle.

* * *

A tall steel archway announced the entrance to the Larson ranch, *Larson* in three-foot high letters, framed by equally large renditions of the Rocking L brand, the letter L resting on a rocking chair runner. Red white and blue ribbons wound around the pillars supporting the archway, and copies of the poster were nailed on the fence posts leading toward the gate.

It was a good half-mile from the entrance to the ranch yard, and that also bore the signs of elaborate preparations for the event. An hour short of starting time, a number of buggies and horses had already gathered, along with two Model-T's. Two Indian women were serving lemonade and other libations from behind a trestle table near the ranch house porch. In contrast to the Sawtooth Wells arrangements, a cedar stump off to the side of the house, six or eight feet in diameter, four feet high, sawed level, with steps hacked into it, was set to serve as a stage.

Andy and Carrie dismounted and approached the house on foot. They were mounting the steps when a blond, square-faced man burst through the door, yelling over his shoulder, "Get at least a dozen more chairs out here, Juana, on the double. Whoa, now." Andy had put out a hand to prevent the man from running into them, and he'd stopped just short of it. "Refreshments out there, folks."

"I'm Andrew Maxwell. This is my mother, Carolyn. Are you Mr. Larson?"

"Ah, the candidate. We were beginning to wonder if you'd decided to show a white feather."

"Why would you think that?" she said.

"A joke, ma'am. Bad one at that. Glad to meet you." He held out a hand big enough to enclose both mother's and son's in one grip. They all traded handshakes.

"We were lucky to make it," Andy said. "No one told us about the change in venue."

"Don't understand that. I sent a telegram to Johnson. He's your boss, isn't he? But never mind. You're here now." He ushered them off the porch. This stump here is a natural stage. We use it for fiddlers and all kinds of musical and oratorical folks. It'll be yours today. Rocking L is my ranch, so I'll introduce you, then you just go ahead and speak your piece. You can sit up there with your son, ma'am, if you want. Plenty of room, and I could introduce you, too."

"I'll sit in the back and watch, if you don't mind."

"Suit yourself. Now is there anything else I can do to make you comfortable?"

"I was expecting some men from Folsom," he said.

"Oh, sure. I know you're concerned about security and all, which is why we moved things out here instead of the store. Once we did that, there was no need for those Folsom men. In fact, they would just get in the way, cause confusion. My men know the lay of the land here. They're all in position. All the rooftops, behind boulders down by the gate. You couldn't be safer."

Carrie said, "You took it on your own authority to cancel our security detail?"

"Why sure. I telegraphed the warden myself. I've known George since childhood, us being brothers and all. We go way back." He winked.

"Mr. Larson, we're dealing with a savage and resourceful enemy. You had no authority to do such a thing," Andy said.

"It's my ranch, and we know our setup best, just like you know yours on the Circle M. No need to worry, like I said."

"How many are covering the crowd itself?" Andy said.

"Enough," Larson said. "I'm telling you, it's tight."

"Excuse us." He pulled Carrie aside.

"Fine. Party starts in half an hour," Larson called.

"We can tell time, Mr. Larson," Carrie shot back over her shoulder. The man flushed, was about to reply, but an old woman emerged from the house, struggling and stumbling with chairs.

"Ah, for God's sake, Juana. Do I have to do everything?"

"This smells, Andy," she said. "You need to cancel."

"You heard him about the white feather. If I pull out now, I'm a coward and the election's over before it starts."

"It's not worth your life."

"Think of this as a dance, Mom."

"A dance?"

"Yes. Call it the vendetta reel. Everyone in position, you in the back, me in the front where Yellow Squirrel can't get to both of us at once. Then we keep moving and stepping till the music's over."

"Till the shooting's over, you mean."

"Keep smiling. We're not hiding any more, remember. You wave if you see trouble. I'll do the same. Do-si-do?"

"There are too many unknowns."

"There always are, aren't there?" He grasped both her shoulders, looked into her eyes. "A wise person I know and love once said this: If I wanted a safe life, I'd live in a cottage and knit sweaters."

"Andy you couldn't knit a stitch even with me holding the needles." She laughed. "Remember?"

"So I'm going to make speeches instead."

"I've got you covered." She patted the holster at her side. They hugged.

* * *

Larson was a one-man show. He delivered the benediction because the preacher didn't show up. Maybe he hadn't gotten a telegram about the new location, either. Then he thanked a list of people for helping organize things. He gave credit to his wife and mother for their share in the preparations, apologizing for their absence, which he didn't explain. Then, in less time than it had taken preacher Moreland of Sawtooth Wells to deliver the opening prayer, he launched into his introduction.

"We had our Democratic candidate here a couple of weeks ago. Now it's only fair to give the other side a chance, even though this man is trying to replace a legend. A moment of silence, please, for that legend, Mr. Harvey Cox."

The moment of silence was very short. Larson continued. "So I know you'll honor today's speaker with the same kind attention you honored Mr. Hale Gentry with a short time ago. Give a good old Hope Valley welcome to Mr. Andrew Maxwell." He clapped and waved, urging the audience into action, then sat down.

The sprint up on the stage went without incident. Andy waved his hat, smiled, scanned the crowd. No Deborah Beasely this time. His mother was seated in the scant shade of sapling at the very edge of the crowd. She clapped vigorously, but she was not looking at him. She was scanning the area for problems. Good.

"Most of you don't know me, but by the time this campaign is over, I'm hoping we'll become friends. It's my hope to become just as good a friend to you in Sacramento as Harvey Cox was to you all these years."

"I got no nigger friends," came the call from the back. It was the same face he'd seen just below him in Sawtooth Wells.

He pulled his pistol. As before, the crowd stirred, shifted, but the man in the back did not duck this time. "Go pick some uh dat ol' cotton," he yelled.

"Don't let the gun make you nervous," Andy said. "I'm only using it to make a point about why your vote for me will help get the railroads off your backs." He looked for the men Larson had promised to deal with the disruption. He saw nothing. Another voice called.

"Stinking black bastard." Suddenly the crowd bristled with weapons—sticks, axe handles, iron rods—and the individual yells melded into a chorus. The audience ran for cover, and the stick-waving mob rushed the stage. He turned toward Larson, but the man's chair was empty. His next thought was for his mother. He fired into the air, which broke the momentum of the crowd's surge, then he leaped off the side of the stage, intending to skirt the edge of the seating area and find his way to her.

Another shot. Not from his gun this time. He hoped it was his mother's. The men were confused now, began milling. He sprinted toward the sapling where Carrie had been sitting, met her halfway.

"I shot over their heads," she said.

"We didn't start this," he said. "Back-to-back, now, to the horses."

"Is this your idea of do-si-do?" Carolyn said.

"I don't much like the caller for his dance," he said.

The dozen or so men surrounded them, looking for an opening or for courage enough to brave the Maxwells' pistols.

"It's the whore and her son," sneered a small man with an intensely black beard.

"The whore and her nigger son, you mean." She paused at that one.

"Let's just keep moving," he said.

"Grab your partner, round and round," she said.

Something flew through the air. He heard a thonk, felt his mother go down. He knelt, covered her body with his. Fired twice into the forest of advancing legs. Cries of pain. Again, the surge halted. He felt his mother struggling to rise.

"I'm okay," she said.

Once again, they were back-to-back, more than halfway to the horses now. Someone rushed from the side. He lifted his hand to fend off the blow. Something struck his thigh. His mother's gun fired. He staggered, but did not go down. Until something struck him on the head, and he saw black, then light, and realized he was on his knees. He fired blindly, his last three shots, as he struggled to his feet, and they were at their horses, using them as shields.

A cordon of men appeared between them and their attackers, and the thugs lowered their weapons and walked away. Two remained moaning on the gravel. One clutching a knee, another a hand.

Larson walked across the lawn. "Get those men to a doctor," he said. "You folks all right?"

"Mom?" Despite his blurred vision, pulsing thigh, and the blood that flowed down his cheek, his first thought was for her.

"Did I get anyone?" she asked.

"A couple, I think. Anyway, they're gone now."

"My God, Andy, you're bleeding."

"Doesn't look so bad," Larson said. They ignored him.

Carrie daubed his cheek with her bandana. "Here we were so concerned about Yellow Squirrel," she said. "What do you think?" She pointed to a spot on her scalp.

"Quite a lump growing. Plum-purple, but no blood."

"Can't say the same for you," she said. She began dabbing at another wound at the base of his skull.

"I'm sorry as can be about all this," Larson said. "No way to prevent it. You know some of us get pretty excited when our taboos are violated."

"Tickle me with a white feather, Mom," he said to Carrie, "but apparently some of us have no taboo against lynching."

"Not even here in California…" she said.

She and Andy spoke the rest of Hiram Johnson's shibboleth in unison, "the finest state in the union."

He turned to Larson. "If you didn't arrange this, you allowed it."

"I'm sorry you found it necessary to fire on unarmed men."

"Unarmed?" she said. "Unarmed?"

"I didn't see any guns except yours," Larson said. "Did you?"

"I didn't see any of your vaunted security force trying to stop the attack," Andy said, "did you?"

"Well, those two men you shot didn't seem seriously injured, so I don't believe it will be necessary to file any charges."

"We may be filing a charge or two of our own," he said.

"Good luck on your campaign, Mr. Maxwell. I'm not sure how many folks are going to turn out to hear a candidate who shoots at them, but time will tell."

"Yes, Mr. Larson, it will," she said. "It certainly will."

FIFTY-SIX

DOCTORING

It was nearly midnight when Carrie and Andy reached the Circle M. Shortly thereafter, the ranch house living room resembled an infirmary. Ling Chu, Amelia, Many Clouds, Nonny, and even Virginia carried cloths and bowls to and fro. Ling Chu readied his arsenal of needles and glass cups. Amelia grabbed a razor and, after soaking and lathering, began scraping hair away from the wound on Carrie's scalp. She handed another razor to Virginia, who held it distastefully at arm's length. Finally, at a nod from Amelia, she took it to Many Clouds, who knelt beside Andy.

"I'd better get some fresh water," Virginia said and headed for the kitchen.

As Many Clouds finished her barbering, Ling Chu approached with a needle and thread. "You see to Mrs. Maxwell, Ling," she said, holding out her uplifted palm for the needle. "I can take care of Andrew."

"You very sure?" Ling Chu said. She nodded.

He winced as she squeezed the wound shut. "Is it that deep that it needs stitches?" he said.

"Yes," she said. "But it's not so very long. Would you like whisky?"

"Is it going to hurt that much?" he said.

"I'll do my best, but I can't promise…"

"Maybe just a towel to bite down on."

She made her initial stab into his flesh. He bit, grunted. "That wasn't as bad as I thought," he said.

"I'm not finished yet," she said.

"I know. And I'm in no hurry for the next jab."

She giggled, drew the thread through. "Here I come again," she warned.

He bit, grunted. "Where did you learn this?"

"From the Mission School doctor," she said.

"You learned a lot at that school," he said.

"Get that towel back in your mouth," she said.

He obeyed, and there was silence between them for a while. Amelia finished with his mother, who was standing. Nonny and Amelia gathered rags and bowls.

"Last one," Many Clouds said finally. She tied a knot, then snipped the thread. She pressed a square of gauze to his scalp. "Hold this." She fastened it with a couple lengths of adhesive tape. "Done," she said.

"Thanks," he said. He turned toward her, and for the first time since they'd both returned to the ranch, for the first time, actually, in two years, their eyes met. He skipped a breath. There was sudden light, a sort of hole in the clouds. Oh, my Lord, no, no, no. Especially not now and on top of everything else, he thought.

"Thank you," he said again, the words floating on a mixture of amazement and fear.

"You're welcome." She lowered her eyes and knelt to collect tools and rags. As she knelt, he caught sight of Virginia standing in the kitchen door, a bowl of clean water in her hands.

"How do I look?" he said.

"Like a fashion plate," she said. There was a smile on her lips, but a chill in her voice.

FIFTY-SEVEN

THE PRESS

The Second Vendetta—III

by Andrew Maxwell

We were not assaulted by the enemy we feared yesterday, but we were nearly done in by an unexpected foe. We thought we had made ample preparations to protect ourselves in Hope Valley for our second campaign appearance, but those protections were withdrawn without warning at the last minute, and a gang of hooligans attacked the rostrum and canceled the speech before it was properly underway. Michael Yellow Squirrel was nowhere in evidence, but we were lucky to get away with our lives, despite having been assured that the staff of the Larson Ranch, where our appearance took place, was equal to the task of turning away any danger that might present itself.

These writings began as a series of articles describing our attempts to turn away the vendetta of one man. It may become a description of our victories over armed assaults from many more sources that we imagined. Obviously, we must widen our strategy.

* * *

Special to The Sacramento Union

by Harold Finch

 A more outrageous attack on the first amendment and to our freedom of the press is hard to imagine than that which took place yesterday when the Union's reporter was turned away from candidate Andrew Maxwell's speech in Hope Valley. When said reporter presented himself at the entrance to the Jack Larson Ranch, where the event was scheduled, he was told that Mr. Maxwell was allowing no press coverage and that we should return to our offices and explain that to our readers.

 The only explanation possible is that Mr. Maxwell is afraid of what honest disclosure will reveal about his message to the voters. In his last speech, he brandished a six-shooter. Now he has trod on our constitution.

 In addition, this reporter heard gunshots emanating from the scene. Given his personal history, one must conclude that Mr. Maxwell is possessed of a hair trigger temper as well as a hair trigger pistol. Those are hardly winning ways for any man who seeks the trust of the public, and The Union *will do all it can to deny him the office for which is obviously unfit.*

* * *

Special to The Elevator

by Deborah Beasley

 Our attempt to report on the Hope Valley campaign speech of Mr. Andrew Maxwell, fourth district assembly candidate, was thwarted yesterday by armed men who claimed they were acting on orders from Mr. Jack Larson, prominent rancher in the area. The location of the speech was changed without notice from the Hope Valley General Store to Mr. Larson's ranch, and Mr. Larson apparently left orders at the entrance to his land that no press would be allowed on the property. Thus was the public denied knowledge of both the particulars of Mr. Maxwell's speech and of the gunfire plainly heard from the vicinity of the area where it was delivered.

 A reporter from the Sacramento Union *was also turned away, but allowed to leave on his own volition. We ourselves were detained forcibly until such time as Mr. Larson deemed it fitting to allow "the nigger lady"(He did not say "lady," and the word he did use is unfit for publication.) to "go peddle her papers."*

FIFTY-EIGHT

LAST MARMOT

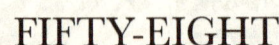

Yellow Squirrel had about decided not to eat his marmot. He'd go over to Shingle Lake for fish or even deer. He shouldn't be here, should be speeding to Wind River in victory with bright stars to light the way. The Hope Valley fiasco had spoiled his moment, his circus moment, and put him in a bad mood. As in Sawtooth Wells, it had been simple to sneak past the so-called security men and get a perfect vantage point. Unlike Sawtooth Wells, however, when only Andrew had showed up, Yellow Squirrel had had both him and his mother in his sights at Hope Valley. But then came Larson's riot, and now he was back with the marmots.

Gravel trickled from above the cave mouth. He grabbed his rifle, and ducked into the cave. He waited until the scratching and scrabbling was almost upon him before he leapt from the cave and trained his weapon uphill.

"Wing," he said, "you were almost dead."

Wing-Without-Feathers dropped lightly the last couple of feet from the canyon bank to the shelf in front of Yellow Squirrel's cave, both hands extended. Yellow Squirrel handed him the flask, watched him take a couple of swallows, then pulled it back. Wing's eyes strayed toward the roasting marmot.

"That nasty thing is all yours if you've brought me good news."

Wing smiled. "Ranch people gone," he said. "Guards. Cowboys. All gone."

Yellow Squirrel puzzled for a moment. "You said before the place only looked deserted and that everyone was hiding. But now they've really abandoned ship?" Wing nodded, reached for the flask. Yellow Squirrel held it out, did not hand it over. "Why?"

Wing shrugged. "Maxwells have big trouble." He snatched the flask from Yellow Squirrel, drained it. He handed it back, held out his palm. Distracted, absorbed, his eyes on the distant peaks, Yellow Squirrel gave him coins. Wing pocketed the money, smiled again. "You won't hurt Washoe people now?"

"You're the one who's keeping them safe, Wing, as long as I get the information I need. Remember that," Yellow Squirrel said. He lifted the spit off the forked sticks that supported the marmot and tossed the whole thing to Wing-without-feathers, who cradled it and smiled gratefully. He gnawed a bite off the haunch.

Yellow Squirrel waved him away, watched him make his way down the rocky trail, still chewing away. Before long, Yellow Squirrel had hatched his new plan of attack.

Thoughts flooded his mind, thoughts that appalled and frightened him, made him queasy, but which he couldn't stop. Maybe he should turn his back on all this. Evidently, the Maxwells were in big trouble, under attack from all directions by forces large and small. If he left right now, they'd wonder where he went, and he'd haunt them for the rest of their lives. Would he come? They'd wonder. When? They'd have to keep their guard up forever. For nothing.

But give up? No, he wouldn't be giving up, just changing tactics. Was it not better to let an enemy suffer long than give him a quick, honorable death? Would he not be a stronger and longer-lasting presence as a ghostly enemy than as a quick avenger?

The fire sputtered. The rocks were still dotted with grease and blood from the vanished marmot. He was a warrior, schooled to discipline, fasting, killing. Impure thoughts like these were white inventions, white diseases, to be purged with scourging and action.

No marmot. No food at all until this was finished. He plunged his hands into the coals and scattered them over the green boulders. "Fear me, Maxwells," he proclaimed to the echoing hills. "Fear Yellow Squirrel above all things."

FIFTY-NINE

CHANGING OF THE GUARD

"You all shouldn't be going up there tomorrow," Cooper said. "For one thing, I bet your head's still pounding to beat the devil."

Carrrie said, "I thought this was settled, Cooper." She paced the living room. Cooper and Amelia sat at the empty table.

"That was before you and Andy got shot up and all the Folsom guards disappeared and half our hands rode off," Amelia said.

"Until this campaign, it was one renegade," Cooper said, "and we had it figured out how to handle him. Now… I just don't know, Miss Carrie. I swear I don't. Without them workers, you can't sell no cows which means you can't buy hay and all what you need for the winter except on Southern Pacific credit, which means the Circle M's pretty nigh on the auction block, don't it?"

Silence. She stopped her pacing, placed her forehead against the mantel. It was pounding more than she wanted to show. "You ought to give classes in optimism, Cooper. I swear you could turn sunshine to darkness with a single word."

A tense stillness followed. Maybe if Andy were here, but he and Ling Chu had sped off to Sawtooth Wells in the Model-T to send one S.O.S. telegram to Hiram Johnson, another to Bierce, and to mail off his latest

Vendetta piece to the *Examiner*. Virginia, Many Clouds, and the children were on duty in the kitchen.

"Might I say a word?" Miller, had been fidgeting silently on the couch.

"Mr. Fitzpatrick," Carolyn said. "You know you needn't request permission to speak."

"Me and the kids, we been feeling kind of useless, so I'm thinking we could take over some of the guarding."

"Why, Willy can't even lift a carbine, let alone—" Cooper interrupted himself. "I'm going out for a smoke while you all decide how a six-year-old's going to save the ranch."

Fitzpatrick started to follow Cooper, but Amelia rose and stopped him. "Don't bother, Mr. Fitzpatrick. When he gets worked up like this, he needs some time alone. Go on and explain your idea." She sat herself on the couch beside Miller, who continued speaking.

"Naturally, we wouldn't want Willy and Maggie doing guard duty full out with rifles and the like, but they got eyes and ears and they's small enough to fit where them Folsom men couldn't never. Plus, knowing them, them kids learned the nooks and crannies around here better than anyone. Between the three of us, you could do a lot worse."

"Well, well, well," Amelia said. "You might actually have something there, Mr. Fitzpatrick."

"Indeed you might," Carrie said.

Amelia rose, took Fitzpatrick's arm and raised him to his feet. "Let's us go out and talk to Cooper. I do believe he will welcome your idea and will be persuaded in the end. At least if I have anything to say about it. And believe me, I do." They headed out the door.

However well-meaning Fitzpatrick's contribution, however much she objected to Cooper's gloomy assessment, Carrie knew that the Circle M was in trouble in exactly the manner he had described. The Southern Pacific dragon could consume the Circle M in a single bite.

SIXTY

ROOFTOP RENDEZVOUS

He wondered for a moment why he'd be out here on the roof knocking at Virginia's window, but it was really no wonder. He had stitches still throbbing in his scalp and a crucial speech coming up the next day. It might make no sense for him to be here, but it was no real mystery, either, because the throbbing in his loins easily drowned out the pulsing in his head.

So, here he was, and here she was welcoming him like he was Aladdin arrived on a magic carpet. And before long, they were spent, lying skin-to-skin under damp sheets, and his mind was drifting toward his speech the next day, but Virginia was talking, and he struggled to pay attention.

"When you think about us, Andy, what do you think about?"

"About thunder, lightning, explosions. The usual."

"No, no. Seriously."

"Didn't you hear or see any of that just now? It sounded like maybe you—"

"It was glorious." She raised up and kissed his brow. "But what about after this? Your career, mine. Our life."

"Hey, let's not get ourselves mixed up here. I'm the stoic, and you're the sybarite. Remember?"

"Nobody's one thing all the time," she said.

He wished he could dash back across the roof. "Is this really the best time for this talk?" he said.

"*This talk.* Men always say that. If you have a situation, you call a meeting, have one conversation and think everything's decided and you don't have to discuss it any more. But Andy, this isn't some kind of academic department problem, it's life. You talk about it all the time, change it while it changes you. Would an artist paint only one picture of a flower or a novelist write only one story?"

He didn't know how to respond.

"All right, then, let me draw some pictures for you." She held up her hands as if to frame an image. Then suddenly dropped them and turned to him. "By the way, I've been doing some sketching of the Circle M landscape while you were off gallivanting—"

He sat up. "Gallivanting?" he said.

She waved him off. "Just a little joke, my love. I know you got a bad knock on the head, but don't let it turn you into a sour apple." He laid back.

"Lord, Virginia, you're confusing. Now you're the jokester and I'm a sour apple."

"Anyway, I think these new sketches are quite good, especially compared to the doodlings I did around here a couple of years ago. I think you'll be impressed."

"I thought those others were very good."

"Your taste is all in your mouth, Andy. But getting back to us and our future. Here's my first picture." She reformed her fingers into a frame. "I can see a staid professor who is exasperated with his flighty wife."

"Wife?" He sat up again.

"Or…" She reshaped the frame. "I see an Indian-fighter-scholar and his eccentric and artistic mistress—"

"You want to be my mistress?"

"Flitting from opening to opening as her paintings hang in galleries worldwide. Or secluding herself on the Circle M, riding hills and forest for more inspiration for the mountain landscapes that have made her famous."

"Riding? You mean horseback?"

"Of course. You remember Daddy has a ranch in the Napa Valley. I've spent much more time in the saddle than your average faculty wife."

"Or mistress?"

She dropped her hands to her lap. "Those are just two pictures of many. All of them very entertaining."

"How many?"

"Nope, Andy. Now it's your turn."

"I don't want a turn. In the middle of all this…" he waved his hands in circles. "Why not just let things unfold as they… unfold?"

"Because waiting for things you want to happen means they never do. Would we be here right now if I hadn't written you that note, even though it took two years for you to react to it?"

"There was so much havoc—"

She sat up in bed, let the sheet fall around her waist. He tried not to look at her breasts, the nipples pert with excitement, sensing that he needed to keep his senses about him.

"See what I mean?" she said. "There's always something. Now come on, Andy. Say all this business with Yellow Squirrel and the university gets settled one way or another, what are you and I doing, in your mind?"

"You're an artist, I'm a graduate student."

"You are maddening, maddening, maddening." She flopped on to her back, speaking to the ceiling, pulled the sheet up to her chin, for which he was grateful, though he never thought he would be glad for those breasts to be hidden from him. "Not you." She held up a palm. "And me." She held up the other. "Us." She twined her fingers.

"Okay, okay," he said. He closed his eyes, cupped his hands and smoothed the air in front of him. "My turn at the crystal ball, then." He tried to imagine a face, a scene, anything. He saw nothing, but he had to at least pretend he did. "Great swami sees in your future—our future—a city house and a country house. He sees classrooms, salons, and cow manure. He sees society editors following us around town and around the range."

"Are we married?"

"Ah. Let's see. Oh, no, Great Swami apologizes, the crystal ball has clouded over."

She turned on her side, propped herself on an elbow, and looked past him to the wall. She looked into his eyes. She smiled and stroked his cheek.

He had either escaped an ambush or stepped into one. He had no idea which.

SIXTY-ONE

MARKLEEVILLE

Fifty or so people had gathered in a clearing just outside the town of Markleeville around a platform of fresh-sawn lumber that had been banged together for the occasion. Andy and Carrie rode into the scene under a bright Saturday sun. A stiff, cool breeze scooped clouds of dust from the red earth and carried the smell of burning oak and cooking meat from the two open fires where women sold fried chicken and beef stew. A collection of Stetson-topped ranchers and overalled herders crowded close to the platform, which was draped in enough bunting to make uniforms for a baseball team. More roosted on the four buckboards, a Model-T, and a chain-driven Brush Runabout parked on the outskirts of they crowd.

As they dismounted, Halstad walked up with the two assistants he had brought along. None of them had official jurisdiction, but no one could stop their acting as private citizens.

"The local sheriff's not happy with the arrangement," Halstad said. "Bill Sutter's his name. Part-time farmer, part-time lawman. He claims him and his two part-time deputies can protect you plenty."

"Mr. Sutter must be highly capable," Carolyn said.

Halstad nodded, smiled. "He did admit they might be a little undermanned if you two decide to open fire on the crowd like you did in Hope Valley."

"I'm not going to use the pistol in my speech after what happened, but I'm not going up there unarmed, either," he said. "And neither is Mom." Ideally, there would have been four or five Folsom professionals in addition to the local lawmen, but Larson had poisoned that well, and Andy had no faith in the commitment of the few left on duty. Wagons and horses continued to come, and it was more than a half-hour till the speech was to begin.

"Looks like there might be a bigger crowd than you drew in Sawtooth Wells," Halstad said.

"I wonder what it is they've come to see?" she said.

"The town was named after a man who was shot and killed. Maybe they're tired of the name and need a new victim," Andy said.

"Enough of that," Halstad said.

"I apologize for my son's macabre sense of humor." Carrie punched Andy's shoulder.

"Maxwellville? Maxwelltown? What do you think?" he said.

A young pudgy fellow in a clerk's apron approached him, hand outstretched.

"Welcome, Mr. Maxwell, Mrs. Maxwell. I'm Jason Barnes."

"Ah, yes, Mr. Barnes. I understand you're the mayor here," Andy said.

Barnes's cheeks turned to red plums when he smiled. Yes, yes. Been my cross to bear for a couple of years now. I have to get back to the store, but I heard you'd come in and wanted to assure you I'll be here to introduce you as promised."

"Do you dare, Mr. Barnes? A notorious pair like us?" Carrie said.

Nervous laughter. "Well, whatever else they may say, Ma'am, you're good for business." He gestured toward the crowd. "I'll see you at two o'clock."

Andy thought of the Circle M, under the protective umbrella of the Fitzpatricks, Virginia, Many Clouds, Ling Chu, Cooper, and Amelia. A fearsome force, augmented by a few of the older workers who had resisted whatever bribes and coercion had sent the others packing. If Yellow Squirrel didn't want to destroy the house, he could certainly get to the cattle, fenced and gathered for shipping. What if he and his mother didn't have their avenger figured out after all? And with all that going on, why was he here? Shelby had said once that when you have only bad choices, the worst choice is no action at all. You got to act. He wondered if George Custer had said that first.

"We figure Sutter ain't going to let you get shot. Not on purpose, nohow," Halstad said. "But he ain't going to worry about the nigger-yellers. So we'll try to keep all that damped down same time as we're looking out for the renegade."

Andy pulled himself out of his gloom. "Thanks, sheriff. I want to get through this alive and win a few votes in the process. Mom, you and I better split up now so he can't pick us off both at once."

She checked her pistol, kissed her son on the cheek. "You know I was reluctant, Andy, but now that we're in it, let's win it."

"If you say so," he said.

Halstad nodded and walked off into the crowd with his men. The crowd had indeed grown, become far larger than his Sawtooth Wells audience. Every one a possible vote, Andy thought, with the potential of convincing someone else who wasn't here. A seat on the board of regents, redemption for himself and Cohen and for the Coopers and Amelias of the future.

Jason Barnes suddenly appeared on stage, shedding his apron as he strode to the front of the platform. There was scattered applause, which he let build as he waved to the crowd, calling out to many people by name. Then he raised his arms, and everyone fell quickly silent.

"Afternoon, folks," Barnes said. "Today, we got our other candidate for assembly here to talk to you. Mr. Hale Gentry give us a heck of a talk last week, and now Andrew Maxwell's here to try and outdo him. It'll be quite a job of work, but we wish him luck. Come on up, Mr. Maxwell."

Barnes beckoned and Andy trotted forward. Applause was light. The wind picked up and tossed some grit into his face as he approached the stage, and he was blinking as he shook Barnes' hand at the top of the steps and made his slight bow to the crowd.

He reminded himself that he was just explaining his thoughts to his friends and neighbors. A quiet chat. But he didn't feel calm and chatty. He was angry. He had not earned whatever enmity kept people from clapping, even politely, for his appearance. His mother, of course, applauded. Beside her stood both Deborah Beasley and Joseph Francis, also clapping. Halstad and his men were too busy with their duties for such frivolities. He'd work with what he had, then.

"Thank you, Mayor Barnes. Good afternoon folks. Being I'm a rancher myself, I know you have chores to do, so I'll not take too much of your time."

Someone clapped and was hushed. "When they asked me to toss my hat in the ring—by the way, what does that mean, toss your hat in the ring? Let me show you." He spotted a bareheaded boy of about fifteen near the front of the crowd. "You, young man, what's your name?" The boy looked around. The man next to him—his father, he supposed—nudged him.

"Kyle, sir," he said.

"Well, Kyle, you look like you could use a hat. Here."

Andy tossed him his hat—a white straw with a braided horsehair band. The boy caught it, looked up at his father, who nodded, and put it on his head, grinning. The hat fell across the boy's forehead to his eyebrows. Those around him laughed.

"You're liable to catch something off that nigger's hat," a man behind Kyle said. One of Halstad's men spun him around and hustled him away before he could say another word.

"You'll grow into it, Kyle, before you know it. Now, folks, why would I pull a stunt like that? Give away a perfectly good hat? Only to illustrate why I got into this campaign. There are too many politicians in this state who get into the legislature so they can use your tax money and the Southern Pacific's bribes to get rich. Our founding fathers meant legislators to be public servants. Servants who bring you the benefits of the hard-earned money you send to Sacramento. Now, that hat will protect Kyle's head from the sun and rain, but you and his pa need other protection, too. Matter of fact I could have used some myself the other day." He pointed to the bandage on his head.

There were a few snickers. "Nigger's head's too hard to break." From the back of the crowd. The man was downed instantly, quietly. No one like Halstad.

"I got this knock on the noggin from the same railroad barons who are ready to buy up your land for a pittance when their shipping rates make it impossible for you to feed your families with the fruit of your labors."

This last remark earned him some applause. He smiled and acknowledged it with a brief wave. Some of the arms came uncrossed. People looked at one another and nodded. There were even smiles from the two hefty gents in the front row, who, to this moment, had been scowling and looking everywhere but at him. A few steps to the left of young Kyle, a bandy-legged fellow with a dark mustache and his arm in a sling nudged his neighbor and smiled. Maybe this wouldn't be such a tough crowd after all.

"Now, Mayor Barnes mentioned my opponent. I'm sure Mr. Gentry touted the virtues of the railroads and explained the benefits they bring you. Am I right?" Several heads nodded. "Of course he did, So why would you believe me and not him?"

He tried to lift his voice and eyes to the rear of the crowd, to make sure everyone could hear and feel included. A nearby movement distracted him. He turned to see the man in the sling raising his injured right arm. He thought immediately of the handkerchief-concealed pistol in the hands of President McKinley's assassin a few years earlier, but, he thought, no one would try an obvious imitation like that. The flame, smoke, and yell of, *Die, nigger*, came simultaneously.

He dropped to one knee. Pistol drawn. The crowd scattered. This time it was Sutter and his deputies who subdued the shooter. In seconds, they had him face down in the dust in front of the platform.

"Bisby, you fool, you ain't never getting out of the hoosegow after this," one of them said. As they led the culprit away, Sutter shouted back over his shoulder. "Go on, Maxwell. You'll get no more trouble now."

Carolyn was kneeling beside him as he holstered his pistol. "Are you shot?" she said.

"No, Mom." They stood and embraced. "Now get back. Let's not give Yellow Squirrel that easy shot."

"Surely you're not going to continue speaking," she said.

"A politician can't keep cutting his appearances short."

"Damn you, Andy, you—"

"Get out there now. Hurry." Reluctantly, she obeyed. He leaped back to the front of the platform. Enraged now, but knowing he couldn't show it.

"Do like sheriff Sutter says, folks. Come on back. I have a few more things to say, and the trouble's all over now. No one's hurt. Don't let a man like Bisby spoil your Saturday. What do you say? Come on."

In the back, Carrie began clapping, then Halstad and his men picked up the applause. Then Jason Barnes was beside him on the podium, applauding as well. Slowly, slowly, but ever so surely, the crowd began to coalesce again.

"Thank you, folks," Barnes said. "We're tougher around here than that little Bisby feller, aren't we?" This time the crowd applauded loudly and the volume swelled when Barnes said, "Mr. Maxwell, I return the stage to you."

Andy stepped forward. "And people wonder why I like to carry this with me," he said. He drew the pistol and looked at it and smiled. Some laughs and cheers from the assembled. "You know, Kyle's hat is one way of demonstrating how Southern Pacific has had its way with us for quite a while now. I can use this gun to show the same thing in another way."

The red, white, and blue bunting on the left side of the platform burst outward. A shot. Someone in back of the crowd fell. Mom? He found himself looking down the barrel of a rifle with Yellow Squirrel at the other end. The security force had been looking up, expecting him to attack from a tree or a rooftop. But he'd lain in wait under the platform.

Fire-streaks, explosions. Andy's pistol jumped, a blow to the head knocked him backwards and set him down. He waited for pain, but felt none. It was just that someone was tightening a cinch around his head and that everything was dark. He heard more noise, shooting. Then, a flaming rocket of pain shot through his skull. Then nothing.

SIXTY-TWO

THE PRESS

The Second Vendetta—IV

by Thomas Redmond

Many readers of The Examiner *and* The Elevator *have pored over Andrew Maxwell's description of his preparations for an attack by his family's enemy, Michael Yellow Squirrel. The attack came Saturday, and Mr. Maxwell lies incapacitated but alive in a hospital bed in Sacramento. That is why this reporter's name rather than Andrew Maxwell's appears above the words in this space. You can read of the circumstances surrounding the incident elsewhere in these pages, but we trust that our intrepid rancher-scholar turned politician will soon be ready to pen his own version of the event, and we look forward to reading it as much as the rest of our audience.*

* * *

Special to The Sacramento Union

by Harold Finch

The SECOND *Vendetta*

 Proving once more that lawlessness and anarchy follows wherever he goes, the violence-plagued campaign of Andrew Maxwell occasioned not just one but two assassination attempts in Markleeville on Saturday.

 First, Silas Bisby, a local ranch hand and former Confederate cavalryman used a gun concealed in a bandaged hand to fire on candidate Maxwell during his speech. Mr. Bisby, who was obviously mimicking the method used to kill President McKinley, though with much less success, was quickly subdued by sheriff William Sutter and charged with attempted murder. It is conjectured that Mr. Bisby's abiding resentment over the south's defeat combined with the provocation of Maxwell's racial heritage proved more than he could tolerate.

 Careless of the public safety, Mr. Maxwell resumed his speech, only to be attacked once more, this time, apparently, by the renegade Indian, Michael Yellow Squirrel, who has been rumored to be stalking the Maxwell family for some time. Yellow Squirrel succeeded in wounding both Mr. Maxwell and his mother, Carolyn Maxwell. Both were transported to Sacramento for treatment.

 Yellow Squirrel was also wounded during the exchange of gunfire between him and Mr. Maxwell, but escaped. Luckily no one in the audience was hurt. Certainly this will spell the end to Mr. Maxwell's dangerous, ill-fated campaign.

* * *

Special to The Elevator

by Deborah Beasley

 A deadly mix of politics, racism, and vengeance marked the Markleeville campaign appearance of Mr. Andrew Maxwell for the fourth district assembly seat on Saturday. As Maxwell attempted to explain his program for ending railroad tyranny over the politics and economy of California, an embittered confederate veteran identified as Silas Bisby opened fire from the audience. He hurled a racial epithet along with his bullet, but both proved ineffective, and sheriff William Sutter arrested and jailed the malefactor in short order.

 Mr. Maxwell courageously resumed his speech, but the notorious Michael Yellow Squirrel, who has been seeking to obliterate the Maxwell family and destroy their Circle M ranch, burst forth from beneath the podium and opened a volley of rifle fire. He felled Mrs. Carolyn Maxwell as well as the candidate, but not *before Mr. Maxwell's bullet wounded him, though we don't know how seriously because he somehow escaped despite his injuries.*

Both Mr. Maxwell and his mother are expected to recover before long; however, there is no word about when and if Mr. Maxwell will resume his campaign.

SIXTY-THREE

THE HOSPITAL ROOM

Wentworth Hospital was a tidy clapboard building that looked more like a private mansion than a medical facility. Clean and well-staffed, if a person had to be hospitalized, it would be hard to improve on Wentworth. But Andy felt jailed. He'd begged his mother, Amelia, and Cooper to take him home, but they'd refused, and he had to admit that their hour-long visit had left him exhausted, that he was not ready to travel. Yellow Squirrel's bullet had torn a path across one side of his face and clipped the edge of his left eye socket. Whether he'd lose the sight of his left eye remained in doubt. Not in doubt was the fact that he'd carry a souvenir scar into his future.

"We won't be going home ourselves, Andy," Amelia said. "Your mother's got us a hotel suite. I never even stayed in a hotel room, and now we got a suite." She smiled, but Cooper shot her a look, suggesting that such levity was inappropriate, and she quickly returned to her more solemn aspect.

"And with your mother's broken wing," Cooper gestured toward Carrie, standing at the foot of the bed, her left shoulder thickly bandaged, arm in a sling, "she needs to be close to a doctor, too."

"My wound is minor," she said. "Ling Chu can take care of it."

"A broken collarbone and fifty stitches?" Amelia said. "You calling that minor?"

"Compared to when Yellow Squirrel shot me two years ago, yes," she said. "And Ling Chu pulled me through that." She turned back to Andy. "The point is, it's too soon to leave you."

"I'm sorry, Mom. After all our planning, and we still didn't get him."

"You most certainly did get him," she said. "You should have seen him go down. like a sack of grain falling off a freight wagon."

"Yes, well, so did I," Andy said. She ignored his remark.

"And if we'd been up on that platform together, we'd both be dead. Your tactic of forcing him to shoot in opposite directions worked just as it was supposed to."

"And he ain't going to get far, boy. He's got at least your bullet in his leg and probably one or two more from Halstad and his men."

"But here it is two days later, and he's not dead and he's not in jail."

"He may not be in jail," Cooper said, "but don't be so sure he ain't bled to death out in the bushes somewhere."

They left, pushing their way through a knot of reporters who had gathered at his door. They responded with a terse, "no comment" to a chorus of questions.

* * *

There was a change of dressing, pain darting and swirling like flames through his scalp, a sledgehammer-pounding around his eye. An injection, sleep, dreams. He was climbing Sawtooth Peaks as he often had as a boy. Then he was scaling the Matterhorn, he and Julian. Julian was singing, jumping from rock to rock, across chasms, unhindered by the ropes or the other climbing gear that fettered Andy. Across a deep canyon, Julian waved to Many Clouds, who sat on another peak, smiling as she watched their progress. Scrambling over boulders toward Many Clouds, knife in his teeth, was Yellow Squirrel. Neither Julian nor she was aware of him. He tried to yell a warning, but he couldn't make a sound no matter how hard or how many times he tried. Finally, he managed a shout, but whether it saved Many Clouds or not, he didn't know because he was suddenly back in his hospital room.

* * *

A nurse whispered softly, "You're safe, Mr. Maxwell." Her fingers held his wrist, gently, warmly, feeling for his pulse. "Everything's going to be fine."

"She's right, my boy." The voice, vague and distant, came from the foot of the bed. It took a moment for the faces of Johnson and Lissner to come into focus.

"Do you feel up to talking to these gentlemen, Mr. Maxwell?" the nurse said. "I personally don't think they should be in here, but my supervisor insisted."

He felt groggy, would rather have waited, but he knew this couldn't be delayed. "I… yes. Okay," he said.

"Fifteen minutes," the nurse said. "No longer." She slid two extra pillows under his back, helped him slide into a sitting position, and disappeared.

"Got you trussed up proper, don't they, son? Like a calf ready to brand." Johnson approached the head of the bed, his florid cheeks and wire-rimmed spectacles floating like spotlights in the fog which was Andy's consciousness at the moment. Lissner crossed the foot of the iron bedstead and stood on the side opposite of Johnson. Things began to clear.

"I could tell you were a quick study, Andy," Lissner said. "But we never covered sharpshooting into the audience. Well done."

"Well done, indeed," Johnson said. "Your stock has gone up enormously, and once the debate—"

"Hiram," Lissner said. "Surely you can see how pale and weak this young man looks. And with that bandage? I'm not sure a debate at this point is the wisest move."

Johnson, however, forged ahead with his usual sanguinity. "What you need, my boy, is to get yourself out of here as soon as you can. Nothing makes a man sicker than being sick. What do you say to rescheduling that debate for a week from Saturday?"

"That's less than two weeks away, Hiram," Lissner said.

"And the election is less than a month away. And we have a wave of public sympathy for this young man. For his injury, yes, but most importantly for his courage. We must capitalize on that."

Andy smiled. "The debate. Yes, I've been thinking I'm not sure I want to go through with it."

Johnson leaned forward. "It's only natural to have second thoughts, son. After what you've been through. But to turn back now—"

Lissner held up a hand. "Let's hear him out, Hiram. What's bothering you, Andy?"

"What matters most?" He said. The two men looked puzzled. "In my life, I mean. What counts? I've got to take care of those things first. I'm not sure politics is the way to do it." The pounding behind his eye had resumed, if moderately.

"This is too much for now," Johnson said. "We'll be back when you feel better. We obviously have a lot to talk about."

Johnson and Lissner approached the door, solemn-faced, then donned smiles to greet the reporters who waited outside. Andy could see nothing of the politicians' approach to the journalists, but he heard Johnson's smiling tenor declare, "The boy's looking great. He'll be ready to rope calves and ride bulls in no time. You can write that we're rescheduling the Hale Gentry debate for a week from Saturday, and nothing will keep him off that platform." Then the door closed and the voices dissolved into an incoherent murmur.

It could very well be you yourself, Hiram, that keeps me off that platform, he thought.

SIXTY-FOUR

ROUNDUP

Many Clouds jabbed her heels into the horse's flanks, hazing a calf toward the branding pen as Virginia drove its mother toward the other end of the corral. She had to admit Virginia could ride a horse. And she wasn't afraid to work. You'd never have guessed it to see her wandering around amid the work and danger in her strange clothes with her sketch pad, oblivious to all but the pictures she was drawing. She said she'd learned riding on an English saddle, but she'd taken to the western outfit as if born to it. Neither of them had known anything about handling cattle, but Miller had taught them a few basics, and the well-trained cutting horses were doing the rest.

Thanks to Hiram Johnson's influence, the Folsom guards had returned to the ranch, but the defecting cowhands had stayed away. Miller, Many Clouds, and Virginia had decided to do what they could to help the few remaining employees complete the dusty tasks that were the lifeblood of a cattle ranch like the Circle M. The herds driven en mass from the summer range had to be culled of animals that would be shipped and sold—fattened steers were the moneymakers, but older bulls and cows no longer fit for breeding would bring in some cash. New calves needed branding. Most of the young bulls had to be castrated. Some would be left whole for breeding. Animals that would not be shipped needed herding to carefully selected winter range—grassy in the fall for grazing, easy of access for delivery of hay once snow covered the grass.

The first crew had completed many of these jobs before they debarked, but there was still plenty of sweaty work left to do. Maggie and Willy pitched in like the troupers they were, scurrying back and forth to open and close the gates that allowed the calves into and out of the branding pen. Willy first spotted the smoke.

"Something's burning. Over yonder hill," he yelled.

All work stopped. Men climbed atop the fences to get a better look, but could see nothing more than a burgeoning swell of distant black. The California Mediterranean climate included several months of drought each year. September and October came near the end of that drought and were both the warmest and driest periods on the calendar, the time when fire was feared most. Flames on the range or in the forest could destroy the work of years and make recovery impossible for years after that. In no situation was the idea of mutual assistance even among sworn enemies as ingrained as it was here.

Everyone on a horse headed out immediately in the direction of the smoke. Many Clouds was certain what they'd find when they got there, and the knowledge chilled her soul.

SIXTY-FIVE

FAIR WARNING

The whole right side of Yellow Squirrel's lower body was an aching, throbbing stump. Maxwell's bullet had torn through his thigh, ripping muscle and flesh its path. What hurt even worse at the moment was the wound in his buttock, the one he thought for a moment was going to stop him as he ran from the scene of the shooting. That bullet was still in there, bumping up against a bone. The thigh wound he thought he could handle with a tourniquet and poultices of herbs. But he had to get that bullet out, and he couldn't do it himself. No white doctor. Even at gunpoint, he couldn't trust one of them not to poison him.

It had taken him two stolen horses and four days to arrive here at the Washoe village, where he'd planned to have Ling Chu kidnapped and brought to him. But the village was deserted. Even Wing was nowhere in sight. Too bad. The little Chinaman had prodigious healing skills, and he knew what would happen to his precious Circle M if he tried anything. Of course, the Circle M would fare none too well in any case, and he would probably suspect as much, but he wouldn't take any chances. Now Yellow Squirrel would have to seek the old man out for himself. First, though, this village.

He dismounted, a bit woozy, he supposed from loss of blood, lowered himself gently to the ground, dragged his stiff and painful leg to the communal fire pit and tested the ashes. Cold. An inspection of two of the wikiups showed that the tribe had left hastily. Scraping and sewing tools remained. They were planning to come back. Well, they might have saved themselves for the moment, but they had been advised of what would happen if they sided with the Maxwells.

Pain stabbed his rear. To go back to Wind River with an injury like this. A coward's wound. At least that's how the other warriors would think of it, a hurt incurred running from an enemy. He knew from past experience that he was a quick healer, so he had no doubt he'd be able to return by spring. But he'd wanted to go home now, before the snows, in triumph.

He found a tattered basket and filled it with dry pine needles. There were eleven huts and a sweat lodge. Soon, he'd piled fuel on the floor of every one. Such hot sun. Yellow Squirrel had to rest before he completed the final task. He sat on the stones beside the communal fire, cursing his weakness.

"Hey, nonny, nonny," came from behind him.

He spun and drew his knife. He'd left his rifle on the horse. Further proof that he wasn't thinking clearly. "What do you want?" he said.

"God has given you one face," she said, "and you make yourself another."

"I have nothing to do with your god."

"Of course you do," she said.

He stood, sheathed his knife. "Get out of here. I have work to do." He picked up a length of wood and began lashing a bundle of pine needles to one end. "On second thought, stay. You can spread the story of what happens to anyone who tries to fight me." He drew a flint and steel from a buckskin bag at his waist.

"Those who don't fight you fare much worse, Michael Yellow Squirrel," she said.

He unsheathed the knife, held it by the blade as if to throw it. "Go away, old lady."

She held her arms toward him. "I'm not your tormentor, Yellow Squirrel. Neither is Carrie. Neither is Andy."

He returned the knife to the sheath. Why would he pull a knife on this dried up old apple, even if she was a Maxwell? He bent to the job of lighting his makeshift torch. The sparks did their job quickly in the dry heat. He stood and limped toward the sweathouse. Might as well start with the biggest hut.

"You can burn the whole world, Yellow Squirrel, but you will still live in anguish."

Again, the voice came from behind him. Again, he spun around, yanked out his knife. He'd had enough of this old witch. Then he felt silly. His knife was poised, but the village was empty. He was alone with his burning branch. The way it should be.

SIXTY-SIX

FIRING RANGE

Carolyn had shown her where the key to the gun cabinet was hidden, and Many Clouds decided there was no better time to arm herself than right now. She pulled out a standard Winchester .30-.30 and an old-fashioned .44 pistol. Weapons she was used to. Ironically, it was her uncle who had seen to her firearms training. He generally adhered to the doctrine that women belonged in the teepee or at the skinning rack, but when it came to opposing the white man, especially using his own weapons against him, Yellow Squirrel believed every Indian should be prepared, women included. He'd been delighted when Many Clouds expressed an interest. She'd see how delighted he was now.

She gathered the children behind the house, facing a small knoll where ground squirrels romped in profusion. Her uncle had preferred to use living things as targets rather than inanimate objects. The object was not just accuracy, he explained, but killing, and you didn't get that feeling by shooting at cans and twigs.

"Watch," she said. Her first rifle shot knocked a squirrel into the air, sent him to a hard landing halfway into the entrance of his hole. Suddenly he became, a small patch of fur swirling in the breeze. Her second caught another in the head as he dived away from the first crack of the gun.

"Jeez," Maggie said. "You're as good as Pa. Maybe better."

"Now you," Many Clouds handed the rifle to her.

"Pa don't allow us to touch no guns, Maggie," Willy said.

"This here's special circumstances, Willy, don't you reckon?"

"Pa don't allow—"

"He would if he was here, but he ain't." Maggie tried to hold the rifle to her shoulder as Many Clouds had, but her arms were too short to reach the forestock, and she wasn't strong enough to hold the barrel up.

"You're going to need a rest, I guess," Many Clouds said. I was older than you when I started, but others of us used them, so here." She pulled up an empty ammunition box and had the girl kneel behind it.

Many Clouds taught them patience, how to wait till the squirrels climbed out of their holes after taking cover from the sound of shots. How to use the sights, how squeeze on the trigger rather than jerking so that their aim remained steady, how to roll with the kick of the weapon instead of fighting it and incurring unnecessary bruises or even broken bones. After an hour or so, they hadn't accounted for a lot of dead squirrels, but they'd come close, and most important, their fear of guns had turned into respect and an expectation of mastery.

"Don't worry about telling your pa," Many Clouds said. "I'll do that. I expect he'll understand the necessity. Now, let me show you how to clean and oil these guns. It's just as important as learning how to pull the trigger."

SIXTY-SEVEN

LING CHU'S KITCHEN

Yellow Squirrel had learned the story of Ling Chu's cot from his interrogation of Many Clouds. Carolyn had offered many times over the years to build him a separate room or even a cabin, but Ling had insisted on sleeping in his little corner in the kitchen where he could see and protect his domain. Yellow Squirrel had spent an agonizing day waiting for the house to go dark. The pain was no longer confined to his leg. His whole body pulsed with it. Spirits stole his thoughts and carried them aloft, through tormenting storms, fire streaming down like rain, himself drenched, burning, unsheltered.

The night before, he'd watched everyone returning late from fighting his Washoe fire, amused to see them straggling through the archway, heads and shoulders drooping with fatigue. If it wasn't so dark, he was sure he'd be even more amused to see the soot smeared all over their clothes and skin. He'd have gone after Ling Chu then, but it was uncertain how much time he'd have. The next night they'd be in bed early, sleep more soundly. More time for the job that needed to be done.

The guards stood on the rooftops and wandered the yard with their bull's eye lanterns, which did more to announce their presence than to reveal intruders. Even as lame as he was, he knew he'd have no trouble getting past them, sneaking into the kitchen, and crawling up to the sleeping man's cot just as he was doing at that moment. He clapped a hand over Ling Chu's mouth, then pressed his full body atop the cot. Ling Chu stiffened and his eyes widened in surprise. However, he did not struggle, and there seemed to be no horror in his eyes. That was not a good sign, that lack of fear. From his back pocket, Yellow Squirrel with an uninterrupted motion pulled a bandanna from his pocket, lifted his hand away from Ling Chu's mouth and inserted the bandanna as a gag.

    He whispered, "I have some doctoring for you to do. I'm going to get up and light that lamp right there. You're going to stay quiet and still while I explain things to you, then you're going to get to work. Do everything just right, or this whole place will disappear just like that Washoe town. Nod that you understand." Ling Chu did so. Too calmly for Yellow Squirrel's taste. Why was the little guy so relaxed? Maybe it was all to the good. He'd need a steady hand to pull out that slug and sew everything up. And Yellow Squirrel knew it was going to take all the powers of endurance he could summon to stand the pain.

SIXTY-EIGHT

FLOUTING THE DOCTORS

This time, there'd be a real stage instead of just a wagon bed. The platform for the next day's debate was being erected directly outside Halstad's office and would be large enough to hold any number of dignitaries. Pine pitch and freshly sawn lumber overwhelmed even the smell of horse droppings in the street.

"Looks like everyone wants in on the act now, Mom," Andy said as Cooper pulled their buggy up before Gilligan's place.

"Now that you're a big celebrity," she said.

"Now that they think they ain't going to get shot at, you mean," Cooper said. He drove the team from a bench seat at the front of the wagon, Amelia beside him, while Andy and Carrie shared a thinly upholstered seat in the back.

"Where's Ling Chu?" Amelia said. "He was supposed to meet us, warn't he?"

For a moment, Andy was relieved. They'd found the softest-springed vehicle they could in Placerville, and it rode considerably more comfortably than the Model-T. Even so, his head was bursting with pain, and he'd hours ago decided he'd been stupid to insist on coming back to the Circle M to spend the night before the debate. He should have listened to the doctors. Right now he not only couldn't imagine his headache disappearing by tomorrow. He couldn't imagine it disappearing ever. Then his mother spoke, and his relief changed to anxiety.

"Yes, Amelia, he was," Carrie said, "and he never misses a chance to drive that car, and he's always on time."

"This team's about wore out," Cooper said. "We'll make better time if I change them. Amelia, get on over to Halstad's office and tell him we got an emergency."

"On the other hand, you know that car's always breaking down," Carrie said.

Andy sat back in his seat, reached over to fold his mother's hand in his. "I knew Yellow Squirrel wouldn't kill that easily, Mom. And think of the defenseless people out there—Many Clouds, the children."

"Ling Chu, Virginia," she said.

"I know. Of course, there are the guards…"

"You know Yellow Squirrel's never had any trouble getting past them, Andy."

Amelia rushed back to the wagon, just as Cooper finished hitching up a new pair of horses. "Mr. Halstad, he's gone out because that Washoe village burned up and Gilligan went with him as a deputy. Won't be back till tonight."

"I guess we don't need any more proof that Yellow Squirrel's still on the rampage, do we?" Andy said.

Cooper disappeared into the barn, returned presently with two rifles. "These was in the tack room," he said. "I done told Feifer a dozen times he ought to lock them up, but this is one time I'm glad he's careless." He handed one rifle to Amelia, kept the other for himself. "Ain't neither one of you two up to shooting right now," he said to Carrie and Andy.

"Let's hope none of us has to," he said. He transferred his sidearm from his hip to his lap.

"Amen," Carrie and Amelia said in unison.

Cooper had the fresh team at a trot before they even got out of the town limits.

SIXTY-NINE

ANOTHER BURN

It was five miles, just short of an hour, from Sawtooth Wells to the Circle M archway. Couldn't they go any faster? He knew the answer was no. The team was cantering now, a risky pace as it was. As side roads like this one went, the surface was good, but it was graded only once a year, in the spring, and a wheel hitting a rock or hole at the wrong angle could put them afoot in an instant.

He checked his grandfather's watch, though there was no real need. He knew the landmarks—they were passing the Crabtree cabin at the moment—as well as he knew his own name.

"Smoke," yelled Cooper as they topped a small rise. He didn't point, but slapped the reins and urged the horses to a gallop.

Carrie and Andy leaned forward and saw the black swirl rising and swelling from the direction of the Circle M. For the first time since Yellow Squirrel's return, he felt true fear. The house? The barn? And who was inside whatever building was burning?

They sped down the slope and around a curve, affording them a full view of a short straightaway. A hundred yards ahead, a rider headed in their direction at full speed. Amelia raised her rifle.

"It's Virginia," Andy yelled. Amelia lowered her gun. That unmistakable blonde hair, unfettered by hat or turban, flew around Virginia like a halo as she goaded her mount to even greater speed. She was riding bareback, only a hackamore for reins, yet she was in full control of her animal, a pinto cutting horse named Pebble, and was pushing him to the maximum. So much for the delicate-maiden image Andy had carried in his head for so long.

She began waving when she saw the wagon, and Cooper reined the team to a halt.

"Yellow Squirrel," she said breathlessly. Her horse was prancing, skipping in circles.

"What's burning?" Carrie said.

"The house," Virginia said. "Oh, God I never imagined how ugly and awful, as if I was looking the devil in the face."

"Girl," said Cooper, "you making no sense."

"What happened, Virginia? Quickly," Carrie urged.

Virginia calmed her horse, an act which seemed to calm her somewhat as well. "We all came to breakfast as usual, but Ling Chu wasn't there. No coffee, no eggs, no nothing. And everything smelled like gasoline. Mr. Fitzpatrick went to look in the kitchen…" She looked to the sky, breathed deeply. "We were all watching him, when we heard Willy yell, then all of a sudden there was Yellow Squirrel behind us and he was holding Willy up by the arm, all twisting and squirming. He had a knife at that little boy's throat." She shook her head and tears flowed.

"Next thing, he made us all go into the kitchen. Ling Chu was tied up and gagged on his cot. Yellow Squirrel told us to stay there and he'd be watching and if we tried anything it would be the end of Willy, then he backed out the door, still holding on to the boy. Mr. Fitzpatrick must have thought he saw an opening of some sort, I guess. Anyway, he jumped at him, and my God, Andy, you should have told me."

"Told you what? What happened."

"Told me what he was like. It was so savage. As if he was glad for the chance to kill. I don't know why Mr. Fitzpatrick thought he could beat him, but instead he ran right up on the knife. Right up on it, and that Indian butchered him. Not just stabbed him. You have no idea."

"Keep going," Carrie said.

"It was Willy made the rest of it happen. He jumped out of Yellow Squirrel's arms like a bird and just kind of flew away. Yellow Squirrel started chasing him, but he was limping too bad to catch him, and we all scattered. We yelled to the guards, and they ran toward the house, but Yellow Squirrel shot down all three of them before they got ten steps. I ran to the barn and jumped on Pebble. Flames were shooting from the windows before I got out of the yard."

"Is Yellow Squirrel still there?" Andy said.

"You can bet on it," Cooper said.

Virginia said, "He knew you were coming back today. He said this was the end of the Maxwells and their ranch and he should have started here in the first place."

"So he's given up on the idea of a public spectacle," Carrie said. "Now we're moths come to immolate ourselves on his pyre."

Virginia said, "He said something about that too. That gasoline was the white man's invention and he'd die by it."

"Amelia," Cooper said, "you drive this wagon back to the Crabtrees. Virginia, you follow them. I'm taking off across this here field. Ten to one, he'll be watching the road for you all and I'll be able to get the jump on him from behind. Might even be able to team up with Many Clouds. She's got plenty of moxie, that one."

"No more moxie than me," Virginia said. "Just give me one chance—"

"Hold it, hold it," Andy said. "This is the Maxwell Ranch and a Maxwell problem. First of all, everyone in this valley is bound to head straight for the fire in no time at all. Amelia, Mom, and the wagon stay right here to head them off. We want no one else dead on our account.

"Cooper, it's a good idea for you circle up behind the house just as you said. Virginia, I'll ride double behind you, and we'll take the trail to behind the barn. I hate to have you in this, but I've got to admit I'm not up to handling that horse myself. Once we're there, we can get to the hayloft where we can see the whole yard and take it from there."

"What if he's already up there waiting?" Cooper said.

"I grew up playing around that barn, Coop. He'll never know we're coming."

"Andy," Carrie said, "you're operating with one eye and a massive headache and you're weak as a puppy."

"You know my eyesight's improving every day, and I can sure see a target as big as Yellow Squirrel, and I'm plenty strong enough to pull a trigger. No time for arguments, now." He climbed to the rail of the buggy. "Come on over here, Virginia," he said. "I need a lift."

SEVENTY

RIDING INTO TROUBLE

The distance was short, but it was in many ways the longest ride he'd had ever taken. Without stirrups to support him, he lay victim to every twist and bump of the horse's gait. Snuggling up to Virginia should have been a delight, but there was nothing romantic about this situation. She was no more sensuous for him now than a fencepost.

"Where did you learn to ride like this?" he said.

"You know."

"The Napa ranch? You always said you were training for dressage or something sissy like that."

"For a professor, you're dreadfully innocent," she said. *Naïve. Innocent. He was acquiring quite a reputation for cluelessness.*

He said nothing, though he acknowledged in his aching, pain-filled head that she was absolutely right.

* * *

They could see flames wrapped like a blanket around the part of the house they could see by the time they approached the barn from the uphill side. Was the whole house like that? And what of the shots they'd heard? The smell of incinerating wood mixed with the odors of burning gasoline and flesh. He hoped that last came from Ling Chu's pantry, not from any trapped or dead human beings. More than a building, this was the house of Maxwell Carter's dreams and his legacy, a symbol of what human effort and ingenuity could accomplish, given free rein. Soon it would be grey ash. At the moment, though, Andy was more concerned about who rather than what was turning to ashes.

Though the barn was nearly forty feet high at the roof, the elevation uphill on its backside made it possible to approach the building from a height above the roof. A trail curled around the foundation and into the yard, so there was about a twenty-foot gap between the hillside and the top of the building. Too far to jump, but some long, sturdy limbs had long served as bridges for Andy and Julian as they played their cowboys and Indians and explorer games. The branches would serve for far more serious adult games now. The problem here was that Andy knew he was too weak to climb the ten feet or so to where the limb branched off the trunk.

"You don't have to lift me," he told Virginia. "Squat down and I'll stand on your shoulders, and you'll just stand up. Your legs are plenty strong enough, and that should give me plenty of height."

"Then what?' she said.

"Then I go after Yellow Squirrel while you take Pebble back to the buggy and wait with Mom and Amelia."

"Sure," Virginia said.

There was something in her tone he didn't like, but he had to move on. She squatted obediently at the bottom of the tree, her back to the trunk. He stepped up on her shoulders, facing the tree, held on for a minute to forestall a surge of dizziness, then said, "Okay."

She stood quickly, and he found himself neck high with his chosen limb. Ordinarily, it would have been a short leap to its topside, but now it was a struggle. Once he finally made it, vertigo forced him to lie prone for a few moments. He must have passed out for a while because the next thing he heard was, "Hey, wake up and move over."

Virginia was draped across the limb at his feet, and he had no idea how she'd gotten there.

"How—"

"In addition to our sissy dressage we did some sissy trick riding up there in Napa, so I know how to stand up on a horse. I figured if you're going to fall asleep on the job you needed some help."

He looked down to see Pebble tethered at the foot of the tree. "You jump right back on that horse and—" He interrupted himself, decided it would be better to save his strength for the enemy. "Okay, okay. See that ladder nailed to the roof?" she nodded. "It's there to make access easier when there's a leak or something to fix. Right at the top, at the peak, there's a hatch, a panel of sheet metal. We lift it off. Lift, not slide. No noise. When we drop through, we'll land on a bed of hay bales. They're stacked up high this time of year. Next, we crawl forward till we see the sliding door where the hay gets loaded in and out. It's a perfect spot for watching the house and yard. If Yellow Squirrel's there, we've got him." He patted his hip where his pistol was holstered. "If he's not, we've got ourselves a perfect lookout. He has to come out there some time."

"I'm with you, partner," she said. She leaned forward and kissed his cheek. Andy wobbled for a moment.

"Whoa, there," he said, recovering. "This is as easy as falling off a log."

SEVENTY-ONE

HUNTING WILLY

Many Clouds and Maggie had fled out the back door, right behind Virginia, when Yellow Squirrel turned his attention to Willy. Virginia sprinted toward the barn, but Many Clouds feared the exposure of all the open space she'd have to cross with Maggie in tow, so she opted to run toward the corrals, then to take cover under the bunkhouse. They heard rifle fire and saw the Folsom guards stagger and drop to the ground. They'd just ducked behind a watering trough when they heard a loud whoosh from within the house.

"What was that?" Maggie said.

"He's burning the place. That was the gasoline we smelled."

"What about Willy?"

"I don't know about him, but I do know about Ling Chu, and I've got to get him out of there."

"But Willy—"

"I'll look for him, too. Get in the trough."

"It's dirty."

"Hold your breath as long as you can, then get back under. No one will look for you there."

"But you—"

"Get in." She pushed her over the brink, and the girl splashed softly into the trough. "I'll be back," she said, and Maggie took a deep breath and plunged under the surface.

Many Clouds felt like a lizard scampering on her belly and knees and elbows through the dust to the kitchen door. She slid inside and came face-to-face with Ling Chu. He had turned over the cot to which he was bound and managed to drag himself and the cot almost to the door. Yellow Squirrel wasn't in sight. She'd worked in the kitchen long enough to know where the knives were, and it wasn't long before she had Ling Chu's gag off and begun sawing at his ropes.

"Willy?" she said.

"Don't know," he said. "We look."

They opened the door to the living room, but the air was blistering hot, the fire an orange curtain, and they closed the door immediately. They circled out the kitchen door to the only other rear door, the one to the hallway next to the office. Looking through the window, they could see the office hadn't been engulfed yet, but that it soon would be.

They looked under the steps and under the house for Willy. Nothing. They couldn't call out for fear of attracting Yellow Squirrel's attention. Wherever he was.

Many Clouds knelt on the top step of the short stairway, reached for the handle. Ling Chu grabbed her wrist.

"Hot," he whispered. "Locked."

"Guns." She whispered.

Ling Chu twisted his way into the crawl space underneath the house and came back with a ring of keys. He held one up. "Office," he said. He whipped off his shirt and wrapped it around his hand. Many Clouds appreciated how much it must have cost this modest little man to expose himself so. He used another key to open the deadbolt, handed Many Clouds the key ring, then twisted the knob with his covered hand and pushed.

Many Clouds lunged through the door, staying as close to the floor as she could, kicked the door shut behind her. The momentary opening had sucked oxygen-hungry flames down the hall, scalding her lungs and skin. Her closing of the door stayed the onslaught, but this was no place for a human being. What air there was was too hot to breathe. She'd have to get in and get out with the one breath she was holding.

Still on the floor, she reached up and unlocked the office door. She had planned to break a window pane and reach inside for the knob, but the key was much better. Once in the office, she found that the key to the gun case was not in its proper place. She looked around frantically. How much longer could she hold her breath? On the floor under the chair. Why? No matter. She picked it up and crossed to the case. Already unlocked. Yellow Squirrel. But he already had guns. Maybe he needed ammunition. All these thoughts raced through her mind as she grabbed all she could and headed for the window. The pane was raised, Ling Chu outside waving frantically. She tossed out two rifles, two pistols, and dove through the open window.

Outside, she lay on the ground, gasping, coughing, burning. Ling Chu was beating her with his shirt. She looked at herself and realized why—her dress had been smoldering. Back to the trough in a hurry.

SEVENTY-TWO

HAY

Progress over the hay bales was slow because they were trying to be so quiet. Plus Virginia had to keep stopping to sneeze. Why had she saved her hay fever till now? He also had to stop to regain strength and clear his dizziness. They crawled in darkness, which meant that the loading door at the barn's front was not open, or only partially so. It meant nothing as far as whether Yellow Squirrel lurked near the door or not.

Finally, he reached out to drag himself forward and grabbed a handful of air. They had come to the forward edge of the stack. The bales would be arranged in stair-steps, about eight or ten bales deep from here to the loft floor. He could see now that light traced the slight gap between the barn walls and the fully-closed rectangular door, a flickering light with an orange cast created by the flames outside.

He signaled Virginia to stop. Yellow Squirrel was almost certainly not here. He would have wanted to keep a watch, and he couldn't do that through a closed door. But to be sure, he yelled, "Yellow Squirrel," then rolled three times to the right in case he drew fire. No shots. Great, though the rolling had exacerbated his vertigo and cost him precious seconds to recover. Virginia was at his side when the world righted itself.

"So much for silence," she said.

He didn't answer, led her down the haystack to the door. He grabbed a handle and rolled the door open a few inches. He felt Virginia peering over his shoulder as they gazed down at the yard.

Three men lay still in the dust. The Folsom guards. The house was indeed swaddled in fire, and the fire was creating its own winds and updrafts, smoke and sparks now sweeping across the yard, now shooting straight up like a fiery geyser. The bunkhouse roof smoldered where a vagrant gust had tossed an ember, and the sawmill shed was about to ignite from the same cause. Would everything go? The barn roof was metal, but that was still no assurance it would escape.

Movement. He raised his pistol. Many Clouds. Ling Chu? Yes. Ling Chu running, bare-chested. He'd never expected to see that. Carrying firearms, yet. He and Many Clouds flattened themselves behind a watering trough. And Maggie rolled out of the water like a beached fish. The little group seemed safe for the moment, but they were exposed from three directions, and where was Yellow Squirrel? Many Clouds turned her head now and pointed toward the bunkhouse, gathered herself to run once more, then saw flames begin to break out on its roof. Flattened herself again.

There was a lot of crawl space under that building, but if it burned, it was no shelter. He put himself in Many Clouds' place. The barn was a bad bet, with all the open ground they'd have to cover. Virginia had been lucky to get here at all, let alone get away on Pebbles. Yellow Squirrel must have been too preoccupied with the guards to deal with her. Andy's mind sped through the possibilities, then he knew where to find him.

He also knew how to thwart him, but he was too weak to do it himself. He'd have to send Virginia. He outlined his plan. She nodded, smiled, kissed him on the lips. He kissed her hand. Then she clambered up the haystack and back in the direction they'd come. He took up his post at the hayloft door.

There was new dust in the near distance. He'd known Mom and Amelia would be able to hold off the neighbors only so long. It wouldn't take much of a breeze in this dry country to lift sparks and embers to surrounding buildings. Dry stubble stood in a harvested wheat field across the road. If that caught, other farms might become involved. Everyone in the valley had a stake in keeping the flames from spreading. And so did he. Well, let the people come. If this idea worked, it would be over by the time they got here. And it had better work. He was tired of things not working.

SEVENTY-THREE

VIGIL

Two tack room windows provided Yellow Squirrel separate views of the archway into the Maxwell yard. They were really glassless miniature doors, one high on the east wall, one on the north. They opened right around the corner from one another, so he had excellent angles.

He couldn't see most of the rest of the yard, though. For that reason, he'd rather have been in the loft. But that had its disadvantages, too. The long distance to his getaway horse, for example, lame as he was. Here, not more than twenty yards distant from the bridge, he'd be able to call out the names of his targets. *Andrew Maxwell*, he'd say. *Carolyn Maxwell*. They'd know exactly who was sending the bullets that finished them. Once they lay dead, his horse stood only a few steps away, and he'd be out of the yard before anyone realized he was even there.

It wasn't quite the circus show he'd first envisioned, but the Maxwells would be just as dead, and the spectacular fire would attract an audience from far and wide. Leaving all those others unscathed bothered him some, but two children and a woman—the old Chinaman was charcoal by now—not worth worrying about. It had been a mistake to try getting him to extract the bullet while in the kitchen. Lots of hidden knives there, and he'd cut himself loose the second Yellow Squirrel's back was turned. Loose or not, though, he could never have gotten out of the inferno.

What bothered him most was the boy. He'd hoped to take him back to Wind River and raise him like a warrior. He had read his spirit, knew his Indian blood dominated his white blood. His heart would be wasted with

Fitzpatrick and the women. He'd proved himself when Fitzpatrick had so stupidly attacked. Yellow Squirrel had loosened his grip ever so slightly while he was dealing with the father, and the boy was away. Well, good for him. If he escaped the fire, it would be a fine idea to return in the spring and take him back to Wind River. A wave of pain sluiced through him. Ling Chu had stopped the bleeding at least, but there was still a lot of healing to be done. He shifted position to stop the hurting.

One of the windows banged shut. His first thought was the wind, but when he pushed against it, it wouldn't give. Latched from the outside. No escape that way. Then the other window slammed. Yellow Squirrel sprang through the tack room door and headed toward the barn's main entrance. Cautiously, he peeked around the doorjamb, first one way, then the other. Saw nothing. Then from deep inside the barn, an explosion and wood splintered a couple of feet from his head. Someone shooting from inside the barn.

His instinct shoved him away from the direction of the bullet, out the doorway into the yard, his rifle pointed back into the barn's dark maw. After that, several things happened fast—almost simultaneously. Yellow Squirrel realized that stepping out of the cover of the barn was probably a mistake. An Arapaho war cry—Ayeeeiii—sounded from his right. A yell—*Yellow Squirrel*—sounded from above. A terrific burn sliced through his neck into his chest, and a sledgehammer-like blow to his ribs knocked him sideways to the left. He felt himself hit the ground, but he couldn't recall falling.

SEVENTY-FOUR

OVER?

From the hayloft loading door, Andy watched Yellow Squirrel drop, then lie quietly, unbelievably, in the dust. He reached and grabbed the block and tackle that was always in place for loading and unloading hay, stepped on to the hook, and lowered himself to the ground. He approached the Indian carefully, skeptically, pistol ready. He kicked the rifle yards away, looked for other weapons. The knife.

He approached from behind, pulled the knife from its sheath and secreted it in his own belt. He toed the body, turned it face down. The dust around it was turning muddy with blood, but he saw nothing else that could be used to attack. No surprises, then. He toed the body again, so that the countenance that had haunted his life lay open to the heavens, tranquil as a sleeping child's. He holstered his weapon and knelt near that face he hated. Yet, it was hard to hate something that seemed so unthreatening. Illusions.

"Yellow Squirrel," he yelled. "Michael Yellow Squirrel. Are you still there?" The eyes opened, fluttered, opened. There was life in them, but barely. "You're still alive. Good. I wanted to make sure you knew it was over. You're done."

Yellow Squirrel's face contorted. Andy bent closer. Yellow Squirrel spat straight at his face. But it was a weak attempt, traveled barely an inch before it fell back on the cheek of the spitter, who tried to raise a hand to wipe it off, but failed. And the eyes closed for good.

With the spit dribbling down the corpse's cheek, Andy's anger at Yellow Squirrel and the horror he had wreaked returned in force. The very sight revolted him. He laid his hat over his dead enemy's face and stood.

Virginia stood beside him. Looking down at the remains of the fearsome enemy.

"Thank you," Andy said. "Without you… Thank you."

Many Clouds walked up, her step tentative, rifle at her side, something like fear in her eyes. He extended a hand to her. She took it, trembling.

"My own uncle." She said. "I shot my own uncle." She lifted her eyes to his.

"You're very brave," he said. Their eyes met, igniting a moment of communion almost identical to the one they'd shared when she'd dressed his wounds after the Hope Valley fracas. This time, too, the swell of emotion caught him off guard. No time or place for this. Many Clouds shook her head slightly, squeezed his hand, drew hers back. She knelt, laid down her weapon, placed her hands above, not quite touching, the body. She began a low keening, swaying back and forth. Virginia stepped forward, laid an awkward hand on Many Clouds' shoulder, shifted her gaze to Andy.

He turned and tried to take in the surrounding scene. The space around Yellow Squirrel was like the eye of a cyclone. Outside the eye, conflagration. Part of the house's roof collapsed, crackling and thundering. Flames engulfed the bunkhouse. Men, horses, wagons poured over the bridge and through the archway. Men and women formed bucket brigades. Across the yard from the corrals came Cooper, carrying Maggie, Ling Chu at his side.

"Squirrel man think I burn, but me and Many Clouds faster than fire, you bet," Ling Chu said.

"It was still too close, Ling," Andy said. "I'm glad you're safe."

Inside the eye, Many Clouds continued her grieving, Virginia her support. Amelia and his mother had arrived, stood hand in hand, staring at the body. Willy stood at Many Clouds' shoulder, opposite Virginia, a pistol almost as long as his leg hanging by his side. So it was his shot that had startled Yellow Squirrel into the clear? Where had he learned to handle that weapon? The boy dropped his pistol and ran to Many Clouds, then collapsed, sobbing, his arms wrapped around her waist.

They had rid themselves of the all-consuming threat to their very existence, but, Andy realized, his life had suddenly become much more complicated.

SEVENTY-FIVE

LOOKING FORWARD, LOOKING BACK

"This don't make no sense," Feifer said. "Between our house and the livery stable we can make you all snug and comfy. Why stay out here in the dust and smoke?" He gestured toward the remains of the ranch house, the bunk house.

In days to come, Carrie would wonder why they had declined Feifer's invitation. No one else would be able to explain it either, but they were unanimous. She supposed they had needed to cling to the familiar for a while, even if the familiar no longer existed. But that explanation seemed facile. They did accept blankets and a little food and drink, but they were paradoxically grateful when Feifer drove his wagon out of the twilit yard and headed toward town.

Embers glowed, occasionally snapped, in the wreckage. Except for a singeing of the sawmill shed, no other buildings had been damaged. The air stank of wood smoke, wet charcoal, and something else Carolyn couldn't identify at first. Feathers? Yes, from the bedding. But the rest was an undifferentiated cloud of repulsive odors. All that remained of her parents'—her own—years of work and dreams was a stench. Yet she could summon up not a sob or a tear. The pain was too deep for crying. In time, perhaps.

Around the campfire, they squatted on odds and ends of furniture and boxes they had scraped together from the barn and other outbuildings. Talk was spare. Willy and Maggie couldn't stop crying, holding tight to Many Clouds. Some fool had left their father's charred skeleton uncovered for them to discover. Hadn't it been enough to witness his murder? They'd be crying to the end of their days, and who could blame them?

"Amelia, darling," Cooper said. This tender remark from Cooper startled her. He never spoke to anyone like this, at least in public. "We could squeeze everyone in our cabin, you know."

"And you're all welcome," Amelia said.

Everyone smiled, shook their heads, just as they had at Feifer. Except the children, who hadn't heard, or weren't listening. She knew that her brother- and sister-in-law felt part of this group, would be leaving their cabin empty and sleeping under the stars with everyone else.

Carolyn's arm with the Markleeville wound still hurt her, especially at night, and sitting on a straightback chair on uneven ground aggravated the pain. She couldn't imagine what Andy must be suffering with an injury many degrees greater than hers and with all he'd been through. And all he had yet to go through, for he'd stubbornly refused to call off the debate, just as she and everyone else had refused to leave the ranch this night.

"Mother." Andy stood. "Can we walk for a moment?" They stepped in the direction of the barn. At least that was still standing. "I wonder if we're hurrying things a bit," he said.

"You're certainly hurrying that debate," she said.

"No more debate about the debate," he said. They were alone in the dark now, the campfire a low torch of light surrounded by silhouettes. "I'm talking about the burials. Is Sunday too soon?"

"Andy, not to be gruesome, but certain things just won't keep."

"But in our family plot. With Julian, father, grandfather. Enoch." He was pacing, looking at the ground.

"You were all approval earlier." Carrie was a little irritated. She did not want to have this discussion again.

"I'm having second thoughts." He faced her now. "And I guess now that I've started talking about it again, I realize it's not really the timing after all. I can see where it's fitting to have Yellow Squirrel laid near them somewhere. He's their murderer. More than that. He's like an evil force all his own. Burying him there makes it feel as if they—and we—have defeated death somehow. But it's the fact that he'd actually lie beside them, in the same position, as if he were their equal and their kind. That's the part that bothers me."

"I can see where that might..." She paused, turned, gazed into the dark for a moment. Then she turned back to her son. "We could bury him separately, at their feet, crossways to them, not parallel."

"Yes," Andy said. "I think so. They'd be sort of standing on him. And no coffin. Let him rot into the dirt."

"All right," she said. They were both silent for a moment. "Do you feel better now?"

He looked at the stars, seemed to consider her question. She hoped he'd be satisfied. Her arm hurt, and all this ritual made little difference to her. Andy seldom set such store by it either. His intensity surprised her. Underground was underground, and the quicker the better and why worry about where or how?

"Yes, that feels perfect for some reason," he said. "And we'll still deliver poor Miller's body—his bones—to that cabin of his and bury him beside his wife. In a nice coffin."

"Yes," she said. She embraced him as best she could with her one good arm.

He took her hand. "Thanks, Mom," he said. "We can go back now."

She tightened her grip, stopped him from stepping back toward the campfire. "No, not yet." She hadn't intended to broach this subject now, or perhaps ever, but it suddenly seemed urgent.

"What happens after Miller's funeral?"

"What do you mean?" he said. She cocked her head, knowing he had understood her. "Oh, you mean with the children." She held her silent pose. "You mean with Many Clouds."

"You have a choice to make, here, Andy. What are you going to do?"

"A choice?"

"I saw what passed between you and Many Clouds this afternoon. So did Virginia. And after all those treks across the rooftops—"

"You knew—"

Carolyn shook her head. It was her turn to look at the stars, roll her eyes. "Children think their parents know nothing, that they never did anything sneaky themselves." She turned her gaze back on him. "There are promises made in bed, you know—"

"I never—"

"Promises are made, spoken or not. I've become quite fond of Many Clouds and of Willy and Maggie. Please don't leave me more of a mess to clean up."

Her son stared at her with his one good eye. She hauled him back toward the campfire.

SEVENTY-SIX

PYRE

It took Many Clouds a good fifteen minutes to disentangle herself from Willy and Maggie without waking them, more endless minutes to creep around the collection of slumbering bodies to where Andy lay beside his mother. She shook Andy three times before he awoke. She pressed a finger to his lips to keep him from speaking, then motioned him into the darkness. She led him to the shadows beside the sawmill. The bodies were laid out behind the little building for easier access when it came to building coffins. Her chest was tight with guilt over what she had done that day. The necessity of it did nothing to relieve her anxiety.

"You're the only one I could come to," she said. "I can't do this alone, and it has to be done now."

"What does?"

"I know my uncle was a bad man, but I can't bear to have his spirit trapped beneath the white man's earth." She saw Andy stiffen, his head begin to shake. "His spirit must be carried to the heavens in the way of our people."

"We don't owe him any honors, Many Clouds."

She had never heard his voice so cold. It wasn't hard to sympathize with him. How was she to make him see why this was so important? She didn't fully understand it herself. She just knew it was essential.

"It's true what you say about him, but perhaps you'd do it for my sake."

"Do what exactly?"

"What you would call a cremation."

"More burning?" He stepped back. His head shaking more vigorously now. She was losing this. She must convince him of the urgency.

"Usually we would lay him out on a high framework, but we don't have to do that. The coals of the house and a little extra wood is all it will take, so his spirit will be freed and neither he nor any of us will be haunted by it again." She grabbed his arms, felt like dropping to her knees in pleading. But she didn't.

"We had other plans for him," he said.

"Yes," she said. She dropped her arms to her sides. "I know. But for me, will you please do this instead?"

He paced in a circle, hands on top of his head. Stopped. Started to speak. Paced again. Finally stopped and grasped her shoulders. "All right. Maybe this will be a purifying fire instead of a destroying one. That would help everyone."

Gilligan's wife had fashioned canvas sacks for the bodies of Yellow Squirrel and Fitzpatrick from a tarpaulin they had found in the barn. For that, Many Clouds was grateful. The fabric would help get the fire going, and they wouldn't have to look at her uncle as they dragged his body across the fifty yards to the house.

"The bunk house ruins are closer," Andy said. "And we won't have to cross so near to the others."

Of course. Why had she been so fixed on the idea of the house? It would make no difference. She supposed at full strength Andy would have been able to do this job on his own, but he wasn't. And, she discovered, there was a reason they called this dead weight. They yanked and hauled and pulled and finally got Yellow Squirrel to the bunk house, but there was a pile of charred timber still to clear. They were in the midst of struggling to heave the corpse over it into the coals when the job suddenly got easier. They discovered Cooper had joined them.

"Looked like you could use a hand," he said. "What is the plan?"

"Many Clouds wants to give our marauder an Arapaho sendoff instead of burying him," Andy said. He was breathing very hard. Many Clouds wondered if she had asked too much of him.

"'Cause he's your uncle even in spite of everything else, I suppose," Cooper said. She nodded. "You did what needed to be done, and a good job of it, too."

She voiced something else that had been bothering her. "I could have let you…"

Cooper pulled her to him. "Girl, you didn't even know I was behind you—way behind you—when you pulled the trigger." He gripped her shoulders, held her at arm's length and looked her in the eyes. "I was slow getting to the house thanks to falling into the irrigation ditch, so I was so far away I had a chancy shot, even if I got it off."

"But Andy already—"

"Did you know I was up there?" Andy said. She shook her head. "So, like Coop says, you did the job you needed to do. Now, let's get on with this."

She'd known all these things, and it did help somewhat to hear them spoken aloud, but guilt still squeezed her heart as they fashioned a low bed from fresh lumber, fueled it with shavings and sawdust. Cooper found a half-burned timber, still glowing, which he blew into flaming life. He held it out to her. She indicated that he should go ahead, but when he leaned over, she stopped him and took the torch herself.

Once the fire was alive, she stood at Andy's side, their shoulders touching. She thought she should step away from his touch, but didn't. There was a comfort there she didn't want to lose. Cooper laid his hand on his other shoulder, and together they watched the fire rise, curl around the corpse, and lift the flesh and soul of her unfortunate uncle into the waiting night.

SEVENTY-SEVEN

THE GREAT DEBATE

As he mixed with the gathering crowd, Andy was conscious of how poor a fashion figure he cut in the face of Hale Gentry's conches and black leather and white teeth. Gentry shook hands, slapped shoulders laughed heartily. Andy tried to do the same, but knew his unpressed clothes and bandages put him at a disadvantage. His wardrobe was a sartorial menagerie which Halstad and Gilligan had managed to put together out of their own closets. It almost fit, but it was tight here, loose there, and a definite drain on the confidence. Lucky he hadn't been dressing fancy for these appearances, or the gap between crowd expectations and reality might have proved ruinous. Maybe it still would.

Then there were the bandages, especially the big one above his eye. At least he could leave the eye uncovered for short periods now, and his periodic headaches had lessened in both frequency and intensity. He thought he could operate passably, though with somewhat blurred vision, for the length of the debate. Sawtooth Wells' Doc Robinson was a poor excuse for a medical man, but he'd fashioned a half-decent clean dressing to replace the soot-blackened one he'd had worn to town this morning.

"You're bleeding, boy," he'd said. "Busted some stitches."

"Just get me through the debate," he'd said. "I'm going back to the hospital right after." And Robinson, at least to this point, had done his job. Nevertheless, for a politician making the most important appearance of his career, he felt he must present a sad spectacle.

"Mr. Maxwell?"

He turned and found himself looking at Deborah Beasley's pleasant smile. He held out his hand. "Thank you for your reporting, miss," he said. "I'm sorry you've suffered some indignities along the way."

"And thank you for your pieces as well, sir. They have served us at *The Elevator* well."

"I'm curious. What exactly happened that I sent them to *The Examiner*, but they ended up in *The Elevator?*"

"Do you object?" A shadow fell across her face.

"Oh, not at all, it's just I heard about it second or third hand and no one seemed to know how it came about or why."

"I believe Mr. Bierce is primarily responsible," she said.

Of course, and he'd suspected as much. Bierce trying to help Francis increase circulation. The cynic wasn't as cynical as he put on.

"But to work, Mr. Maxwell. May I ask a couple of questions?" Beasley had produced a notebook and pencil.

"Certainly. I haven't much time, though."

"As you know, the election is only three weeks away now. How would you assess your chances of winning?"

"I expect to be the next assemblyman from the fourth district," he said.

"Despite your race?"

"I think the voters are intelligent enough to see past that," he said.

"And how are you and your family coping with all the recent calamities—the fires, the murders, all the rest?"

"We know how to weather calamities, Miss Beasley, believe me. We've had experience at that."

Someone clanged the bell on the fire wagon.

"Excuse me. Time to start the show."

"Good luck, Mr. Maxwell. You carry the hopes of many on your shoulders." Beasley smiled.

"Is that a proper comment for an objective journalist?" he said.

"No," she said, grinning now. Beaming, actually.

"Thanks for the good wishes," he said.

Before he mounted the platform, he pulled from his pocket the final rules Jack Johnson had handed him just an hour or so earlier. After their prickly conversation, Andy had composed what he thought was a pithy challenge for Gentry along with a proposed structure for the debate. He might have saved himself the trouble and just signed the blank paper as Johnson had asked him to do in the first place. The final rules read little or nothing like his proposal.

For one thing, he wasn't allowed to sprint on stage as usual. "dignified entrance," the rules stated. There were timed statements and rebuttals, but no rebuttals to the rebuttals, which left room for all sorts of unfounded allegations. And the moderator. Harold Lancaster, publisher of the *Mountain Messenger* in Downieville. Sure, *The Messenger* was California's oldest newpaper, but didn't Johnson and Lissner know that Lancaster had a running feud with the Maxwells over Carrie's refusal to open Green Canyon to mining? And so on.

Nevertheless, here he was. He'd play the hand that was dealt him. He mounted the stairs and walked to his designated chair on the left side of the stage. With no threat from Yellow Squirrel, his whole family was here and safe, plus Virginia, plus Many Clouds, plus Willy and Maggie. Despite urgings from everyone, Ling Chu concealed himself somewhere far offstage and anonymous. He still wouldn't miss a word, though.

He sat down on the front corner of the platform, facing Gentry who had seated himself on the opposite corner. His opponent gave him a little salute, touching fingers to hat brim. He responded in kind. Such good sports we are, he thought. The entire main street of Sawtooth Wells was filled with people, a sprinkling of dark faces among them. Everyone loves a scandal, a disaster, a brawl—even if it's only a political one.

Pastor Moreland delivered another interminable benediction. Gilligan followed with a—thank goodness—shortened opening speech and introduction of the moderator. Michael Lancaster introduced the various officials and dignitaries who had turned out. And there were plenty. Both gubernatorial candidates were there. The speaker of the assembly. The Mayor of Sacramento. And on and on. Each had a wave, a smile, and a "few brief words" to say. An hour passed. It was hot. Andy wondered how many would stay for how long. But it seemed to him that the crowd had grown, not shrunk, during the preliminaries.

At last Lancaster said, "Now, to the main event. Before we begin, however, no matter on which side of the political fence your sympathies lie, I think it appropriate to offer a word of condolence to Mr. Maxwell and his family for the events of yesterday. For those of you who may not have heard, the violence that has so pursued his campaign found its way to hearth and home. The Circle M family manse and several other buildings were burned, and a family friend was caught in the crossfire between the Maxwells and the renegade Indian who has been pursuing them. Luckily, that villain has also met a just and final end. Let's together express our sympathies to the Maxwell family for their loss along with congratulations for their victory over this murderer."

Lancaster began the applause, which spread quickly throughout the crowd. Even Gentry was on his feet. Andy stood and waved, signaled to his mother in the crowd to do the same. He sat, somewhat embarrassed, as quickly as he thought he could politely do so.

Lancaster's good will toward him, however, did not extend past that moment. After outlining the ground rules—questions from him followed by a two-minute answer and one-minute rebuttal from each candidate—he laid out the first question to Gentry:

"How would you respond to the scurrilous attacks on Southern Pacific's beneficent efforts to advance the prosperity of citizens in the fourth district?"

There was generous applause, which Gentry acknowledged with a three-hundred-and-sixty-degree wave of his hat and that beaming smile. Then he turned to Lancaster.

"I hope that applause won't cut into my two minutes."

"Of course not, Mr. Gentry. Your time begins… now." He pressed the button on a large stopwatch.

"I will use some of my two minutes to express personally my compassion for Mr. Maxwell's misfortune. I've spent many happy hours on the grounds of the Circle M and in its splendid ranch house. Its loss is a loss to us all.

"However, personal misfortunes aside, this is an election in which we must address issues head-on. Southern Pacific has spent a fortune to bring the railroad to these hills, and everyone in the corporation is delighted to see how it has enabled the area to prosper. As with all business, the money spent must be recouped or there would be no railroad at all."

He went on to recount tales of the days when ranchers were compelled to drive their stock to market in Sacramento, or lug their produce on wagons to nearby towns and villages. He painted the railroad as the benefactor that had saved them from all that isolation and toil. He then delivered a lesson in homespun economics.

"I ask you to consider this: Would any of you ask Mr. Gilligan to let his stables for free? Of course not. And which of you would require Mrs. Adams simply to give away her pies? That would be unthinkable, wouldn't it? And would it be possible for my own business establishment to exist if I could not get a fair price for my products? The answer is obvious. And it's just as obvious that Mr. Stanford, Mr. Crocker, and the rest cannot afford to provide space on their rail cars without just recompense. If they are criminals, as Mr. Maxwell has claimed, then so is Mr. Gilligan and so is Mrs. Adams, and Sheriff Halstad's jail would fill up faster than a rain barrel in January."

Gentry seated himself to the same general applause. Lancaster stepped forward.

"Well done, Mr. Gentry, and well short of your allotted time. Let's see how you do with the same question, Mr. Maxwell."

The clapping for Andy was enthusiastic, but not as general as Gentry's. He acknowledged it with a wave of his hand, left his hat in place.

"I apologize first for the way I look. When you shoot a man in the head and burn up his wardrobe, it tends to affect his appearance." Some laughter. "However, none of this has affected my thinking or my ability to recognize the truth. It's true Southern Pacific spent some money to build the rails. But they also received generous land grants—alternate sections along the entire route—from the government. I would wager that the worth of the land they now hold—received *gratis* from us taxpayers—is at least equal to the worth of their rolling stock and their steel road combined. Their land stretches from San Diego to Sacramento and beyond, more land than any rancher in the state. And it's not just farmland either."

He recited a short list of areas that had been nearly worthless grasslands when deeded to the railroad, but were now thriving towns and cities whose value now added up to several fortunes.

"And they're adding to that real estate by putting small farmers out of business and grabbing their land. Everyone in this assembly probably knows or knows of at least one such case, but let me recount just a few from here in Sawtooth Valley—"

"Time," Lancaster said.

"Impossible," Andy said. There were a few boos, quickly drowned out by applause. He looked to Johnson for help. The man shrugged his shoulders.

"Can't argue with the clock," Lancaster said. He held up the large silver watch, which did, indeed, register two minutes. He wondered when the moderator had pushed the button. He doubted he'd had much more than a minute. He started to protest further, then sat.

"Thank you, gentlemen." Now, Mr. Maxwell, this question is for you.

"Are we not allowed rebuttal time?" Andy said.

"I don't think that will be necessary in this case." He turned to Gentry. "Mr. Gentry?" Gentry shook his head. "Since Mr. Gentry has forgone his rebuttal, I'm sure you agree it wouldn't be fair to offer it to you. Now, are you ready for the next question?"

He fought off the urge to continue the argument, made a mock bow. "At your service, Mr. Lancaster."

"Excellent. Do you plan to continue your prevaricating efforts to discredit and besmirch Mr. Gentry's reputation throughout this district?"

Even Johnson rose to his feet on that note. No pretense of fairness, then. Andy waved Johnson to sit down.

"When did you stop rustling cattle, Mr. Lancaster?" he said.

Lancaster looked flustered. "Why—"

"Never mind. Of course there's no way a man can answer that question without incriminating himself, which is exactly the position which you've placed me in, Lancaster." He turned to the crowd. "Mr. Lancaster's accusation resembles a question about as much as a camel resembles a monkey, but I'll answer it anyhow.

"There's no need for me to besmirch Mr. Gentry's reputation. His own actions indict him. I'm certain the huge majority of men here are virtuous fellows who have never placed a bet on one of his backroom roulette wheels or patronized one of his back-alley brothels or swallowed a drink of his cut-rate, tax-evading liquor. But I'll bet there's no one—man or woman—who doesn't know someone who has."

"Time," yelled Lancaster. He waved his watch.

"Yes it is time," Andy said, "time to call an end to this fraud of a debate."

"He's going to cut and run," someone yelled.

"Just as yellow as he is black," called another.

But he continued. "And it's time to shovel the manure out of the legislative stables. Your ballots are your shovels. Hiram Johnson for governor. Andrew Maxwell for the assembly."

He descended the steps waving and smiling to a mixture of boos and applause. His head throbbed. Had he just lost himself the election? He felt less like a politician, but more like a man.

SEVENTY-EIGHT

THE PRESS

MAXWELL-GENTRY DEBATE CUT SHORT

Special to The Elevator *by Deborah Beasley*

No event the size or importance of Saturday's debate between the fourth district candidates for the assembly had ever happened in Sawtooth Wells. Mr. Hale Gentry and Mr. Andrew Maxwell squared off for the first of two scheduled debates before a large crowd on a sunny afternoon, and sparks flew.

Mr. Gentry received the first question from the moderator and master of ceremonies, Mr. Michael Lancaster, editor of the Mountain Messenger.

Gentry's response credited Southern Pacific with creating prosperity in the area. Mr. Maxwell attempted a rebuttal, but appeared to be cut short by the moderator. Mr. Lancaster then delivered a question that was in fact a thinly-veiled accusation that Maxwell had been spreading lies about Gentry's business, accusing him of illegal and corrupt activities. Maxwell replied that any such rumors were the result of the activities themselves, not any statements he had made. He then declared the debate a "fraud" and left the arena.

Mr. Gentry branded Maxwell a coward for his action and called for the citizens' votes for himself as the only legitimate candidate.

* * *

MAXWELL IN RETREAT

Special to The Sacramento Union

by *Harold Finch*

Apparently piqued by a challenging question from the moderator, Andrew Maxwell continued his pattern of impulsive and irrational behavior by abandoning the stage to his opponent, Mr. Hale Gentry, at Saturday's debate between fourth district assembly candidates.

Asked about his accusations that Gentry has been involved in a variety of illegal activities, Maxwell repeated the unproven allegations and walked away from the debate.

Combined with the gunplay that has dominated so many of his appearances, this latest fiasco seems to bode ill for his candidacy and thus for Republican chances of retaining the fourth district seat in next month's election.

SEVENTY-NINE

SURGERY

"Very gutsy move, Andy," Hiram Johnson stood at one side of his bedside, Lissner at the other.

Andy had spent a long time under ether for two surgeries to repair his stitches and dig bone chips out of the area in and around his wound. One of the chips had been lodged near the back of his eyeball, and pressure on the optic nerve had been responsible for the problems with headaches and vision. The doctors were optimistic that he'd regain the full sight of his left eye as more bone chips worked their way to the surface. The swelling had diminished, and the pain in his head had changed from an aching throb to a variety of sharp stabs, like someone was jabbing needles around his eye. But it wasn't as intense, and the ether hangover was fading.

"Gutsy, yes," Lissner said. "But not very smart."

"I'm going to win," he said. The two men looked across at one another. Skeptical, he thought. They think I'm done for. "You two picked me because I was a native of Sawtooth Valley, and I know those people have conscience, and their consciences won't let them vote for Gentry now that his seamy side is in the open. I ought to write Lancaster a thank-you note."

"I don't know," Lissner said, "people don't like a quitter."

"Who's quitting?" Andy said. "In another week, doc says this bandage will be no bigger than a silver dollar and won't cover my eye at all, so I figure if I make one more speech, say in Angel's Camp, looking like I'm on the mend so people don't wonder about my health, and then you, Hiram, give me a plug in Placerville. We'll have it sewed up."

"Your optimism is admirable, my boy. But, Meyer, what do you think?"

"'sewed up' might be overstating the case, but—"

"Gentlemen, gentlemen. I'm not going to argue. The results will tell the story. Two appearances. Are you with me?" He held out a hand to each of them. They hesitated, but shook.

"And one more thing."

"Yes?" Johnson said.

"What about a press conference?"

Lissner leaned on the bed. "I don't think you have the slightest idea how to handle the press, Andy. You're blunt, argumentative, and thin-skinned. They'll kill you. Stick to speeches and no questions."

Lissner's vehemence took him aback. "You think I'm that much of a disaster?"

"Nothing of the kind, my boy." Johnson's voice was a tad too hearty as he patted his shoulder. "Just tactics. Trying not hand the opposition any ammunition."

Lissner was suddenly as affable as his boss. "We're agreed, then. A rousing speech from you and one from Hiram, and then we'll see." He checked his watch, turned to Johnson. "Speaking of rousing speeches, you're due to deliver one to the Stockton Chamber of Commerce dinner this evening, so we'd better get cracking."

"Right you are, Meyer. And listen, boy, don't get discouraged."

"Me get discouraged?" he said. "It seems to me I'm the only one in this room who thinks I have a chance."

"Not at all, Andy," Lissner said. "I'm paid to look for trouble, so I go overboard sometimes. You'll do fine." He nodded to Johnson, and the two headed for the door. It seemed to him he was out of their minds before they left the room. These guys were the pros, and they'd given up on him. If he was that bad off, what did he have to gain by playing it safe?

He tossed back the covers and swung his feet to the floor. You didn't win an election or anything else lying flat on your back.

EIGHTY

BENEATH THE GROUND BENEATH THE TREE

Many Clouds watched the box containing Miller Fitzpatrick's bones descend into the hole where it would rest forever, beside his wife, under the apple tree she had planted a year before her death. Cooper and Andy slowly let the ropes slide through their hands. It seemed wrong to put Miller in a prison in the earth instead of freeing him to join with the wind and the sun and the rain. She wanted the coffin to never reach bottom because when it did, this part would be over, and she was terrified of what would follow.

All too soon, the ropes went slack and Miller Fitzpatrick came gently to his final resting place. Over the last day or so, Maggie and Willy had gone from weepy to stoic, which Many Clouds found even more disturbing. She felt Maggie shudder when the coffin's movement stopped. The little girl, then, sensed the magnitude of the shift in their lives that would follow.

"Lord, forgive us all for wasting the gifts you bestow upon us," Carrie said, "of which Miller Fitzpatrick was one of the best." Everyone looked at her, a bit surprised, for she had never been given to such pious and biblical-sounding talk. Another measure of the impact that this—and all—the recent events had had on them. "I meant it," she said.

"Bye-bye, Papa," Willy said. "Have fun in heaven."

"Willy," Maggie said, "You don't have—" she stopped because Many Clouds had squeezed her hand hard. No bickering here. "I'm glad Mama and Papa can be together," she said.

"Willy's eyes turned sorrowfully up to Many Clouds. "Are we orphans now?"

Many Clouds saw the others trading glances—Cooper, Amelia, Carolyn, Virginia, Andy, Ling Chu, Nonny. Willy had asked the question they'd all been avoiding. She knelt and wrapped an arm around each of the children. "No one with a family is an orphan," she said, "and I'll bet the three of us would make a wonderful family. What do you think?"

"So you'll be our mama?" Willy said.

"As close to it as I can possibly get," she said.

"All right," he said, his voice faint.

Many Clouds turned to Maggie. "And what about you?"

Maggie's answer was to break down in sobs and hug Many Clouds, who looked up at the audience, all of whom were smiling, the women—even Carrie—weeping, except for Nonny, who had wandered off toward the surrounding trees, humming her melody.

"I hope you know you won't be doing this all alone," Amelia said.

Many Clouds smiled up at Amelia, then turned back to comforting Maggie. She'd made her promise now, spoken it aloud. There would be a price to pay. She knew it. There was no escaping the price for letting yourself get pulled into this white world where disaster always waited.

EIGHTY-ONE

SOLICITING VOTES

District four covered well over six hundred square miles, but less than a thousand registered voters lived in the whole area. More cows than people, Carrie, had said, and she was quite right. Of those, a maximum of six hundred and fifty would turn out for a given election. Since this campaign had attracted so much attention, that maximum was likely to be reached. Thus, Andy figured, three hundred and fifty votes would make him a winner.

He accepted the doctors' verdict that he wouldn't be up to barnstorming for at least another week, but that didn't mean he couldn't make a direct appeal. With Lissner's help, he'd gotten the county clerk to provide an annotated list of voters showing who had submitted ballots in the last two general elections, and he spent every waking hour sitting in an alcove of Wentworth Hospital scribbling personal notes to nearly every single voter, leaving out the fifty or so who were definite no votes because of their association with Gentry or the railroad or both.

"You need to rest, Mr. Maxwell." A nurse tugged at his sleeve.

"Ten more," he said.

"No," she said.

"Five," he said.

"And then you're going back to your room."

"Yes," he said. But he had written fifteen more before she was finally able to drag him away.

EIGHTY-TWO

AWAITING THE TALLY

Carrie had rented a suite in Placerville's Cary House Hotel to be on hand for the tallying of the votes. Because of the long distances from local polling places to here in the county seat, it would not be till the evening on the day after the election that the formal totals would be in, but they'd checked in on election afternoon anyway.

It had taken a healthy bribe to lower the staff's raised eyebrows over when Amelia and Cooper appeared, but their presence was essential on more than just the principle that they belonged in the family. Now, after nearly three hours agonizing with Cooper and Andy over the Circle M's financial picture—made extremely hazy by the destruction of fifty years worth of ledgers—she acceded to Ling Chu's insistence that they tackle the platter of sandwiches and beverages he'd fetched from the hotel kitchen. Even the food, though, hadn't helped cheer up the conversation.

"The only thing that bothers me much is this damn bandage, and that will be gone in no time."

Carrie didn't quite agree. All of it bothered her. The incipient scar on his cheekbone, the misshapen area where the bullet had grazed his eye socket, the doubt over whether he'd regain the full sight of that eye.

"I never was much of a pretty boy anyhow," he continued. "Maybe this will make up in character what I lacked in handsome."

"Ain't nothing wrong with your handsome, Andy," Amelia said. "It's your sense we wonder about sometimes."

Andy grinned. "You dare say that to the man who is about to become an assemblyman, a regent, and a professor?"

"And who has two women pining after him and ain't neither one of them here on one of the biggest days of his life?"

Andy lost his grin.

Carrie said, "Amelia, maybe this isn't the time." She was secretly glad that Amelia dared to bring up a subject they'd been tiptoeing around for days, but it still made her squirm. Wasn't it really Andy's business, not theirs? And so much was going on.

"I'm sorry, Carrie—"

"Thank you for calling me 'Carrie' instead of 'Miss Carrie.' Maybe we're getting somewhere, you and I," Carrie said.

"Maybe, maybe not, but don't change the subject. Anyhow, no reason to put it off. You and me been talking, why not bring the boy hisself in on it?" she turned back to Andy. "Many Clouds sittin' up in that cabin by herself with them children, and no one's seen Virginia since the burial. What do you think happened to her? You know something we don't?"

"I'm not sure, Amelia. I haven't talked to her."

"See what I mean about you ain't got good sense? You can take care of a murdering Indian, but can't deal with a female who don't mean you no harm at all."

Andy appeared to be struck dumb. Carrie hoped her smile didn't show. Cooper finally broke the silence.

"Don't never assume the female don't mean you no harm at all, especially when she says she means well, boy."

"And what's that supposed to mean?" Amelia said.

The squabbling was entertaining, but it was still squabbling, and Carrie suddenly wanted no more of it on the eve of what promised to be a great celebration following a series of catastrophes.

Afterwards, in the suite, no one felt like retiring despite their fatigue.

"Ling Chu," Carrie called, "I think I saw a bottle of whisky in those supplies you brought up earlier?"

"Oh, yes, indeed, Miss Carrie." He hurried toward a box on the other side of the room."

"If I can't say 'Miss Carrie'," Amelia said, "neither can he."

"You hear that, Ling?" Carrie said. Ling had uncorked the bottle and was lining up glasses.

He answered without hesitation. "Yes, Carrie, I hear." Everyone laughed, applauded.

"Your whisky, Mr. Andrew." Ling Chu passed him a glass.

"Call me 'Andy,'" he said.

"Too much for now," Ling said. "Mr. Cooper." He passed him a glass.

"And for me, please," Carrie said.

"And I wouldn't mind a drop myself," Amelia said.

"Oh, now, Lord help us." Cooper rolled his eyes.

Once he had supplied everyone else, Ling Chu poured one more glass, which he raised high. "To victory for Mr. Andrew," he said. He threw down two fingers of bourbon in one gulp. For a moment, they were all too astonished to move.

"Drink up, you all," Ling Chu said. "What are you waiting for?"

* * *

The next morning, the messages came thick and fast.

EIGHTY-THREE

CABIN FEVER

Five days after Miller Fitzpatrick's burial someone lassoed the apple tree—still a scrawny sapling, yet to bear fruit, yet to even push forth a blossom—and uprooted it. Normally, no more than two or three wagons or riders passed by the Fitzpatrick cabin in a week. Suddenly, more traffic than that traveled the road every day. Sometimes the passersby would just ride past and jeer, call out derisive names like "half-breed bastards" or "squaw bitch." Sometimes they spit or threw rocks. Occasionally, men in suits, with the look of bankers, or gamblers, would stop and take notes as they perused the property.

The Maxwells had left Many Clouds with a rifle and a pistol and some cash. They'd also given her a horse, a young mare named Molly, and a buckboard. They had not wanted to leave her at the cabin, but she thought it was best for Willy and Maggie to be close to their parents, at least for the time being.

She had killed and butchered a deer not long after the crowd from the Circle M had left. The children had become adept at trapping small game. Combined with produce from the garden, this would feed the three of them for a time. She thought they could survive the winter, relatively mild in these parts, then they would travel together to Wind River in the spring. Maybe she wouldn't have to be as dependent on the Maxwells after that. After all, they would be very busy rebuilding their ranch, too busy to bother with her, whatever their good intentions. Not to mention Andy's election. She wasn't sure whether that had happened yet, or whether he had won, but it was sure to take a great deal of their time and attention.

It had been almost as painful as burying Miller to be so constantly in Andy's company, then to watch him leave. To have him embrace her, hold her hand, knowing it was all part of the sympathy and ceremony, nothing quite personal. Sometimes, as when they stood together watching Yellow Squirrel's spirit climb to the stars, or when he wrapped her in his arms before he left the burial, she fancied something deeper. But it was surely her imagination and would come to nothing and she needed to put the notion aside as she had so often before. Stay away, she told herself. Nothing else made sense.

She tried to establish a routine, keep the children's lessons going, focus on their chores and other activities, distract them from their grief. But the tree's destruction had been a major blow. Whoever had done it had been sure to chop it into the smallest bits possible and scatter it all over the lot. Maggie had cried all day. Willy had just sat against the cabin wall, looking at his parents' headstones.

A few days afterwards, when she'd managed to resurrect the schedule in a makeshift way, one of the dark-suited men parked his buggy on the road and actually walked up to the cabin. She shooed the children inside and met the man with a rifle in her hands. It was pointed at the ground, but she was fully prepared to raise it higher if the need arose.

The man, plump, mustachioed, and in his thirties, looked startled by the firearm. He raised his hands and opened his coat. "Hey, miss, I'm unarmed. I don't intend to hurt anyone, and I hope no one intends to hurt me."

Many Clouds didn't move, said nothing.

"I'm Zeke Barnes of First Miner's Bank." He reached into his vest pocket, pulled out a business card, and extended it toward her. Many Clouds remained still and silent. "Well, I'll just lay the card down here on the ground. You can pick it up later, perhaps. Now, the reason I'm here is, Mr. Fitzpatrick, the owner of this property, we understand he is deceased?"

Many Clouds nodded.

"Can you show me the title? The deed?"

"Why should I?"

"Because my bank... Look, I can explain better if I can see the deed."

Many Clouds was beginning to feel the same fear as when Yellow Squirrel had suddenly appeared. She raised the rifle a few inches.

"With Mr. Fitzpatrick... gone," Harris said, "the property reverts to my bank, you see."

"Your bank didn't homestead this place. Miller did."

"True enough. But we loaned him some money, and the loan's in default, so the property is now ours."

"No." She raised the rifle still higher.

"Whoa, I'm not going to stop a bullet over this," Harris, said, backing away, his hands still in the air, his pink face turning red. "That's what the sheriff is for. Good day." He turned his back and scampered downhill to his buggy.

Willy and Maggie poked their way out of the cabin and stood with Many Clouds as Jason Barnes' vehicle clattered down the road.

Just as he turned the curve that put him out of sight, rocks and dirt clods rained down on the cabin roof from the trees on the hillside above. Shouts and laughter followed. Boys, from the sound of it. Many Clouds levered a shell into the Winchester's chamber and brought the weapon to her shoulder. Then she eased the hammer back to half-cock. One bullet would likely invite another. She picked up Zeke Harris' business card. Paper. She understood that white men fought battles with it. "Come on, children," she said, "let's hitch up Molly. We're going to town."

EIGHTY-FOUR

TOTE BOARD

On the wall opposite the bar in the Cary House's saloon hung a huge blackboard. It had gone up in the gold rush days when Placerville was called Hangtown, had been used over the decades to record the results of everything from hangings to horse races. Tonight, a slick-haired dandy on a ladder was chalking up the votes for the 1910 elections. Andy had tried sitting inconspicuously in a corner to watch, but he was soon spotted and the resultant demands for autographs and answers forced him to retreat to the suite, where he relied on periodic reports from Cooper.

The process turned his insides into a hot an agonizing coil. The first posted counts were from the south end of the district around Columbia and Angel's Camp. Disappointing. Even though he'd known the Southern Pacific was strong around there because of the jobs its maintenance and repair facilities generated, he'd counted his post-operation speech there quite a success He'd been able to deal easily with the catcalls—ignoring some, wisecracking others to silence ("I see Simon Legree has joined us this afternoon.") and it felt good to be sporting only small bandage instead of the huge bandage he'd been wearing ever since Markleeville. The cheers had been loud.

"Andy, get rid of the long face," his mother said. "You almost beat Gentry in his strongest area. You should be happy."

"Almost, Mom? Almost? I have to do better than almost."

"And you will, Andy," Amelia said. "You wait."

"Wait, wait, wait," he said. "I can't stand to wait any more." *But I don't want to know the results either. Is this insanity?*

Cooper entered the room. "Sutter Creek," he said. "Things looking up." He handed Carrie the slip of paper and headed back downstairs.

It was better, but it was still a loss. Why? Maybe because Sutter Creek was just over the hill from Hope Valley? Larson country? Useless and painful speculation. Well, so what if he lost? He'd still be a regent, wouldn't he, and he'd be able to pry open the university's closed doors for himself and many others. Not only that, but Deborah Beasley said his newspaper pieces had been well-received. Maybe a career in journalism? *Kidding yourself, Andy. Losing is worth no more than what the bull leaves behind in the barnyard.*

Cooper's next report was from Hope Valley itself. His first clear win. Not by much, but a victory. Surprise. Had the campaign speech fiasco disgusted the constituency that much, or had Larson been so confident he hadn't bothered to stuff the ballot box? Again, useless and painful speculation. Maybe he was on his way to Sacramento after all.

Suddenly, he had misgivings about winning. He'd become a politician. With constituents to listen to and legislative colleagues he had to make deals with, and would he be beholden to governor Hiram Johnson? And what would that mean to his professorship?

Incipient elation replaced that particular anxiety when Cooper brought in the count from Jackson. A substantial margin over Gentry there.

"It's starting to smell awful sweet, Andy," he said. "Sure you don't want to come down with me?"

"Great idea, Coop," he said. "I can't stand being shut up here another minute."

"Nor can I," Carrie said. "Let's all go."

They descended the staircase just as the recorder chalked up the results from Sawtooth Wells, giving him a nearly 2 to 1 margin over Hale Gentry, and the crowd cheered—there were scattered boo's, but very few—to see the Maxwells on the staircase. It was nearly midnight before the full count was in, but when the tote board was full, Hiram Johnson was governor, and Andy ended the evening standing on the bar of the Cary House thanking a smiling and noisy crowd for his seat in the California legislature.

* * *

The SECOND *Vendetta*

TO ANDREW MAXWELL, ASSEMBLYMAN WELL DONE ALL OUR BEST STOP

BIERCE AND REDMOND

* * *

TO A. MAXWELL

WELCOME TO THE TEAM STOP SHOULD NOT HAVE DOUBTED STOP MEYER AND I ELATED STOP JOHNSON

* * *

TO HIRAM JOHNSON, GOVERNOR

CONGRATULATIONS GOVERNOR STOP LOOKING FORWARD TO AN EXCITING TERM STOP THANKS FOR THE HELP TO BOTH YOU AND MEYER STOP

ANDREW MAXWELL

* * *

THE PRESS

Vendetta Victory

Special to The Examiner *from* Mr. Andrew Maxwell

Well, we got him. The cost was enormous—two orphaned children, multiple deaths, a ranch burned—but Yellow Squirrel is dead and his evil with him. He could have vanished after he was wounded at my speech in Markleeville. We would have had to live with his specter, wondering always if, when, how he would reappear. But his nature couldn't be content with that. He needed blood unto his last breath.

Still other, more subtle, evils remain in the world, however. It is to those that I turn now as I conclude this vendetta series, prepare to represent my constituents in the assembly, and to help our new governor put the ax to the tentacles of the octopus that has been strangling our citizens for so long.

* * *

Andy spent three days on horseback thanking the voters who had put him in office. He heard plenty of negative comments about Hale Gentry, but most often, people told him that his handwritten notes had tipped the scales. "Though your handwriting could do with some polishing, boy," one schoolteacher said. "I don't really believe you all are going to be able to do anything about the railroads," the blacksmith in Markleeville said, "but I thought you was worth a try, especially considering the other fella."

He nodded, smiled, took notes, shared ideas. This was what it was to be a public servant. Maybe a politician's life didn't have to be such a mire of graft and corruption as he'd feared. Then he was back in Sacramento, where he got the news the same way everyone else did—from the newspaper.

* * *

JUDGE GRANTS INJUNCTION AGAINST MAXWELL ELECTION

EIGHTY-FIVE

LEGAL TENDER

Many Clouds had never had a substantial amount of money before. She understood that what seemed enormous to her might be nowhere near enough for her purpose. However, she figured that Andy and Carrie would not have left her a pittance, so she drove slowly the length of Auburn's main street looking for a lawyer's office. She saw three signs. How to choose? Who to trust? She knew no one to ask. Send a telegram to Andy? Not if she could help it. Besides, she couldn't sit around for the day or more it would take to get an answer, especially with Maggie and Willy to look after. No one was about to deliver the reply to their cabin door.

She turned the buckboard around and headed back down the street. The first time through town, she had passed notice as just another squaw and her brood. Now, she began to draw stares. People stopped. Talked. They had begun to recognize her as connected to Miller Fitzpatrick, to the cabin. She needed to finish her business and get out.

The first sign she came to hung next to the Liberty Belle Saloon, was hand-carved, and read, "G. Noble, Atty." She hitched the wagon, gathered the children and the small leather satchel with Miller's documents enclosed, and climbed the stairs to G. Noble's second floor office. A muffled voice answered her knock. She had to put a shoulder to the sticking door to open it. They stepped into an office dominated by a huge walnut desk, behind which sat a very old man, white-haired and balding, with an unlit meerschaum pipe in his mouth.

He waved her toward the only chair in front of the desk without looking up from the pile of papers in front of him. She had Willy sit and Maggie stand beside her while she waited before the desk for the man to finish whatever he was working on. The pen scratched. The man hummed. She was on the point of leaving. Finally, he capped his pen, slid the paper to the side, and looked up.

"Mmm. Injun, huh? Not many of you all come in here." She hadn't heard anyone speak in his soft, drawn out way before. It sounded gentle, made her want to trust him.

"Mr. Noble?"

"Mmm." He leaned back in his chair and pulled the pipe from his mouth.

"I'm Many Clouds. This is Willy and Maggie Fitzpatrick."

"Mmm. Fitzpatrick. Fitzpatrick. Why are you all coming to see a lawyer?"

"This man," she laid Zeke Harris' card on the desk, "came to see us today. He says his bank owns the cabin, but it must be a mistake."

"Cabin?" He picked up the card. "Harris. Harris. Not as bad a scallywag as some of them moneylenders, but a scallywag nonetheless. But you better back up, Miss Clouds, because I haven't the faintest notion what you're talking about." He smiled, stood. The man was short—barely five feet, she guessed. He reached under the desk, groaning about his arthritis as he leaned down and came back up with a milking stool in each hand. "My footstools. I love this oversized desk. Allows me to spread out my work, but when I use a chair tall enough to work at it, my feet barely touch the floor. Bad for the circulation. Here, children, why don't you sit on these and let your mother—"

"Oh, I'm not their mother," Many Clouds said.

"But she is almost," Maggie said.

"My Lord in heaven," Noble said. "Sounds to me like we have more tales to tell than Mr. Twain. Best get started or we'll miss supper."

The three of them talked. Noble listened.

"You say the Maxwells are tied up in all this?"

"But I don't want to bother them," Many Clouds said. "I thought that if you could look at Mr. Fitzpatrick's papers in that satchel, you could talk to Mr. Harris and explain better than I can that he's wrong. I have some money to pay you." She hoped he wouldn't name a price yet, ask her pay in advance. He pulled the papers out, went over them.

"Well, on the face of things our Mr. Harris is technically in the right, I'm afraid."

"So there's nothing we can do?"

"Oh, I didn't say that, didn't say that at all. Tell you what. You leave all this with me, and I'll go have a talk with our banker friend." He rose, took a moment to steady himself on the desk. "You can go on back home. I'll ride out that way tomorrow and let you know the results of my little meeting."

He grabbed a beat-up silk top-hat from the rack and ushered them out of the office and down the stairs. Molly stood where she had been hitched, but the wagon shafts lay in the dust, along with the sliced ends of the leather traces.

"Now that," Mr. Noble said, "is the height of skullduggery. Willy, you run over to the livery stable and give Mr. Michaels this." He dug in his pocket and handed Willy a coin. "Tell him it's from the giant, and that he's got a little repair job across the street here. Good lad."

"Who's the giant?" Willy said.

"Why me, of course. See the sign? G. Noble? Officially, 'G' stands for 'Gerald,' but folks around here dubbed me 'Giant.' Obvious reasons, of course." He giggled, stretched his arm above his head. "Hurry along, now."

Willy did as he was told. "Thank you," Many Clouds said. She reached for the purse that hung at her waist. "Let me pay—"

"Plenty of time for that," Noble said. "You shouldn't have any more trouble for the moment. I'm off to my appointments, now." He tottered off down the sidewalk. looking barely able to navigate. What had she gotten into?

From the other direction, Willy appeared followed by a pasty-faced youth whose skin was blotchy with pimples and who looked incapable of fixing so much as a glass of water. Many Clouds remembered a Bible verse about the lame and the halt. Was it really so wise, she wondered, not to involve Andrew?

EIGHTY-SIX

INJUNCTION (1)

"What does this mean, exactly?" Andy asked Lissner.

"The election can't be certified until this works its way through the courts," Lissner said.

"That much I understand," he said. "My question is how do we fight it?"

"I don't think they have a chance of winning. Southern Pacific's behind the suit, of course. As long as they keep the seat vacant, Hiram's a vote short in the legislature, But there is nothing in the state constitution barring Negroes from holding office. It's just that proving it all will take time. Lawyers argue, judges judge. I'm sure you're familiar with the process."

"All too well. Which lawyers and which judges?"

"The attorney general's office vs. Southern Pacific in the guise of the Citizens for Fair Election Practices."

"So we can't hire our own lawyers?"

"We will of course file an *amicus curiae*, but neither the party nor you have any official standing in the court at the moment. If we lose, you can file suit yourself."

"The Maxwell fortune was never vast enough to go up against SP, especially now. How long do you think?"

"Perhaps a month or two," Lissner said. "Now, should the decision go against us—"

"How could it, if the law doesn't exist?"

"Anything can happen."

"So Gentry could still take the office."

Lissner laughed. "Oh, no. That's one thing that cannot happen. Even if they invalidate your victory, Gentry's lost. Hiram would appoint someone else until the next election."

"So I'm in limbo, then," Andy said.

"Regrettably, I'm afraid so. I wish there were something more I could do."

"Well, at least I can take my seat on the board of regents and devote myself to the reason I started this whole thing in the first place."

"The regents? Oh, Andy, surely you appreciate that under the circumstances—"

"You're not going to renege on that, are you?"

"You had the impression—"

"Impression, hell. He promised me that seat, win or lose, if I campaigned for the office." He jumped out of his chair, leaned across Lissner's desk.

"Governor Johnson never meant to convey with certainty—"

"Governor Johnson is not going to get away with this," he said. And he headed out the door. But behind his brave words, came the thought that he'd become the naïve and innocent lamb on his way to the slaughterhouse. Maybe all those remarks about his naïvite had been on target after all.

* * *

Two days later, he stood at the peak of Nob Hill, gazing down the steep grade of California Street to where its silver cable car rails swept across the bottom of the hill to Market Street and to the green water beyond. It was noon, the light flat, the sidewalks crowded. He was standing at the top of the mountain, he thought, and that's where he meant to stay. Where he could accomplish something. Where he counted. Where he mattered.

Behind him rose the Fairmont Hotel, named for the silver baron who was one of the legendary figures of a frontier California that was disappearing quickly. In an elegant suite at the top, the new governor was putting together a new government for a new age, one which Andy meant to make sure included him.

An hour later, he paced the anteroom of Hiram Johnson's suite, his fury growing by the moment. Since he had stomped his way out of Lissner's office in Sacramento, his rage had simmered without respite. He'd been McNulty's protégé, then his fool. Then Johnson's protégé, now his fool. He slammed a fist into his palm. Checked his watch. He'd been scheduled to enter the suite thirty minutes ago. No more waiting.

He threw open the door, saw Johnson huddled with two other men he didn't know. The room was smoky, half-full bourbon glasses rested on the table in front of the men.

"Governor," he said, "I need to see you."

"Yes, Andy." Johnson rose, smiling. "Tell you what, gentlemen. Why don't we come back to this later? Over dinner, say. Mr. Maxwell and I have some unfinished business." He ushered the men out amid handshakes and laughter, then gestured to Andy to sit down.

"I'd rather stand," he declared. "Meyer said you're not going to put me on the regents after all."

"Before we get to that, I have some good news for you, if you can sit still for it."

"The injunction's been lifted?"

"No, I'm afraid not. However, the news does concern legal matters. Judge Bailey has dismissed the charges against you in the little matter with sheriff O'Neil. Insufficient evidence. You should be receiving paperwork shortly."

"Your influence… Thank you, Mr. Johnson." How could a right thing seem so wrong?

"A matter of what's fair, Andy. Justice must be served. Now, as for this misunderstanding about the regents, I don't think Mr. Lissner had a chance to finish what he wanted to say to you the other day. It's just that the appointment can't be immediate, under the circumstances." Now Johnson sat, picked up a burning cigar and began chewing on it.

"And what circumstances are those?" he felt a bit foolish now, standing stiff and agitated in front of this relaxed man. He was not in control.

"The injunction, for one thing."

Finally, he sat, but he sat on the edge of a chair, leaned toward the almost-lounging Johnson.

"They have nothing to do with each other as far as I can see. You said I was on the board, win or lose."

"Oh, did I? And when did I say that?"

"The morning I agreed to run. I laid down my conditions. You agreed."

"I recall complimenting your negotiating skills. I don't recall saying I agreed to your conditions. Do you, Jack?"

Andy looked behind him. Hiram's son had stepped into the room at some point. "No sir, not in my hearing," he said.

"Don't try to weasel out of this." Andy was back on his feet now. "You know I never would have run if you hadn't made a commitment."

"I'm sorry if you inferred what I never meant to imply, Mr. Maxwell. If you think back over our conversation, I think you'll realize I never promised you anything." He paused, blew some smoke. "Now did I?"

He was stunned, speechless. He could not recall the exact words, but every gesture, smile, movement had implied… Feeling as much a fool as if he'd just turned over the wrong card in a game of three-card monte. He looked back and forth between the new governor and his son, who wore a decided smirk.

"Now, Mr. Maxwell," the elder Johnson continued, "you did a first rate job with that campaign. Went way beyond the call. No doubt about it. The party and I owe you a debt. Whether this injunction succeeds or not, the fourth district seat belongs to the Republicans."

Something made Andy glance back and forth at father and son. Had they shared a look, or had it been his imagination?

"I note and acknowledge your desire for a place on the board of regents," Johnson continued. "Such an outcome is still within the realm of possibility. But an absolute promise? Not then. Not now. Are we clear?"

Many words—Liar. Judas. Fraud.—swam through Andy's mind. But only one emotion snaked through his gut. Fury.

"Yellow Squirrel was at least true to his evil heart all the way to the end," he said. "You, apparently, are true to nothing at all."

EIGHTY-SEVEN

INJUNCTION (2)

Noble did not show up at the cabin the next day as he had promised. Nor the day after that. On the other hand, neither did Zeke Harris or the sheriff. Many Clouds decided to wait one more day until… until what? She wasn't sure.

It was Willy, playing mumblety-peg after morning chores, who spotted him first, a short man on a tall mule, ambling down the road from town.

"Many Clouds, the giant's here," he yelled. He scampered breathlessly to the cabin.

Noble slid off his mule, literally. To accommodate his short legs, the stirrups had to be pulled up so high that he couldn't step directly from them to the ground. So he freed both feet, swung his right leg over the saddle and slid belly down to the ground. Many Clouds wondered if he should help him dismount, but decided that if he didn't ask, it wasn't her place.

"I don't have much to offer but cool water and a bite of venison jerky," she said, "but please come into the shade."

"Many Clouds, you are a model hostess, able to spot exactly what a guest needs most. Water and shade. Yes, yes, yes."

Seated and refreshed, Noble pulled out the leather wallet of papers that Many Clouds had left with him and handed them to her. "Here you are, my dear. I'm sure you'll find everything in order." He took another sip of creek water.

"What did you find out, sir?" Many Clouds said.

"Now, about Mr. Harris. And about Mr. Fitzpatrick. They indeed had a contract of some years standing. Mr. Fitzpatrick borrowed money from the First Miners Bank to buy a wagon and horse, and he put up this homestead as security. At an interest rate I would consider usurious, but entirely legal, I'm afraid."

"Usurious?" Many Clouds said.

"High beyond all reason. Fifteen per cent. The loan had one more year to go, and Mr. Fitzpatrick had already paid the price of his purchase twice over. But that's neither here nor there. Payments had been more or less regular all this time, but one payment was missed in September. Then of course, nothing came in during October. The contact specifies that two missing payments in succession cause the land to revert to the bank."

"But if we can make up the payments… "

"So one would assume, but not according to the contract, nor according to Mr. Harris, who claims to be acting on the orders of higher-ups and with no authority to be flexible."

"Do we have to move?" Maggie said.

"I think I can make a case that Mr. Fitzpatrick's untimely death invalidates the contract and that it must be renegotiated with his heirs. I filed an injunction—or will file when the circuit judge holds his next sessions in a couple of weeks or so—stopping the bank from seizing the property until we can straighten all this out. Then, Mr. Harris was kind enough to arrange an appointment with the president of the bank, whom I have known for some time, so an injunction may not be necessary."

"So we're saved?" Many Clouds said.

"I've bought you some time, is all. Eventually the bank will get its money or this property, so whatever resources you can muster I'd advise you to act quickly."

"How much?" Many Clouds said.

"One hundred and thirteen dollars and forty-two cents, give or take. We could get it reduced if the judge disallows some penalties. It could be more if he doesn't."

It was more than twice what Many Clouds had in her purse. "And what do we owe you, Mr. Noble?"

"Shade and water is quite enough. I've done some inquiring, and I believe you have enough trouble without having to finance my pedestrian errands. I wish, in fact, that I had enough set aside to pay the debt entirely, but it is beyond my means. Nevertheless, you must eventually pay the piper or vacate the premises."

"You are the kindest man alive, Mr. Noble. I wish…"

He waved his hand. "Too much wishing, not enough doing. That's what's the matter with this world. Now I must return to my office. There could be a paying client waiting there right now."

They stood, shook hands. On impulse, Many Clouds threw her arms around him, and the children followed suit.

"Oh, no, no, no," he said. "None of that now." His eyes were wet as he pushed them away and walked back downhill to his horse. "If you can just give me a hand up to the saddle, I'll be on my way."

Many Clouds cupped her hands. Noble stepped into her improvised stirrup with his left leg, swung his right leg over the saddle, slid off the horse on the opposite side, and dropped to the dust, where he lay still as a brick.

EIGHTY-EIGHT

WHAT BIERCE IS UP TO

"What else can I do?" Andy asked Bierce. He paced the office.

"'He also serves who only stands and waits,'" Bierce said. He struck a match and applied the flame to his stogy.

"Don't throw Milton at me, Ambrose." He fanned at the rank cloud of smoke. "The man is an absolute liar. I wouldn't doubt he rigged the injunction himself."

"Doubtful. But it's also doubtful he's too upset about it. Win or lose in court, he gets to fill the seat, and if you lose he'll probably get himself a man more pliable than Andy Maxwell. Word is, his backup minion would be one Jason Barnes."

"The grocer-mayor of Markleeville?"

"The same."

Andy sat down, eager to get Bierce's cooperation. "That proves he wants me out of the picture. So you'll go after him in 'The Tattler?'"

"Perhaps, if more pressing issues don't arise."

"But he's a Judas. He needs to be exposed." Andy was back on his feet.

"Then do it."

"I don't have a platform."

"Then get one." Bierce rolled his eyes and stared at the ceiling. "For an elected representative of the people, you have a miniscule understanding of the so-called *art* of politics."

"It seems more like the art of street thuggery to me right now."

"At last you're beginning to understand." A knock on the door. "Ah, that should be him now."

"Him?" Andy said. "Who?"

"Come in." Bierce stood as he called. "Ah, Joseph, good. You know Mr. Maxwell. Have a seat, have a seat."

The Joseph in question was Joseph Francis, publisher of the *Elevator*. He and Andy shook hands, exchanged greetings.

"Now," Bierce said. "Am I right, Joseph, that Andy here helped you sell a few extra newspapers during the late unpleasantness of his campaign?"

"Yes, indeed. And thanks to you as well for arranging his writing to appear in *The Elevator*. Our readers were naturally interested in your exploits, but many citizens crossed the color line to read your contributions to our publication and to read Deborah's accounts of your campaign."

"Thank you," he said. "But what—"

"You're acting mystified, Andy," Bierce said, his tone irritated now. "I have brought together two individuals who have an obvious need for one another, so my job is done. Go forth. Have lunch, have a walk, have a talk, but leave me to my work."

He stood shook hands with each man, opened the door and ushered them into the hallway.

* * *

It was a far cry from his sybaritic meal with Bierce at the Palace, the modest plate of frankfurters and beans and coffee he shared with Joseph Francis and Deborah Beasley in a small café south of Market Street. But he felt somehow more at home among the mottled crowd of diners at the half-dozen battered tables than he had among the linen crystal of the expansive Garden Court.

"We can't offer you much of anything but column inches, Mr. Maxwell," Francis said. "A few pennies here and there when we have them."

"You'll have to call me Andy, or we'll never be able to do business," he said.

"Of course, Andy," Deborah said. "And you must think of this as a chance to speak for the cause in a way that the big papers will never allow. And believe me, I know. I'm known and respected at *The Examiner, The Call-Bulletin, The Oakland Tribune,*" but only if I tone down the message almost beyond recognition."

He thought of Cooper and Amelia, of his father. Of the dreams he'd nurtured, imagining himself as a respected and accomplished academic. Did he have to choose one or the other? If so, what counted? What mattered? Maybe he wasn't so naïve after all.

If it turned out to be to his political advantage, Johnson might overlook his outburst and put him on the regents after all, but there was no controlling that. Nor could he control whether the court would allow him to take the office he'd won. Nor could he, for the moment, control the university's decision about his entrance into the graduate program. And after all the *sturm und drang* and Yellow Squirrel's defeat did he still care so much about all that? Yes, he realized, he did. He cared about all of it. And now he had before him the offer from *The Elevator*. Something he'd be settling for after failing at everything else? Or simply a different road up this mountain he was climbing? It all depended, he realized once again, on what counted, what mattered.

EIGHTY-NINE

A GIANT FAVOR

Many Clouds remembered Amelia's words, "You won't be doing this all alone." And she recalled her own determined, if silent, vow to do it by herself anyway. But after carting Gerald Noble's body to town, waiting hours for an undertaker, only to find that the price for embalming and burial was beyond even the cost of paying Miller's loan, she finally accepted that she'd reached the limits of what she could accomplish on her own. Without the help of this generous man whose forsaken body lay wrapped in canvas in the back of the buckboard, she and the children might be on foot and on the road. That could still happen, but because of him, hope remained. Not, however, if she tried to stand alone. What's more, she appreciated anew the meaning of her new responsibilities—the children and the land. She could not simply load her belongings on her back and walk away as she would have in days past. Thus, the telegram:

* * *

TO MRS. CAROLYN MAXWELL

PLEASE COME EARLIEST CONVENIENCE WILL EXPLAIN

* * *

She waited and watched until the telegraph operator sent the message. Or maybe just pretended to. She had no way of verifying that the tapping and clicking represented what she had written. She thought the fact that it was going to a Maxwell might ensure its delivery, otherwise she might never know.

When she returned to the wagon, there was a bouquet of sweet peas on the seat, others strung through the horse's bridle. Maybe she wasn't entirely alone after all, but she'd have felt better if the benefactors had felt safe enough to make themselves known.

* * *

It took Many Clouds and the children almost two days to dig the grave. They could have buried him in a Potter's Field outside of town, but they'd agreed Gerald Noble deserved better, that he deserved a place with Maggie's and Willy's parents beside the stump of Swallow's apple tree.

Finally, on their hands and knees with ropes, they eased him into the hole as gently as they could. It took only an hour to fill the hole it had taken so long to dig. Willy had scavenged a two-foot piece of one-by-six, and he and Maggie had carved on it with his mumblety-peg knife, "GIANT NOBLE ??-1910". They dug a trench at the head of the grave and propped it up with stones. Maybe they'd be able to commission something more permanent some day, but, Many Clouds thought, not even a piece of polished marble would be more heartfelt than this.

"Ashes to ashes, dust to dust, and Lord commend your soul to heaven," she said.

"Say hi to mama and papa," Willy said.

"Amen," they chorused.

NINETY

WHERE'S VIRGINIA?

"No, Andy, I haven't seen her." Nathan Cohen signaled the Merry Widow's bartender for another round.

"I've left notes all over town, Nathan. Not a word."

"Maybe that's the message."

"What?"

"No answer. No romance. It's all over."

He took a sip of his fresh beer. Thought for a moment, remembering those nights of snuggling with Virginia at the Circle M, how she had thrown herself into helping even with the dirtiest jobs when the chips were down. "No. It's something else."

"You want to hear what McNulty's done now?"

"McNulty?"

"I know it must seem like small potatoes to you at the moment, but you might, just might, dimly recall him."

He smiled at his friend's sarcasm. "I'm sorry, Nathan. That's not what I meant. What's the little dictator up to?"

"He approved my thesis."

"No." He clapped Nathan on the shoulder. "Congratulations. Probably just a token ploy, but so what, eh?"

"Man, you are so cynical."

"I've come by it honestly, my friend, believe me."

"It just seems like that for the moment, Andy. This whole exclusion policy will dissolve pretty soon. You've got them beat every which way. You'll see."

But at the moment, Andy couldn't see that he'd beaten anyone but himself.

* * *

He decided to try the Sketch Club once more. On the ferry, a bright and sparkling ride beneath a warm fall sun, he pondered what he'd say to Virginia once he found her. Mom had said to straighten it out, and that's what he'd do. He'd tell her it was time to come to some defined arrangement. They'd talk it over, and then… what? Well, that would depend on the conversation, wouldn't it? What she felt, said. What he felt, wanted. Too vague. Shouldn't he be more clear going in? But why, when so much depended on her response? By the time they docked, he was no closer to a resolution.

Then, as he walked toward the Sketch Club, he had another thought. He stepped back into some overhanging shrubbery and waited watching the club house. Two hours. More. Finally Evelyn Withrow stepped through the front door and headed downhill. Even on the fairly deserted street, it proved easy to remain undetected as he followed her down the hill and aboard a trolley for a long ride to a modest hillside house on Forty-Eighth Avenue. Again, he waited, though in this residential area it was not so easy to remain undetected. If it weren't for the thick-trunked cypress on a nearby vacant lot anyone looking out a streetside window would have spotted him for the wandering voyeur he was. Maybe someone already had. He could just knock on the door, but if Virginia were avoiding him and someone else opened the door they'd just say she wasn't there and he'd be back to the beginning. Again, finally, patience paid off.

Carrying easel, canvas, and a case of paints, Evelyn descended the front steps and walked toward the nearby ocean. She joined Virginia at a lookout point above the Sutro Baths. The enormous domed glass roofs of the public swimming pools reflected the crimson disk of the setting sun. The Cliff House restaurant with its castle-like spires, perched gingerly on the finger of rock called Land's End, which jutted into the roiling surf. The roaring, barking, and whining of the sea lion colony on guano-whitened Seal Rock a couple of hundred yards offshore mixed with the sounds and briny smell of waves crashing against the rocky coast. The scene was any painter's dream. But he was not focused on nature's beauty. He watched Evelyn and Virginia greet, embrace, and kiss. Then he approached.

"Hello, Virginia."

"Oh, Andy. How special." She seemed neither flustered nor surprised, but reached out, took his hand and wrapped him in a hug, pressed her whole body firmly against him. His own body responded in kind.

"You see, Evelyn," she said. Her smile at Withrow was assured, almost smug. "I told you he cared enough to seek me out."

Her words made it suddenly clear what he needed to say. "Excuse us, Miss Withrow." He took Virginia's arm and led her aside.

"Oh, Andy," she said, "I was so afraid it was over. Us, I mean. The way you looked at Pocahontas—"

"Many Clouds," he said.

"Yes. I thought maybe… But never mind. Here you are and everything's—"

"Stop," he said. And he stopped walking. "I'm a bit of a dolt, I guess, or I would have figured it out a long time ago."

"Figured out what?" She stepped back.

"I loved you, chased after you all these years, and it took me till now to realize what a creature of endless games, manipulations, and fantasies you are. This vanishing act you just did, this little test of my devotion. It's only one in a long line of those past and those to come, *if* I let it continue. If *I* let it. I always assumed it was up to you. But I know it's up to me, after all."

"What are you accusing me of?" She turned her back.

"Accusing? No. Or accusing myself, if anyone. You're a woman of wonder and delight and endless surprises, but you're like a circus to me."

"A circus?" She spun around, flustered now.

"A ten-ringer where there's spectacle and performance everywhere and no telling what's illusion and what's not." He took her face between his hands and kissed her tenderly on the lips. She answered with passion, throwing her arms around his shoulders. He pulled back, letting the taste of her linger before he spoke again. "Take care, love. As the poet said, I never will forget you, nor ever be the same."

*　*　*

Andy knew he wasn't supposed to feel this elated, or elated at all. The governor had, probably, refused his appointment to the regents, some venal judge was trying to yank away his election win, a yapping pack of mealy-mouthed academics wanted to deny him a doctorate, and he'd just broken up with his lover. Nevertheless, he fairly floated his way across the bay, his mind a kaleidoscope of images—mostly now of Many Clouds—her calm, pleading eyes on the night they cremated her uncle, the startling moments their gazes had joined—when she'd ministered to his Hope Valley wounds, beside Yellow Squirrel's body—her warm cuddling of the children at their father's graveside.

He sprinted up the front steps of his rooming house, opened the door, glanced at the little table in the foyer. A yellow envelope. Telegram.

* * *

MANY CLOUDS NEEDS HELP STOP BEST WISHES AND LOVE STOP

MOTHER

* * *

Andy smiled. I was already on my way, Mom, telegram or not. Why it took me all this time to realize it, I don't know, but I've been on my way to Many Clouds for quite a long while.

CARL R. BRUSH

Who's who in The Second Vendetta

In 1913, Bierce said he was headed south to investigate the Mexican Revolution. He disappeared and was never seen or heard of again.

Ambrose Bierce. He really did write for *The Examiner*. He wrote a column called "The Tattler" and penned *The Devil's Dictionary*.

Delilah Beasley. She was a prominent journalist and writer of a number of bay area newspapers as well as the author of classic works on Negro History (as it was termed in her day), especially *Slavery in California (1918) and Negro Trail-Blazers of California (1919).*

Joseph Francis. He published *The Elevator,* one of several minority publications of the late nineteenth and early twentieth century. *The Elevator* did not last until 1910, but Francis was still around as far as I know. I invented the relationship between him and Beasley but it would be odd if they hadn't teamed up professionally.

Hiram Johnson. He really was elected governor in 1910 and brought a slew of progressive changes to California—Women's Suffrage, the recall and referendum, and a number of other reforms that loosened the railroads' stranglehold on the government. He served only two years, after which the legislature made him a U.S. Senator (No popular election of senators in those days), where he became an arch-conservative and served for decades. I used this political change of heart as a motivation to make him the less-that-desirable guy you meet in *The Second Vendetta*.

Meyer Lissner. He actually was Johnson's aide.

Thomas F. O'Neil. Indeed, he was Sheriff of the City and County of San Francisco from 1906-1908, though I extended his term by two years in the novel. I have no evidence that he was anything like the rascal I created for *The Second Vendetta*.

Tom Redmond. Redmon is a fictional character I lifted from the late Oakley Hall's superb detective series set in San Francisco of the same period (*Ambrose Bierce and the Queen of Spades* is the first of the series.) Redmond is Bierce's sidekick in those stories, and I intended my use of his name as an homage to Hall, whom I greatly admire as a writer, as a nurturer of writers and as a general man of letters.

Benjamin Ide Wheeler. Wheeler was president of the University of California, which had only one campus at the time—from 1899-1919.

www.ingramcontent.com/pod-product-compliance
Lightning Source LLC
LaVergne TN
LVHW091531060526
838200LV00036B/560